NEALE OSBORNE

Lydia's Tin Lid Drum

OXFORD
UNIVERSITY PRESS

OXFORD
UNIVERSITY PRESS

Great Clarendon Street, Oxford OX2 6DP

Oxford University Press is a department of the University of Oxford.
It furthers the University's objective of excellence in research, scholarship,
and education by publishing worldwide in

Oxford   New York

Auckland   Cape Town   Dar es Salaam   Hong Kong   Karachi
Kuala Lumpur   Madrid   Melbourne   Mexico City   Nairobi
New Delhi   Shanghai   Taipei   Toronto

With offices in

Argentina   Austria   Brazil   Chile   Czech Republic   France   Greece
Guatemala   Hungary   Italy   Japan   Poland   Portugal   Singapore
South Korea   Switzerland   Thailand   Turkey   Ukraine   Vietnam

Oxford is a registered trade mark of Oxford University Press
in the UK and in certain other countries

British Library Cataloguing in Publication Data

Data available

ISBN: 978-0-19-276356-3

1 3 5 7 9 10 8 6 4 2

Printed in Great Britain

Paper used in the production of this book is a natural,
recyclable product made from wood grown in sustainable forests.
The manufacturing process conforms to the environmental
regulations of the country of origin.

*Written in memory of
my dear friend Wendy.*

Lydia's Tin Lid Drum
MENU

Appetizer

Two figures raced at a breakneck pace, the branches and creepers of the night-time jungle *shoosh slish* whipping past their ears. And close behind them, frightening sounds, the sounds of trunks, the trunks of sweet trees hacked aside by giant knives.

Two figures ran. A girl and a man. And though the two were father and daughter, the man's skin, tanned from a lifetime hunting in hot sunny climes, was pale next to the deep bronze-brown of the girl's complexion; and while his hair was fair, hers streaked from her scalp in thick black strands as she dashed through the jungle, ducking, brushing foliage branches, sensitive to plant scents shooting past her: bursts of pepper, piercing spearmint, arrowroot, grapefruit, all the sweet aroma trails.

The man, Alazandr, a strapping chap accustomed to tough, to tougher terrain—even he had difficulty staying in stride with his fleet-footed ten-year-old child.

Far behind them, fire raged. A royal palace consumed by flames; its butchery kitchens and sinister laboratories, serums, potions, and magic liqueurs sizzling away in a fearsome blaze, bright against the midnight moon.

'Eli—*Elixa!* Imminti saltia!' Alazandr called to his daughter in her native Tangi-tongue.

The girl Elixa stopped at his request, waiting under a gum tree as Alazandr stumbled up, careful of the child he carried in his arms: a younger girl, only four years old, barefoot and wearing a plain vanilla robe. This simple dress was so unlike Elixa's rich attire: a blood red sari of finest silk, dripping with ruby berries and jewels.

The man placed the four-year-old girl upon the ground against the gummy trunk of the tree. The child said nothing; she stared oblivious as if in a trance, insensitive to the pain of the trio of star marks branded onto her face. Alazandr looked back frantically. He could hear, so near, the splintering crackle and *chop-chop* of branches. He rifled through his khaki jacket, looking for the last of his confectionery weapons.

Elixa merely rummaged in a satchel she had slung around her shoulder—a satchel full of stolen sweets, enchanted chocolates, mystery liqueurs; and from the assortment, she picked out a single crystalline mint.

'Isi, Popka,' Elixa hissed, shaking her father's forearm. '*Popka!* Glasseer minta.'

Alazandr shook his head. 'Tu skoot!' He ordered Elixa to go, showing her the handful of tiny red

2

grenades he'd just dug out of his jacket pocket. 'Kirshay kabooma,' he uttered grimly.

Elixa narrowed her emerald eyes. She nodded, then popped the mint into her mouth. Alazandr watched in wonder as the girl began to disappear. Her liquorice hair bleached white then flickered clear; likewise her bronze flesh, leaving faint X-ray bones, till in moments there was nothing to see of Elixa but a glassy glimmer in a sari and tiara.

Meanwhile, the rapid slash of metal fast approached and, an instant later—

Alazandr turned to these monstrous insects hacking quickly through the trees. Three vile metallic mantids, antennae twitching, detecting their prey; the tall copper creatures reared above him, raising their sabre-like limbs to strike.

Elixa was away, slinking into the depths of the jungle, the glassy mint transforming the very clothes she wore into an aura of invisibility. Suddenly she heard *one two three* successive explosions. She dared to look back. Afraid for her father, for the four-year-old child he'd saved from a bloody death. Afraid he'd never make it to his boat at the cappuccino delta. Afraid he had given his life to protect her.

And now the sky erupted with thunder. Warm black coffee rain pelted down. Still, in the distance, it was possible to see fire fizz above the Mokachini jungle.

Elixa promised her father that one day she'd find a way to eliminate the sinister sect that threatened

her land, and finish off its bloodthirsty sorcery for good.

And so, with her satchel wrapped safe in her robes, Elixa fled the cruelty of her home, her glassy mocassins splashing through the *dash dash dash* of coffee rain.

The girl inhaled the tastes of the forest—its syrup saps, citrus layers, and musky mocha notes; Elixa gave herself to the forest. On what was meant to be her Night of Sweet Initiation.

Chapter 1
Master Chef

Thunderous sounds like a rumbling kettledrum erupted in Lydia's slumbering mind.

The little girl raced at a terror-stricken pace—kicking litter, crisp packets, wrappers—along the alleyway behind the flats. And behind her: frightening sounds. Junk being crunched in metal teeth.

Lydia ran, hand in hand, with a man who looked just like her daddy Petro; and though he was older and stronger than she was, he could barely keep up with the nine-year-old girl.

'Lydia—*Lydia*,' he called. 'Don't let me go. *Please.*'

But as Lydia scampered ahead, her grip slipped. The man stumbled over a tumbling dustbin. Lydia looked back frantically; she could hear, so near, the munching and crunching of unseen machines. Then, amidst the trish-trash of packets and bottles and discarded cartons, the little girl noticed this silvery container.

She rummaged through the rubbish and dug out a rectangular tin; Lydia prised its lid. Nuggets of toffee lay inside.

She turned back and shook her father's arm. '*Daddy, Daddy!*' Lydia cried. '*It's toffee!*'

Daddy Petro lifted his head, and Lydia watched in horror as he began to turn to tin: his hands became metallic gauntlets; his whole body covered in dull grey tones. Soon there was nothing left of the man but an emotionless robot in armoured clothes.

Meanwhile, a mechanical *clunk* and *clank* came closer and, an instant later—

Lydia saw these canine contraptions lurch into the alleyway. Two robot doggy guards, ears twitching, seeking the truant child. The brutal metal hounds bolted towards her. Opened their jagged jaws, ready to bite—

Lydia jarred herself awake, and she stirred from the depths of the nightmare. Even in sleep there was no respite from the sadness that overshadowed her life. Lydia didn't like to go to bed some nights; this was the time when the fears that lurked at the back of her mind would bubble up as bad dreams. Night after night. Nightmare after nightmare.

The girl sat up, in the gloom of her bedroom. Tired and tearful, she thought for a moment; there had been something different about this latest dream: the added torment of the tin. The tin with the toffee in.

For Lydia, finding a real tin of toffee would be like discovering a trove full of treasure. To her, toffee was the most wonderful thing in the world. But Lydia wasn't allowed her toffee any more.

She hadn't been allowed toffee for over four years. Ever since Stannic, the man who ruled her land of Likrishka, had introduced rationing and prevented children from eating sweets. And by taking toffee from her life, Stannic had taken away Lydia's drum, for the little girl used to use the tin as an instrument. And, when she hit its lid, weird things would happen to metal objects nearby.

The first time this occurred was when Lydia was nearly three, and she'd received a gift on Midwinter's Eve: a tin of special toffee, all the way from the country of Tangiya. (That was where Auntie Elixa came from. Mummy had told her that Elixa was a toffee-chef who lived in a faraway village called Karamesh.)

Lydia could still recall the pattern printed on the tin: exotic birds and forest trees in shiny pink and purple. She still retained the memory of Mummy opening the tin and taking out the inner packet with all the chunks of toffee in. And Lydia still cherished that very first taste, her very first piece of Karamesh toffee: *mmm* that unique treacly tang, buttery smooth, chewy and rich—

Her little fingers had started to twitch. Instinctively, Lydia had pounded at the tin lid, let her hands make a

satisfying *thud-a-dubbadum*. And as she had done, all the metal nails had shuddered loose from the walls, making a clock and a couple of picture frames clatter to the floor. And yet Lydia hadn't found this unusual at all—it was as if, through the tin, through the lid of the tin, she felt somehow magically magnetically connected to the world around her. To her startled parents though, it must have seemed as if there'd been a miniature earthquake.

It had been like that for the next few weeks. Toddler Lydia touring her home. Stomping up and down stairs, with the tin under her arm. Drubbing it with her fingertips, or a rock-hard stick of liquorice. And as she'd gone by, all the metal objects mysteriously misbehaved: clockwork watches would start winding backwards; taps in the bathroom would splash on and off; mantelpiece candlesticks would somersault into the air, and cans in the pantry would rattle topple roll; cutlery in kitchen drawers did jingly acrobatics, while the woks and pots and pans, in the cupboards, clashed like bickering cymbals.

Then, as months passed, Lydia taught herself a range of percussive gestures: purry rolls, crisp tattoo tip-taps, repetitive ruffle riffs, snarey rhythmic snaps, faster tempo hammer bam slams or slower softer skiffle scuffs; thus she'd learned to play a variety of musical phrases, full of rolling vowels and bongo consonants.

And, with the 'tin lid drum' channelling her thoughts, Lydia had discovered she could bend metal to

her will: agitate it, animate it, make it obey her drummy commands.

It was the eating of the toffee though that determined her ability—'Must be something special in the recipe'—because without the confection from within the tin, Lydia's drumming became a dull dud *dunk* which seldom made a paper clip jump.

All this was a distant memory now, and thoughts of presents no longer entered her head. Lydia's life had changed so much since her early childhood—indeed everyone's life changed after Stannic came to power. Mostly for the worse too.

Stannic had been ruler of Likrishka for as long as Lydia had been alive. And since she was five, not long after her mummy died, Likrishka had been overrun by Stannic's robot army.

The Likrish ruler had always been famous, a Master Chef celebrated throughout the world; he had a metal tongue with enchanted taste, and was often referred to as 'Stannic the Tin Man'.

Lydia had accepted all this as normal, and it was only as the years had passed that she realized how odd Stannic really was: his face (in fact, the whole of his body) was made entirely of tin. A flexible kind of living tin. But how he got that way, she couldn't say.

What Lydia *did* know was that Stannic made everybody do what he wanted them to; he even told mummies and daddies what to do. The Tin Man had taken

everything from Lydia. He'd taken everything from all the other children too.

But at least there was one person Lydia knew who seemed to lead a better life: that was her elder half-sister Celine, a top dessert-chef for Stannic's regime.

Lydia never saw Celine. Not properly. Not in person. To speak to. To listen to. Sometimes she would see her on the TV in official news bulletins. The last time that happened, though, was months ago and showed Celine in her luxury house in the district of Muesli. She was Head of Desserts at a trendy restaurant, the '*Mint Julep Mill*', and she served her exquisite sweets to its select clientele, those of the wealthy Dinner-Jacket Class.

'I miss Celine *so* much,' Lydia wept to herself. 'Miss her as much as I miss Mummy.'

Her mummy Mari. The loveliest kindest person Lydia would ever know.

Every day, Lydia thought of her mother and their times together, moments so precious for their rarity and never-to-be; the girl's mind would wander back— *Remember when Mummy and me, remember when Mummy*, her train of thought travelling to a motherly stop: *Maple Syrup, swimming, shopping, Redberry, trip-a-day, story-time, birthday*. Then that out-of-the-blue day when Mummy had gone to the hospital. That day when, in Lydia's mind, her mother had boarded a never-ending sleeper train—and her life was soon to pass away. And so, Lydia's world derailed around her, leaving her stranded, sad and confused.

It was only a few days after that when robot soldiers suddenly appeared and took control of Likrishka. An unexplained state-of-emergency had been declared, and all the power and communications had been shut down across the land. Soon giant tin soldiers blocked the streets, wielding weird yellow weapons resembling bottles of cloudy lemonade. And with these robots came orders for the people to pack.

Near her home on Redberry Common, a big orange double-decker bus pulled up. Then five-year-old Lydia was hustled aboard with the other local kids.

Lydia had only a vague recollection of the crowded noisy bus ride to the seaside. The children were told they were going to Peachbourne, one of Likrishka's nicest resorts.

But Peachbourne resort had been turned into Tinport. Tinport Detainer Zone: a town patrolled by robot soldiers; all the infants were to be isolated in detainer flats, and educated in the ways and tastes of the State.

For the last four years or so, Lydia had lived in Tinport town, locked up in one such ground floor flat. And now she had no tin to drum. No toffee. No Mummy to help her unwrap it.

After her nightmare, Lydia sat up in bed. She squinted at her bedside cake-clock; it was almost a quarter portion past dawn. Daylight began to glow through the curtainless window and, somewhere above the town, there came a bizarre buzzing noise like an enormous food mixer chopping up the sky. The blender-blade *chudder chudder chudder* came closer. Lydia sprang from her bed and went to the window, glimpsing a wasp-shaped helicopter rasping through the air overhead.

A helicopter was a very rare sight. The Likrish people never travelled anywhere—and Lydia's last trip was the seaside bus ride. Everyone had orders to stay inside; only a fool would disobey anyway, as metal hounds now prowled the streets. These were the same mechanical hounds that stole into Lydia's nightly nightmares. She sometimes saw them from the flat's front window, dustbins on legs with dog-shaped heads. That was their original use, after all: litter collectors designed to scoop up packets in their paws, or scrape up wrappers with their claws, or even scrunch larger junk in their jaws.

Now their computer brains were programmed to attack, and it was people who were treated as trash.

Lydia continued to peer through the window while the helicopter circled circled descended—suddenly *scritscratch!* She jumped as claws scratched at the glass; an animal had appeared at the pane, tapped with its paws to get inside.

'*Ooh*, it's only Smokey.' Lydia opened the window a little, and a thin black tomcat leapt through into the room. 'You do know there's no food for you, Smokey. Not that you'd want the muck Mater D cooks up.'

Mummy had bought Smokey when he was a kitten; Lydia adored him, the lovely little fluffy thing, even though he had this strange forked tongue. Lydia had brought Smokey with her to the seaside, but pets were confiscated here in Tinport, and so she'd let him escape outside. He did keep coming back to the flat, though sometimes Lydia didn't see her cat for days; he must have lived on plants or mice, and she was always afraid a robot hound would catch him.

The helicopter-wasp had landed now and with the racket from the rotor blades cutting out, Lydia could hear an electronic *bark-bark* echo in the alleyway behind the flats.

'Rotten robot dog,' she whispered, stroking Smokey's night-cold back. 'This isn't a nice place for a nice kitt-cat.' Smokey half-closed his big green eyes and gave a contented mew. 'Sh-hush. No *miaow*. Don't want Mater D to hear you. Mater D doesn't like animals, does she? Mater D doesn't like anybody.'

Mater D was the bitter old spinster appointed as Lydia's nanny. Mater D wasn't her real name; it was a title such as 'Ms' or 'Madam' and stood for 'Mater Detainer'. (Lydia nicknamed her *Mater Doggy-Bag* but that was something she had never said out loud.)

The Mater Detainers were women of retirement age that Stannic had assigned to raise the infant under-tens; and while the threat of robotic police would keep the women and children in line, it was left to custom-made interactive televisions to teach the Tin Man's cookery lessons to the luncheon-age youngsters.

Likrish children had been given these mealtime labels according to how old they were: babies were '*brekkers*' (who grew up so fast), toddlers were '*brunchers*', infants '*lunchers*', and when children reached the age of ten they took taste-tests, the results of which determined their future once they passed the '*elevenses*'. Those who failed these exams would most likely be expelled to work camps, while those who showed promise as potential chefs would go on to study at Stannic's academies.

Hence Mater D was meant to be there to cook and clean for Lydia; however, as the old crone often moaned: '*I never snot ask to snot be no slavey to some wuz else's lazy brat.*'

On one occasion, Mater D mentioned she much preferred her previous job, at some pseudo-wood recycling plant, feeding the machines with old sugar-paper. *Poor machines*, Lydia had thought, *being fed by Mater D*.

Mater D, you see, was an awful cook, and in Likrishka—which, after all, was *ruled* by a chef—it took unusual stupidity for a person to stink at cookery. Each meal Mater D made was revolting (she even ruined instant soup) and Lydia had to eat whatever

tummy-ache-making fare the detainer prepared; while she'd never dare complain about the nasty taste, Lydia couldn't help but pull 'unsavoury' faces.

'*My cookings not snot good nuff for Lidl Mess Silver Slimy Spoons?*' Mater D would say in snide reference to Celine. (Lydia's beloved half-sister had been the youngest-ever winner of the prestigious Likrish Silver-Spoon, and so Celine had got stuck with the title '*Silver One*'.) Mater D also insulted the two of them by saying they were '*dirty Deli leftovers*' because, while Celine and Lydia were born in Likrishka, Mari, their mother, had first lived in Delisha, a province to the north.

They both had different fathers too: Lydia's daddy Petro was definitely a local man, but she knew nothing about Celine's dad.

'Anyway, what did it matter where she come from?' Lydia would answer back in her mind. 'Celine is still the best sweetie-maker in the land.'

Celine had indeed been Stannic's star academy graduate, and a role model to all Likrish cooks; not only was she extraordinarily talented, she was chic and beautiful too, and in recent years Celine had been sent around the country as a confectioner-ambassador, and the media-frenzy dinners she'd attended provided good publicity for Stannic. Lydia never questioned her sister's involvement in the Tin Man's schemes; Celine *had* to serve him, and if she didn't do as she was told, he—he'd probably whack her with a big tin frying pan, just as Mater D hit Lydia with her rotten wooden spoon.

'Someday soon, Celine, someday soon—' Day after day, Lydia would inwardly say, 'Someday soon Celine's going to take me away to live with her. Away from mean old Mater Doggy-Bag.'

Every day, she'd hoped for this, ever since she was packed off to this poky flat. But each detainer-day her hopes grew fainter; nearly half of Lydia's life had gone by without seeing or hearing from her famous half-sister. Maybe Celine had forgotten all about her.

Perhaps that's what happens when mothers die. Families disintegrate. Sisters forget.

But Lydia would never forget. And while Mater D didn't let her keep any personal belongings ('*Don't snot want none o' your junk cluttin' up my flat,*' she'd said) Lydia *had* saved a single photograph and managed to hide it from the old detainer: there were five people in this picture, including herself as a baby cradled in her mother's arms (Mari, in the centre, with a lovely wide smile); on Mummy's left was her younger brother (silly Uncle Terri, hardly looking at the camera); and on her right was their own mother Rosé (Grandpa Pyrus had died by that time). Celine was there too, about ten years old, half the age she would be now; holding on to Granny's pinny, Celine stared rather stern as though the fate of the world weighed upon her childish shoulders. Behind them all was a decorative wall, the wooden wall of some old place where Mummy's family used to live.

Here in Tinport though, Lydia's room had no decor; it was bare and as boring as an empty cake box.

Now, her only preoccupation was gaining a cookery qualification. (She wasn't allowed any toys or games, although her favourite pastime had involved playing with the toffee tin, making metal move around and drumming it to do things.)

For more than four years now, Lydia had endured a daily diet of televised luncheon-lessons. The cookery course had gone way beyond the basics; she had to learn complex recipe variations and dinner combinations— whether to boil, to braise or roast, to fry or grill, to poach or toast. There were menus to memorize, and she had to work out difficult calculations, cooking rates, temperatures, ingredient quantities, all the important formulae for meals.

It wasn't that learning how to cook was so bad; but maybe if the lessons had included the actual baking of cakes or something nice—*Oo*, Lydia often daydreamed about going to stay with her Aunt Elixa, living in her kitchen in Karamesh, cooking and eating toffee all day—But the television lessons were so long and dull, and Lydia wouldn't have access to a proper stove to prepare proper food until she was older. And only then if she proved worthy enough to join the next generation of Likrish chefs.

For those who met Stannic's highest standards, there might be the honour of serving in the Sweet Elite: a group of only half-a-dozen top government cooks.

Anyway, Lydia didn't fancy going to one of Stannic's *queasy academies*; she wanted to go to a normal school

with friends her age. With playtime, painting, sports days, storybooks, dancing and music, different subjects to keep her interest.

But for children belonging to her class, there were no normal schools any more.

Chapter 2
Microwave Oven

And so, for Lydia, it was going to be another glum day. Another glum day to fritter away. Another day spent following Stannic's cookery curriculum.

Piles of computer printouts lay on the tatty mat of her room, and Smokey the cat had sat on one; Lydia had to nudge him off it, let him lie under the bed instead. She brushed the printout with her fingers, glancing over the bewildering tables of sums and text. She felt she was going to fail her tests, and shuddered to recall one of Mater D's taunts: '*Yuz flunk your lessonings it be the workscamps for you, same ones whur they in-prisons your dad in!*'

Lydia decided to get dressed, swapping her plain nightshirt for her State-approved uniform: a dark grey pinafore, dark grey socks, and a pale pink smock that buttoned tight at the top. Back home she'd had a variety of clothing, but here this 'ration-kit' was provided,

kept in a flimsy balsam-wood wardrobe. Lydia had to handwash this kit herself, in a sink of chilly water. (The flat had an easy-to-use washy-machine, but Mater D broke it, trying to overload it. She would never iron any of Lydia's clothes either, so her kit was always crumply creased.) At mealtimes, Lydia was made to wear a garish yellow poncho made from recycled lemon rind and, even though it was easy to wipe clean, she found its plasticky fabric uncomfortable. She had a sole pair of shoes, too, she'd only wear on Ration Day: the one time per week when she would accompany her Mater Detainer to the store. Here everyone was given their ration of groceries: drinking powders, tablets of tea, and supplies of food ingredients from which Mater D was supposed to make a range of meals; for Lydia, though, every dinner was the same, the same stodgy doggy-baggy stew, same mucked-up mashed-up mush.

Mater D's been quiet this morning, Lydia thought as she tied up her pinafore. She normally heard the old detainer clattering around in the flat's kitchenette, cobbling together what she referred to as 'breks-fussed'; it was very cramped accommodation the two of them shared, and sounds in adjoining rooms often thudded through.

As Lydia left her bedroom, she was surprised to see Mater D at the end of the hall, standing with her back to her, hunched by the front door; the nosy old woman seemed preoccupied, keeping a beady eye on something outside.

Lydia said nothing, and nipped into the bathroom; after she'd been to the toilet, washed her hands, and cleaned her teeth, she went into the study.

Each morning, before lessons began, all Likrish children had to register their presence. Lydia sat up straight in the swivel chair positioned in front of the workstation; then she faced the cube-shaped machine that she'd had to answer to ever since she moved to Tinport. Lydia had first thought it was a microwave oven, but it turned out to be a weird type of television: for starters, at designated times, its screen would automatically switch on and off; then there was only one channel to watch, the one that showed the cookery lessons. (Lydia also had to sit through newscasts full of bulletins about how prosperous Likrishka had become thanks to Stannic. And how he now had similar ambitions for the whole of the country.

Likrishka was part of a country called Candi, which was split into seven different lands: the others being Franjipan, Froza, Delisha, Nooga, the Winelands, and the isles of Baykari. Likrishka was the southernmost piece of Candi, and with Lydia's homeland under total control, Stannic was greedy for the rest of the regions; his robot soldiers had recently invaded Likrishka's six neighbours, and already the Tin Man's mechanical forces and fearsome hounds were capturing their towns. Stannic now proclaimed himself ruler of all the Candi-Lands. And possessor of their ingredient riches.

Over the years, he had often appeared on TV, in his starchy white coat and chef's hat crown, to address the Likrish children. At first, Stannic had offered words of encouragement, but those words soon turned sour; the Tin Man demanded better results, describing what life would be like for 'failures': a tougher life. In an allotment camp, or a ration factory, or prison farm. All places where the grown-ups were. And where Lydia knew her daddy had been taken.

There was something creepy about the way the Tin Man never showed any emotion. Even when he was issuing threats, he expressed only deadly seriousness. Lydia had nicknamed him *'Mister Tinny-Bin'*. It turned her stomach just to think of him. She knew every nuance of Stannic's metallic face, the colourless steely eyes, strong tin chin, his ageless armoured features.

Lydia had grown to hate the Tin Man: for taking daddy Petro, for sending her to Tinport, for putting her with Mater D. Lydia was very scared of him too, and of whatever fate awaited her.)

The sound from Lydia's oven-like television came through a lightbulb-shaped set-top device: a cartoony goose head with webcam eyes and a speaker beak. During the lessons, this gander goose would constantly honk out instructions, and Lydia would have to type responses on a keypad. (She could hear the honking from next door too, and assumed that an oven-TV had been installed in every flat in Tinport.) A slot, at the bottom, would spew up printouts, ration vouchers, and test-receipts. These were to be handed over to Mater D.

With Lydia's tenth birthday less than a year away, Mater D was being extra-strict, fretting that poor results would reflect badly on her. It wasn't good to make Mater D mad. If she didn't like what she read on the receipts, the woman would fetch her wooden spoon and smack Lydia with it. Then Mater D would burn the receipt, mash it into a distasteful paste and force the girl to eat it for her tea.

For now though it was neither test time nor lesson time, and Lydia simply sat upright in the swivel chair while the webcam gander scanned her retinas.

'*I-dent-if-eye*,' the gander ordered.

'I am Lydia Rhodium of Tinport, Likrishka; server of Stannic and the Nation of Candi.'

Once Lydia had finished this pledge of allegiance,

the speaker-beak gave out a double *honk-honk* to show that the child had been correctly identified, and was free to go until lessons after breakfast.

Leaving the study, Lydia saw Mater D still in the hall, nosing through the window beside the front door; the old woman was bent down stiff in her detainer outfit (starchy white shirt with long grey skirt); her wiry hair was set in a net and, as ever, she wore her spectacles with their pebble lenses like two boiled sweets pegged upon her nose. Mater D seemed agitated, *nn*-gnawing on a length of tough liquorice, and clicking two more sticks of it between her bony fingers. Lydia found it very irritating, that constant *tic-tac* of liquorice. This particular brand was yucky too, and Mater D used up their rations on packs of them (liquorice permitted as a medicinal confection). Over the years, the synthetic sticks had stained the old woman's hands and made a black line around her mouth; Lydia felt quite sick when she saw those filthy lips up close.

Hearing the girl at the end of the hall, Mater D jerked her head round; she narrowed her eyes behind her pebbly specs, and beckoned Lydia with stabs of her forefinger: 'Gets yur!' she ordered. 'Chop-chops!'

Lydia timidly sidled along the hallway and, when she was within reach, Mater D hooked on to her with a mucky knuckly hand, and she pressed the girl to the window. Now Lydia could see what had got Mater D's false teeth in a twist.

Blocking the door was a brutish-looking robot sentry.

'Just *standed* thur. Snot movin' nor not nothin',' Mater D muttered nervously as she stared at the robot. 'What's it *thur* for? What's it *wants*?' She gnawed her liquorice, and glowered meaner than normal.

Lydia was nervous too. Studying the imposing robot, she noticed it was different from the can-droid soldiers that trudged around town: the Tinport police with their big bucket heads, vizor eyes, and mouth-like slots (Lydia didn't know what the slots were for—the robots never spoke through them; they were just dumb waiters carrying out Stannic's orders). This sentry looked more advanced, broader-shouldered, longer-legged, with one of its hands like an oversized can-opener.

It must have arrived in the helicopter-wasp. But what was it doing at her front door?

As Lydia chewed her thumbnail, and Mater D anxiously clicked her sticks of liquorice, they saw someone drive up in a black limousine; this was another rare sight, as nobody was allowed to travel by car except important government types. The limousine was parked on the forecourt of the sea-front flats. Lydia could see that the grill of the car was emblazoned with a metal emblem: a tin plate and two crossed knives. Stannic's dreaded emblem.

Then as her gaze moved from grill to windscreen, Lydia's heart fluttered faster in her chest. But not out of fright. Her heart and mind raced with sheer delight as a young lady could be seen behind the driver of the limousine; she had bobbed dark hair with a silvery sheen.

'Celine!' Lydia cried, pushing Mater D out of the way, and reaching for the door handle. At the sound, the robot's body spun round; it raised its hand with the can-opener device which sparked into life with a zap of electricity. Mater D squawked and ducked, but this *zap* was just a warning.

Celine now emerged from the black limousine. She was stylishly dressed in a charcoal-grey suit, and she carried a large posh government lunchbox which Lydia presumed to be chock-full of documents, speeches, and (best of all) top secret recipes.

Celine addressed the robot sentry, issuing a short command: 'Prime, let me pass.' Like a great iron gate, the sentry turned aside, letting the young woman enter the flat. 'Thank you, Prime,' she said, then smiled down at Lydia. 'Prime is his name. As in "prime beef cake". Stannic doesn't like anyone going round unguarded, so Prime was sent to wait for me here.' Celine closed the door behind her. 'I hope he didn't alarm you, Mater D.'

The old woman said nothing, and pebble-eyed this surprise visitor.

'I have something special for you, Mater D.' Celine placed a paper bag into her hand. 'For taking care of my sister.'

Mater D dug out a clawful of curly green sweets; these were Celine's famous 'jade snails' (lime fondant jellies in mint-chocolate shells), handmade treats that no one could resist. Lydia looked on jealously. Mater D simply sniffed at the snails, then stuffed them back in

the bag, without a word of gratitude, even though Celine must have gone to some trouble to make them. The misery-guts detainer didn't even offer their guest a cup of tea, but this was probably for the best as, according to Lydia, Mater D made 'the worst cuppa teas in the world *ever*'.

'I hope you enjoy those sweets, Mater D,' Celine said with a friendly smile. 'Now I'd like a few moments to talk to my sister, please.' She took hold of Lydia's hand, and whispered to her: 'Let's go to your room.'

'*Fnuh!*' Mater D grunted. 'No one snot tells me few mumments,' she grumbled as she shuffled off to the kitchenette. 'It's me what bosses this place.'

Only when they were in her bedroom, did Lydia say (but not too loud): 'Why did you give Mater D a present, Celine? She's nasty to me.'

Celine didn't seem to be listening; she surveyed the sparsely furnished room, then went to the window, peering out on a muddy back garden and its delapidated fence.

When Lydia had moved in, the garden was pretty, the lawn lush with camomile flowers sprouting alongside the path; birds were frequent callers, so too butterflies and honey bees. But Mater D spent her idler hours there, bodging about with a spatula-trowel, and shooing all the wildlife away. She had ripped out the flowers, dug up the grass, and tried to grow her own liquorice by sowing two rows of the sticks in the mud.

Even Lydia knew 'you can't grow liquorice from sticks without roots. Stoopid Mater Doggy-Bag'.

So the garden was now a mossy soppy mud patch with scraps of scrubby crabgrass that made a crummy view. Mater D had ruined that too.

'There are alleyways between these buildings, aren't there?' Celine asked.

'Rotten robot dogs run up and down them some-times,' Lydia replied.

'Be very careful of those, won't you?' Celine said seriously.

'You won't catch *me* going outside, Celine. Have to be stuck in here with Mater D. Eating her yucky din-ners, yucky tea.'

'And what about lessons?'

Lydia shrugged. 'Don't like lessons. And Mater D says I don't study enough. My marks aren't *that* bad. Mater D's just mean to me. She hits me—'

Celine seemed to ignore this comment. 'A certain cookery knowledge can be very useful,' she said.

'Not everyone can be as good a chef as you are.'

'I seem to remember,' whispered Celine, 'even when you were very young, you had Mum's taste skills . . . ' She paused. It had been such a long time since Celine had seen her nine-year-old sister; and Lydia had the same golden iris eyes as their much-loved mother.

'Miss Mummy every day,' Lydia said. 'And Daddy Petro too.'

'He's in one of the Black Root confection camps,' Celine told her. 'I can only make enquiries. Nothing more.' She glanced at her designer watch with its silver face and minute spoon hands. 'I can't stay long here either,' she said, but removed her jacket and laid it on the bed. Then she sat beside it, with the lunchbox brief-case on her lap.

Beneath her jacket, Celine wore a pristine cream tunic, the top left pocket of which was garnished with medals and cake decorations: the jelly diamond, silver circle, bars of chocolate, rose and gold. Lydia went to get a closer look. 'Oo, I haven't seen that one before,' she pointed, so proud of her half-a-big-sister. 'What d'you win that for?'

'The *gold* one? That's the Cordon d'Or. For distinction in Likrish dessert.'

Lydia lifted the charcoal jacket to see if there were any medals there. 'Lovely suit, Celine, so soft and clean.' It had the scent of pear drop perfume too, the girl remembered from home. Then Lydia gasped as, inside the lapel, she recognized the badge for 'The Sweet Elite'!

'I've just been promoted,' Celine told her. 'To the Confection Division at Stannic's headquarters.'

'In Burnville? *Wow.*' Lydia smiled. 'It's lovely there. Mummy took me to the fudge factory once. Showed me where she used to work.'

'Well, *I'll* be working full-time at Burnville now. And I'm moving back to our home on Redberry Common.'

'Maple Syrup House?'

'Yes.'

'Oh!' Lydia's mind lit up like a candle on a birthday cake. 'And I can come and live with you?'

'I'm afraid not,' said Celine. 'I'd be too busy to look after you.'

'But I *hate* this place.'

'It won't always be like this, I promise.'

'But I bet if you asked Mister Tinny-Bin—I mean, the Tin Man—really *really* nicely, I could stay a bit?'

'I'm sorry, Liddy. All children your age have to remain in Detainer Zones.'

'But I won't be any bother, I'll do my lessons and—'

'It's Stannic's orders. I had to get special permission to come here.'

'Then why d'you bother coming at all?' Lydia was nearly in tears.

'Oh, Liddy.' Celine held her half-sister to her, felt her cold pinafore crinkling against her. 'Oh, look at your clothes. All crumpled and smudgy.'

'Mater D won't do my washing. That's why she makes me wear the "easy-wipes".'

'The *what?*'

Lydia showed Celine the squeaky peely poncho. 'Makes me look like a lemon.'

Celine laughed. 'Never mind. I have something here to cheer you up.' And immediately she added: 'But don't open it now. Wait till it's safe to.' Celine unclicked

the locks of her lunch-case and, from it, she took a plain grey cake box.

Lydia was disappointed to see the words '*Official Ration Pudding*' stamped on the box, but she knew better than to judge a cake by its cover, and guessed that Celine had prepared one of her wonderful desserts. Lydia leaned forward, put her nose to the cardboard. She couldn't detect anything specific inside; it must have been well-sealed.

'Is there toffee in the pudding?' she whispered excited. 'Even just a flavour?'

'Toffee isn't permitted here, you know that. Anyway I've something else for you.'

Celine tucked the cake box under the pillow, and was about to reach inside her jacket, when Lydia asked: 'Celine? Do you ever hear from Auntie Elixa?'

Celine gave a wry smile. 'You and your toffee, Liddy. And Elixa isn't really your auntie. In fact, she's my half-sister.'

Lydia frowned confused. 'But *I'm* your half-a-sister.'

'Elixa is too. We both have the same father. A sweet-hunter named Alazandr.'

Chapter 3
Peaches and Cream

'Do you ever see your daddy, Celine?' Lydia asked. 'Is he still alive?'

'Oh yes. But it might have been a different story if he and Elixa hadn't escaped from Mokachino many years ago.'

'What were they escaping from?'

'Elixa's mother,' Celine replied. 'A powerful kitchen witch. A very bad lady who used to punish Elixa, keep her locked away, forcing her to memorize recipes—'

'That's like *me* and Mater D,' Lydia interrupted.

'Well, about twenty years ago, on her tenth birthday, Elixa fled her home and settled safe in a village in the forests of Tangiya. A village called Karamesh.'

'*Karamesh,*' Lydia said, relishing that magic word. 'Where my toffee comes from.'

'Oh, there are toffee-kitchens all over Tangiya. Yet Elixa's genius set Karamesh apart. She created, oh,

un*dreamed-of* luxuries, sumptuous combinations of exotic plants and natural toffee. It became a most sought-after confection. Our mother loved it.' Celine smiled sadly.

'And it comes in tins,' added Lydia. 'Tins that do weird things.'

'It's only *you* who could do weird things with the tins. Quite amazing things when you wanted to. The number of my pans you dented, making them dance and stuff. What else was it you used to do?'

'Nothing, Celine. Doesn't matter. Don't do anything any more. Sorry about your pans.'

'Well, as you know,' Celine continued, 'since Stannic took over, ten odd years ago, your tins have been impossible to get. Karamesh stopped sending toffee to Likrishka.'

'Why?'

'Because Elixa has never liked the Tin Man.'

'I like Elixa,' Lydia smiled. 'She sent toffee to *me*.'

'And it had to be smuggled in specially. In fact, Karamesh has to smuggle out *all* of its toffee, as its whereabouts is a secret.'

'What do you mean, it's a secret?'

'Soon after Elixa reached Karamesh, the toffee-kitchen moved to a new location. It simply disappeared. Just vanished in the forest. And Karamesh has never been discovered since. *Although*,' Celine whispered, 'one outsider knows where to find it: my father, Alazandr Argenta.'

'I won't tell,' Lydia said. 'So where's your daddy Alazandr now?'

'Oh, here. And there. I get messages from him. From time to time.' Celine glanced at her watch again: its silver spoons had scooped out a quarter of an hour. 'Now I have to go. Duty calls.' Celine rose from the bed and put on her jacket. 'Oh, you almost made me forget. I'm here to give you this.' From one of her inside pockets, she took out a silken handkerchief, pressed her palms around it. 'Our mother's heart wouldn't melt when she was cremated.' Celine held out her hands to her little sister. 'Take it. Keep it very safe.'

Without a word, Lydia put the handkerchief into the pocket of her pinafore; then she hugged Celine around the waist, feeling she may never see her again.

'I really have to go now,' Celine repeated as she opened the bedroom door. 'Make sure you do everything your Mater D tells you.'

'Don't leave, Celine, *please*. Mater D hits me, and her dinners make me *sick*—'

Lydia stopped. Mater D was right outside the door; she was about to pop one of the jelly snails into her mouth (unable to resist them after all), but dropped it back in the bag as soon as she saw Celine.

'Ex-cuse *me*, Mater *Dee*,' Celine said through clenched teeth.

The detainer took a couple of steps to the side, discomfited by the angry look in the young woman's eyes as she passed by.

Mater D's own expression grew scowlier as she turned her pebble-lens gaze on Lydia.

'*I'll* sees Messes Slimy Spoons out,' she seethed, shoving the girl back into her room. 'I dids ears what you snitched about me,' she added threateningly before slamming the door.

Alone by her bed, Lydia heard the sound of car tyres crackle across the forecourt gravel, the sound of the limousine purring away as Celine was driven from her life again.

The front door shut. Then came Mater D's shifty foot shuffle, all the while muttering: '*Who's she think she? Bossy me. My place.*'

Lydia retreated to the window as the old woman barged her way into the room, brandishing her wooden spoon.

'Who is she think she is?' Mater D sneered. 'Her robotty bossy guards, *skewers-is-meez* an' limo cars.'

'Celine's important,' Lydia said. 'She's in the Sweet Elite now.'

'Sweetie *Leet*.' Mater D spat out her words as though they were poisonous pastilles. 'Stannic shun't haves no filty foreigners-nuz ruin in his kitchens.'

'Celine *is* a Likrishkan.'

'Everybods knows hers mam's Delish *leftovers*. Sully-een Sur-*lie*-ver Spoons an' her fancied *zurts* an' slimy *snails*.'

'They're *not* slimy,' Lydia mumbled. 'I wouldn't mind them.'

'*Aww*, don't you snot back-talk *me*!' Mater D screamed and stamped her foot furiously, and Smokey, who was still under the bed, darted out giving her a fright.

The black cat turned and hissed at Mater D, before Lydia opened the window wide, letting Smokey leap straight out.

Mater D was more livid than ever. 'You lets that filty rat-a-cat in *my* flat!'

Her whole body trembled, contorted with rage, her beastly face frothed at the mouth. Mater D staggered at the girl, swishing her wooden spoon, intent on dishing up some instant punishment, but Lydia climbed to the window ledge and, just before she jumped out, she shouted:

'*I hate you, Mater Doggy-Bag! I hate you!*'

Lydia scampered up the garden path and lifted a broken slat in the back fence.

'You sorrib litter dreg!' Mater D yelled after her. 'You can't leggit far!' And the woman slammed the window so hard, Lydia heard a smash of glass as she squeezed through the fence, and tumbled into the alleyway.

Straightaway she checked there were no robot hounds around. Then it occurred to Lydia, the dogs may be back in their kennels recharging. (The oven-TV said they spend most of the day souping up their battery bones; it was so they stayed fully alert at night.) In any case, she needed to be wary of patrolling soldiers.

Where did Smokey go? Lydia thought as she crept

along the alley. Where am *I* going to go? Mater D's
flat was right on the sea front, so her first idea was
maybe the beach. Or maybe the pier. Could try to hide
there.

Lydia wished she had her shoes on, as the alley was
ow ow stony on her stockinged feet; it led to a side-street
that went towards the beach, and she slipped past the
terrace of detainer flats, the chained-up gates and garden fences. Suddenly a noise made her tense. A buzzing
up above, as the helicopter-wasp rasped back across
town, carrying Prime, Celine's beefy bodyguard. *Dagger-
dagger-dagger* it sped away from Tinport, headed inland
towards Burnville and Stannic's factory headquarters.

After that momentary jitter, Lydia made it to the end
of the alley, about to venture out into the side-street—
She flinched again, hearing heavy rhythmic footsteps; a
shadow appeared on the road ahead. A robot soldier
stomping by.

Lydia waited. Waited some more. Made sure the soldier was well down the road, the clinking din of its tin
limbs diminishing. She only had to pass between the
houses now, and then it was over the road to the beach.
At least she didn't have to worry about traffic. Lydia
brushed her long blonde hair out of her eyes, had a
quick peek round, then skipped across the street. After
descending a few stone steps, she reached the beach,
and its sand was soft on her shoeless feet.

Just as she'd expected, there was no one around. The
shoreline clear of soldiers and hounds.

Peaches and Cream

Even on Ration Days, it was only safe to go outside when the town's loudspeakers said so; Lydia could see them now, all along the sea front: duck-headed megaphones fixed to all the lampposts.

The ducks, like a flock of hysterical trumpets, would blare out a series of raucous quacks: *Quack-wak-wak*. The call to queue. *Quick walk quick walk*, then *quack* the way back.

During this weekly walk to the ration store, Lydia would see the other children, hundreds of them in single file, hundreds of children in the same grey uniform, most with sloppy-sliced lopsided haircuts, and each escorted by an elderly woman gripping them by the hand. They would queue up at an automated depot that used to be the Peachbourne Post Office; then Lydia and all the other youngsters would present their lunchervouchers to a row of dispensing machines. Even then she wouldn't utter a word, and the children would stand there staring at the ground, afraid of making eye contact with anyone and making their Mater Detainers mad.

It turned out that these soulless depots and zones had been set up all over Likrishka.

Aah, when the place had been Peachbourne, it was genteel retired folk or seaside-goers that used to inhabit the pretty white gateau flats; most of the buildings were tiered guest houses, one family to each layer maybe. Now their icing facades had decayed, and the hotels

39

converted into boarding houses, dismal prisons for silenced children.

For Lydia, it was bittersweet to remember the one-time funfair town. Filled with bell-like merry-go-round sounds. Vanilla, lime, and strawberry flags. The colourful kiosks selling all their goodies to summer-dressed day-trippers. Fresh pom-frit fish, candy shrimp, lobster rock, and tangerine eels to take-out from the jel-lyfish-and-chip shops.

Ice-cream trams would *binga-bong* by. These were mobile parlours that customers could hop on to, then sit at the counter, eating their favourite icy dessert as the tramcars travelled on their tracks, up and down the promenade. Past the pier, the amusements and sweet emporiums, the deco cake houses . . .

Only tin soldiers roamed the tramlines now and, while glittering illuminations used to light up Peachbourne, Tinport town was blacked-out and curfew-cursed. Nothing good happened there any more; it had ceased to be a place of week-away fun, and was now one of everyday drudgery.

Even the beach wasn't as it once was; portions of it had been devastated by excavators, great chunks shov-elled out by robotic buckets-and-spades, leaving the shore full of shaly craters.

The sand, which Lydia shambled along, was soft and fudgy; she even decided to nibble a pinch—it was much nicer than Mater D's dinners. The unrefined fudge sand

had a fruity tang from the peachy sea that spilt across the coast. The sea's creamy spray refreshed the air, but even this was tainted by fumes from a dockyard in the middle distance. A great big gob of a harbour, it was, with amalgam tankers filling the bay.

Streamboats used to sail around the coastline, depositing sightseers on the rocks, to picnic and pick-'n'-lick the barnacle confections there. But the only boat Lydia could see was a great metal freighter waiting at the harbour, the sort of vessel that might bring shipments of sugar and spice from abroad. Stannic had turned the seaside resort into an industrial port.

Gazing out to sea inspired Lydia to ponder on the vastness of the world, and the epic voyages explorers used to make to destinations beyond the horizon. She knew Tangiya was just across the sea, to the south-west of Candi; Lydia had seen it on a globe. A colourful blue-green gobstopper globe that Daddy had at home. This globe showed the whole of Lydia's world. A sweetie-world called Planet Plenti.

Though it had been some years ago, Lydia still remembered the bedtime stories Mummy had told her, teaching her all about the world. A world bursting with sugary minerals and milky liquids that, over time, had combined to make all kinds of natural confections. Confections like toffee, nougat, and fudge. Like cookie dough, jellies, and buttery sludge.

The Candi-Lands themselves comprised a remarkable country, and Mummy had summed them up in a funny chiming rhyme:

'In Franjipan, there's marzipan, jelly beans,
    and lemon trees (chip chop timberrr!).
The land of Froza is frozen over with drifts of sorbet
    and whipped ice-creams (brrr brrr brrr).
In Delisha's forests, there's cherries and berries,
    snaffle-wolves and truffle boars (grrr grrr grrr).
The Winelands are lushy with gum bushy vines,
    barley-sugar fields, and rivers of wine (glug glug
    glug).
Nooga is glutty with nutty orchards, smarty
    arty boutiques and canals (ship shop ship shop).
Likrishka's a mixture of raw fudge sands, allsort
    allotments, and factory lands (dig-dug chug-chug).
Then there are the isles of Baykari:
Krackatucka, Kukido, Krustikob, and Layakayk.
One! Filled with savoury snacks.
Two! All layered with biscuit packs.
Three! With beaches of crusty bread.
Four! Full of cake on an edible bed.'

Mummy Mari had also told Lydia of a rich tea sea with islands of mint (the largest called Mentha) and beyond this sea were the lands of Tangiya.

Tangiya featured four varied territories, overflowing with magical confectionery:

'Hot, chocolatey Mixakoko with tutti-fruit groves
    and a coast of cocoa.

*Darkest treacle-rich Mokachino where the jungle drips
   with sappy cappuccino.*
*Dry buttery Dairipan with its milk-like lakes and hills
   of cheesecake.*
*And hubbly-bubbly Jamatarta, with its soda pop gey-
   sers and jammy marshes.'*

And now it seemed that Lydia would never ever see
these delicious locations; and all those tantalizing sweets
were destined to remain untasted.

Lydia continued to wander the beach, keeping close to
the promenade wall so she couldn't be seen from the
road. After a while, she reached the pier; the words
'*Peachy Arcade*' were still visible along the side, but the
candy-stripe paint was peeling away and the flake-tex-
tured timbers showed through. There she settled, in her
pink smock and pinafore, on the sand beneath the pier.
It was cool in the shade. Quiet too. Just the far *craa* cries
of circling seagulls. The *plushy plash* of the breakfast-
time breakers. The creak of crackerbread board above
her head. The pier's underside was encrusted with sea
sugar, and years and years of juicy tides had yellowed
the wood of the pillars and beams, left them with the
scent of peaches and cream.

Now she was here, under the pier, Lydia had no clue
what to do. Rotten Mater D was right. Lydia couldn't
'leg it' anywhere. In time, she'd have to return to the
flat. And if Mater D reported her missing to the author-
ities, that would mean a *much* harsher punishment than

one the old woman could cook up. Still, Lydia feared that, when she got back, she would suffer a black-and-blue spoon-smacking.

As she sat there, licking the air, Lydia detected movement in the water; she got up and approached the far end of the pier and there, amidst the shallow sea-swirls, she saw a gully bird strutting about, its hook-beak pecking at what appeared to be some floppy spaghetti. When it caught sight of Lydia, the gull took flight, arcing away into the sky, leaving her to see what had washed up on the current: it was a jellyfish. Gently afloat on the foam of a wave. A pale yellow jellyfish like those once found in the seafood sweet shops. Lydia took hold of a cold trailing tentacle and pulled the lifeless creature ashore; the jellyfish lay limp on the sand, its body a wobbly bowl filled with a thick fruity soup. The girl dug her fingers in, broke its soft transparent skin, and scooped out some of the jelly to eat. It was slippery, slimy and tasted of apricot. 'Hmm. Not bad.' A little bitter, but edible.

She carried on dipping in and supping on the jellyfish till suddenly, right across the beach, Lydia heard a tinny screech:

'*Security breach! Security breach!*'

The loudspeaker ducks, along the promenade, had started up with alarming quacks. Had Mater D gone and snitched on Lydia? Reported her missing, after all?

'*Security breach at Warehouse One!*
Security breach at Ration Store Four!'

44

What was that about a warehouse and ration store? Lydia hadn't been anywhere near them. Still, too afraid to stay outside, Lydia wiped her sticky fingers on her pinafore, then she dashed back towards the flat, her socks slip-sliding on the soft fudgy sand.

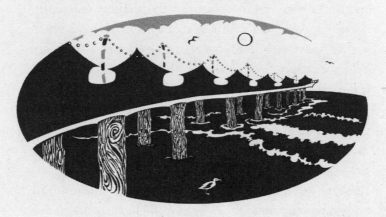

Chapter 4
Love Heart

As Lydia crept back in through the broken fence, she reminded herself to look out for snakes. Not that she'd ever seen a real living snake before, but only just yesterday Mater D claimed she'd found one in the garden:

Lydia had barely finished morning lessons when she'd heard a shriek from outside; she'd run to her room and looked through the window to see Mater D, plainly shaken, fallen on her backside in the mud.

'Thur wurz a *snake*!' she had squawked at Lydia. 'And I choppied at it with my spudja-la. And its burnts up as a snizzly snossage.'

'Where is it then?' Lydia had asked.

'Thur!' Mater D had stabbed her finger at a shrivelled bit of root that was meant to be some burnt-up serpent. 'Thats bits its *thur*.'

'The old bag's gone fruit-loops,' Lydia had mumbled, furrowing her brow. 'Never get snakes round here.'

'Ooh, don't you snot lurks at *me* likes that!' Mater D had scowled. 'Orrib litter brat!' Then she'd raised her fist in a threatening way. 'Gets back to your lessonings before I *thwacks* ya with me spoon!'

Wish there *had* been a snake, Lydia now thought. A poison one that bit her on the bottom.

As she inched down the garden path, the first things she *did* see were her spare clothes scattered about and flung in the mud; the bedroom window had indeed been smashed, shards of sugary glass lying below it. Lydia's fear intensified as she climbed inside, mindful of the pane's jagged edges.

Mater D had wrecked everything in her rage; smashed the cake-clock, torn up the computer print-outs, strewn the bedclothes around the room; she'd emptied Lydia's wardrobe and drawers, and found and ripped her family photo into bits. Now she had nothing of value except—

She stepped towards the bed. 'Oh *noo*.'

The pillow had been moved. Celine's cake box was missing.

Lydia felt faint, fell on the dishevelled bed. 'Why did Celine bother visit?' she murmured sorrowfully to herself. For years she had hoped her half-sister would whisk her away, but instead had only stirred things up.

Lydia knew that life with Mater D would be even worse from now on; it hurt just to think of the thrashing she'd get from the rotten wooden spoon.

Lydia wept for a bit, then gingerly got up. She would

have to sort this mess out later. Her only thought now was: Where's Mater D? Lying in wait in her room maybe.

Lydia tiptoed through the hall, listening out for the telltale clicks of liquorice sticks. On the carpet she noticed a part of the cake box torn into shreds. She followed the trail of cardboard into the kitchen where she found the remainder of the box with its contents untouched. Lydia could hardly believe what she saw—

Suddenly a gurgling made her jump, and she turned to see Mater D seated at the kitchen table. The wooden spoon in her bony hand was poised above a bowl full of mushy milky cereal; a pack of liquorice sticks had been tipped onto the tabletop, and the bag of jade snails lay by the bowl. The old crone said nothing. In fact, she didn't move at all, just sat with her eyes wide, kind of petrified. Her black lips were all puckery as though she sucked on a sour sweet, and her throat continued to make gurgling noises like croaky yelps for help. Lydia stood silent for several seconds. The elderly detainer remained stock-still.

Still slightly frightened, Lydia edged closer to Mater D. She dared to pinch her arm, then flinched back quick, but the woman merely sat there, stuck in her chair, gripping the spoon, and staring into space. Had Mater D got into such a mad state that she'd knotted herself into a statue? In the middle of her breakfast? Lydia was completely perplexed.

So she switched her attention to the contents of the cake box. It wasn't just some fancy dessert her half-sister had brought. It was more wonderful than she could ever have expected. Thrown down beside the box was a tin. A tin in pink and purple lacquer. Lydia trembled as she held it in her hands, transfixed by the picture on the lid, its florid border of trees and birds, the snaky lettering in Tangi-language: *'Karamesh Taffee'*. Lydia's special toffee. Excitedly she lifted the lid, gaped upon the packet within; she couldn't wait to open it, went to pull the waxy paper apart and—

Another sound distracted her. This time 'What's that?' the automatic oven-TV.

Lydia resealed the tin, and ran to the study where the speaker-goose was honking up a hullaballoo, shouting out: *'Soundbite! Soundbite! Soundbite!'*

An urgent bulletin was shooting through. Text appeared on the TV screen, and Lydia read that a number of thefts had just been detected in Tinport Zone. 'Who'd be daft enough to do that?' she wondered but, whoever it was, they'd got away with it for now.

The oven-TV showed camera footage recorded at the ration stores, but instead of the thieves being caught on site, all Lydia saw was a flicker of light. Things then simply vanished from shelves. There were also shots of a robot guard dog, its head a frazzled scrap of circuits; the locks of doors were melted too, with nothing to see of the destructive culprits.

There are *lots* of kooky doings going on today, Lydia thought to herself.

The TV goose now delivered these orders:

*'All will remain in detainer quarters! Lessons today will
be postponed. Identity of perpetrators inconclusive.
Camera retina data unknown.
All Luncheon Children and Mater Detainers will
undergo immediate scan registration.'*

Lydia heard all manner of commotion coming from the neighbouring flats: geese *honk-honk*ing, old women yelling for the children in their care to obey the TV. Under the eyes of the cartoony goosey ganders, no one would now be allowed to wander. Outdoors. To ration stores. All would stay in their detainer chambers.

'I-dent-if-eye,' the TV stated. *'Luncheon child, identify!'*

Lydia did as she was told; again she stared at the oven-screen while the webcam gander scanned her eyes: 'I am Lydi—Lydia Rhodium,' she stammered. 'Lydia Rhodium of Tinport, Likrishka; server of Stannic and the Nation of Candi.'

The goose-head gave a double *honk-honk* confirming Lydia was present and correct. But, of course, the scanning procedure wasn't finished.

'Mater Detainer, identify!' ordered the goose.

Then, after a pause, the speaker repeated:

'Mater Detainer. Penny Chew, identify!'

'Penny Chew?' Lydia said to herself. 'That must be Mater D's real name.'

Now, from outside, she heard the loudspeaker ducks trumpeting instructions to the robot police, telling them to target Lydia's flat:

'*Robot unit. Go to Two-One Tinmuth Court. Mater Detainer not responding. Robot unit. Two-One Tinmuth Court. Mater Detainer in breach of request.*'

Lydia dashed to the kitchenette. 'Mater D! Mater D!' she cried, nudging the rigid woman, shaking her chair. 'Wake up, Mater D! You have to be scanned. Soldiers are going to come to the flat!' Lydia dreaded the consequences of being found with a tin of forbidden toffee. (And how would she explain where she got it from? Celine would be in trouble too.) Lydia shook and shook Mater D's chair, and the pebble-specs fell from the old crone's nose and splat into her cereal bowl. 'Mater D! Mater Doggy!' Lydia sobbed. 'You rotten old bag. The robots are coming here. I hate you, I hate you.' She got so vexed that she picked up the breakfast bowl and plonked it upside-down on Mater D's head. And all the detainer did was sit there and gurgle while milky mushy slop dripped ickily down her wrinkled face.

Lydia knew that she had to get out. She had the tin of toffee now. Celine must have wanted her to use it to escape. Out of the back door—oh. The door was locked. So, putting the tin down onto the floor, Lydia prised the lid again; she ripped open the inner packet to reveal the lovely amber-brown toffee all in uneven nuggets.

Lydia took a piece, hungrily shoved it into her mouth; the toffee chunk clacked tough against her teeth

and, as she gradually chewed it gooier, its rich salivary flavour oozed out. Lydia felt that tang on her tongue, the long-forgotten tingle in her fingers. She hadn't drummed for quite some time, she hoped she'd be able to remember how.

After swallowing the toffee, Lydia looked for something to hit the tin with. At once, she saw Mater D's sticks of liquorice. She took two from the pack, then tapped them tentative at the tin lid; after a few beats, anything metal in the kitchenette—tap fittings, saucepans, a broken bread-maker—anything metal started to shake. Then Lydia concentrated on the door. As she drummed, her mind could somehow feel its way around the lock, as though she had reached out and run her fingers over it.

She kept it simple: '*pick-a-lock and jolt-a-bolt*'.

A pattern of taps and a delicate drumroll.

The back door lock clicked, the handle turned, the top latch slid back and opened on demand. 'Easy peasy.' Lydia was pleased. 'Like falling off a chocolate log.'

Just then, she heard, along the road, the rattle of jointed metal. A unit of robot soldier police crunching their feet across the forecourt. *Crunching crunching* towards her door.

Lydia put the toffee packet back inside the tin; she dropped the liquorice sticks in her pinafore, and snatched up the bag of jelly snails, crammed those in her pocket too.

Robots now battered their fists at the front door,

forcing their way into the hall of the flat. Lydia raced out the back and, clutching the toffee tin to her chest, she nipped up the path, and got out through the fence. Then she negotiated the alleyway, reaching the connecting street.

She looked left and right to see if it was clear—Lydia thought she saw someone there, a child darting between the buildings. A child made of golden light. Ever so quick quick. The child flit out of sight. Lydia shook her head. Surely her imagination. Probably the morning sun reflecting off a window.

Wasting little time, she left the flats behind, and found herself amid streets full of shops and cafés all shut with their windows boarded up. Lydia was in the town centre now and, as she crept through, she kept looking around, noticing this flicker of light that seemed to follow her. She was beginning to feel spooked.

'Silly to be scared of the light,' she told herself. It was solid soldier robots she should be afraid of. Because of these, her first concern was to get out of town. And fast.

Tinport sloped towards the sea, so for Lydia, heading away from the front, it was a steady climb through winding crescents and interconnected streets. In her mucky stockinged feet, she scurried up to the outskirts of town, keeping away from any main roads. Then she rested for a moment, crouched hidden in a side-street.

Lydia gobbled some more of her toffee. 'Just a piece.

Or maybe two.' After all, she'd had nothing to eat this morning, except a few scoops of apricot jellyfish.

She was about to set off again when, upon the concrete, there came a scrape of metal feet. Lydia froze. It was exactly what the girl had feared. The robot hounds had been released. She dared to peek around the corner of the street. There was one of the tinny binny doggy things, its ugly muzzle sniffing at something in the shadows. Then with a screechy creak of its joints, the hound opened its mouth, and barked a terrible loud

'Rult! Rult!'

Smokey the cat darted out of the shadows, and Lydia was so startled, she dropped her toffee tin *Clank!* to the ground. The robot's head jolted round. Its camera eyes zoomed in on the child. The metal hound bounded towards her. Lydia knelt and felt for the tin; she struck the lid quick with the palms of her hands. *Dud-dur-um! Dud-dur-um!* She focused her mind to snare the hound, drummed it to suddenly turn and roll over, as though she'd wrenched an invisible leash. Its dustbin-body went spinning down the street, *clatter batter batter bump* against a brick wall.

The robot struggled to its clawed pawed feet, scratching and scraping and kicking up a clunky din. Lydia fumbled for the liquorice sticks next, got them in her grip as the brutal hound bolted back, snapping its jagged jaws, ready to bite— She beat the sticks upon the tin, made the metal dog stop abrupt. Then she bashed the lid *thump thump*, flattened the head of the robot mutt, as if she'd whacked it with an invisible hammer. The dog keeled over, mindless, motionless. Lydia let it lie in the road. She picked up her toffee tin, and ran. She sorely needed to get away now.

Smokey followed Lydia too, and he weaved around her legs, almost tripping her.

However, as she reached the edge of town, something brought her to a definite halt: a barrier built around Tinport's perimeter. A tall thick plastic wall, stretching left, stretching right, in colourful swirls of pink and lime. A giant sweet-wrapper securing the entire town.

Lydia was trapped; this was one obstacle she wouldn't be able to overcome with her tin lid drum. In utter despair, she sank to the pavement, leant against the perimeter wall. Lydia put the tin beside her, and tucked her hands inside her pinafore; she thought she may as well eat a snail sweet, but deep in her pocket she felt something else.

A handkerchief; the second present Celine had given her. Lydia carefully unfolded the silk to find an object, no bigger than her palm, wrapped in silver paper. Daddy had told her, long ago, her mummy Mari had suffered from an illness that had turned her insides to a kind of stone. And, as Lydia uncrinkled the paper, a red crystal heart could be seen within, iridescent in the sunlight. She squinted into its bloodless chambers—but no, there was nothing to see inside. No images nor fondant memories. Sadly, Lydia kissed the crystal heart. Then,

just as she was about to wrap it up again, she saw writing on the inside of the paper; it seemed to be a list of sweets Celine had made:

Diamond Sun Bean. Chilly Jelly Amethyst.
Sapphire Fizzweed. Jet Heart Truffle.
Winter Pearl Drop. Ruby Red Shortbread.

She must have meant to give this list to her. That was why she put it with her mother's precious heart. But what was Lydia supposed to do with it?

She placed the handkerchief back in her pocket, and took out the bag of jade snails instead. Smokey nuzzled against her arm, and Lydia tipped one of the snails into her palm. 'Here, Smokey. Would you like a sweetie?'

At the offer of the snail, Smokey hissed, then suddenly his ears twitched; he turned and shrank away, raising an arched back of black hackle-fur.

What was spooking Smokey? thought Lydia. Another robot dog?

She reached for her toffee tin—It was gone. The toffee tin had gone from her side.

Then she thought she sniffed a faint whiff of fruit juice. Lydia looked up and there, standing a short distance away, was a slender child. A girl dressed, not in detainer kit, but a chic ensemble of buttery colours: a caramel polo-necked sweater and skirt, yellow stockings, sneakers and shades, and topping off her long golden hair was a little beret like a yolky soufflé. The face of the girl was caramel too, and she flashed a wicked white grin as she held out the toffee tin. 'Here,

Lydia, here,' the girl whispered with a giggly laugh but, instead of giving back the tin, she darted away.

Lydia scrambled to her feet. She scooped Smokey up in her arms, and tried to trail the caramel child.

It was difficult to keep up with her; she moved in such a slippery fashion her body appeared to be nothing more than a ghost of buttery light.

For some while, Lydia scampered beside the wrapper perimeter barrier wall. And then the caramel girl disappeared. Seemed to float right through the wrapper. When Lydia got to this particular spot, she found a hole where the plastic had been melted, and it was easy for her to stoop through too.

Beyond the wrapper there were no buildings, no more alleyways, no paved streets. Before her now were country lanes, overgrown verges and verdant meadows. Lydia had made it. She'd escaped from Tinport Detainer Zone.

Smokey wriggle-jiggled from her arms, and Lydia watched him run free in the grass. Then she saw the caramel child, up ahead, grinning and teasingly waving the tin, and so Lydia began to amble after her along the grassy lanes. She walked for fifteen minutes, maybe more. Passing fences, trees, and fields—at one point Lydia hopped around a cattle-grid—still in pursuit of this buttery ghost who'd pinched her tin of toffee. Lydia had to keep on going. Wherever this mysterious child was leading her, she had to keep on going.

Eventually she spotted the girl leave the road. It

took Lydia a little while to catch up. And there, down a country lane, was an old abandoned railway station. The ghostly child must have gone inside.

A ticket office, at the entrance of the station, had its window shuttered up; there was a turnstile too, rusted stuck, but Lydia was able to squeeze under it, and cautiously go on in.

It looked as though no one had been there for years. The station was run-down and weed-ridden; spider webs glimmered between the beams, bramble bushes encroached upon the walkways. A sign for 'Lost and Found' had faded. The waiting-room was shut too.

Lydia searched the length of the platform; her feet *scuff-scuff scuff-scuff*ed upon the wooden boards. She peered under benches and behind the fences for any sign of the girl with her tin. And, as she neared the waiting-room, she heard children's voices arguing within.

Chapter 5
Sweet Assortment

Suddenly the door swung wide. Lydia was confronted by a hooded buglike creature child with light blue skin and black-striped eyes, and four clawed hands that jittered out and grasped at her. Lydia ducked and backed away, terrified, but the claws of the child hooked onto her pinafore, snared her messy long blonde hair, and Lydia screamed and struggled as she was dragged to the creature's waiting-room lair.

A second black-cloaked child then grabbed her, and in the flurry of arms and hands and claws, Lydia saw it was a kooky-looking girl with red-centred eyes and sickle-like horns.

'Get in here, *you*,' she whispered harshly, shoving Lydia into the waiting-room, causing her to stumble into another child with a chubby body that bumped her to the floor.

Lydia found herself surrounded by seven girls, all

about her age. Six of them wore sleek black cloaks, and a couple had the hoods up around their heads.

The chubby girl she'd stumbled against had puffed-up pastel purple hair, and a face all floury pale; her cloak covered half of her round pudding body, the rest being dressed in a plum-coloured robe. She looked very cross as she loomed over Lydia and, reaching down, she hauled her to her feet. 'Oh, look at you, you messy waifer.' The girl, though, wasn't cross with Lydia, but with the red-eyed child who'd shoved her inside. 'Why can't you be careful, Zye?' she said to her. 'You could have hurt her.'

'We're s'posed to stay outta sight, ain't we?' the girl answered with a sour sneer. 'I wasn't gonna leave *her* yowlin' out there with robot-copters buzzin' about.'

'No need to push her around, though,' the chubby child replied. 'And, Cocoa-*Butter*. How could you just run off and leave her?'

She turned to the girl all in caramel and yellow, the ghostly child who'd led Lydia here. The girl called Cocoa-Butter flashed a wicked white grin again; then she teased Lydia by shaking her tin. 'We do what we want,' she whispered, and stuck out her tongue.

The chubby child snatched the tin from her, and gave it back to Lydia.

'I'm ever so sorry she took your sweets,' she said. 'Coco's always playing up. It's a tin of toffee, isn't it? Oh, that's what we could call you. *Toffee*. We've all got code names. Sugar thought it would be a good idea. I'm

Marshmallow, *Marsha* for short. I'll tell you who the others are, while we wait, if you want.'

Marshmallow

First, Marshmallow introduced Lydia to a tomboyish girl in a patched-up jumper, baggy shorts, and trainers; she had mussed-up champagne curls of hair pouring over her forehead and, most noticeably, a very broad mouth and heavy lower jaw. Meeting Lydia, the girl smiled wide, showing a great set of shiny teeth.

'This is Jawbreaker,' Marshmallow said.

'Jus' shay Jawji,' the tomboy shrugged in a casual way.

Jawbreaker

The next girl was taller than all the others, and she stood up straight, posing with her hand on her hip;

beneath her cloak she wore a knee-length chocolate-coloured frock and ballet slippers with scuffed toe-tips. 'This is Hazel Whirl,' presented Marshmallow.

Hazel Whirl

'Helloo,' Hazel said to Lydia, went to give a wave, then changed her mind and, with her hand, she preened her swirly auburn hairstyle instead.

'I'm Dolly Mix—*Dolly Mixture!*' a smaller girl blurted out. She seemed to be the most bubbly of the group, with sweet cheerful features, flutter-pretty cherry eyes, and flossy pink hair twisted into pigtails.

Dolly Mixture

'Calm down, Dolly,' Marshmallow said.

'But I like meeting new friends,' Dolly replied.

Lydia had already 'met' Cocoa-Butter, so Marsha now pointed out the last two girls. Whilst most of the others seemed pleasant enough, Lydia still felt uneasy at these two: there was the sour-faced one with red eyes like targets and, of course, the pair of weird cream horns that curved from her head of ginger hair.

'This is Bull's-Eye,' Marsha said with a sigh.

Bull's-Eye stood with her arms folded, trying to look tough. 'It's *Zye*,' was all she uttered back.

Bull's Eye

Finally, there was the thin blue-skinned girl with her shiny white lips and eyes striped like humbugs. She sat sullen and hooded on the floor in the corner, her four arms tucked inside her cloak.

'That's Peppermint,' Marshmallow whispered.

'Hell—hello,' Lydia said nervously.

The girl simply stared up at her with the black-and-white slits of her eyes.

'Peppermint's mute,' Marsha explained. 'She has this note pad thingy Sugar gave her. But she only ever uses it to talk to *her*, and doesn't like it when Sugar's not here.'

'Who's this Sugar person you keep talking about?' Lydia asked.

'Sugar Cube. Our leader,' Marshmallow replied. 'She told us to make sure you got here safe.'

'Oh. Why me?' Lydia asked.

'Because you're coming with us. That's why.'

There was nothing for the girls to do except wait.

The room was quite big, but had only one bench, against the far wall facing the door, so a few of the children had to squat on the floor, with their cloaks tucked under their legs.

'Come on,' Marshmallow said to those on the bench. 'Bunch up and let Toffee sit down.'

'Thank you,' Lydia said, and perched on the end, hugging her toffee tin, and swinging her feet beneath the seat.

The sun shone dim through the dusty windows. Nobody said anything. Some fidgeted about to get comfortable, or stared at the ceiling or the door or the walls. The waiting-room was littered with cartons, wrappers, and packets, and a pile of knapsacks lay by the door: all signs that the girls had temporarily camped here. But far from smelling lived-in and stale, the room had a lovely sweet aroma, a blend of chocolate, fruit, and mint.

'We've got some food, Toffee,' Dolly said, breaking the awkward quiet. 'You hungry?'

'Don't eat that now, please,' added Marsha. 'Sugar said to save the food for the trip.'

'But it be all right to have a bit—'

'Do as you're told, Doll!' Bull's-Eye growled.

'Sorry, Zye,' Dolly replied.

The tension in the room could be scooped with a spoon, and it suddenly became more scoopable when the girls heard noises from outside. A wasp-like buzzing overhead. Then sounds of footsteps clacking on the platform. Lydia looked anxiously towards the door.

'Hope it's Sugar,' Marsha whispered. 'She never said how long she'd be.'

'Pepper, go check again,' Bull's-Eye ordered.

But before anyone could move, the door handle turned and this petite girl nipped inside the room; the girl had a cascade of spiky dark hair, and she wore a chunky dark brown coat, long black trousers, and pink-rimmed goggles.

'Shugz has churned up.' Jawbreaker smiled.

The girl in the goggles leant against the door, her breathing rapid and erratic. Her coat was really a thin brown coating hiding a bright white jacket beneath; this jacket had so many padded pockets, she appeared to be wrapped in a bar of chunky chocolate; from one of these pockets, she took some gum, a stick of glistening glucose gum. Then the girl called Sugar Cube chewed and chewed it, and this seemed to help to steady her breath. So this little girl's their *leader*? Lydia wondered, unimpressed.

'You know you mustn't run yourself flat, Sugar,' Marsha said.

'I *had* to dash back,' Sugar Cube told her, her voice with a faint electronic edge. 'There are helicopters on the lookout now.'

Lydia noticed the stripy-eyed Peppermint hunched over a hand-held wafer device; she jotted on it with a little metal toothpick, and Sugar somehow knew what she'd written, as she frowned at Peppermint, then nodded.

'Yes, Pepper, I know. I could hear the duck alarm quacking in the distance. I was hoping the thefts wouldn't be discovered till we were gone.'

'We be safe in here though, won't we?' said Dolly.

'If we keep inside,' Sugar replied. 'Coco? Did you manage to get everything I asked for?'

Cocoa-Butter handed over a black plastic binbag, and Lydia watched while Sugar took out an assortment of items from the Tinport stores: tubes of chewy toothpaste pastilles, children's clothes in a range of sizes, and sets of underwear sealed in cling film.

'Goodie, Coco. You too, Pepper.' Sugar then scanned the room through her goggles. She stepped towards Lydia. 'Welcome to our sisterhood,' she said. 'I hope you got here without much trouble.'

'I've already told her who everyone is,' mentioned Marsha. 'And I thought we ought to call her Toffee.'

Sugar looked Lydia up and down: this tousle-haired urchin in a jelly-stained pinafore, crumpled smock, and mucky socks.

'Hmm. We need to get you kitted out. We have one knapsack spare. A hidey-hood. And you'll want some shoes, if we have a pair.'

'Zye?' Marshmallow said. 'Where are those pumps we pinched for you? Toffee can have them instead.'

Bull's-Eye huffed and trudged over to the knapsacks; she rummaged around and found a new pair of gym shoes. *Thump!* one. *Thump!* two. She slung the pumps real hard at Marsha. The footwear just bounced harmlessly off her. Marshmallow tutted, then she picked up the shoes, and passed them to Lydia.

'Thank you,' Lydia said, trying on the pumps; they were a little loose, but laced up comfy. She wondered why Bull's-Eye didn't want them, and took a peek at her feet; one foot had on a worn leather boot, while the other appeared to be a rock hard hoof.

'What you gawpin' at, *you?*' snapped Bull's-Eye; and she glared at Lydia with her cold red eyes.

Lydia said nothing; she turned away, and wandered over to the other side of the room.

Hazel was there gazing into a mirror, brushing her hair and straightening her cloak; when she noticed Lydia, she smiled down at her. 'There's one of these cokey-cloakies over there for you.' Hazel spoke quickly with a lilting voice. 'What did Marshar say your name was? Toffee? *My* name's not really Hazel, it's Shelley. It is. Though I suppose I could pretend I'm playing a character. Like a part in a ballet. I'm a dancer, you know, did you know?'

'Oh, I used to like dancers and ballet,' replied Lydia. 'But no one's allowed to do anything fun where I come from.'

'Dancing isn't *fun*,' Hazel went on. 'Well, it is a bit. But, as I keep telling everyone, ballet dance is a very sophisticated after-dinner entertainment. It is.'

Believing her point to be well understood, Hazel fetched Lydia a spare 'hidey-hood'.

She helped her into the sleek black cloak, and fastened a clip that was sewn in the collar; the hood was snug and nice and warm, the material of fleece with a lining of cream.

'Of course, I'm used to tutus and lovely silken costumes,' Hazel twittered on.

'She's Shelley Janduya, you know,' whispered Coco, the ghostly girl sneaking up and making Lydia jump. 'We stole in to see her at ze Pralini Palais.'

'Oh that's right,' said Hazel. 'I did a little cameo role with the BonBon Broil Ballet.'

'Are you a really famous ballerina then?' Lydia asked.

'Hey, Toffs,' Jawbreaker broke in. 'I use to be on a show, ush well.'

'Yes, but you weren't a dancer though, were you?' Hazel said sniffily.

'Nah. I jus' use to stuff stuff in me gob.' Jawbreaker grinned, giving Hazel a playful push, a gesture she didn't particularly appreciate.

'Oo! Can we have our sweets before we go?' asked Dolly. 'Can we, Shuggy, can we?'

'Yeah, when *are* we leavin'?' Bull's-Eye moaned. 'I'm sicka bein' tinned up in here.'

'We'll be getting on the next train,' Sugar Cube said. 'In one and a quarter hours and seven slices,' she added precisely, as though she'd just consulted a digital clock inside her head.

'Do trains still stop here?' Lydia asked, confused.

'They do if I tell them to,' Sugar replied. 'Now then, sisters,' she called out to everyone. 'We've a long journey ahead of us. So we'll eat our sweets now, and then pack them away.'

Each girl fetched a knapsack from the pile by the door (apart from Coco who owned a trendy golden handbag, and Hazel who carried a royal blue holdall). As it turned out, they all had supplies of some favourite confectionery, in essence similar to Lydia's toffee:

Dolly Mixture, for instance, had packets of bite-size candy, and she tipped out the pieces and nibbled at a few.

Hazel Whirl, meanwhile, had a jar of nutty chocolate spread; she even used a teaspoon to daintily eat a mouthful or two.

Bull's-Eye produced a tie-up purse that *click-clack*ed with gobstoppers of every hue; the grumpy girl bared her teeth as she crunched on one of the marbled sweets.

Cocoa-Butter dipped into her handbag and took out a bar wrapped in golden foil; from it she broke off two squares of white chocolate, let them *mmm* melt in her pouty mouth.

Marsha, naturally, munched on marshmallows; and Jawji chewed on a bunch of wine gums, kept in paper bags.

Sugar Cube had a cardboard tube containing doses of brightly-coloured sugar pills. And last of all, there was Peppermint who held a pouch of minty pastilles; moving with a twitchy stiffness, Peppermint clawed out one of the sweets; then she slipped it between her white lips and sucked the pastille secretively.

Not wanting to feel left out, Lydia opened her tin of toffee. 'Anybody else want a piece?' she asked.

Most of the girls ignored her offer, but Coco tiptoed across and nabbed a nugget of toffee from her.

Cocoa-Butter

'*Cocoa-Butter!*' scolded Marsha. 'That's not for you. Give it back.'

'But Toffee give ze toffee to us.' Coco smiled all sweet and innocent.

'Coco,' sighed Sugar. 'Please.'

Coco reluctantly returned the piece. 'Pinch what we want,' she muttered to herself.

Sugar then got up and frowned at Lydia. 'Toffee,' she said in a lecturing electro-tone, 'this tin is probably the only one you'll see for a while. I suggest you save it. Maybe eat that one piece now, and eat some more when you feel you need it.'

'Sugar does know what she's talking about,' Marsha said to Lydia. 'She's very clever.'

'Yeah, Shugz is a right smartie-pants,' Jawbreaker added, making Dolly giggle.

Lydia scoffed the nugget of toffee. Anyhow, one piece was enough for now. Starved of the toffee as she had been, it was more nourishing, more satisfying than she could have imagined, and it reminded her of happier times.

The girls now equipped their bags for the trip; they put away their packets or paper bags, pouches, purses, bars, or jars of sweets. Then Sugar Cube handed out the stolen goods.

Marshmallow prepared the spare backpack for Lydia; she included a toothbrush and toothpaste chews, crammed in some clothes and clingfilmed undies, and a packed lunch in a plastic tub. 'Here you go, Toffee. You can put your tin in it too.'

'I'd rather carry my tin myself,' Lydia said, clasping it close to her tummy.

'But it'll be better in the backpack for now,' Marsha insisted.

'Do what we *tell* you, Toffee,' scowled Bull's-Eye. 'An' stop wastin' time.'

'No need to be like that, Zye,' said Marsha, thinking for a moment. 'Does anyone have some string or something?'

Hazel kept a few ribbons in her holdall. 'Here you are, Marshar. Borrow one of these.'

'Thank you, Hazel. Now see, Toffee? If you take out the sweets, I'll show you.'

Lydia put the packet of toffee in her pinafore while Marsha took the tin and clamped the ends of the ribbon in the lid; then she looped the loose part around Lydia's neck.

'There you go. You can carry it hands-free now.'

With the tin hung right in front of her, Lydia really did appear to be a little drummer-girl.

Chapter 6
Chocolate Bars

The time for departure was drawing near. After the girls had packed, Lydia noticed them nipping outside; when one child returned, another went out, and so on, until Dolly turned to her:

'Need to go to the loo?' she said. 'Come on, Toffee, I'll take you where it is.'

The very first day they'd arrived at the station, Sugar and the others had discovered a washroom.

Lydia and Dolly now made the short walk to it, across the platform. Lydia could hear the robotic heli-copters *chop-chop-chopp*ing over distant Tinport and, as she looked up, she saw dark grey clouds, and felt drizzle in the Likrish air.

'Going to rain soon,' she told Dolly.

'Oh. I din't bring a brolly.'

Dolly led Lydia round the back of the ticket office to a door printed with the words '*Staff only*'. A melted

padlock lay nearby. The door wouldn't close properly either, and a splintery hoof-mark halfway up it told Lydia that Bull's-Eye must have kicked it in.

Behind the dusty office was the washroom the girls had used these past few days. The boxy room had a drinking fountain, a sink, and a cubicle where a toilet could be found. It was dark inside—the electricity disconnected long ago—the only daylight coming through a window near the ceiling; the walls were all green, being smothered in fungus, and *drip plip* puddles had collected on the floor.

Lydia saw Hazel Whirl standing outside, with a squeamish expression upon her face. 'I absolutely *detest* this place,' Hazel complained. 'I do. It's a dirty old dump. And it's full of bacteria and horrid green mould and—and scum and "jums".'

'It's all right *really*,' said Dolly. 'We used some slooshy juice.' She was referring to a limeade disinfectant carelessly sloshed across the place. 'And Shuggy Cube fixed the taps, so the soda's drinkable. Anyhoo,' Dolly waffled on, 'it's the last proper loo we may see for a bit. So if you have to tinkle, tinkle now. Otherwise it have to be behind a tree.'

The girls took turns to use the toilet.

Hazel grudgingly went first. Then Dolly.

And finally Lydia. When she was finished, she went to use the sink; after wrestling with its rusty tap, she washed her hands with a dribble of water, and dried her fingers on her pinafore. Then, just before she left, she sip-slurped some soda from the fountain.

Lydia found Hazel and Dolly waiting for her, nosing about the ticket office.

'Do you two know what's going on?' she asked them. 'And where we're all supposed to be going?'

'Oh, I never got a clue where we're off to,' said Dolly. 'But Shuggy Cube said she specially picked me out. To save my life. In't that nice?'

'And Sugar rescued me from all these robots before they invaded my village,' added Hazel. 'She told me we were trying to find a safe place to hide for now.'

It was time to rejoin the rest of the group, the three girls ducking out of the kicked-in door. Hazel skipped back incredibly quick; her figure was a whirly blur and, in a second or two, she had covered over fifty metres to reach the waiting-room.

'I can run fast as that,' cried Dolly, but she couldn't really, and set off flat out, dashing slackly, looking as though her limbs might fly off; predictably she tripped and fell, and her feet clattered on the wood of the platform. 'Hoops-a-dizzy,' she giggled. 'I'm all right, though.' Dolly Mixture picked herself up straightaway, but she seemed to have injured her leg, and limped the rest of the way.

At the door of the waiting-room, she came face to face with a frowning Sugar. 'What was all that *noise?*'

'D'you wanna loada *robots* to find us?' added Bull's-Eye.

'Sorry,' Dolly smiled sweetly. 'I twipped.'

'You have to be more careful, please,' Marsha whispered diplomatically. 'Now, we'll all be going in a few minutes. So put your leg back on properly.'

Lydia thought this was an odd thing to say, but Dolly jiggled her hips a bit, and she didn't limp any more.

The girls were now ready to leave the station. With knapsacks under their fleecy black cloaks, the sisterhood resembled a pack of hunchbacked animals. Drizzle began to patter upon their hidey-hoods as they prowled beyond the platform and down to the train track; the track itself was made of liquorice rail embedded in crispy cereal shale.

The children walked past the fences and hedgerows that separated the railway from the fields and country lanes and, as they continued along the track, the shale *snap-crackl*ed and *popp*ed underfoot.

Eventually crunchily they reached a set of signals similar to traffic lights high up on posts.

Sugar told the others to lie low in the hedgerows while she went and prised open a box at the base of one of the posts; after pressing a couple of buttons inside, she joined the rest as they crouched out of sight.

Sugar explained this was where she'd been earlier: hacking into Stannic's computer network to find out about the next scheduled train; then she had tampered with the signal box to rig the lights and delay it when it came; the 'sisters' would have to get aboard before the signal corrected itself.

Seconds ticked by. The darkening sky filled with clotted clouds of rain.

Then, through a rumble of thunder, the girls heard the *chew-chew-chew* of a train.

'Spot on time. Get ready,' urged Sugar.

A grey locomotive trundled towards them, dragging a freight train of wagons and wagons, twenty-two in total, not about to stop. The engine was horse-shaped with steam billowing out from its head and, as it neared, the trackside signal starting flashing red red red.

The great grey freight train screeched to a halt, its autopilot detecting the fault; Lydia read the words '*Candi-Pan Express*' upon the flank of the locomotive as it passed the place where the girls were waiting, and stopped a dozen wagon-lengths ahead.

Rain now poured uncomfortably down. Coco was first to scurry over. She nimbly climbed the closest coupling, then slid the door of a wagon aside. Marsha was next to creep up to the train, and she crouched down on the ground below the open door, and waved for the others to jump up off her back. One by one, the sisters used her body as a bouncy step, and however much they stamped and stomped, they didn't seem to hurt her.

They let their leader Sugar hop up first.

Bull's-Eye made sure she stepped aboard second.

Then Jawji. Then Dolly clambered clumsily in.

Then Hazel, who didn't need Marsha's assistance; she tiptoed a couple of steps, spun and leapt high into the wagon. It was Lydia's turn to get on next.

'Hurry, Toffee, hurry,' Marshmallow said, glancing at the signal light, now amber bright against the overcast sky. The engine horse snorted impatient.

Lydia put her foot on Marshmallow's cloak, ready to hop up off her back. The signal turned green. The train jerked forward. Lydia slipped, and she grabbed for the edge of the slidey door. The toffee tin was in the way, clunking against her like a cumbersome medallion. She couldn't hold on, about to fall back to the liquorice track, when a pair of caramel hands gripped her hood and yanked her up. Coco set Lydia down in the wagon, just as the train began to move away.

Marshmallow, who was lighter than she looked, got off her knees, and sprang up fast, the others helped to haul her aboard, leaving Peppermint to scamper along— suddenly, almost locust-like, Pepper launched herself at the wagon, grasped at the door with her four clawed hands before tumbling untidily inside. Her hood fell back, exposing her hair tied back in bands of black and white, just like the stripes of her eyes.

Sugar Cube sighed, relieved. 'You'd think we'd be better at this by now. With all the trains we've had to get on.'

'It was that *Toffee*'s fault,' uttered Bull's-Eye. 'Better not slow us down again.'

'Nobody's to blame,' Marshmallow said. 'We're all aboard now. Safe and sweet.'

The sisters wriggled out of their knapsacks, and laid them at their feet.

It was cold and dim inside the wagon; there wasn't much room to move about in either, the interior being stacked with storage pallets. Opposite the door, the girls found a shutter that slid back like a serving hatch, but it let in little light.

The locomotive picked up pace, from a canter to trot, to trot to trot, across the rails of liquorice track. And as the train rattled along, the floor, on which the sisterhood stood, shuddered unsteady, all wobbly like a jelly on a trembly plate. Thunder continued to crunch up above, and torrents of rain hammered down on the land. Sugar had to close the door to cut out the downpour, and this plunged the wagon into total darkness.

Lydia happened to be standing by the shutter and, up on her tiptoes, she peered through the hatch, catching a glimpse of the countryside as the steam train puffed its way past. This morning, she would never have thought she'd be making any sort of journey. And such an unlikely journey too: as a stowaway on a train with eight strange girls. *And* with a tinful of toffee to hand. Just feeling the tin there, pressed against her, gave Lydia so much comfort; she felt she was able to do anything with her toffee. A world of possibility, just a mouthful away. And it was all because of her lovely half-sister:

Celine will be in her car, Lydia thought wistfully, off to Burnville with its wonderful fudge factory. She'll be all right. Working for Stannic. Maybe she can bake him some kind of happy-cake. Then he won't be so nasty any more.

Lydia soon left behind her miserable life with Mater D, and an unfamiliar rail route of *liquorice sticks liquorice sticks* spirited her away.

The 'horse-drawn' freight train ate up track, travelling north towards the part of Likrishka known as the Black Rootry. Through the hatch, Lydia watched the rain-lashed landscape judder past, the silhouettes of silenced towns, and their outskirts with warehouses, junkyards, and factories. All the while, raindrops drumrolled down, *ta-ta-ta*cking on the metal of the roof of the wagon. Lydia could also hear rustles in the darkness, and suddenly the wagon lit up behind her.

'Better close that shutter,' ordered Sugar.

'Yeah, shut that hatch, *Toff*,' Bull's-Eye added, seeing Lydia standing there.

Lydia did as she was told; she slid the shutter shut, turning to find that Sugar Cube had a luminous tube whose light glowed turquoise across the girls' faces. She held this tube aloft to inspect the stacks of pallets.

There were six such stacks the sisters had to squeeze between. Each pallet contained an oblong slab, about the size of a mattress, coated in foil. The slabs had a strong saccharine scent, and Sugar knocked the nearest with her knuckles. *Thunk thunk.* The slab was rock hard, and looked really heavy too. Bull's-Eye *shripp*ed back the foil sheet to reveal a deep brown bar beneath.

'Oo, look look,' Coco smiled. 'Shocolart.'

'That's choca-lut?' Jawbreaker asked, seizing the

corner block of the bar. 'Hmm, not try choca-lut before.'
And saying that, she opened her immense mouth
wide and bit straight through the giant bar. The brittle
chocolate shattered into chunks, and Jawji choked
down a chip of it. 'Urh, thish shocky-lut sh'orrible,'
she grimaced.

Coco then nibbled at one of the bits. '*Yurk*. Is not
deluxe shocolart *we* know,' she said. 'Oo, Shawshi,' she
added excitedly, 'you shou' try tasty shocolar-char of ze
BonBon bistros. Is our favouritz. Is gourmet. Is *mwaa*.'
Cocoa-Butter kissed the air.

Jawji just shrugged, Coco's accent a bit too rich for
her.

'*Ohh*,' Marshmallow groaned, disappointed. She'd
also popped a bit of the bar in her mouth, but it tasted
so nasty she'd had to spit it out. 'A truck-a-load-a chocolate and none of it to eat.'

'We'd better settle down for the night,' Sugar suggested. 'I don't want to waste the light.'

'You don't expect me to sleep in here, do you?'
Hazel sniffed.

'Ah, I'm use to bunkin' up rougher than this,' said
Jawji.

'Yes, I'm not surprised *you* are,' said Hazel. 'But I
prefer my own boudoir.'

'Oh, stop moanin', ya girly Whirly,' Bull's-Eye
huffed.

'I'm sure we can all find a space on the floor,' said
Marsha.

83

'Hmm, maybe,' Sugar wondered aloud, 'we could make blankets out of that foil.'

By the turquoise light, the girls helped Sugar rip sheets of foil from five of the chocolate bars. They folded them over to form makeshift sleeping bags, then laid them down by the pallet stacks.

'If we share two to a sheet,' Sugar said, 'it'll save space and be warmer that way.'

Lydia stood there as the others paired up; she guessed they'd known each other a while and were already friends: the posh girl Hazel Whirl went with Coco; Peppermint with Sugar; Marshmallow and Dolly Mixture, Bull's-Eye and Jawbreaker. Leaving Lydia to wrap up alone.

And so, like cosy candy bars, the sisters huddled in the tin foil sheets. Their fleecy cloaks helped to keep out the cold and, once she was certain the girls had settled, Sugar doused her luminous tube, closing it up telescopically. The wagon went dark and, as Lydia shuffled to get comfortable, her foil sheet scraped upon the floor.

'Whoever's scuffin' rustlin', shut up!' came Bull's-Eye's voice.

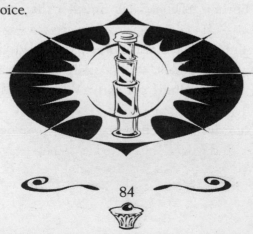

Chapter 7
Sugar Lumps

The 'Candi-Pan Express' horse continued across the liquorice rails; the guts of the wagon train grumbled and rumbled; then there was the constant rattle of the pallet stacks, slabs of yucky chocolate quivering within them.

Although it had been an exhausting day, Lydia found it difficult to sleep; her mind was full of uncertainty, bubbling over with so many questions. She could feel the turning wheels of the train, the drizzling away of the rooftop rain. She heard a crackle of foil too and then, soon after, faint clicking sounds coming from somewhere within the wagon. Lydia thought it best not to alert the others; she certainly didn't want to wake up Bull's-Eye and get another ticking off from her.

She folded back her foil sheet and ever so quietly got to her feet. In the dark, she started to feel her way along

the cold metallic pallets and, when she came to a gap at the back of the stacks, she turned to investigate the strange clicky snaps. Lydia froze as two eyes stared up at her. Robot eyes glowing infrared.

'Toffee?' came a voice with an electronic edge. The glowing eyes were Sugar's goggles. 'I hope I didn't wake you,' she whispered, switching on a teaspoon-torch. This pocket light was just bright enough to illuminate her pale features. 'If you wait a digit. I've nearly finished.'

Sugar Cube

As Lydia sat beside her, she could see that Sugar had scrunched up the sleeves of her jacket, exposing her arms marked with rectangular scars; then she gasped as Sugar used her finger to open a slot in one arm. From the slot, she flicked out what appeared to be a sugar lump, replaced it with a new cube, carefully clicked the slot shut again and pulled down her sleeve.

Lydia had thought there was something unnatural about Sugar the first time she'd heard her speak. She also had a scent of cough drops or some similar medicinal sweet. 'What's wrong with your arms?' Lydia asked. 'And your funny voice and glasses?'

'I was disabled as a baby,' Sugar replied. 'I could hardly hear, talk, or see. Couldn't move or do anything.'

'But you're better now.'

'I've spent my life in a sweet institute. On the isle of Layakayk. Treated by my mother. Her speciality was Sucro-Bionics.'

'Soo-croo-bye? Oh. What's those?'

'It's a bit complicated to explain.'

'Oh, *please*,' Lydia said, glad to be speaking privately like this.

'Well, it's to do with sugary energy cells and putting them into living things. Like with me. My muscles have been replaced with sucron batteries and, to function, I need my daily dose of sugar pills. I'm sure you saw me eating them earlier.'

'Is that like the sugar you put in your tea?' Lydia asked.

'Not quite,' Sugar Cube replied. 'It's really a medicine. Glucose tablets. And time to time I need to change the sugar lumps in my limbs. I do that when the others are asleep.'

'How could you tell what you're doing in the dark?'

'I don't see like other people do, Toffee. These goggles I wear are a pair of viewers that send real-time images to my eyes. My voice-box is artificial too, and I have to wear hearing aids.' Sugar pushed aside the spikes of her hair to show Lydia the pink disc inserted in her ear. 'Thing is, with all this sucro-technology, my senses are much better than they ever would be normally. As long as my sugar levels don't drop.'

She smiled, then frowned, and looked blankly at the crumbling lumps in her hand.

'So where's this train taking us?' Lydia had been dying to ask.

'We're off to find some rare sweets,' Sugar replied. 'But I'm still waiting for a list.'

'The *list*,' Lydia realized. 'I've got this list of sweets!' she whispered excited.

'You do? Where?' Sugar looked on as Lydia gave her the silver paper wrapped around the crystal heart. 'Can I see that red stone?' she asked.

'Be careful with it. It was my mummy's.'

Sugar took the heart in her gloved hands, and used her teaspoon-torch to analyse the intricate crystal. 'Hmm. Ultracoronary corallosis. Very unusual illness. I'm sorry about your mother, Toffee.'

'Mummy was lovely,' Lydia said sadly, folding the heart back into the hankie.

Sugar now studied the silver paper, and its list of sweets they were supposed to find:

Diamond Sun Bean. Chilly Jelly Amethyst.
Sapphire Fizzweed. Jet Heart Truffle.
Winter Pearl Drop. Ruby Red Shortbread.

'Hmm. These sweets will be tricky to track down,' she said. 'They're bound to be found in different parts of the country.'

'But the Tin Man's got robot soldiers everywhere, hasn't he?'

'That's why we need you and your tin, Toffee. You can help us stop Stannic's machines.'

'How do you know about me and my tin?'

'I have a file about you. It arrived on my computer. And data for the others too.'

'What do the others do then?' Lydia asked.

'Oh, they each have their own ability. You saw how Jawji chomped through that chocolate. And you know how good Coco is at stealing things without being seen.'

'How did you all meet?'

'I've been getting everyone together for a while now. Tracking them down. Breaking out of prison towns, stowing away on trains. I've seen more of the world these past few weeks than the rest of my life,' Sugar said. 'You were one of the most awkward to free. Someone had to get a toffee tin to you, watch out for robots, time your escape right.'

Lydia suddenly remembered Celine's jade snails; she took them from her pinafore and offered the bag to Sugar. 'Would you like one of these?'

'What are they?'

'Fancy sweets my half-sister made. I pinched them from rotten Mater D.'

'You say they were made *for* your Mater Detainer?' Sugar took a jade snail from the bag, but instead of eating it, she crushed it in her glove, and sniffed the jelly shelly fragments. 'Ooh!' she winced. 'This sweet's been spiked with alcola.'

'Is that good?'

'It's a rare spice used in medicine. Just a taste can paralyse a person for hours.'

Lydia grinned as she understood why Celine had given the sweets to old misery-guts. 'Mater D must have eaten one for breakfast!'

'Only an expert chemist-chef could have prepared these snails.'

'Oh, Celine's amazing. She's really famous—'

'I know. Celine Argenta, your half-sister. I've read all about her.'

'Wow. You are a right smartie-pants,' Lydia said.

'It's my memory,' answered Sugar. 'Everything sticks in my brain like treacle. I can even speed-feed computer data direct into my digital eyes. Gigabytes, dinnabytes, entire encyclopaedic meals. Maps of cities. Candi-Tangi dictionaries—'

Lydia gave an enormous yawn. 'Oo, sorry.'

'You look tired, Toffee. Get some sleep. There's hours of our journey to go yet.'

'The floor isn't very comfy.'

'Here.' From one of her many buttoned pockets, Sugar took a red-capped plastic tube; she tipped out a small round gumdrop onto the palm of her glove. 'Here, eat this.'

'What is it?' Lydia asked, taking the gumdrop and popping it into her mouth.

'It's a Slumber Bonbon,' Sugar said. 'Perfectly harmless. It's a goodie gumdrop.'

The bonbon tasted a little like liquorice, and straightaway Lydia felt woozy drowsy. She rested her head against Sugar Cube's coat, and her mind drifted into a dreamless aniseedy sleep—the first time, in a long time, that Lydia hadn't been beset by nightmares.

When Lydia stirred, she found herself curled up in a sheet of crinkly foil, her backpack and toffee tin placed beside her. The sluggish *chew-chew chunk* of the train wheels seemed to be much louder now; someone had pulled back the slidey door, and daylight flickered into the wagon.

From under the foil, Lydia could see that the others were awake and stood in the space at the end of the carriage. She recalled last night's talk with Sugar: whatever abilities they possessed, surely this assortment of girls wouldn't get far in a country run by Stannic's robots. How could Hazel, Dolly, or Coco hope to overcome an army of machines? What could Jawji or Marshmallow do to keep them all from ending up in factory prisons?

This morning, even Bull's-Eye looked subdued, yawning, and rubbing her eyes with her fists.

A few of the girls had opened their lunch tubs, and sat down to eat the snacks packed inside—snacks from kiosks and vending machines they'd broken into on their travels.

Lydia glanced at Peppermint. The strange blue child hardly ever looked up and, with her two pairs of claws, she jittered open a bag of crisps, and stabbed a straw into a carton of fruit juice; then she ate squirrel-like, nibbling crisps and slurping on her carton in turn.

Lydia also saw Cocoa-Butter eating creamy crackers and shortcake biscuits. Her face looked paler now, framed by frosty whipped-cream hair; even her soufflé-beret seemed flatter and sat on her head like a pat of butter. But that was until Coco swallowed two squares of her pure white chocolate—for 'afters' the sisters dipped into their sweet supplies—and Lydia watched as the caramel colour returned to her cheeks, her hair turned utterly butter-rich gold, and Coco became more lively and somehow slippery to the eye.

Lydia felt hungry as well, and so she decided to get up. Clutching her tin, she dragged her backpack over to join the others. *Hmm*, toffee for breakfast (even if it was only one piece). No more of Mater D's meals for her.

After they had eaten, the girls packed up their things and prepared to while away the time remaining on the train.

Coco snapped open a compact that was varnished brown like a big chocolate button, and she peered in its mirror, grinning and pouting, putting on a little caramel lipstick.

Hazel also had cosmetics in her holdall and, after she'd brushed the swirls of her hair, she applied a creamy moisturizer, circling it into her cheeks.

Marshmallow, meanwhile, was peeking through the gap by the door, and Lydia went and knelt beside her, hoping to catch sight of their surroundings. During the night, the express horse had bypassed the Black Rootry, and there were no more industrial districts to see. The view was now one of open countryside: vanilla plains and flat patch pastures, hills and hills in wave formation, yellow crops as bright as lemon drops.

'This is Franjipan,' Marsha said. 'It looks a nice place to hide. I've seen it in picture books.'

Lydia heard Sugar's distinctive voice next; she sounded very serious too, asking the girls to gather round as she had something important to say to them all:

'Now then, sisters, listen please—I think that now's a good time to tell you about the person who helped us all escape.'

'In't that *you*?' said Dolly. 'And Peppy-mint and Zye?'

'We three did our bit, I admit,' replied Sugar. 'But how do you think we knew about you all? And precisely where we'd find you?'

93

'I assumed it's because you were ever-so-clever,' said Hazel.

'Well, none of us would be here right now, if it wasn't for someone called Mam-ba-Hisska.'

'Oo who is zis Hisska person, Shoogar?' asked Coco.

'In Tangi-language *Mam-ba-Hisska* means Lady of the Snakes.'

'Oh that's right,' said Hazel. 'People in Tangiya speak differently, don't they? They do.'

'Lady Hisska told me to track you all down,' Sugar continued. 'She also knew we had unusual abilities. Hisska promised to assist us, guide us, and said we were her chosen Sisterhood.'

'But how did she know about our abilities?' quizzed Hazel. 'I mean, I know you know I'm a famous dancer, but I'd kept my super-speed a secret, so I thought.'

'Why'd she care about us, anyway?' asked Bull's-Eye. 'Nobody bother 'bout me before.'

'She needs our help in stopping the Tin Man,' Sugar said. 'So she's sent us to find these six special sweets. You could call it a confectionery treasure hunt.'

'How will these sweets defeat the Tin Man?' said Marsha.

'I'm not sure exactly,' Sugar Cube frowned.

'What'sh this "Ishka" person look like then, Shugz?' asked Jawji.

'Don't know.'

'For someone who knows everything, you don't know much,' said Hazel.

94

'I've never seen Hisska face to *face*,' Sugar explained. 'It was weeks ago, she sent all this coded data to my computer. At the science centre where I lived. It was right before Stannic's robots took it over. I only just got away, and I couldn't even help my mum. This Snake Lady Hisska saved us *all* from being captured. So we have to trust her. And try to help her.'

'I reckon this Snake Lady's a witch,' pondered Dolly, 'who lives in a walnut hut in the Tangi jungle. And we s'pose to find all these special sweeties to spice up her magic's potions.'

'So we gotta go all these dangerous places?' Bull's-Eye said. 'Findin' sweets for some mouldy old witch?'

'Oh I don't mind helping finding things,' said Hazel. 'But I'm not going near any robottos. I'm not.'

'I don't want to go near any robots either,' Sugar told her. 'If we're careful, we can avoid them.'

'Where we go now then?' Jawji asked.

'We're on our way to the White Forest first. We've got to start our hunt for these sweets, and there's a girl in Franjipan who can help us. Speaking of which,' Sugar said, 'we'd better get ready to get off. The train's about to stop.' Sugar then adjusted a button on her outer coat, and the colour of the garment changed, from chocolate brown to a pale almond yellow.

'Wow,' smiled Lydia. 'Your coat can be any colour you want?'

'I invented it myself,' Sugar explained. 'It's a fibre-optic fabric with rainbow drop plasma—'

'Oh, don't bore us all stupid with *that* again,' Bull's-Eye griped.

'I was only telling Toffee about my coat,' Sugar frowned. She also showed the girls how their fleeces turned inside out, so they now became cream with a lining of black. It was going to be lighter where they were headed, and creamy cloaks would blend in better.

And so, on their leader's advice, the rest of the sisters rearranged their hidey-hoods; then they shrugged themselves back into their knapsacks and waited by the wagon door, ready to alight.

The liquorice tracks passed the countryside sights, and veered into a shimmering forest: a forest full of tall nut trees with whitish trunks and creamy leaves. It was here that the steam train came to a halt, just as Sugar had predicted.

Lydia looked out from the wagon to see it had stopped at a temporary depot complete with water tanks, supply pipes, and troughs. With the arrival of the long grey locomotive, pairs of articulated metal limbs unfolded from their trackside positions and, as the arms creaked and clanked into action, Sugar Cube ordered the girls from the train.

One at a time, they clambered from the wagon and scurried into the surrounding forest. From the trees, the sisters watched as the metal limbs fixed a funnel to the horse; then wielding great iron spoons, they swung across from trough to funnel, trough to funnel, shovelling a black sludge into the engine.

'What's that stuff they're shovin' in, Shugz?' Jawbreaker asked.

'It's gruelly fuel,' Sugar told her. 'A mix of coke 'n' oats.'

'The train runs on coconuts?' said Dolly.

'No, you sherbet *dip*,' sneered Bull's-Eye. 'It's like a black rock, coke is. Isn' it, Sugar? So there.'

'Hmm,' Sugar nodded. 'It's liquidized then thickened with grain. Makes an energy porridge for lorries and trains.'

Once the automated limbs had finished feeding the engine, they removed the funnel, and folded back into place, allowing the train to trundle off with its twenty-two trucks of chocolate blocks.

Chew chew chunk. Chew chew chunk.

The '*Candi-Pan Express*' left its nine stowaways to the stillness of the vast White Forest.

Chapter 8
Marzipan

The girls were glad to be outside. It was pleasantly quiet in the forest shade with no sounds except the twittering of birds, and occasional crackle of branches.

Sugar Cube stood concentrating, trying to detect something deep within the trees. 'There!' She turned her feet precise degrees and proceeded to pace in a straight direction. The other girls followed in a disorderly line, with Lydia timidly lagging behind.

Between the tall cream trees they went, breathing the sweet autumnal air. Golden light filtered through the canopy, illuminating the spacious forest, and the triangular leaves that glittered down over the slopes of soil (soil that was all crumbly white, supporting pale or yellow plant life: feathery ferns, thickets of gorse, daisy flowers, and dandelions). The forest floor was crisp and dry, and the light *choc choc* of the children's footsteps mixed with the *chicori clicks* and *buzzy zizzes* of unseen insects.

Occasionally they did glimpse these cricketty creatures looking like strips of citron peel nestling in the tree-trunk cracks; and then there were silvery wrapper-flies orbiting in clusters. The girls did their best to avoid these insects, and continued to shadow their leader Sugar along the forest trails.

Still feeling left out, Lydia dawdled, yawning and peering into brooks they passed; she noticed goldfish, and gelatinous newts nipping in and out of the whitish sugar-water.

'Keep up, *Toffee*!' Lydia heard, and she looked up to see Bull's-Eye scowling at her.

'Stop being mean to her, Zye,' said Marsha.

So distracted by the novelty forest, Lydia hadn't realized the others had stopped; they watched as leaves were disturbed on the ground, accompanied by a soft slishing sound.

'Whassat wotsit?' Coco whispered.

'Eee!' Dolly squealed. 'It's a sneak!'

And there, slithering swiftly towards them, was a lemon-chequered rattlesnake. The serpent slipped up close to Sugar, then lay in the leaves, its tail rattling:

Shug-a-shug-a-shug. Shug-a-shug-a-shug.

'Nothing to worry about,' said Sugar. 'It's one of Hisska's snakes. I can tell.'

From inside her jacket, she took out a case the size of a small plate; this green case had a shiny outer shell that made it resemble a flattened apple, and Sugar

clicked it in half to reveal a laptop screen and rows of multicoloured keys.

'That's a smartie computer,' said Lydia. She'd never seen a device quite like it before. Nicer than the oven-TV, she thought. *And it doesn't have a nasty goose on top.*

Sugar put her apple-green laptop on the ground and, to the sisters' astonishment, the serpent slithered up to the computer, and inserted its forked tongue into a side port. 'So it isn't a *real* sneak?' Dolly said, nosing closer.

'It's how I get sent all this coded data.'

Sugar nudged Dolly out of the way, and she knelt in the leaves while the wiry serpent loaded its bits and bytes into the computer. Sugar then tapped away at the keys, typing so speedily her fingers were a blur across the multicoloured keyboard.

'I've got a bigger computer than *that* back home,' said Hazel. 'And it plays multimedia music disks on it. I bet Sugar's doesn't.'

'Hazel, don't be such a boaster,' said Marsha. 'Sugar does important things with her computer.'

'And I have a mobile phone to play games on,' Hazel muttered. 'I do.'

'My little brother Matt likes 'puter games,' said Dolly Mixture. 'He's got Manic Baker, ehm, Sim City Teashop, Spice Invaders . . .'

While Dolly waffled on about her brother's computer, Sugar Cube perused the data crackling off the tongue of Hisska's serpent:

'The sister we're looking for,' she read, 'was last seen near the village of Miniegg.'

The snake unplugged its tongue, rattled its tail again, and slithered away slowly.

Sugar closed up her apple laptop and tucked it back in a jacket pocket. 'Come on,' she beckoned, 'we'll soon track her down.'

The lemon-chequered rattlesnake led the girls on, deeper into the bright White Forest, its sinuous body threading them through the hazy maze of trees. The children walked and walked and walked, and became so bored they started to natter:

Hazel Whirl, the elegant dancer who Lydia wanted to befriend, was already talking with Cocoa-Butter; they both had similar fancy tastes, and gushed about make-up and fashion and things—things which Lydia knew nothing about. Dolly and Marsha chatted to each other too; they came from neighbouring regions of Delisha, and had joined this sisterhood about the same time. Even Bull's-Eye had a friend in Jawbreaker, and made occasional comments to her. Meanwhile, Peppermint and Sugar shared a conversation, Pepper jotting on her note pad wafer, sending wireless whispers to Sugar's hearing aids.

In addition to the chatter and the *slish-slish* slither of their serpentine guide, Lydia heard these intermittent croaks, croaks which always sounded close by. 'That *your* shtumach gugglin', Marsha?' Jawbreaker asked.

'Sounds as though you swallowed a toad,' said Hazel, making Dolly laugh.

'Well, I'm *hungry*,' Marshmallow said.

'You're always hungry,' Bull's-Eye remarked.

'Well, I assume it takes a lot of food to fill up a body that big and tubby,' Hazel uttered tactlessly.

'I can't help being big,' Marshmallow said.

'Sh-mostly mallowy flab, ay, Marsh?' Jawbreaker joshed, harmlessly thumping her fists into Marshmallow's punchball body.

'Stop that!' Marsha bounced the tomboy away with a nudge from her bumper hip.

'We famish also,' added Coco. 'And we cannot keep monching our shocolart.'

'Isn't everything in the forest eatable?' mentioned Lydia.

'Oh, shut up, Toffee,' Bull's-Eye said. 'Like you know more than *we* do.'

'Most things *are* edible if they're prepared right,' said Sugar, but then added it would be better to wait till they found the Franjipani girl who was the real expert on the subject of plant life.

'Yeah,' mentioned Jawji. 'When's she gonna show—?'

Sugar shushed her. '*Listen.*' Her sensitive hearing detected something. Lydia heard the noises too. Scratchy sounds and animal cries. Then she was startled to see a clutch of wildcats slinking around the roots of the trees. There must have been at least ten of them, all

with yellow-striped off-white coats, pointed tufty ear-tips and curly whiskers with a twist.

'Lemon lynx,' Sugar whispered. 'Stay quite still.'

'They come near me,' said Bull's-Eye, 'I'll *kick* 'em.'

The lemon lynx surrounded the girls, miaowed at them and showed their fangs.

All of a sudden, from up in the trees, these golden cereal grains rained down, pattering upon the ground and scattering the lemon lynx who jumped away excited, pouncing on the golden nuggets, *cru-crunch*ing them crisp with their teeth.

Lydia looked up into the tall tall trees; she assumed there must be someone there, but all she could see was a mesh of twigs and quivering leaves. Then the branches appeared to move and, with a *snap-crack-crackle*, a leaf-covered little girl fell from a tree. However, instead of crashing to the ground, she descended by grasping branch after branch, using the tree as an elaborate ladder, before landing in a crumpled heap, unhurt.

She was an unusual girl (though no more so than the other children Lydia was with): she was willowy thin with an oval face, and her yellowish hair was tied back and knotted tight in a plait. Her skin was white, like the bark of the trees; indeed, she appeared to be *made* of wood but, as she got up, her face colour changed to a light nut brown, and her skin became soft and human. She also wore this long-sleeved dress composed of layers of creamy foliage, a garment to help her blend in with the forest.

Her almond eyes stared at the sisters. 'Who are you?' she said softly.

'We're here to help you, Alma,' smiled Sugar.

'You know my name,' said the leaf-covered girl. Then she glanced at the snake at Sugar's feet. 'I see this serpent sometime. It follow me.'

'It's a harmless tracker-snake,' Sugar told her. 'It would have been impossible to find you without it.'

The sisters welcomed Alma to the group, once Sugar had explained about Hisska and the list of sweets, and how they might help stop Stannic's machines.

Alma understood only too well; she spoke of 'metal scare-men' that captured her people some time ago.

Alma

By now, the prowling lemon lynx cats had eaten all the cereal grain, and began to close in on the girls again. Alma raised one of her hands so the sleeve of her leafy dress spread wide, and inside Lydia could see lots of pouches like fruit hanging down from her arm. In one of these pouches there were more golden nuggets, which Alma sprinkled around for the cats.

'Aah,' sighed Dolly, kneeling by one of the lynx. 'It so cutie-pie. Lookit its twisty whiskiers.'

'Mind yourself,' Alma warned her. 'It is not a domesti-cat.'

Dolly didn't listen and went to pet it. The lynx hissed and lashed out with a clawed paw. 'Oo, naughty cat!' Dolly swatted back. The lynx then leapt at her, bit her hand, and scampered away. 'Aah, din't be scared of me.' Dolly waved. And she left the rest of the lynx undisturbed to gnaw at the last of their cereal nuggets.

Lydia was puzzled. 'Didn't that cat just bite you, Dolly?'

Dolly smiled, and showed Lydia her hand. It was scarred with teeth marks, but with no sign of bleeding. Then, to Lydia's continued surprise, Dolly rubbed her skin and caused the bite to disappear. 'I'm all right, though,' she said.

'We have to think of a code name for you,' Marsha said to Alma.

'Oo!' cried Dolly. 'What about *Nut Wood*? Cuz you look like a tree. Oh. We couldn't call you Nutty, could we?'

'And it's not the name of a sweet,' snorted Bull's-Eye.

'I've got one,' suggested Hazel. 'Franjipani cake? A nice slice of lemon-flavoured Franjipani cake.'

'Oh, *that's* catchy,' joked Jawji.

'I like *Marzipan*,' Alma said, and that was that.

The lemon-chequered tracker-snake now slipped away into the forest, leaving the girls with their latest companion, Marzipan of Franjipan.

And so they set off to her village of Miniegg to plan their next what-do-we-do.

As Marzipan showed them a way through the wood, Lydia noticed the plants on the ground beginning to crop up in distinctive patterns. Soon the girls were passing through what appeared to be a street of trees paved with turf and lined with wokky pots, salad bushes, and untrimmed bonsai.

At the end of this woodland avenue, the children arrived at a village built about the tree-trunks. Lydia was giddy with wonder, turning every which way to see the houses up in the branches, living pods like giant eggs, some of them put atop platformed towers.

The village had been fashioned from creamy logs, giving it the appearance of pieced-together pasta. Spaghetti-like vines stretched between the buildings, and birdfeeders and wickerwork cages had been suspended from them.

The cream eggs were also linked by bamboo tubes,

in segments like oversized rolls of macaroni; these were the village's plumbing pipes, but they'd all been neglected and some tubes had split and were dribbling water. All the cages were empty too, and their swaying lent an air of desolation to the place.

All the cages, that is, except one: across from the girls perched a silvery bird with the hooked beak of a hawk. Lydia stared at it. The bird stared back with beady eyes that *click-click*ed like cameras. Then the hawk launched from the open cage and, with a terrible screeching, it swooped straight at them.

Sugar cried out and winced in pain as a fizz of interference trilled through her brain.

Bull's-Eye scrabbled for a pebble from the ground and, with a whip of her arm, she slung it—*Clunk!* It struck the moving hawk with deadly accuracy— but, to her surprise, the bird turned and tried to fly away.

'That bird's . . . metal,' Sugar said weakly. 'Toffee, *do* something. Don't let it get away.'

Lydia snatched up her liquorice sticks and improvised a complicated beat upon the toffee tin, trying to snare the metal hawk as it circled overhead, its flight all stuttery, interrupted by ropes and trees and towers at every turn. The hawk's wings flapped slower and slower as though attracted by a potent magnet; yet still it fought the pull of her drum, all the while trilling out its irritating tinny cries. For Lydia it was a real struggle, like tugging at a wayward wind-blown kite.

'*Oo* . . . it . . . dun't wunt to—' Lydia hammered a command upon the tin lid, made the bird swoop and smack into a tree trunk; after which, with one of its wings smashed, it dropped to the ground and stopped its screeching.

The children gathered round this strange metallic bird.

'Well done, Toffee,' Sugar said, relieved. 'I could feel that hawk squawking in computer code. It cut right through me.'

'I got the bird before *Toffee* did,' Bull's-Eye bragged, pointing out the rounded dent in its beak. 'If I'd had a bigger rock I would've knocked its head off.'

'Stopping that horrid birdy though,' said Hazel, 'by drumming on a tin. I am very impressed.'

'How did you *do* it, Toffee?' asked Dolly.

'Erm, it's like—' Lydia tried to explain—'it's like my mind can stick to metal things, and then, if I concentrate, my drumming can pull the metal about, or cause it to crunch up or jump or stop. Or whatever I want to, really.'

Much of the hawk was still intact, and now its body started twitching, its beak began clicking, so Bull's-Eye stamped her hoof on it quick, shattering its lightweight casing. Sugar crouched down to examine the remains; the innards of the bird were a mixture of circuits powered by solar cells along its wings; she also discovered the head unscrewed, and she shook out a tiny digital camera.

'I see these silver bird before,' said Marzipan. 'They arrive with the metal men. Their poison-eyes pick out people that hide.'

'There must be lots more of them, then,' said Sugar. 'Stannic's flying spies.'

Chapter 9
Coconut Mushrooms

Marzipan guided the girls to a tower that reached up to one of the cream egg buildings. Near the base of the tower was a lock like a nutshell and, using a key, Marzipan cracked the shell in half; this caused a door to swing up flappily, and she invited the others inside. One by one, the sisterhood ducked through, careful not to catch their backpacks on the flap. Then, once they'd all squeezed in, Marzipan snapped the nutshell shut, and the door lowered and locked.

The tower was built out of slightly spaced logs, and this allowed slits of sunlight in to fall in pretty patterns upon their faces. Lydia could see a narrow staircase wind up and up to the treehouse at the top, and Marzipan led them all into the tower, the assorted sounds of the sisters' feet—scrapey shoes and thuddy trainers, scuffy pumps and ballet slippers, a leather boot, a single hoof—clacking up the spiral stairs.

At the top, a flap flipped up, and the girls climbed into the cream egg treehouse.

The first thing that struck Lydia was the colour of the walls; the treehouse's interior had been painted yolky yellow, and this made the room seem warm and homely. Mats of plaited grass lay around a low dining table, and all the furniture and fittings were made of a type of papier mâché in marbled blues and limes.

'I used to live here with my mother,' said Marzipan. 'I stay here alone now. Only go out to look for food. I try to find others who hide same as me. But there is never anybody.'

'What happened to the people, Marzi?' asked Marsha.

'They were rounded up by metal men. I climbed high in the trees. Hid like wood. I see them use bottles that spray fizzy gas. They put people in fields then spray them to sleep.'

'Where are the robottos now?' quizzed Hazel.

'The metal men move on, long ago,' said Marzipan. 'In trucks like giant soup can.'

'That means we be free to find those treasure-sweeties, won't we?' said Dolly.

'*Diamond Sun Beans* we need to find first,' Sugar recalled. 'Are they somewhere near here, Marzi?'

Marzipan shook her head. 'They are a type of jelly bean. And the jelly bean trees are very far away. Even on transport, we won't get to them today.'

Marzi now invited the sisters to sit around the table,

and they rustled down on the grassy mats, while she brought out a number of picnic baskets.

Lydia didn't expect very much. After all, what could one little girl find while hiding in the woods? A pocketful of paltry nuts? A few bitter berries? A bit of tough lemon bark torn off the trees? The baskets, though, were filled with dozens of homemade delicacies. Marzi must have hoarded a hundred ingredients to produce so much, and Lydia was '*Wow!*' won over by the food on offer: almonds set in pastry pats, nut-glut biscuits and fruity shoots; soft doughy rolls and cinnamon scones; seed-encrusted bread sticks to be dipped into pots of lemon jam, and mini flans filled with frangipane. The tum-grumbly girls tucked into the food.

Only Sugar didn't eat, and sat there chewing on her thoughts instead. Lydia was sad to see she didn't partake of the delightful spread, so she got up and offered Sugar one of the cookies: 'These taste quite sugary,' she said. 'Why don't you have one of these?'

'I'm fine, Toffee, really,' Sugar replied. 'I have to be careful what I eat.'

'Yeah, leave her alone, Toffee!' Bull's-Eye snapped. 'You'll make her *sick*.'

'Um lucky,' Jawji spluttered with her mouth full. 'I can spritzy much munch *any*fink.'

To complete the brunch, Marzipan fetched cups of water fresh from the kitchen's pasta-taps. 'I don't have enough cups for everyone,' she said.

'Sh-all right, Marz,' Jawji smiled, spitting crumbs as she spoke, 'I jush share mine wiv Marsha or summink.'

'I'd like my own cup if you *don't* mind,' Hazel was sure to stress. 'And can I have a serviette? I really don't want to mess up my dress. Marzipan? Marzi? Excuse me—' Hazel tugged on the girl's leaves as she passed. 'A serviette, please.'

'I'll see what I can find.' Marzipan nodded, and left the room.

'She isn't your *servant*,' Marshmallow said to Hazel. 'Why are you always so fussy?'

Marzipan returned with a pile of paper towels, and handed one to each of the girls.

'Is there anywhere where I can freshen up, Marzi?' asked Hazel, ignoring Marsha's comment.

Marzipan pointed Hazel to a bathroom and, once the other girls had finished eating (and stocked their lunchboxes with yummy leftovers), they took turns to use it too. Marzi, meanwhile, gathered her things; she was sure to take all of her stock of yellow blocks, blocks of almond fondant she had stashed in a box. Lydia could see why Alma had chosen that name for herself. Her special sweet *was* marzipan.

Lastly she bagged some peach tea powder, and favourite biscuits, nuts, and scones; Marzi didn't need a knapsack, her pouches would suffice.

'Food was lovely,' Lydia said to Marzipan. 'I haven't had snacks so nice since my mummy—' She stopped herself. 'It doesn't matter now.'

114

Peppermint wrote something on her note pad.

'Pepper says *thank you* too,' relayed Sugar Cube.

'And I don't feel empty any more,' said Marsha, giving her tummy a squeeze.

The sisters spent no more time in the treehouse; Marzi cracked open an oval hatch, an exit onto a platform balcony, and the children stepped from there to these wickerwork walkways.

The walkways were quite high up in the trees; they curved around the egg-topped towers, linking balconies, railings, and ladders, thus enabling the girls to pick a course through the village. It was, however, something of an obstacle course: the carved wooden railings overflowed with foliage; yellow creepers tangled down, encroached on some of the living pods, and made it look as though dribbles of yolk were running down the giant eggs. The girls made their way from platform to platform, treehouse to treehouse, the white wood wickerwork creaking with their weight. Marzi assured them the walkways were safe; in any case, peering down, Lydia saw that the woven vines formed spaghetti nets just below them.

Up and down the ladders they went, step hup to the bamboo balconies; the walkways continued around the trees, around the branches and creamy leaves. Marzi then led them down to the ground, through yet another tower and spiral staircase.

The tower came out by an animal enclosure with a penne-like fence and a horse inside.

'Oo, a pony!' Dolly cried. 'In't he lovely?' She ran up excited, and fell over the fence.

Marzipan, with more composure, opened a gate to let the girls in. They went over to the small sorrel horse, a franji-pony, all patchy brown with mint white rings and fluffy fetlock feet.

'Hello, Polo-mino,' Marzi said, stroking the pony's creamy mane, feeding him sugar shoots from a pouch, and making *pruf-pruf* sounds with her mouth. 'My village look after lots of animals as pets. I let them all go. Though I couldn't leave Polo.'

'Can I ride on him?' Dolly pleaded. 'Can I, *please?*'

'Of course,' said Marzi. 'But treat him gently.'

The other sisters went to pat the pony, but when Pepper approached him, he acted perturbed, bucked a bit and backed away. Marzi managed to calm the animal, lead him from the pen, while Peppermint hunched in her hidey-hood ashamed.

Marzi now went to a little wooden garage, and rolled out a two-wheeled egg-shaped carriage: a light papier mâché trap with rigatoni axles and spokes.

Marzipan tethered the pony to the trap; she and Dolly got up on his back, and the other eight children bundled into the egg.

And so they set off from Marzi's village. Through the eerily quiet White Forest, up and down the leafy slopes, bobbing along on the franji-pony trap. Even with its cushioned omelette-seats, enough to accommodate four

adults, it was quite a squeeze for the sisters in the carriage: Jawji bunching up to get comfy, Marshmallow mushed up in the corner; Peppermint all fidgety elbows; Coco, making mischief, wriggled for the fun of it; Hazel complaining about the crowded bumpy ride, Sugar as usual frowned and sighed, while fed-up Bull's-Eye shoved and huffed, with Lydi'-in-the-middle getting squashed and pushed.

On their travels, from time to time, Marzi got Polo the pony to stop; then the children left the trap, and took their knapsacks to go and find food. Now that they were with Marzipan, they discovered that the forest was stuffed full of edible nibblable treats.

Sweet-hunting really appealed 'to Lydia; when she was very young, she used to go out brambling with Mummy, looking for currants around Redberry Common. (She was good at finding fruity sweetie things—had a 'nose' for it, so Mummy told her: a sweet-hunter's nose just like her father's—Of course, now Lydia thought about it, Mummy was probably talking about Celine's dad, not her daddy Petro.)

Once Marzipan had shown the sisters the best sweet plants and where to find them, Lydia was soon sniffing around all on her own, locating shrubs of gooseberry chews, and sugary asparagus spears, to save in her knapsack for later.

In one place, the creamy bark was peeling from the trees, and Marzipan started handpicking it—she shook off a beetle first—putting the bark in a pouch.

'Whatcha kept that for?' Jawji asked.

'Make a mock chocolate soup.' Marzipan smiled. She encouraged the others to take some too; then she could boil some soup for all of them later.

Marzi was a kid in a candy wood, picking and pouching the plentiful plants, a variety of sweets and fruits and nuts. And then there were trees with nutty pods yielding her favourite almond fondant. Light yellow moss had also spread across these trees, a flossy moss that was perfectly lickable; Marzipan scraped it off with her fingers. 'Umm *yes*,' she tasted, 'is nice and fresh.'

Elsewhere, the children helped themselves to sticks of yellow rhubarb.

'In't rhubarb *red*?' Dolly said, pulling up a custard-coloured stalk.

'That's *Black* Forest rhubarb,' Marzipan put her right. 'White Forest's is light. Has a mellower flavour.'

Marzi uncovered unusual shoots and fruits and flowers both nutritional and medicinal and rich in vital vitamins and minerals. There were yellow berries, a remedy for tummy aches; a fever-relieving eucalyptus, the sap of which could cure the shiver shakes. There were little white dock leaves that, if eaten neat, could clear the skin of a nasty rash. Or spicy nuts that pepped a person up if they were feeling bored or sad.

The wonderful White Forest was also where certain honey-centred lozenges grew, the ones Lydia remembered Mummy giving her, to soothe a rotten cough she'd got.

This sweet does this. That plant does that. Marzi was an utter botany swot.

And she was an expert in zoology too, pointing out any animals in the forest: there were pale brown chipmunk creatures that scurried squirrelly across the branches; thin lemon chameleons dozing almost unnoticed in the leaves; an albino mole nosed shyly from its hole, while canaries and finches chirruped *syrup-syrup* from nooks in the trees. Lydia even saw a small bear with pale pink fur.

'That *is* a rare bear,' Marzi whispered to her: 'A franji-panda.'

Lydia had never heard of a pink bear before. But there it was. A pink panda. A candy pink panda. Now that was a kooky something. And it proved to be a scaredy-cat, did a runner when Lydia tried to pat its back. She lost the pink panda in this shaded glade and, instead, came across what looked like miniature dishes scattered across the forest floor; they turned out to be the caps of coconut mushrooms.

Lydia called the other girls over.

'Oo. *We* like zese,' Coco clapped. 'And zez so so much.'

'That's because there's been no one to pick them,' said Marzi.

They all collected a few tubs full, plucking the stalks from the coarse white soil.

Jawbreaker went to tuck into her mushrooms straightaway.

'Ah-ah,' said Marzi. 'We wash them first.'

'Yes, *Jaw*ji,' Hazel agreed. 'Don't you have any manners? Miss *Muck*.'

The children found a nearby brook, dipping the coconut mushrooms in and cleaning off the soil. Then they settled on a stretch of grass.

Marzi made the sisters sit in a circle, while she performed a tea ceremony important to her people. First, she filled a wooden cup with water, and mixed in some peach tea powder from her pouch.

Marzipan sat in a lotus position, looking like a pile of leaves; she bowed towards the centre of the circle, picked up the cup in both of her hands, raised it slowly to her lips, closed her eyes and took a sip. Then she passed the cup to the girl on her left.

'Franjipani people begin picnics like this,' said Marzi. It was easy to see the quiet joy with which she shared this ritual with her newfound friends; and yet Lydia also saw in Marzi—deep inside her almond eyes—similar sorrows to her own, sorrows fresher in her mind; her loss of family, village, community. All of these feelings in a single cup of tea.

And so, one by one, sister to sister, they sipped the tea, and passed the cup.

Lydia treated it like some mealtime game; she hadn't played games nor shared anything with anyone for many years. So, when it was her turn, she made sure she did everything correctly. '*Mmm*, the tea was really tasty.' Its peach flavour sparkled with the water from the

brook. Once all ten sisters had sipped the tea, they were free to eat their forest treats. The mushrooms proved to be lovely and filling. The light brown caps were all flaky with coconut, but to Lydia's delight they were a bit like toffee too. Chewy and gooey, they stuck to the teeth. And as for their stalks, they were softer and candy-sweet.

The children finished with handfuls of refreshing water. Marzi also brought Polo over, and once the pony had had a drink, it was all aboard the carriage again.

Polo the pony pulled them on, and the two-wheeled egg rolled slowly northwards.

'Where are we going to sleep?' asked Marsha. 'In the middle of the forest?'

'Oh I wouldn't like *that* at all,' said Hazel.

'Betcha you get use to it, livin' rough an' stuff,' said Jawji, patting Hazel's shoulder.

'I don't *want* to get used to it, thank you very much, Miss *Scruff*.' And Hazel slapped Jawji's hand and turned away in a huff.

'We can go to a farm I know,' Marzi called back to them. 'A stop on the way, where we can stay.'

Chapter 10
Chipsticks

After hours of travelling, the light beyond the leafy canopy began to grow dim. Lydia was thinking just how pleasant the White Forest was, when, after a while, the scenery changed: the girls stumbled upon a trail of devastation, hundreds and hundreds of metres wide, with rows and rows of stubbly stumps, this stretch of the forest now a graveyard of greying trees. Lydia also sniffed a whiff of chip fat.

'The metal beast has been here,' uttered Marzi. 'It eats up the nut woods. Scares away the animals.'

This metal beast, whatever it was, had left a track of thick-cut chips—inedible wood chips—some of which had been fried in oil. The trap crunched uncomfortably across the splintery trails and, as Polo's hooves *clop-clip* clopped upon the chipsticks, Lydia saw something happening to Marzipan: the longer they lingered among the cutaway woodland, the greyer the leaves of her

dress became, turning as ashen as the sad surroundings. Marzi became less talkative too, still and starey-eyed as though her very personality had perished with the forest.

Polo the pony took them on. Bull's-Eye kept a sharp lookout; with a couple of heavy rocks at hand, she watched the woodland all around, checking for any of Stannic's spy-hawks that might still be about. But there was nothing to see except the remains of trees. No landmarks. No wildlife. And no sign of people.

In time they crossed the 'forest graveyard' and Marzipan snapped back into life.

By the supper-light sun, the sisters arrived at a desolate farm: *Sweet Wheat Fields*, a typical Franjipani farm, that grew a range of cereal crops to feed the isolated forest communities. Polo clopped past flat white meadows dotted with a mix of birds—nuthatches, fieldfares, wheatears, buntings—pecking seeds from the sugary soil. Eventually the children reached the farmhouse, a country-style cottage half-demolished by some long-gone spoon-scoop creature machine.

Nearby was a cereal boxy barn. The sisters climbed a ladder up to its hayloft; it would be warmer than the draughty half-a-house. Marzi made sure that Polo the pony was settled in a stable area below them; then the girls sat down to eat an evening meal. Next to the barn was a stack of huge storage bowls in which they found cereals, seeds, and grains: crisp rice, sugar flakes, and honeyed nutty loopy shapes; it was lucky these bowls had tight plastic lids, as field mice now seemed to have the run of the farm.

'*Shoo*, shoogar mousses!' Cocoa-Butter hustled them away.

And so, after a few handfuls of cereal, the sisters slept among the shredded wheat hay. It was dark. Quiet. Just the shuffling of sugar mice.

Dawn brought a wholesome golden sunrise breaking through the flaky clouds. It also brought a wake-up call, the sisterhood roused by a loud loud crowing:

'*Chicki-noodle-soop! Chicki-noodle-soop!*'

'What's making that noise, Marzi?' Marsha asked as she blinked around the hayloft.

'That's Coq-a-Leeky the rooster,' Marzipan replied; and she leant out of the barn to cluck a response, and their cockerel alarm quietened down.

Rise and shine, breakfast time, the sisters were soon up and about. The first thing they did was eat some of their special sweets to keep them strong for whatever lay ahead.

The morning in Franjipan was cool and fresh with a chirpy bird chorus, simple signs of life to inspire the girls, and tell them not all was so desolate in their world.

And yet, they were nowhere near a main road or railway, and Sugar Cube needed to find a vehicle tough enough to take them through the forest, then on to the northern province of Froza. She found what she was looking for in the shape of a strawy-yellow tractor abandoned in a sunflower field. This sturdy machine had a two-seater cab and four huge wheels with pie crust tyres; it was hitched to a trailer holding one of the storage bowls, big enough to carry all the children in. Also, though it may have looked old-fashioned, the tractor cab had a modern push-button auto-drive inside (it could be programmed to steer around a field, for instance). And, once Lydia had drummed on the lid of her tin to open its door and access the controls, Sugar could easily operate the tractor, and so the sisters prepared to set off again.

It took them a while to get ready for their journey and treasure-sweet search: filling bottles from a chicken-shaped pump (pushing on its hingey-wings made water spout out of its beak); topping up the tractor from its tanker-jug of corn oil fuel; kitting out the trailer with pillow bales of shredded wheat; stuffing food tubs with seeds and nuts and tasty crunchy breakfast rusks. And last of all, Marzi said farewell to her pony pet.

'Bye-bye, Polo-mino!' she waved with bittersweet-ness.

'Yeah, cheers, Polo,' Jawji added, as they set the pony free in a lemon grass paddock.

'So then, Marzi,' Sugar Cube said, 'what about these Diamond Sun Beans we need to find?'

'They very scarce,' Marzi replied. 'But I do know where they grow. We need to find a golden thicket.'

Bull's-Eye, Sugar, and Marzipan crammed into the chunky tractor, while the other seven girls sat in the trailer, leaving its clear plastic lid slightly open to let in the air.

With Marzi giving directions, Sugar drove across the fields, back to the silence of the forest once more. Another rough and bumpy ride; the tractor rocked from side to side, and branches clattered against the windows as it rumbled over potholed tracks. The children in the trailer bowl were bounced about too, between the pillows of shredded wheat, but at least they were on the move again in transport more spacious than the crampy trap.

Further through the forest, the creamy trees grew ever yellow. Emerald leaves covered their branches, and Sugar took the tractor to where the trees were brightest, their bark thick like lemon rind.

'This must be the golden thicket!' cried Dolly, excited at the prospect of finding treasure-sweets.

Sugar stopped the tractor and trailer, and everyone got out.

Lydia could sense the thicket's heady atmosphere; she sniffed lemonade fizzing in the air. However, she could also see that parts of this thicket had been chopped down. Another of those chipstick trails cut across the forest here, and the fried fat smell was stronger now.

'*Ur* poor *fume*!' Coco exclaimed and, dipping into her trendy handbag, she found a little scent bottle and sprayed its fruity fragrance all about her.

'Mmm, that's nice niff,' said Dolly Mix. 'It really masks the stink.'

Marzipan glared around the thicket, littered as it was with lemon tree stumps. 'This is where I hoped we would find the diamond jelly beans. But cutters and the metal beast may already have ruined the trees.'

Sugar asked Hazel Whirl to scout around the area, and the girl spun away with super speed, kicking up chipsticks as she went along the trail.

Barely a minute later, Hazel's twirling figure returned. 'I've seen it, I've seen it,' she fluttered, all flustered. 'A great metal beast. And it's coming back this way! It *is*.'

The sisters left the tractor behind to follow the trail of splintery chips; after a while, they could hear a far-off roar, and saw plumes of smoke from the forest up ahead. The children kept off the chipstick track to creep through the uncut forest instead.

It took a lot more than a minute to walk the distance Hazel had covered so quickly, but soon they were close enough to spy on the tree-eating beast.

This colossal machine towered above them. A virtual factory-on-wheels, it was four or five compatible contraptions all jolting and bolted together as one. A powerful traction-engine, at the front, dragged the other sections behind it: one consisted of a pair of great oven gloves operated by crane arms connected to a body with pipes that pumped up smelly yellow fumes; at the side of the body were four wide waste-tubes pooping out the trail of tasteless chips, and finally, under all this tonnage, was a big belly section groaning along on rows of claw-edged lemon squeezer wheels.

Ahead of it were the woodcutters Marzipan had mentioned: a trio of chain-sawing robots floating above the stumpy ground on huge sponge cake hovercraft devices. Lydia thought the woodcutters looked birdlike, gigantic metal woodpeckers perhaps. Connected to the tree-eater by flexible fuel pipes, the robots roamed in a curved formation, flying low from tree to tree, their chain-saw beaks *c-c-cut* into the trunks; the trunks would crunch to the forest floor where they lay like giant white chocolate logs. Then the advancing tree-eater beast would grab the fallen logs with its oven mitts and lift them—two, sometimes three at a time—over the top of the engine, to feed them into the body section. That was the roaring Lydia could hear; the buzz-saws inside it, the steely teeth biting crunching chewing timber. A sawdust stink filled the children's nostrils as the beastly machine creaked its way along, tirelessly devouring trees, the weighty tread of its metal wheels churning the earth and crushing the stumps.

'*Why is it eating the sweet trees?*' asked Dolly, having to yell above the buzz-saw roar.

'To clear the forest,' Sugar guessed. 'Create new roads. Stannic could have all sorts of reasons. What I can't figure out, though, is what the machines are using as power sauce.'

'These trees contain oily sap,' Marzipan informed her.

'Citral petrol, of *course*,' Sugar realized: 'they're self-feeding. The body part chips and spits out the tree, extracts the oil which collects in the belly of the beast for fuel.'

'It eats away the White Forest's very spirit,' Marzi said. 'Think of the villages, the animals, the many precious plants that will be lost if it isn't stopped.'

'There's gotta be sumfin *we* can do, Shugz,' Jawji said. 'Before all the trees are trashed.'

Lydia saw the frown on Sugar's face become extra-serious; she mulled ideas in her mind for a moment. 'Do you think you could shut off the woodcutters, Toffee?' she asked.

'Oh.' Lydia hugged her tin, and nodded. 'Yes. I guess.'

'Goodie, Toffee,' Sugar replied. 'Now, the engine must have a driving device.'

She discussed her plan with Jawbreaker and Marzipan who would help her gain control of the beast. Lydia would handle the floating woodcutters with Marshmallow there to offer protection.

Lastly she had some stern words for Peppermint, and though Lydia couldn't hear what Sugar said to her, she saw her wag her finger as though to forbid Pepper from using her powers here. Peppermint narrowed her white-striped eyes, and nodded in reply.

Peppermint

And so it was that five of the sisters prepared to stop the monstrous contraptions.

Marzipan scurried over first. The lumbering tree-eater was easy to sneak up on, and she dashed to the very front of the engine, careful to avoid the sharp ridged hubs of the grinding lemon squeezer wheels. Marzi then turned her body to wood; she attached herself with a jump to the bumper and, most amazingly, she started to twine her way up the machine: her branching arms extended from her leafy dress, her body became similarly long and thin, clinging to the engine,

and stretching across it like a climbing plant, all the way up to the door of a control cab many metres off the ground.

Sugar and Jawbreaker now approached; Jawji took hold of Marzi's tough leafy limbs and used them to climb the traction-engine, hauling herself up from bumper to mudguard, then from one metal ledge to another, gradually scaling the side of the vehicle.

Sugar Cube followed, but the effort proved more difficult for her. Tremors from the engine shuddered through her arms and shoulders, but she gritted her teeth, and carried on climbing, holding tight to Marzipan's ladder body. Jawbreaker reached the cab, and she bit off its lock with her awesome jaws. The door swung wide, and she squeezed inside. Sugar soon joined her; she opened the cab's control panel, and started to analyse its switches, settings, sensors and radar dishes.

Next it was Lydia's turn to act. The woodpecker woodcutters had to be stopped. No doubt it would be the hardest drumming she'd ever had to do so far. These robots were large and armed and dangerous. And there were three of them too. She couldn't show how afraid she was though, and imagined how the others would make fun of her if they knew that she used to be scared of a spoon. And so with her toffee tin around her neck, and liquorice sticks held tight in her fists, Lydia scampered between the trees. Marshmallow followed her towards the metal woodpeckers as they hovered on their sponge cake bases.

The din of the machines was nearly deafening: the growling engine, tree-shredder teeth, the flush of chips and splinters from the waste-pipes, the hum of the sponge cakes, vibration of the chain-saws. Chopped and toppled trees crackling down.

And now another sound cut through the din: a poison-eyed hawk suddenly flapped from the trees, screeching its high-pitched screech as it circled.

Bull's-Eye hurled a rock at the metal bird, a shot that knocked it out of the air; then she ran over to where it landed to finish it off with her hoof.

The screeching hawk had alerted the woodcutters, and the three of them swerved around to attack the girls. Lydia wasn't sure how she could stop them; she began to batter at the lid of her tin, but the trio of woodpeckers swooped too fast. She let her concentration lapse. The first of them dipped its beak towards the ground, swinging its chain-saw to cut her down. Lydia squealed and ducked behind a tree stump. The blade buzzed over whisker-close, hacking out chunks of wood beside her. Another woodpecker had gone for Marshmallow; she flung herself out of the way of the saw, but the hovercake base thumped into her body and sent her bouncing tumbling rolling across the forest floor. Lydia was relieved to see her get up unhurt from a collision that would have killed anyone else.

The third woodcutter had zeroed in on Bull's-Eye who stood there stamping, smashing the hawk, unable to hear the chain-saw behind her.

Hazel saw her and spun past the tree stumps; she skipped over to Bull's-Eye and pulled her out of the way in time as a jagged beaky blade chopped at the place she'd stood a split-second ago.

Then the woodpeckers rotated for another strike, swinging on their flexible pipes.

Lydia got back onto her feet; she beat the tin lid brisk and clear. She focused on the foremost robot, thinking she could force it to turn against the other two. The woodcutter started to sputter forwards. Closer and closer. She drummed faster and faster. Lydia could feel the metal weighing heavy and magnetic inside her mind. She concentrated extra hard. Her drumming halted the robot's charge. It revved and grunted, stopped and started—then she ordered it twirling back, its chain-saw whirly nutty whipping in attack. The woodpeckers clashed with devastating impact. Screeching duelling chain-saws shattered. Fiery sparks and metal sawteeth shot out hot and showered down. *Kabang! Kabang!* Their hover-cakes burst, sending the robots spinning to the ground and whizzing madly round, severing their fuel pipes which lashed out scalding lemon petrol.

The sisters fled, in fear for their lives.

Even those watching from the uncut forest had to retreat, as one woodcutter hurtled haywire into the trees, slicing through the trunks and branches. Dolly Mixture ran screaming from it, stumbling over furrows as the machine smashed past.

Coco and Peppermint hid in a ditch, just as the woodcutter hit the floor with a fountain of soil. It stirred and whirred there for a while, digging itself powerless into the earth.

The second woodpecker went bucking into the tree-eater and, as the hefty beast rolled forward, the robot was caught beneath its claws; squeezer wheel after squeezer wheel crushed the woodcutter flat.

As for the last of the chain-saw robots, it had wedged between two fallen trunks. The tree-eater's oven gloves clapped down on them, hoisting the woodcutter into the shredder.

Sugar Cube tried to shut down the buzz-saws, but the tree-eater roared like a giant lion, its shredding chipping munching functions mangling the robot stuck in its throat. Jawbreaker panicked and climbed from the cab; when she reached the bumper she jumped, falling badly and scraping her knees. Sugar wasn't far behind, she grasped onto Marzi's branching limbs and tried to descend as quick as she could.

Marshmallow rushed over. 'Sugar!' she shouted. 'Jump! I'll catch you!'

Sugar dared to jump from the mudguard, thumping into Marsha who cushioned her otherwise bone-breaking fall. Last of all, Marzipan detached herself and tumbled to the ground. Then the girls scrambled from the massive machine, feeling the terrible tremors increase. The unstable beast blew its gaskets, spitting out woodpecker metal and chips; oily flames began to flare from its rear as the sisters raced to the safety of the trees. With a tremendous wrench of nuts and bolts. The tree-munching neck. The trunk-chipping body. And finally the beast's tanker-belly broke down. Its throat spurted smoke, while its bottom piped out boiling fuel, a gurgly gush of greasy sap that splashed and splat to make a leaky slicky lake.

It took some time for the beast to simmer down and, with a strangled groan, it ground to a halt. Crane arms, oven gloves, squeezer wheels, buzz-saws. All lay useless.

It was suddenly peaceful without the roar of the machines. And now that the woodpeckers were out of action, Lydia wondered how much woodland they'd saved from the chop. And just how much wood would the chipper-contraption have chipped if the nonstop chipper-contraption hadn't been stopped?

Chapter 11
Jelly Beans

The girls regrouped to see who needed first aid; Sugar had a pocket full of rice paper plaster squares and minty antiseptic cream that Jawji used to patch up her knees.

Marsha nursed some minor aches too, while Sugar herself had to eat some glucose pills and rest a while to recharge her energy.

Marzipan then took the sisters back to the heart of the golden thicket, hoping that their treasure-sweet had not been devoured by the forest-eating beast.

She led them into this tangle of trees with the leaves above glowing emerald and gold. Beams of sunlight spilt spotlit upon them, and this cool place oozed with citrus juice; Lydia could feel it sharp in the soil, could smell it in the saps that seeped from the trees.

Marzi wandered from trunk to trunk until—

'Here. A Diamond Sun Beech,' she smiled.

The sisters stood beneath a tall lush tree. Lydia could see the clusters of bright white jelly beans high up amidst the green leaves.

'Why are they called Sun Beans?' Hazel asked.

'The juice has a certain pleasing sunny effect on people,' Marzi told her.

Sun Beans, Lydia thought to herself. They sound nice.

Marzipan admitted that this tall smooth tree would be tricky and time-consuming to climb. And the jelly beans hung from the very top branches.

'Yeah, a bit outta reach, ain't they?' squinted Jawji.

'Oo, let me, let me!' Dolly volunteered, waving her hand and jumping up. 'I can reach them.'

She *is* a bit of a sherbet dip, Lydia thought, because Dolly was the smallest of the group. Although, what with the abilities of the other girls, she was curious to know what it was that Dolly could do (besides look pretty and giggle a lot).

Dolly began by wriggling a little and, to Lydia's astonishment, she split herself in half at the waist; then she got Bull's-Eye and Jawbreaker to lift her, take the top half of her body by the arms, and swing her and fling her, 'One two three—*Wheee!*'

Dolly flew up high into the tree, while her lower body stood weirdly below, shuffling her feet excitedly. Up above, Dolly Mixture clambered through the treetop, grabbing for the branches with the bright white sweets.

Leaves and lemon twigs sprinkled down; Lydia

heard snaps and crackles from up high—The sisters scattered as Dolly's top half suddenly plummeted *Thud!* to the ground and, in her hand, a cluster of jelly beans with glistening diamond-like coatings.

'Sorry, Dolly,' Marsha said, stepping forth to pick her up, 'I should've caught you.'

'I'm all right though,' Dolly smiled, and she let Marshmallow fit her back together as though it were the most natural thing in the world. Dolly then handed the jelly beans to Sugar Cube who sealed them in a carton in one of her pockets.

They now had the first of the treasure-sweets for their mysterious helper, Snake Lady Hisska.

As the children turned to leave, Lydia noticed a bunch of these Sun Beans lying almost hidden in the grass: these beans were less brilliant than the ones Dolly had plucked. Still they seemed about the same. Looked tasty too. 'Might try one or two.'

Lydia scooped the fruit up, and nibbled at one of the jelly bean bunch. Ooo, it was chewy with a juicy centre, tangy like strong lemonade. She would save the rest of the bunch for the others. They *would* be pleased with her. Already Lydia was feeling sunnier, quite lightheaded too. 'I think I'll have another.'

The sisters were making their way back to the tractor when they realized one of their group was missing.

'What happen to Toffee?' Coco mentioned.

'Ah, she's always laggin' behind,' said Bull's-Eye.

'Toffee?' Marshmallow called softly. 'Toffee? We're over *here*.'

No answer. The sisters had to retrace their steps, and found Lydia still there in the lemony thicket, sitting on the grass, gazing at the jelly beans in her hands.

'What you got there, Toffee?' Sugar enquired.

Lydia looked up with a dazed expression. She held out the half-eaten bunch.

'Oh *no*,' uttered Marzipan.

'What sup?' Jawbreaker asked.

'She's eaten some Sun Beans.'

'That's all right,' said Dolly. 'Sugar saved the ones *I* picked.'

'You do not understand,' said Marzipan. 'Sun juice is prized by my people. We use it to make grown-up wine. Drink too much it cause memory loss. This is why Sun Beans are also known as Forget-Me-Nuts.'

'Oh, T-*Toffee*,' tutted Marsha.

Lydia looked wide-eyed at her, a silly smirk on her face.

'How long will the effects last, Marzi?' Sugar said concerned.

'Depend how many she eat. You are not meant to eat them neat. She may be forgetful for days.'

'Stupid Toff,' Bull's-Eye huffed.

'She wasn't to know,' said Marzipan.

'Yes,' Dolly added. 'Poor Toffee. She'll have forgot how to drum and *every*thing.'

'Well, she's no use to us now then, is she?' said Bull's-Eye. 'Why don't we just leave her here?'

Lydia did in fact begin to crawl away. Marshmallow had to toddle on after, and grab her by the hand. 'It's me, Marsha. Remember? Marshmallow.'

'Mar-Mar?' Lydia muttered all dopey, and she let the kind roundy girl lead her back.

The sisters got into the trailer, while Sugar started the tractor again. She drove along tracks to the edge of the woodland, where she located a stony road. The children were free of the White Forest now, and soon were cruising past deserted farmsteads, fields of sugar-frosted wheat, and bales of cotton candy uncollected.

Marzipan had never been so far from her village before. But it was just the same for the rest of the sisters. Not one of them had a proper home any more.

As the rough road ran through remote Franjipan, the land became hillier, got hillier and chillier. Then further north, the road got stonier and lonelier.

The girls could see their breaths misty in the bowl and, as it grew colder, so they drew their fleeces closer, and huddled in the hay. Marsha said they'd be better wearing the spare clothes that Coco had stolen; these included leggings and stockings for those in skirts or shorts. Hazel also put on a pair of legwarmers she had in her holdall.

Before long, their journey had taken them to hills of broken tablet, and Sugar followed a man-made route through these rugged lime stone highlands. Tractor and

trailer bowl trundled on, slowly along the rocky road. When it got dark, Sugar stopped the tractor and, not long after, a lime-chequered tracker-snake slithered by with information: data about giant walls of glacier ice blocking the border roads.

Chilling confirmation that Stannic's robots had started invading Froza.

And so the sisters spent a quiet night upon the hillside. All ten of them safe in the hay-filled bowl.

'Never seen such chunky hillucks as these before,' said Jawbreaker.

'These are the Limer-Layers,' Sugar told her.

'Spritzy much flattish where I live,' added Jawji. 'All fields an' gum farms.'

'That sound nice,' Marzipan said. 'It is town and city I don't think I'd like.'

'Nah, me neither,' Jawji agreed.

'My home city's a *lovely* city,' Dolly stated proudly. 'A giant tea set, white and pretty.'

'Is it where we head next?' asked Coco. 'Dolly Mix's tea set city?'

'Not yet,' Sugar Cube replied. 'We're off to Froza. To find one last sister.'

'I hope we reach her before the Tin Man's robots do,' said Marsha.

'Me too,' frowned Sugar, concerned that the girl was all alone in the Frozan cold.

'Oo, one more friend to find?' Dolly smiled. 'I hope she's nice.'

'As long as she's more use to us than *Toffee*,' said Bull's-Eye. Lydia perked up at the mention of toffee. She still had that silly smirk on her face, and this irked Bull's-Eye even more. 'What you gawpin' at, *you?*' she glared, but Lydia just stared back and smiled.

The sisters slept as best they could, nestled in the bales of hay; they rested their poor little aching bodies, so tired from another eventful day.

The next morning, a pale lime light woke them, shining through the lid of the bowl.

The children opened their lunchboxes, and ate the remainder of the White Forest food. They were lucky they'd kept some because, here in the hills, there was nothing at all worth foraging for, the only plants being stringy grasses and acrid snowberry bushes.

Lydia's mind was still tied in forgetty-knots; she had to be tended to by Marsha who fed her half-a-stick of custardy rhubarb and a couple of coconut mush-rooms.

'Why don't we let her have some toffee?' said Marzipan. 'It may help cure her.'

Marsha took a toffee nugget and offered it to Lydia. She looked wide-eyed at the lovely sweet, then grabbed it greedily and stuck it in her mouth. As she chewed, the tang of toffee on her tongue brought back *mmm* kinda *mmm* Mum 'n' me memories. Some kind of smiling sadness filled Lydia's mind.

Their tractor ride continued along the hilly road, rumbling past cracky caves and chalky blocky rock-strewn trails prowled by one or two lime-striped tigers.

'Puddi-tart!' Lydia pointed, almost climbing out of the bowl through curiosity.

'*No*, Toffee.' Marsha pulled her back. 'That's a tiger. *Grr. Grr.* Eat you up.'

Outside, the air grew colder still. The sisters noticed frosting on the cone-like peaks above them; saucy springs spilled from the cones, the lick-a-rock all glorious with swirly layers of colour. 'Are we in Froza yet?' said Dolly, nosing from the bowl.

'Sure, we must be,' answered Jawji.

Delicately-tinted flakes, a sorbet sleet, began to sweep down upon them and, all across the sundae highlands, the falling sleet thickened to slush. Everyone in the trailer perked up as the tractor passed the last of the sauce-topped rocks.

Before the enchanted children lay a place covered in frozen sorbet. Drifts of pastel peach and lemon,

of icy lime shining in the morning sun. The colourful drifts were intercut by trails of ground roasted nuts, forming grippy gritty roads in decorative curves across the land. Sugar drove the tractor over to one of these nut grit roads, and soon the vehicle was grinding its way north through the drifts of sleety sorbet. It was getting harder to see past the ice-encrusted windows, but Sugar did her best to keep the tractor steady, could hear its pie-tyres *crunch crunch crunch* on the crushy nutshells. Wary of upcoming road blocks, though, she decided to cut across the drifts and leave the nutty route behind.

Then, somewhere within this icy wilderness, Sugar detected the presence of yet another tracker-snake (her hearing aids could pick up their microwaves).

The tractor pushed on across the ice, ploughing through the pastel sleet and spraying up a mush of slush. The girls in the trailer-bowl could feel it trundle slower and slower, till eventually it slid to a halt.

They lifted up the plastic lid, and jumped down onto the icy sorbet.

'Do we *have* to go out in this drizzle?' said Hazel. 'Hope my hairdo doesn't get wet.'

The sisterhood had come to a place where the green ice rose in big solid blocks. The areas between the blocks were patched with pale pink pools; creamy soda bubbled within them, and the air was dreamy with the smell of vanilla.

After a while, the lime sleet ceased, and the sisters

145

made their way around the blocks, searching for the tracker-snake Sugar had detected. Bull's-Eye spotted it, a green-and-white serpent lying still in the sorbet ice. This snake didn't even give a *shug-a-shug*, its rattle-tail was frozen up.

'The girl must be somewhere close,' said Sugar, and she sent the others to play hunt-the-sister amongst the blocks of ice.

It was Cocoa-Butter who soon called them together, and they gathered by a steep sorbet slope beside a soda pool. 'Look look,' she whispered, pointing out a silhouette almost invisible against the icy lime.

Yes, the others could see it too. A tint, the faintest hint of green. The outline of a standing child frosted inside the sorbet. Sugar used her gloved hands to sweep away the frost. Then she stepped back, and the sisterhood stared at this figure up against the slope.

This slim little sip of a girl. Her eyes were closed, and her whitish face, with its soft stained lips, was framed by blue-tinged shoulder-length hair, icicle-like hair that spiked straight down. And for such bitter conditions, she was surely underdressed; while the others were in their cosy fleeces, this girl wore only a pale green blouse, and slippers which were more like icy clogs. It looked as though she had run away, still in her nightdress, and frozen to death.

'Her name's Liise,' Sugar told them.

Just then, there came a distant scraping, and *pick pick pick* sounds, getting louder all the while. The girl called

Liise opened her eyes and, without a word, she darted away towards the pool of soda water.

Looking back at the ominous sounds, the sisters saw a giant metal crab looming suddenly over the slope: a monster crustacean with a chromium shell, a dome at least twenty metres in diameter; it sported a pair of fearsome pincers and sets of rhythmic ice-pick legs, using them to cling to the frozen slopes. A second crab then appeared behind the tractor. The sisters sprinted away, after Liise, but there seemed to be no way out for them, trapped between these mechanical crabs and a deep pink pool. Liise dropped to her knees at the soda's edge, and she held her hands just above the bubbles; the other girls watched amazed, as the surface of the soda started to freeze over. Whiter and whiter, wider and wider, a sheet of ice spread all the way across the pool; then Liise skipped lightly onto the ice and scampered across without looking back.

The others followed her. Hesitant at first. But when they heard the oncoming crabs—metal limbs *shuk-shuk shuk-shuk*, pincer claws *clack-clack clack-clack*—the frightened children had no choice, and trod gingerly onto the icy surface, soda deep beneath their feet.

Liise continued to scamper across the pool, only pausing to freeze it more securely with the power of her touch. At last, she reached the opposite side and climbed the sorbet bank to safety.

The pair of crabs clattered into the tractor, wrecking

it with their powerful pincers, tearing pieces off the vehicle and casting them at the girls as they fled. Hazel had already skipped across the frozen pool and got to the edge ahead of the others; Peppermint too, had clawed her way across the ice, typically jittery quick. And as chunks of tractor hurtled at them, the rest of the sisters scrambled clear, awkwardly slipping and sliding away as tyres whizzed past their heads, the bowl skimmed by like a flying saucer, engine portions and axle parts smashed into the soda around them, cracking the surface ice into floes. The squealing girls had to hurry across the thinning rink, jumping desperately from floe to floe, till they reached the far side of the soda pool, and clambered onto solid land. All of them staggered up the sorbet shore, safe, thinking that the metal crabs could never get across. However, to their utter horror, the crabs began to *pick-pick pick-pick*, steadily up and around the blocks. Almost spider-like they climbed, clinging to the steep sorbet slopes, manoeuvring around the pool to attack the sisters on the other side.

It was then that Lydia noticed Peppermint move towards the edge of the block. The weird stripy-eyed girl just stayed there. The monstrous crabs scuttled closer to her. They'd almost picked their way around when, all of a sudden, Pepper lurched forward and her mouth hurled a stream of fire, minty fire, to soften the block.

The white-hot flame cut through the sorbet, cut it

away in melted layers, and the crabs floundered on the slushy slope. They tumbled down and crashed into the soda pool. Chrome domes clashed and pincers thrashed as the crab machines struggled to stay afloat. Swirls of liquid quickly engulfed them and, as they sank, the soda surface flashed with pink electricity.

Bubbles, creamily luminous bubbles, sizzled in the air for a while. Peppermint spat out the last of the fire; then she closed her humbug eyes, and took a few exhausted breaths.

Much relieved, the group of girls turned to find Liise some way away. The shy ice maiden sat in the sorbet, peeping from behind a fringe of icicle hair. A wide-eyed look of intense anxiety showed upon her frost-freckled face, and Sugar Cube gently explained how they found her, how the sisterhood needed her, and how she would be safer with them.

Ice Lolly

Liise sat there quiet, and listened, timidly brushed a bit of ice from her nightdress.

They didn't have any problem choosing a code name for her: 'Ice Lolly' was agreed on straight away, and Liise didn't argue with them; in fact, she said nothing at all.

And when the others set off across the sorbet, she simply got up and tagged along.

Chapter 12
Raspberry Ripple

The children were seemingly nowhere now, and their tractor was a scattered wreck.

'I s'pose we'll have to stupid walk all across this ice,' said Bull's-Eye.

Even wearing extra clothes, the thought of no transport made the sisters really feel the cold.

'I think now's the best time to share these out,' said Sugar, unbuttoning one of her pockets and taking out a packet of pastilles: 'I call them Hot-Tots. They'll stop us all getting the chills.'

Sugar handed out the pastilles, letting Peppermint take one first: Pepper stared her humbug stare, and swallowed the Hot-Tot quick. Cocoa-Butter snatched one next and ate it just as fast.

Marzipan was most grateful for the heat-sweet; she wasn't wearing a fleece like the others, just her leafy dress that had turned pale green.

151

As for the rest of the Hot-Tots, there were just enough to go round. (Ice Lolly didn't need one, of course.)

Marshmallow made sure Lydia had hers. 'Eat it up, there's a good girl.' The sweet tasted of papaya with a menthol centre that left a whooshy freshness in her mouth; and then, within a moment or two, Lydia felt this wonderful warmth building inside her.

'Veez shweets are shmashin',' Jawji said as she chewed her Hot-Tot.

'You really do think of everything, don't you, Sugar?' Hazel added. 'You do.'

'I wasn't going to leave my home without sweets for any eventuality,' Sugar said. 'Anyway, Lady Hisska sent some of these recipes for me to make.'

'Who cares where you got the sweets from?' Bull's-Eye said. 'Let's hurry up and get to the next place we're s'posed to.'

'We need to reach the jelly valley next.' Sugar turned to Ice Lolly. 'Do you think *you* can help us?'

Lolly blinked her crystalline eyes, and stared beyond the soda pools. Then, without a word, she began to run away. She did stop, at one point, to wait for the others, then she dashed off again across the frosted drifts.

The sisters trudged after Lolly, their mouths exhaling breathy menthol, their shoes crunching watery footprints in the sorbet ice.

'C'mon, Toffee,' Marshmallow called to Lydia. 'Come along. Hold my hand.'

Lydia squeezed her fingers around Marsha's podgy mitt, and the two of them toddled behind the others. Lydia, still all forget-me-nutty, playfully kicked her feet through the ice.

'Shishy *whoop*lush,' she cried. 'Sloopid snooslush.'

'*Shush*,' said Marsha, 'Toffee, quiet.'

Over the sorbet the sisters stepped, up glacial slopes where fruity streams seeped into and coloured fields of parfait, till they found Ice Lolly poised upon a ledge, looking out over the wintry hinterland.

'Ice-cream scoops,' Lolly uttered.

The girls feasted their eyes upon the sights: beyond the parfait lay a snowy panorama flowing with misty softy drifts. The sisters had reached the ice-cream plains for which this frozen region was famous. Lydia had never seen ice-cream in its natural state before. And in such vast quantities too. Enough to fill a billion bowls, enough to chill a trillion tummies.

Ice Lolly led them from the ledge, down the final blocks of sorbet to the freshly fallen snow below. An eager Lydia licked at a handful; the snow was creamy whippy smooth, and she laughed as it trickled ticklish inside her sleeve. The other sisters joined in too, some of them using their lunchbox lids to dig out curls of the cold ice-cream.

'Oo, it tastes so pure and freshy,' Hazel smiled, supping up spoonful after spoonful of snow.

Everyone agreed, but soon they had to leave, as Ice Lolly had already run off again. Lolly now led them

to the top of a ridge from where they could see across the snowy expanse; here the land was far from featureless, undulating in scoopy dunes between which seams of colour rippled richly. Creamulous clouds rolled across the sunlit sky, all the way to a raspberry horizon where Lydia could just distinguish glistening glassy mountains.

'What is it we are looking for now?' asked Marzipan.

'A sweet called Chilly Jelly Amethyst,' Sugar replied. 'That's why we're heading for the jelly valley. *There*. You see? Way in the distance? Those mountains that look like glass.'

Also across the ice-cream seams, Bull's-Eye spied these snow-covered shapes. What appeared to be a line of fallen animals with antlers and legs sticking out straight.

Sugar decided to investigate, and the girls descended the icy ridge to traipse through more of the soft scoop snow. As they proceeded, the dunes got deeper; dollops of ice-cream came over their knees, and they had to take big clumsy steps. The children waded past the colourful seams, and could see that rivulets and whirlpool sauces were staining and flavouring the ice-cream. Tutti-frutti juices had squeezed through fissures in the ground making strawberry, cherry, vanilla, lemon, even chocolatey and minty combinations.

The girls jumped from seam to seam, sampling all the different flavours, till eventually, munchily, they reached the line of unusual snow-animals.

'What *are* they?' said Dolly.

'Carry boo sloops,' was Lolly's odd reply.

'They're sled-bikes,' Sugar realized. 'They must have been left some time ago, judging by the snow.'

'Why would you want to park your bike in the middle of nowhere here?' asked Hazel.

'My guess is robots capture their owners as they try to escape the crabs,' said Marzi.

The girls went along the higgledy-piggledy parade of sledges, wiping off some of the snow; they revealed an assortment of motorized vehicles all designed to resemble animals: there were scooters on skis in the guise of husky dogs, and reindeer sleighs (or, as Lolly had called them, 'caribou') with curving antler handlebars. Then there were sleds shaped like leopards or bears. People's possessions had been loaded onto them: cases, bags, and folded tents. These sights brought back memories frozen in Lolly's mind. Of her family's community fleeing in a convoy.

Some of the snowmobiles showed signs of pincer damage, but the girls managed to find one still intact: it had a scooter (with a kettle-motor) in the design of a caribou, and this pulled a leopard-sled behind. The children made room for themselves and their knapsacks by chucking any cases and bags in the snow. Then they huddled in a pack on the back, while Sugar grabbed the handlebar antlers and set the scooter's button controls.

In no time, they were sledding along, across the ice-cream seams, travelling at a decent speed towards the glassy mountains. A tailpipe at the back of the scooter puffed out rings of cokey smoke that momentarily hung in the air as ghostly chocolate doughnuts. The air grew strangely warmer too, the further north they went, and the girls appreciated the heat.

As the scooter-sled continued across the creamy plain, so the texture of the landscape changed again: the ground around became bumpy and swampy, the pristine cream splodgy and blotchy. The glassy blue mountains towered before them, sweet-smelling steam seen floating over their icy slopes. The children knew they were near the jelly valley now as, from the summit of one mountain, rivers of jelly lava flowed, thick and slow, raspberry red. Lydia had never seen natural jelly before. And here it ran in vast cascades. Enough to fill a trillion tummies, or wobble in a billion bellies.

'What's that *noise?*' Hazel mentioned. 'Sounds like a great big vacuum cleaner.'

'Licky tricky mill,' Ice Lolly said.

Sugar had also sensed this rumbling, and she took the scooter over towards it, along the bank of a lava river where the raspberry current continued down into a vast crater basin of snow. The sisters' sled slid to a halt at the rim of the glacial basin, and from there they saw a metallic building in the centre of the crater. Even though Lolly had mentioned a mill—suggesting something smaller scale with waterwheels or maybe sails—here was a gigantic kidney-shaped structure enclosed in a complex rib-cage of pipes. Red steam

hissed from the innards of the mill, turning the surrounding snow rosy pink and as tacky as candy floss.

The mill was a kind of hydroelectric station but, instead of using water, this installation used raspberry jelly for the source of its power. It had been built where several lava rivers converged, and used stripy pipes like giant straws to slurp up the slow-flowing jelly; these were making the vacuum sound. And as the jelly was swallowed by the mill, so it was liquefied and electrified, then piped out underground.

'Candi-Land's main powerplant,' Sugar told the others. 'It feeds electric-jelly all across the country. Stannic's robots must be running it now.'

Down below, they saw dozens of mechanical crabs lurking around the crater. Guarding the electric mill. Feeding off the jelly. Siphoning off its energy using smaller stripy pipey straws. 'How we gonna reach the jelly valley?' asked Jawji. 'Wiv them 'orrid crabs about?'

'I'm not going anywhere near any more of those,' said Hazel. 'I'm not.'

Sugar thought for a moment. 'There may be a way to get rid of them,' she said. 'If you give me Toffee's tin, I'll show you.'

'Let me have the tin, Toffee,' Marshmallow said, lifting the ribbon from around Lydia's neck.

'Ma din din?' Lydia reached out tearfully as Marsha handed Sugar the tin.

'Oh, don't worry, Toffee. We'll give it back later.'

'Yeah, if we *feel* like it,' added Bull's-Eye.

As the raspberry lava flowed further from the mountains, so it cooled and began to congeal; now only gravity and the pressure of the jelly pushing behind took it into the flossy basin and on towards the mill. And so, Sugar settled on a spot where the raspberry lava was not too hot, and she took the empty toffee tin over, and dipped it in the river to collect the warm jelly. With the lava in a semi-liquid state, Sugar was able to add a wad of pink gum; then she told Lolly to place her hands around the tin and freeze the jelly to set it. Sugar turned the tin over, and the raspberry oblong slipped out solid *sluup* onto the ground.

'What was that wodge o' gum ya shoved in, Shugz?' Jawji asked.

'I call it Combusta-Gum,' Sugar replied.

'You mean it's a bom-bom?' Dolly said.

'That's right, Dolly. When it gets very hot it explodes.'

'How will we get it to hot up by the mill?' said Hazel. 'I'm not going down there, I told you. I'm *not*.'

'We'll let the lava river take it,' Sugar explained. 'Then when the pipes eat it up—'

'*Krabboom*,' grinned Bull's-Eye.

Sugar and Lolly knelt in the snow, preparing another of the wobbly bombs; and then they pushed both jellies in the river, and watched them float on the raspberry current slowly rippling down the slope towards the electric mill.

'We'd best eat these as well,' Sugar suggested, issuing

these black-and-yellow mallows to the girls: 'I call them Goo-Goo-Ga Chews. They'll cause honey-wax to block your ears. Protect your hearing from the boom of the gum.'

'They plug up ya lugholes?' Jawji said, giving Dolly the giggles.

Sugar simply took out her hearing aids, as the others ate the mallows and their honeycomb centres. After a little while, Lydia had a funny feeling; sticky wax began to build in her ears, making her hearing soundproof, boom-proof.

And so, with their ears all weird and waxy, the girls got back on the animal-sleigh; Sugar on the scooter was already sledding away, around the crater, towards the mountains, when these almighty *Boom-booms!* echoed across the ice-cream basin. As the jelly mill ignited, so its pipes set alight too. All the electric-drinking crabs were blown up in a flaring ring of fire. And then came the *rasp burr ripply crush* of flossy pink snow tumbling in torrents. The crater, a great grumbling belly, filled with lashings of ice-cream and jelly. The sizzling mill and its guardian crabs buried under an avalanche of floss.

Even with their ears bunged up, the girls felt shock waves rumbling under them. Their sled raced downhill just ahead of this flossy snowslide. Down down to a place of jumbled jelly shapes, moulded hills and pillars of jello in orange and yellow, all riddled with dribbly streams of ice-cream.

In areas where the cream had evaporated, a hard transparent glaze showed through, and Sugar had to use her cybernetic reactions to steer the scooter over these slopes. Her fast-fingered button-pressing swerved them one way, narrowly missing a lava reservoir, tearing past at a dangerous pace. The scooter slalomed through the jelly arches, weaving around these wobbling boulders, taking them deeper into the valley, and leaving the avalanche of floss to crystallize across the lava, sizzling into it with hot sweet aromas.

The effects of the ear-block-it sweets wore off, and the gooey wax crumbled from Lydia's ears; the first things she heard were the *whoosh* of the scooter skis and ice-cream spurting out from under the sled. Sugar switched off the kettle-motor, and the caribou-scooter scraped to a standstill. Then the sisters left the sled and, as they stepped across the glassy ground, it thudded hollow beneath their feet.

'How safe is this glacey ice?' Hazel Whirl asked.

'It isn't ice,' Sugar told her. 'The whole of Froza sits on top of a layer of boiled sweet. That's how snow and jelly settles in it.'

The sisters picked a path, far from the lava reservoirs, to a part of the valley where solid globes lay cold in the snow: jello globes of differing sizes, from amber pebbles to huge translucent golden boulders. As they got closer, they could see that the jelly had gemstone sweets suspended in them. Lydia stood before a boulder. She gave the wobbly globe a shove and gazed mesmerized

as the gemstones shimmered. 'Oo, Jelloo! Jelloo ahoo!' Lydia cooed, her voice reverberating loud across the valley.

'Will somebody shut Toffee up?' moaned Bull's-Eye.

'What's matter with her?' Ice Lolly whispered.

'She ate some forgetty-beans,' Dolly replied. 'Now her brain's all fuggy.'

Lydia soon quietened down, staring boggly-eyed into the boulder.

'Where is all zis jellay ooze from?' Cocoa-Butter said.

'It comes up from the earth as magma,' Sugar Cube replied. 'Minerals and jewel sweets get brought up with it, trapped inside.'

'And we are looking for a *Chilly Jelly Amethyst*, you say?' said Marzi.

Sugar asked Peppermint to heat the sweet-filled jelly, and she wandered from boulder to boulder, smothering them with mint-white fire. Globe after globe slowly melted away, and the sisters had to slop through the glop to see what sweets now sparkled there.

'An amethyst is a purple gemstone,' Sugar said. 'Anyone see anything like that?'

The girls scanned the melted puddles. Cocoa-Butter got all excited seeing these tantalizing jewels; nipping tiptoe, pool to pool, she dipped her hand in the warm sticky jelly, picking out and pocketing sweet upon sweet, collecting an assortment of the mineral jewels.

She even tried one or two after slurping off the liquid goo. 'Oo, these jewelly jelly bonbons soo yum yum.'

After a while, the sisters spotted a puddle full of purple crystals glittering on a patch of glassy ground. Sugar popped a couple of the sweets into a capsule, and sealed it in one of her jacket pockets.

She smiled, satisfied. 'Chilly Jelly Amethysts.'

Now they had the second confection from the treasure list.

The sisters left the puddles of jelly slush, and began their walk back to the sled. Marsha took Lydia by the hand, and led her from the globe she'd been gazing into; she was sad to leave the pretty glitter-stones. Coco too was still pinching the jewel sweets, and now she was about to try one of the amethysts.

'Come on, Coco,' Sugar called. 'We're going—*Coco!* Don't eat one of those!'

'Yes, Coco,' Marzi added. 'The amethyst must possess some special property.'

Cocoa-Butter pouted. 'We munch what we want.' But she thought for a moment, pretended to obey, and skipped over to the others as they got on the sleigh. Coco sneaked up to Lydia instead, and offered the amethyst to her. 'Here, Toffee, here.'

Marshmallow noticed Lydia put the sweet in her mouth. 'Oh, *naughty* Toffee. Spit it out,' she ordered, but Lydia's teeth crunched the sweet, and she swallowed most of the jelly-centred amethyst. 'Oh, Sugar!' Marsha cried. 'Oh—*Co! Co!*'

Coco grinned her mischievous grin. 'Whassit taste like, Toffee?' she whispered.

Lydia was suddenly filled with a chill, as if lashings of ice-cream were being whipped around her tummy. She shivered and shrugged her fleece tight around her shoulders, but she only grew colder. And, as the others watched, something even weirder began to happen to her.

'Oo, what's going on with Toffee?' said Dolly. 'She's going all glowy.'

The whites of Lydia's eyes did indeed begin to glow. Like purple gems set inside her skull.

Sugar Cube didn't know what to do, and decided to take the dithering Lydia over to the rivers of lava. Some place to warm her up, perhaps. Soon they stood on a glassy bank, peering into the hot red jelly; Lydia knelt to inhale the aroma of raspberries steaming up from the river. However, she shivered more than ever, and strange blue tears began to seep from her eyes.

'We have to move on,' Sugar said. 'It'll be night soon, and we need to find shelter.'

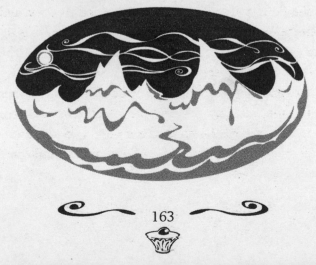

Chapter 13
Ice-Cream Cone

Back on the caribou-scooter and sled, the children made their way south-west, hoping to find some place to rest.

Days were shorter in the lands of Froza, and soon the sky darkened over the snow plains; behind them, a spectral sunset licked at the edges of the boiled sweet mountains. Coils of cool mist settled across the scoopy drifts and, in this unfamiliar place, ice-cream snow started to fall all fluffily.

It wasn't only Lydia who dithered there on the leopard-sled; now far from the warmth of the jellostone swamps, the other girls' teeth began to chatter with the chilly chomps.

'We shi-shivry,' said Coco cold.

'This breeze is brisky,' shuddered Marzi.

'It's all *offul*,' Hazel complained. 'I've never been so frozey. My toes are numb. And I can't feel my bum—'

'We get it, Haze,' Bull's-Eye said. 'You're *cold*. We're *all* cold. So shu-shut up.'

Peppermint was especially unhappy and, taking deep freezing breaths, she clawed her cloak to her close.

Their lengthy sleigh ride continued through a blizzard, and Sugar drove them sleddy steady, the caribou-scooter's cream beam light illuminating the way ahead. Snow fell more heavily and from that first flitter of fluffy flakes, the air around them became an icy creamy mass. The girls were afraid that they may freeze, lost in the midst of the Frozan fields. They could barely see through the flurries of snow, and now the scooter's light flickered low. The snowmobile ran out of fuel. Sputtered to a halt. Its kettle-motor boiled dry.

'Why we stoppin', Shugz?' Jawji called.

'This kettle's kaputty.'

'How can a kettle be a cuppa tea?' asked Dolly.

'She means the stupid scooter's useless,' said Bull's-Eye.

'I'd love a nice cuppa tea,' continued Dolly. 'Or a mugga cocoa. Or a cream eggnoggy. We have those Midwinter—'

While Dolly waffled on about her favourite hot drinks, Sugar asked Bull's-Eye to use her super-sight to scan the ice-cream fields for any sign of shelter. Through the snowfall, through the gloom, Bull's-Eye glimpsed some far-off woodland. The sisters had to gather their knapsacks, abandon the sled, and trudge all the way over to the cover of the trees. Marshmallow helped pull

Lydia along, her eyes still glowing eerily blue. The children entered the wood, with Lydia's eyes lighting up pine trees sugar-bright with lichen. The ground was less creamy, more powdery here. Animal tracks were the sole signs of life: the hoofprints of reindeer, and paw marks of gummi-bears visible in the icing soil.

'Do *you* know where we are, Lolly?' Marsha asked.

Ice Lolly shook her head. 'Never dare the woods,' she dithered.

'We'll be safe as long as we stick together,' said Sugar.

'You don't know that though, do you?' worried Hazel. 'There might be pepper-leopards or grizzly-wizzlies or—or *snaffle-woffuls* everywhere.'

'What'sh a wofful?' Jawji whispered to Marzi.

'I think Hazel meant to say *wolves*,' Marzipan replied with a smile.

The sisters kept on through the wood, huddled in their hidey-hoods; their peeping faces were cold and wet, their fingers bitter-nipped to the knuckles. The blueberry glow from Lydia's eyes was the only light they had to see by, and they walked for some time, past the brittle brown trees; twiglet bracken and pine cones cracked and snapped beneath their feet, making the sisters jumpy and worrisome. And the *hoo-hoo-hoot* of an unseen owl, and the *howoo-howl* of an unseen beast made them even more some.

Eventually the jelly chill faded from Lydia's tum, and so her eyes glowed dimmer and dimmer. The children imagined all kinds of dangers skulking closer.

Sugar got Jawbreaker to bite off a couple of twiglet branches; then she asked Peppermint to spit a bit of flame to set alight the ends.

'Careful, Pepper,' Sugar said to her. 'Don't want to start a forest fire.'

Pepper with gentle *phwuffs* of flame made torches from the snacky brown branches and, as the children continued through the wood, the slow-toasting twiglets gave off twists of yeasty smoke. After a while, the light from the torches picked out a glistening line on the ground, and the sisters could see a trail of salt had been laid across the icing.

'It's a man-made path,' said Marzipan. 'It must lead somewhere.'

'But which way gets us somewhere quickest?' pondered Sugar.

'I know, I know,' said Dolly Mixture, and she stood there pointing one way then the other, reciting a rhyme to herself: 'Lemonadey limeade pop. Oh where will my finger stop? If it fizzes, let it drop. Lemonadey limeade pop. Tish flish *whush*. This way. My finger say so.'

'We're not going to go by Dolly's silly fingers?' said Hazel. 'Are we, Sugar Cube?'

Sugar shrugged. 'Just as much chance as being right as being wrong.'

'You better not be wrong, Doll,' muttered Bull's-Eye.

And so the sisters followed the path, in the direction Dolly had chosen; they crunched along the rock-salt

trail, noticing that some of the pine trees had been axed of their branches; twiglets lay in untidy piles, sprinkled with icing sugar frost. The path of salt became wetter too, and soon they came to the end of the trail. Staring through the icy pines, the girls saw tall triangular shapes beyond the trees.

Though they were tired, they began to run. Out of the wood, the children found themselves knee-deep in ice-cream again. And ahead of them, silhouetted in the moonlight, was the welcoming sight of a village. A village of upturned cornet houses blanketed with snow. The ice-cream storm had eased by now, and the sisters shivered themselves towards the nearest cottage. The houses were all two-storey cones with diagonal-patterned walls, and arched porches with lolly-shaped doors. All was quiet. All was dark. No porch lights or window lights. The cottage door had been left partly open, and the girls stood outside it, puffing and sniffing, their breaths lingering long in the air. Dolly rang the doorbell, which sounded out a tinkly ice-cream van chime. 'No one in,' she said.

Bull's-Eye pushed past her, and shoulder-barged the door. '*Course* there's no one in, Dippy.' The others filed into the cottage after her, and closed the lolly-door behind them.

Inside was a hallway with a stairwell curving up. They tried the light switch, but there was no electricity, a result of them having destroyed the jelly mill. Sugar had to get out her luminous tube, and the girls shuffled

through the cottage, stamping their damp feet on the carpet, and dumping their bags in the hall. Sugar led them into a cold dining-room, and Peppermint lit some stick-of-rock candles found upon the table. These now gave them enough light to see by, and Sugar put her tube away.

Even though the sisters needed sleep, their hungry stomachs decided it was supper time. Marzipan used a twiglet-log stove to make them all mock chocolate soup from the bark they'd collected back in Franjipan. Marzi was determined to keep the meal formal, getting Dolly to lay the table with place mats, bowls, and spoons; there weren't enough chairs to go round, so half of the sisterhood stood up to eat. Soon the candlelit dining-room was filled with a lovely cocoa aroma wafting in from the kitchen stove, and Marzipan brought out a saucepan of hot creamy soup, served a bowl to each of the children.

Lolly placed her hands around hers, and made a thin frozen skin form on top; then she cracked the skin with her spoon, and sipped the liquid cold. 'I like icy soups,' she said.

All of the girls (even Sugar Cube) gratefully drank the mock choc soup. It was something of a novelty for most of them though, to sup together, like this, in a group. There were those, such as Dolly and Marzipan, who were used to chatting with their families at the table; but these two were the exception. For the rest, their meals had been trays of food in a theatre canteen,

doses of pills in a solitary laboratory, a strict dismal diet in a juvenile institute, or self-prepared snacks in a home without parents.

For Lydia, of course, mealtimes had meant some yucky muck in the kitchenette, choked down under the eyes of Mater D. (*'You sits thur and eats every litter spittle scrap, you ungrated brat!'*) And Jawbreaker had never even eaten at a table; she would normally have had the bowl on her lap, sitting around a campfire with others in her caravan.

To follow the creamy chocolate soup, the sisters had these soft choc ices Marzi had found in a half-defrosted freezer. And then it was time for them to sleep.

There were upstairs beds or blanket-covered couches for the girls to snuggle up in. Lolly, though, still in her pale green nightdress, curled up on a pillow on the cold kitchen floor.

In the morning, Sugar caught her rifling through the freezer, foraging for lollies and popsicles. These fruit-flavoured treats were obviously what sustained her, the source of Ice Lolly's unusual powers.

'Do you have anything to carry them in?' Sugar asked her. Little Lolly shook her head. Sugar looked in the cupboards, and found a handy flask or two. 'These thermo-stable containers should do.'

''Kyou,' Lolly thanked her succinctly, and popped some popsicles inside the flasks.

During the night, the ice had melted from her slippers too, so Sugar looked around for some footwear that would better protect Lolly's feet. In a cloakroom, under the stairs, she found a pair of goloshy gumshoes, along with a small school satchel, and a crinkly green anorak called a cagoule. 'I don't really like stealing people's things,' Sugar said, getting Lolly kitted out. 'But it's for a good cause.'

The rest of the sisters soon came down for breakfast; there were cookies and cereals for them, in the kitchen, and they topped those off with their special sweets. (Lolly quietly licked a popsicle.) After Lydia had eaten a piece of her toffee, Sugar Cube returned her tin.

Lydia snatched at it eagerly. '*Karamesh Taffee!*' she read on the lid, banging it with her fingers, and making all the table's spoons flip into the air.

'Well, she seems to remember how to drum on her tin,' said Marsha. 'Can you remember our names as well, Toffee?'

Lydia swept her hair out of her eyes, and looked around at the children's faces, trying ever so hard to name them: *Shirly Whirly? Jujube Brekky? Peppsi? Cokey-Butty?* So many names. *Silly Dippy? Almond Nutty?* And looking at one, the word '*Bully*' came to mind.

'Try to remember,' Sugar encouraged. 'Who am I?'

'Erm. *Bagga-Shugga!*' Lydia blurted out, making the other sisters snigger.

'Nnn*no*.' Sugar frowned. 'Have another go. Shee-*ooga* Kee-*oob*.'

'Shoo-who-goo-koob?' Lydia uttered.

'Tell us your *real* name, Toffee,' said Dolly. 'Mine's Candice. Candice Battenburg. Then there's my sister Madeleine, my brother Matt. Mommy and daddy Battenburg . . .'

And while Dolly waffled on about her family, Sugar asked Lydia if she could indeed remember her proper name.

'Hoo, I dunnoo,' she sighed in reply, still a bit forget-ful from the Sun Beans.

'Come on, Toffee, *try*, *try*,' said Sugar, and this order to 'identify' seemed to spark words in Lydia's mind:

'I um . . . Liddy Nobody yum, minty-port, liquorice sticks—and serve Mister Tinny-Bin who noshes all the candy,' she recited, getting her pledge of allegiance wrong.

'She's nearly better,' Dolly said brightly. 'And I get mixed up like that—'

'*Achoo!*' Jawji suddenly sneezed, interrupting the conversation.

'You fine there, Jawji?' Marshmallow asked. 'Your eyes look all watery.'

'I dink I catched a-*chooo*!' Jawji sneezed again. 'A code.'

'Oh, cover your mouth when you *choo*, Jawji,' Hazel said. 'Or at least use a hanky.'

'Shugz?' sniffed Jawji. 'Do you hab any o' dose hot-toddy dweets left?'

'Sorry,' replied Sugar. 'We ate all the Hot-Tots. You might try one or two of *these* though.' She took a foil-wrapped capsule from her pocket. 'I call it a Tishoo-Zuzube. It should relieve any cold-related symptoms.'

'Better stay in the warm today,' said Marzipan. 'I'll make some more hot soup.'

'Cheers, Barzi,' Jawji smiled; she ate her Zuzube too. 'Cheers, Shugz.'

While Marzipan got busy with the stove, most of the others ventured outside to look around the village. The settlement was set out in blocks, with all the cornet properties separated by wafer fences. As the children *chuf-chuff*ed along the neat nut lanes, they found evidence that Stannic's robots had already driven the inhabitants away: some of the cottages had been demolished. A few cones looked half-eaten by crabs, with great pincer-chunks clawed out of the walls.

There were no other signs of scuffle though, fresh cream snow having settled on the scene. The village all clean and white and serene. (The sisters did see a line of pawprints, and came upon a glacier fox rummaging for scraps in a back garden litter bag.) At the centre of the village was a square complete with skating rink, market stalls, and kiosks. They found the name of the settlement on a sign there: '*Vanilla-Ville*' it read.

'Vanilla-Ville's a fishing village,' Sugar said, recalling

one of the maps stored in her memory. 'It's on the western coast of Froza.'

Beyond the block of cornet cottages was a little dock with coracle boats; the boats were round and had candied yellow hulls making them look like great half-grapefruits floating there in the orange-tinged water.

By the time the girls returned to the cottage, Marzipan had managed to rustle up some lunch; there was soup with vegetables she'd found in the larder, followed by jelly.

They stayed in the cornet cottage that day, and spent another night there too, content to make the most of the comfy beds, running water, and proper loo.

As the days were shorter, so the Frozan nights were longer, and it took a while for the dawn to sneak up on the dark. Peeping out through the cottage windows, the girls could see the sunrise stir with streams of pink and purple aurorae, a rippling ice-cream sundae sky sprinkled with the sediments of stars.

That morning, it was time for the sisters to move on, and Sugar clued them in on the next sweet in their treasure hunt: 'Sapphire Fizzweed is third on the list,' she said.

'Fizzweed is a type of sherbet seaweed,' said Marzi.

'Oo!' cried Dolly, excitable as ever. 'You get sherbet sweets on Delish beaches. I ate some on a daytrip once to—*Oo*, where was it? We went to Paistrihaven last year, Brandiburg before that. I think it must have been at Stroodle—'

While Dolly waffled on about her family vacations, Sugar considered the important question about how they might get to Delisha first. 'We'll take one of those yellow boats along the coast,' she said. 'And look for the sapphire seaweed there.'

'Why do you suppose that snaky witchy Hissy woman wants these weird sweets anyway?' said Hazel. 'I mean, what use is a jelly bean that makes you forget things? And why eat a sweet that makes you chilly and glowy?'

But none of the others could give her an answer; they guessed, however, there was something very special and powerful about this 'Snake Lady' Hisska.

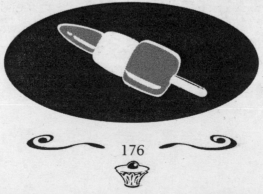

Chapter 14
Sherbet Dips

All the sisters wrapped up warm; all except Ice Lolly, of course, who preferred to keep cool in her crinkly cagoule (with gummy shoes on her bare feet).

Lydia's memory was fully restored. Jawbreaker felt better as well, though she still had a bit of a runny nose that she smeared on the sleeve of her jumper.

Leaving the village of Vanilla-Ville, the children made their way to the coast and the grapefruity boats bobbing in the dock; the coracles were fastened to popsicle posts by ribbon-candy ropes and, underneath peely tarpaulin covers, fishing equipment could be found: basket creels and mesh nets, and oars like two big wooden spoons. The sisters hopped aboard one of the coracles, its curved hull creaking and rocking as each of them clambered in.

'Is it *safe*?' asked Dolly.

'It'll be fine,' Sugar replied, 'if we sit evenly on each side.'

'I'm not sitting next to Miss *Snuffle*-Scruff,' Hazel said, referring to Jawbreaker.

'There's plenty of room,' sighed Marsha. 'Sit over there. I'm sure Jawji don't care.'

Lydia sat beside one of the oars, using it to spoon up the strange orange squashy water.

'*I'm* rowing,' Bull's-Eye insisted, grabbing the oar out of her hands. 'So there.'

Lydia was happy to move. Anywhere away from Bull's-Eye.

'Who else wants to help paddle?' said Sugar. 'How about you, Pepper?'

Peppermint nodded, and she took the other wooden oar, placing her four hands around the handle. Once all the girls were settled, Sugar Cube untied the vessel, winding up the stripy rope, before pushing the coracle away from the shore.

Pull. Scoop. Pull. Scoop. Bull's-Eye and Peppermint rowed in synch, using the spoons to move the boat slowly through the water. Leaving the frozen shores of Froza, they went south-west along the coast of Delisha.

Aurorae flickered purple above the sea-wide horizon, the sky shining weird and red, a fiery colour that belied the cold. As the girls progressed across the chilled morning waters, the sea became thicker, more concentrated like orange juice, and the air became misty and white. Lydia leaned over the side of the boat to see fleeting jaffa fish swimming through the juice, and an orange squash squid that pulsed pulsed past.

Along the coast was a crystal cliff glistening orange through the mist; yet it was the sight of ghosts rising from the rock, and their haunting sighs that made Lydia nervous.

'Froozy spooks,' Ice Lolly whispered, her eyes wide with fright.

More of these faceless spirits shimmered up, then dispersed in wisps from the tips of the cliff; they seemed to reach out with freezing fingers feeling for the children's faces.

'They're only sherbet fountains,' Sugar said to allay their fear. 'They spurt up from the rocks round here.'

'Who's making ze moanies then?' said Coco.

'It's hollows in the cliffs,' replied Sugar. 'The crystal's echo acoustics.'

'In our caravans in winter,' Jawji whispered, 'we use to shay stories 'bout sherbet ghosts. They gum up from the core o' the world, and getchup your nose in the night.'

'That's like Delish fairy tales,' added Dolly. 'There's one about spirits that live in fiery orange pits. I bet it's a bit like this place.'

'Where I come from,' said Marzipan, 'they tell of an underworld with lakes of bitter lemon.'

'And in Spyssian mythology,' Sugar Cube said, 'there's an Isle of the Dead with knifing winds that freeze people's souls and cut at their bones. And all the sweetie secrets of the world are said to bubble up from crying kettles.'

'*Yurh*, sounds grooshum,' grimaced Jawji.

'It's not real,' Sugar assured her. 'We won't have to go there or anything.'

'Only go there when you're dead,' Ice Lolly said.

'Don't want to hear about things like that. Thank you very much, *Lolly*,' Hazel added.

As they carried on past the ghostly cliff, sherbet sprays fell in a fizzy haze and tingled quite pleasantly in Lydia's nose. Now, across the orange water, the girls saw signs of the seaweed they sought; tiny pods of tangerine algae all along the crystal rock.

They made their way to where the weed seemed most abundant. 'That'll be the best place to look,' said Sugar. 'Where all that seaweed's stuck.'

'Oo, watch out for those orange rocks!' cried Dolly.

A sudden surge of juicy waves pushed the boat into these crystal outcrops. The sisters braced themselves for a crash, their coracle soon to be grapefruit crush—but the hull just deflected against the rocks, and fragments broke off and crumbled into the boat. They were ice lolly rocks, citrussy and lickable.

Panic over, they floated past the orange lollies, using the spoons to propel the coracle on towards the misty shore, making for a gap in the cliffs. Closer to the Delish coast were hazardous banks of harder quartz, and Bull's-Eye and Peppermint rowed with care, between the jagged craggy rocks, to a circular lagoon.

Sherbet Dips

It was as if the children had entered a giant orange. On all sides were crystal coves, and at the far side of the lagoon was a beach of peel from which the cliffs rose in segments; fresh-squeezed streams of juice trickled between them, and spilled into the water—if, indeed, it could be called 'water'—for, here, the surface of the sea flowed thicker still, forming marmaladey waves with peely eels slithering beneath.

This place (a place where fisherfolk might come to dip their breakfast toast) was also covered with sea-weed: masses of candied strands washed up along the beach or draped across the frosted coves; tangled leaves of it, pods upon pods of it, overlain in bobbly bundles as though big tubs of tangerine gumballs had been scattered upon the shore.

Bull's-Eye and Pepper prepared to paddle to the beach, but the marmalade was almost too thick to row through. Marsha and Jawbreaker went to help, and they sat like galley slaves, two to a spoon, pushing and pulling through the orange goo.

'Urh, this joosh is shorrible,' Jawji moaned as she tried to shove the oar through the waves of marmalade.

'Something moving down there,' Lydia noted, still nosing over the side of the boat.

'Probably only eels,' said Dolly.

But suddenly they heard a *crunch* of wood. Peppermint pulled up her oar to find that something had bitten off half the spoon.

Lydia looked across the lagoon; she saw long sharp

tails and dorsal fins knifing through the marmalade around them. These were no spooky sherbet apparitions, but a famished family of arga-sharks.

The anxious children pulled at the marmalade with the one-and-a-half spoons. Heaving, rowing, ebbing flowing. Till at last the hull of the grapefruit boat bumped against the beach. The girls jumped ashore, hurriedly dragging the coracle after them.

They stared around the tangy lagoon. Up at the cliffs and crystal coves, and around the rim of frosted peel.

'Oo, look at zis,' Coco whispered, skipping nimbly over the seaweed. She had found another electric spy-hawk, flat on its back at the foot of a cliff.

'The stupid bird musta hit the rocks or summit,' Bull's-Eye said. And snatching up the fallen hawk, she dashed it to bits by slinging it at the cliff.

'Do you have to be so destructive, Zye?' winced Hazel. 'You could see it was already bust.'

'Sisters, sisters. Please,' frowned Sugar. 'Now, we need to concentrate.'

She got them all lined up on the beach, and even invited Dolly Mixture to give a demonstration: Dolly took a length of seaweed, and showed the others how the pods could be peeled to reveal sherbet sweets inside. (Some pods had nothing in them at all, being bladders of air to keep the weed afloat in water.)

'It be best if we do this methodically,' said Sugar. And so she assigned each girl a portion of the shore, and told them to check as many pods as possible. 'We're

after a Sapphire Fizzweed,' she reminded them. 'So look for a sweet that's blue and glittery.'

The sisters spread out and started their search. At first, they quite enjoyed the task; it was fun to unwrap the seaweed pods and try the fizzy sweets within. Coco, in particular, pared the seaweed with speed and then started flinging the orange rind at everyone.

'Cocoa-*Butter*, stop it!' Marsha tutted, swatting bits of peel from her hair.

'Oo, shush you, Marsho,' Coco retorted. 'We chuck what we want.'

Lydia playfully hopped along the shore; the peel of the beach was unexpectedly springy, and she found she could bound about, stop to sort through a few strands of tangerines, and hop along some more. Her part of the shore was pitted with juicy pools around which the sea-weed collected in clumps. Lydia had to unravel the interweaving leaves and pods before she could tell one weed from another. Although the pods looked similar, the sweets inside were different, and so finding a sap-phire would be a case of lucky sherbet dip. A patient sift through every pod.

'*Orange one. No good. Lemon one. I've eaten that one. Empty one. That's no use. Oo, a red one. That's a new one. Lemon. Noo. Nother norange.*'

Oranges and lemons were the seaweed most common. If only Lydia could find a sapphire, here on the shores of Delisha. They were something of a rarity, so said Sugar of the list's confectionery. One might

make you rich. Could be treasure anywhere on the beach. Which pod? Which pod would it be? Lydia didn't know. Was is it this one? No.

And now, after tasting so many of the sherbet sweets, she was properly floppily lightheaded. Sea sounds effervesced in her ears, marmalade waves seemed to spread around her head. Lydia felt dizzier, dizzier and fizzier, her legs all wibbly wobbly with the sherbet dips. She could only imagine what the treasure-sweet would do, if ordinary fizzweed sweets made her feel like this.

Meanwhile, the others searched and searched, but still without finding any sapphires.

After an hour of fruitless hunting, and fizzy sweet munching, Sugar told them to take a break. As the girls got up, they felt similarly Lydi-dizzy, walking all wonky, off-balance and silly. Sugar had refrained from eating any of the sweets herself, and looked on concerned.

'I think you all better have one of these,' she said, taking a packet of lozenges from her pocket, and distributing them amongst the others.

'What are theys?' asked Bull's-Eye in a daze.

'Giddy Gumdrops,' Sugar said. 'To quell lightheadedness and steady any dizziness.'

The gumdrop tasted of ginger pop, and Lydia found that the seesaw sea sounds in her ears soon stopped. And so the sisters crouched in a cove, and chewed their Giddy Gumdrop lozenges; it wasn't so cold there, under cover of the rocks, and growing in some of the crystal

nooks were shrubs with orange marshmallow flowers. Peppermint scrunched a pile of seaweed on the ground, spat a bit of flame to ignite it, and the girls sat around this fizzy campfire, holding stalks of mallows over the flames; then they plucked the toasted flowers and ate them. Crispy petal melty.

As the ginger pop gumdrops got to work, it made the girls feel gassy too. A series of unladylike burps could soon be heard around the cove. '*Urp*, excuse me, *burp burp*, 'scuse us, *oorp*, oh pardon *me*.'

'Better find this fizzweed soon,' Hazel complained. 'And that marmalade's creeping up the lagoon.'

'Hazel's right,' Sugar said. 'Let's get back to it. We haven't got all day.'

And so the sisters dawdled back along the beach, and set about the seaweed again—without eating any of the sweets this time. They grabbed more stalks, picked off and peeled a load more pods, decided they were no good, and discarded the sweets and leaves.

Orange one. *Lemon* one. *Orange* one. *Red* one. But never the blue weed they were after.

The search had now become something of a chore. The girls' fingers were getting sore from handling the pods, and then there were these little lizardy things ('salamandarins', Marzipan said they were called) that scurried out from under the weed, nipped at their hands and made them jump. And as if that wasn't horrid enough, waves of marmalade slopped up the shore, making the peely beach icky and sticky. The tide also brought with it a wriggling mush of jelly eels; like sidewinding slimy tongues, they lapped and snapped around the ankles. Lydia didn't dare go near them, and confined her hunting to high up the beach.

'There's more weed up there on the cliffs,' pointed Dolly. 'And all over the coves.'

'I suppose they got stuck there at high tide,' said Sugar, and told the others that every pod had to be tried. Any one might have a sapphire inside.

Some seaweed hung down the cliffs, like knotted string, and the sisters bounced up off the trampoliney peel, to grasp and pull down the trailing strands.

As for those pods too remote to reach—pods wedged on ledges or snagged on rocks across the lagoon—to reach those, they needed Dolly's unique ability: Sugar fetched a rope from the boat, and Dolly snapped off one of her forearms, tying the rope around the wrist. Bull's-Eye was able to cast this handy grappling hook, and when the rope neared the faraway weed, Dolly made her fingers grip onto a pod. Then Bull's-Eye pulled the rope back, seaweed and all, and once Dolly had let go of it, they got ready to throw her arm back for another go. This way, they made a pile of new pods for the others to open.

Slop blup. Minute after minute. Marmalade *slop blup* curling closer. The girls were really fed up now. Pod after pod. Scraping away the sticky peel. Pod after pod.

Orange. *No*. Lemon. *No*. Another orange. Red one, blue one—*A blue one!*

Suddenly Cocoa-Butter called out: 'We got it! We got it! A sapphire sweetie!'

The sisters gathered round her as Coco held up a large blue bauble, a sherbet sweet that seemed to glitter with an inner flame.

'Oo, I wonder what it tastes like,' giggled Dolly, unwrapping more sapphires from the same string of fizzweed.

'Cannot risk eating it,' Marzipan warned. 'Like the others, it must have some special effect.'

Sugar took the Fizzweed sweets then sealed them away, along with the Sun Beans and Chilly Jelly Amethysts.

By now, the tide of marmalade had pushed so far up the peely beach that the coracle had drifted off on it, bobbing there in the middle of the lagoon surrounded by a ring-a-ring of rising shark fins.

'How we going to get out again?' asked Hazel Whirl. 'Without a boat?'

'There may be a way up the cliffs,' said Marsha.

But the sisters looked up at the sheer orange rock. Slick and sharp and too steep to climb.

It seemed that they were stranded.

Sugar, however, was scanning the lagoon having detected a familiar signal; soon they all heard a familiar sound:

'*Jug-a-jug-a-jug. Jug-a-jug-a-jug.*'

An orange-striped rattlesnake slithered across the shore.

'It must have slipped down the cliffs to find us,' Marzipan surmised.

Chapter 15
Pineapple Cubes

The synthetic serpent slithered away into one of the crystal caves.

'We'd better follow,' Sugar said. 'It seems to know a way out of here.'

'Is spooky dark in there,' uttered Lolly.

Sugar Cube checked her luminous tube. 'Hmm,' she frowned. 'I don't want to keep using this. It'll run out of spearmint oil.'

She looked about, then went and tugged up some marshmallow shrubs. Sugar showed the girls how to make a sparkler by winding seaweed around the mallow stalks and, once all eleven of them had a sparkler each, they were ready to trail the snake. Peppermint lit her sparkler-stalk first, blowing on the tip so it glowed with a glistening flame. Then the girls followed her into the cave, listening out for the maracca-shakey snake.

Though they were pleased to leave the lagoon, it felt

as if they were entering the mouth of a monster; the cave was filled with stalagmite teeth, and the sounds of distant sherbet fountains wheezing through the crystal walls could easily have been the monster's breathing. *Joosh joosh*. The sisters sloshed through puddles of juice, and the tang of orange in the air stung their eyes and noses.

Peppermint's sparkler glinted across the prismic rock and, as it burned down the mallow-stem, the seaweed turned to a tangerine ash. After a minute or two, it had almost fizzled out, so the children changed places, Marsha stepped up next, and Peppermint '*fwoo*' blew to light her sparkler, so they could carry on after the snake.

The stripy serpent stayed just ahead of them, moving smooth through the rocky caves. On and on. Around the jags and stalagmites, twisting and turning through the segments of quartz. It would have been easy to have got lost in these interconnected caverns; the sisterhood just had to trust the snake as it slithered further into the cliff. Marsha's sparkler soon sizzled its last. The sisters swapped places again, Marzi at the front this time; Peppermint lit her sparkler-stalk, and then they continued their underground walk.

'How much longer does this stinky cave go on for?' Bull's-Eye griped.

Marzi's sparkler *siss*ed to the bottom; then Hazel Whirl's. And once Hazel's fire had fizzled, Pepper lit the next, leaving seven sisters' seaweed sparklers tied around the stalks.

On and on, after the orange snake. *Fizzle*. Six spark-lers left. *Fizzle*. Five. *Fizzle*. Four.

It was Dolly Mixture's turn now, and she held her sparkler above her head and delighted in swirling it in the air, making the light shimmer around them.

'Dolly, hold it *still*,' frowned Sugar. 'It's very annoy-ing. And I've lost track of the snake.'

Bull's-Eye pushed forward and snatched at Dolly's arm, rudely pulling it off at the elbow; then she strode ahead of the others, searching for the stripy serpent. In fact, none of the girls could see it now; it seemed to have slithered away on its own. The crystal rock came to a sudden end too.

Bull's-Eye held Dolly's arm aloft, and the sparkler lit up a wall in front of them. A wall built entirely of huge pineapple cubes.

'Stupid snake,' said Zye. 'Wotsit led us up a dead end for?'

'We have to break through the wall,' said Sugar. 'How many sparklers do we have left?'

'I've got one,' Lydia replied.

'We too,' said Coco.

'An' me,' said Jawji. 'I still got mine ash well.'

By now, Dolly's sparkler-stalk had almost fizzled out, so Bull's-Eye chucked her arm back to her. Peppermint then lit Lydia's fizzweed, and she held it up while Bull's-Eye kicked at the wall with her hoof, viciously smashing at it, kicking and kicking.

She only managed to chip and crack it. 'Take ages to kick through that,' she panted.

Jawbreaker also tried to take a bite, but she couldn't get her teeth around the smooth cemented cubes. Now Lydia's sparkler had burned down too.

'Why don't we get Peppy-mint to light some of Sugar's bom-bom gum?' suggested Dolly. 'Bet that would blow away the wall in no time.'

'And probably blow us all up with it,' Marshmallow said.

'You really *are* a dip sometimes, Dolly,' added Hazel.

'What if we only use a teeny tiny bit of it?' Dolly continued.

'We could use one of the sparklers for a fuse,' said Sugar. 'Give Pepper plenty of time to get back.' And so she stuck a crumb of Combusta-Gum into the crack Zye had made in the wall. Then she wedged the sparkler-stalk on top of it, and while the others stayed well away, Peppermint lit the seaweed fuse and retreated to where they waited.

After a minute or two, the gum blew. *Shishoo! Shoo-shoo. Shoo.* A short sharp blast echoed through the cave.

Once the shattering sounds had died down, the girls went back to see what had happened.

With Jawbreaker holding the last of the sparklers, they made their way up to the pineapple wall, crunching across shards of fallen crystal with orange crushy footsteps.

'*Whoah!*' Jawji exclaimed. 'It's boshed.' A great

gaping hole had been blown through the cubes, and she stuck her head in for a look. 'Yesh, there's an empchy chewb froo 'ere.'

'Why did the snake lead us to this place, though?' asked Hazel.

'Let's see, shall we?' said Sugar, climbing through.

Behind the cubes was a tubular tunnel. A tunnel with a channel. An aluminium channel like a smooth gutter chute. As soon as Sugar set foot on the chute, tiles of pineapple light shone above her; and wherever she went, the light would follow, no doubt triggered by her movement.

'Looks like some kind of slidey railway,' said Lydia, looking up and down the gutter.

'It's Delisha's underground transport system.'

'Oh, I've been on the subby-tube,' Dolly said to Sugar Cube.

'How come the lights work?' Bull's-Eye asked. 'They never did in that snow-cone house.'

'Not all of Candi-Land relies on electric,' Sugar replied. 'This underground system runs on pop.'

The tiles continued to blink on and off as the girls strolled along the chute. Soon they saw a stationary object blocking the tunnel up ahead and, when they approached, a cubic platform lit up all around them. The sisters stepped up to inspect the object, and Lydia could see it was a giant drink can sitting in the gutter-chute. The can had small triangular windows, and a ring-pull handle beside its door.

'It's a pop-a-stop shuttle,' Sugar told them.

'And ze shuttle shut,' said Coco, trying the ring-pull.

'Toffee? Do you think you can open the door?' asked Marsha.

'I can try,' Lydia replied. She had to retrieve the tin from her backpack, and loop its ribbon around her neck. Then she decided to eat a piece of toffee, before picking up her liquorice sticks and tapping them at the tin lid.

It was the first time in days that Lydia had done any drumming but, as she concentrated on the door, she felt an immediate connection to the lock. Her toffee-fuelled mind got stuck into its mechanism, and her drum beat made the ring-pull snap up.

The door slid back with a sudden _tish!_ making some of the sisters jump.

'Well done, Toffee,' Sugar said, entering the drink-can-car.

The shuttle could accommodate up to twenty passengers and, once the girls had hopped aboard, they took off their knapsacks, and spread out on the seats. Whilst the outside of the can was blank and grey, the interior was patterned with bubbles of colour, and padded with cushions of comfy sponge cake.

'Oo, it's _very_ posh, this can-o-pop,' said Hazel. 'But then I'm used to travelling first-class.'

Sugar plonked herself in the driver's seat, in front of a circular control screen; it automatically lit up bright orange when she touched its liquid crystal segments.

'D'ya know how ta work this shuttle, Shugz?' Jawji asked.

'Seems straightforward enough,' said Sugar. 'I think I need to press this—'

Tish! The door slid shut. *Whush!* They were off with a push. The sisters sank back in their seats as the shuttle shot forwards with a hiccup of pop. Once the girls had got over the initial rush, the can-car zoomed so smooth along the chute it felt as if it wasn't moving at all. Yet Lydia could hear faint *ta-popper ta-popper ta-popper ta-pops*, as the pipe-a-papple propulsion gas packs, at the back of the can, pushed them on.

The sisters loosened their fleeces, and settled in the cosy seats. Time to relax. Time to munch their lunchtime sweets. Pale pineapple light glimmered in beyond the windows and, as the drink-can-car carried on, stations whizzed by in a blur of tiles. Lydia noticed the tunnels sometimes opened out, with two chutes, three chutes running alongside each other; thus they were able to overtake other can-o-pop cars, simply seen as shooting *tin-tin-tin-tin* streaks too quick to clock.

Ta-popper ta-popper ta-popper ta-pop. The children must have been travelling for at least an hour, when their own shuttle can-car slid to a stop. The interior's lights went out. Sugar's control screen switched off too.

Lydia had to fumble for her drumsticks, and she unlocked the door with a toffee tin command.

Tish! The door slid back at her bidding.

Immediately she smelled heated pop bubbling from the rear of the can, with the pleasant scent of a hot fruit pie. The girls left the shuttle, and hopped to a platform lit with mats of lemon light. Lydia could see the name of the station printed on a wall in tiles of white:

TEA SET CITY CENTRAL

'We've reached my home city!' Dolly piped up.

'Where's that then?' Jawbreaker asked.

'What's the matter with you?' Hazel scoffed. 'It's written perfectly clearly. Can't you read?'

'Nah,' Jawji said, with a shrug. 'Never taught to.'

'We're still in Delisha,' Sugar told them. 'Right in the heart of Tin Man territory. So everyone be extra careful.'

Not wishing to exit the station by the main doors, the girls climbed the emergency stairs; in single-file, they shuffled up flight after flight of narrow steps till eventually they reached a street-level exit.

Coco slipped outside for a look, and she soon returned to report to the others. 'Is busy-busy,' she whispered. 'Best we sneak away queak.'

The girls reversed their hidey-hoods, back again to black again. Sugar then set her coat to dark grey after taking a peek at the sky and, as the sisters crept into the open, Lydia could clearly see why. Although it was only early afternoon, the city was overcast, and smog spread overhead.

'Sky smells scalded,' Marzipan said.

'Pongy poops,' added Ice Lolly.

'Don't be *rude*, Lolly,' said Dolly. 'I live here. And it never niff like this before.'

Coco got out her perfume again, spraying her clothes with a sweet 'odour vee'.

The emergency exit had brought them outside, right beside a railway junction; the place was noisy with dozens of steam trains waiting at forks of liquorice rail. *Chuffle truffle chuffle chew*. Locomotives shunted and snorted. *Huff-n-puff* and *truffle truff*. Hot cross horses stuck on the tracks. *Delish. Likrish. Franji Express. Noogari. Froza*. Trains from all over.

Coke can tanker wagons were gridlocked along the liquorice too, unable to deliver their energy porridge; the signal boxes, between the rails, remaining blank and unresponsive. 'The power's cut,' Sugar explained. 'When we blew up the jelly mill, it must have caused a blackout or power surge. The trains can't run properly without electricity.'

'I thought the horses only needed cokey-oaty pudding,' said Hazel.

'That's right. To make them go. But the signals tell them *where* to go.'

Along the tracks, Lydia watched the trains and engines judder to a stop. And then came ranks of robot soldiers up to unload the rolling stock; these were similar to the tin police that still controlled the Likrish zones: bucket-headed robots awkwardly lifting their tin-can legs to step across the tracks.

'Rotten *clunks 'n' clanks*,' Lydia whispered to herself.

The robot soldiers worked to clear the backed-up backlog of cargo wagons, rattling open the corrugated doors and lifting off pallets and barrels and crates. The scene was one of utter disarray. Trains all in each other's way. While the trackside mechanisms—levers, lifters, and automated trays-on-wheels—all stood useless. Out of order. And the robots carried on without their assistance, dithering turning sidestepping one another.

Thus, with the robots so preoccupied, Coco led the sisters from the railway, walking quiet city streets towards the heart of town.

Lydia tucked her tin under her cloak; she didn't want it hanging loose but, just in case there was danger to come, she wanted the tin at the ready to drum. And yet no robots patrolled the city. No people were meant to be there anyhow. Lydia peeped out from her fleece, seeing the curvy buildings around her; some were shaped like colossal pieces of pottery, oversized sugar bowls or egg cup domes, whereas others were round with spout-style chimneys, teapots, coffee pots with lid-like rooftops. Smoke stains tainted the white of this china town, the glazey surfaces dulled by a sky gravy-thick with dumpling clouds.

Below the smog, the tea set city was pretty yet desolate; the girls wandered through its spacious piazzas, past cake shops, snack bars, and quaint tea gardens with spouty fountains full of stagnant herbal water. 'Daddy used to have a teapot shop round here,' said Dolly.

They had soon passed through the city centre, reaching chintzy crescents full of teacup houses with upturned saucer roofs.

'Your home's near here, Dolly?' Marsha said. 'It'll be somewhere to stay, won't it?'

Dolly took a look around. 'Er, let's go this way.'

The flossy-haired girl skipped along, leading the others; a little bit dippy she may have been, but Dolly knew her city very well. It all looked the same to Lydia: avenues and avenues of white-painted teacups, biscuit-brick bungalows trimmed with icing.

As they went, though, she saw that some of the houses were cracked and chipped; doors broken open, gardens untended, tea leaf hedges overgrown, with trampled bluebells and rockery nutshells and crockery bits all in the road in rows, with topiary grown out of control. Bull's-Eye, bored, kicked stones along the pavement, making clinking clacky echoes down the lightless streets. After a while, Dolly reached her home. A giant teacup with the back door still open.

The eleven children nipped inside.

The dimly-lit place had hardly changed in the weeks since Sugar had led Dolly away. It was chilly though. And soulless. Minus the presence of her family. The sisters dispersed through the rooms of the bungalow, claiming beds, bagging sofas.

Lydia found Dolly tidying up the dining-room,

setting the table, putting out coasters, cups and spoons. 'I brought some friends round for tea,' she whispered to herself, though less than cheerily.

'Who you talking to?' Lydia asked.

'Mummy's and Daddy's ghosts might be in the house,' Dolly replied. 'Listening.'

'Won't they be in one of the work camps? With all the other parents?'

'Shuggy said they get put to sleep. Then taken away to a place without sweets.'

Dolly continued to tidy the table, stopping to wipe away tears from her face.

'They'll be all right, Dolly,' Lydia said. 'My daddy was taken away *years* ago. And he still works in one of the confection camps.'

Dolly looked at Lydia, forced a smile and fluttered her eyelids. 'Why don't we all have a nice cuppa tea?' she said.

The two of them went into the kitchen. Jawbreaker was already there, tucking into something she'd discovered in a cupboard. 'Found these bishkitch,' she munched. 'Oh, but I 'ad to trash shum loafa bread. It gone green wiv mouldy,' Jawji said.

'Would you like a cuppa tea with your biccies?' Dolly asked.

'Yeah. Jeers, Jolly,' Jawji nodded with her mouth full.

Tea came straight from the tap in Delisha; Dolly filled a kettle full and put it on the hob to heat; the gas flame caused the kettle to whistle and, when the other

girls heard this high flutey tooting, they all converged on the kitchen, snooping.

Dolly got out her tea party play set; Lydia was pleased to see she'd brightened up a bit. Busy with teacups, cakes and biscuits; she even found some packets of crackers and crisps.

'Got plenty blends of teas,' she said, mixing in different flavoured sauces, and serving cups to all the girls now seated in the dining-room. '*Lemon* tea for *Marzipan*. Strawberry for *Zye*. Nectarine for *Marsha*. Peppermint for *Pepper*. Peachy tea for *Toffee*. Cold tea for *Lolly* . . . '

For dessert, there were tins of fruit cocktail in syrup and, once Dolly had declared her party to be over, she fetched the sisters blankets and gowns, and they all snuggled down to sleep in the teacup.

Chapter 16
Soup Kitchen

Early next morning, Lydia rose from her sofa bed; she went through into the dining-room to find Sugar asleep, slumped over the table. Her goggles lay next to her, along with six discarded sugar lumps; she sat there without her jacket too, in a sleeveless white serviette shirt. Lydia fetched a blanket and put it around Sugar Cube's cold shoulders. Sugar woke with a start, and she peered at Lydia, nearly blind, shiny tears of sleep seeping from her eyes.

'Is that you, Toffee?' she whispered, her voice sounding weak and crackly. She fumbled for her goggles and switched them on so she could see.

'Yes,' said Lydia. 'It's only me.'

Sugar took her jacket off the back of a chair, and opened a pocket for the tube of glucose pills in there. Lydia went and filled a tumbler with tap water, and it helped Sugar swallow her life-saving medicine.

The other girls soon joined them for breakfast. Dolly made them all a pot of tea (according to Lydia, Dolly made the best tea she'd ever tasted ever) and after their drink, Sugar told them to eat a good dose of their special sweets. It was at this moment, though, that Marsha let on she was down to only one or two marshmallows. Most of the other sisters admitted similarly low supplies, giving Sugar cause for concern.

'Should we save them for another day?' Dolly Mixture asked.

'We'd better eat what we can now,' replied Sugar. 'We might need all our powers and abilities to get out of this robot-controlled city.'

'Where we gone next then, Shugz?' Jawji asked.

'The Black Forest,' Sugar replied. 'That means we have to go through Stannic's main prison camp.'

'What d'you mean *through* it?' questioned Hazel. 'I thought we were trying to avoid dangerous places.'

'What sweet do we need to find in the Black Forest?' Marzi asked.

'*Oh!*' cried Dolly making everybody jump. 'I din't show anyone my animal collection.'

She dashed away into her room, and returned with a big pink cardboard box which she placed upon the table. Dolly lifted the lid to reveal rows of ornamental porcelain eggs with whimsical alfeñique figurines inside, all depicting fauna from Delish folklore:

Creamy unicorns, cherry griffins, wafer-winged wyverns, truffle boars, and torte-hogs.

'Now, I want you all to pick your favourite to keep,' Dolly smiled. 'You first, Shuggy Cube, as you're our leader—'

'Dolly, we don't have time for this,' Sugar frowned. 'Best if we leave in a bit.'

Dolly blushed, embarrassed, and put her egg box back in her room; then she joined the others in the hallway as they gathered their knapsacks, ready to go.

It was still early morning, barely light, when the sisters left the bungalow. They ventured out onto the quiet street, and ambled through the teacup crescents, heading towards the edge of the city.

The roads and pavements and private driveways were curiously free of vehicles. No parked cars, no baker's vans. Every one of them towed away. Deserted street after deserted street.

The further they walked, the more damage they saw: crockery houses partly demolished, half-a-cup structures, abandoned shops. And spilling around the fine china ruins, Lydia shuddered at black tea-leaf rats picking at piles of uncollected refuse.

'Doesn't even look like my home any more,' Dolly said sadly.

The girls soon reached a ring road overpass encircling the city like a giant doughnut; and so they went from the smoke-stained teapots towards the outskirt factories and bakeries. They walked for some time beyond the doughnut road and, as they neared the bakery quarter, certain sounds, ponderous sounds, began to

reach the children's ears. Sounds of a mechanical army marching marching marching.

The sisters sneaked behind a wall, beside a wide paved site: a filling station like an outdoor canteen with rows of huge ceramic bowls connected to taps and pipes. There stood the robot soldiers, hundreds of tin men in orderly lines. And what Lydia had first thought to be regimented marching was really munching, mass mass munching. The robots were programmed to eat as one, a hundred at a time, a line at a time. Tucking into blocks of chocolate. The chocolate looked the same as the bars from the train; unwrapped and broken into squares, they now fitted into the robots' mouth slots. *Munch munch crunch crunch*. A hundred pairs of lever-arms held a hundred chocolate squares. *Munch crunch crunch munch*. A hundred denture mechanisms, inside a hundred metal mouths, broke the blocks into manageable chunks. *Crunch munch crunch munch*.

Lydia could see that it took each robot two or three bites to break down the block—showing how powerful Jawji's jaws were: she had bit it in one.

Automated trolleys, bearing more of the chocolate, trundled between the assembled ranks, and the soldiers shoved the squares into their gob-slots. Block after block, line after line, a parade of chocoholic robots.

'Look at them, the greedy machines,' Dolly Mixture whispered.

'Actually,' said Sugar, 'their intake is strictly regulated. So if one were to upset their eating routine—'

Now, at the back of the canteen site, the taps on the pipes were turning mechanically, and the ceramic bowls began to fill with a cool gasoline soup. Liquid fuel to swill down the chocolate.

Sugar thought that some sort of distraction, some sabotage action, might help them get past so many robots. And so she took Cocoa-Butter aside, and gave her a packet from one of her pockets. Coco ripped it open, and peeked at these cube-shaped sweets.

'Drop the cubes into the soup,' Sugar instructed her. 'One in each bowl should do. Now. Before the robots finish their chocolate.'

'One plunk in each bowl?' nodded Coco. 'We return in a momo.' She handed her handbag and hood to Hazel, then slid from behind the wall slippery quick.

Lydia saw golden glimmer glimpses of Coco as she stole between the lines of soldiers, over to the far side of the site. To camera eyes, to robot eyes, she'd seem nothing more than a flicker of light. Even the sounds of her feet didn't alert them, covered by the noise of the crunching munching. Coco didn't dilly-dally either. Swiftly swiftly, one by one, she stopped at the twenty-odd waist-high bowls, reached up and dropped the cubes into the soup of gasoline. Then she slipped from the site unseen, to join the others in their hiding place.

'I plunk ze sweeties in ze soup,' she grinned. Coco couldn't resist causing such potential mischief.

'What will those cubes do then?' asked Hazel.

'Wait and see,' whispered Sugar.

The sisters jostled for position behind the wall, to watch what would happen next.

By now, the rows and rows of robots had finished scoffing their chocolate blocks and had turned to form queues, disciplined dinner queues, queues of hundreds of robot troops standing in line for the bowls of soup. Beside each bowl was a big tin cup and, once the robots had stepped on up, they gripped the cup, dunked it in the gasoline, took a drink, and *clunked* it down. Then moved along for the next in line. Take a step forward. Dunk the cup. *Dunk* drink *clunk*. *Dunk* drink *clunk*.

Once each robot had finished this process, it turned and plodded back in line on the other side of the site.

Minute after minute, the drinking continued. The canteen resounded with clanking sounds, and the stamping sounds of mechanical boots, as robot troops tramped up in queues to guzzle down their cups of soup.

'Nothing's happen-ning,' said Dolly, bouncing up and down, impatient.

'Give it a moment,' Sugar replied. 'The sweets need to dissolve then bubble up inside.'

Now, across the canteen site, Lydia saw a few of the soldiers frothing from the slots of their mouths. All along the lines of robots, this awful gurgling racket could be heard; their hot pot bodies began to boil, started to bubble, to hiccup and pop. The metal men collapsed and clanged against each other, falling off-balance as though they were drunk.

And yet the dunking and drinking went on, the dumb droids sticking to their programmed menu. Blocks of chocolate followed by soup. Soon the scene was utter mayhem as blasts occurred along the rows. The mess of ticking timebomb bots—tummy rumbling tum-tum *Pop!* Fuel-filled belly-pots exploded with sprays of scalding cocoa. Kettle guts and plated limbs were blown across the canteen site, and the girls had to duck behind the wall as hot machine parts flew through the air. Dolly managed to stifle a squeal when a robot's bucket head smacked down nearby.

Pop-a-froth! Froth-a-pop! Double-bubble-bang! Lydia wondered if the pandemonium would ever stop. There were hundreds of robots, and all had drunk their share of the broth. *Froth-a-pop. Fizzle. Guzzle.*

Dunk. Clunk. Groan. Eventually the blasts subsided, and Sugar decided it was safe enough for the sisters to risk a dash around the depot. From wall to wall, they scurried quickly, ducking behind the pipes and bowls, skirting the chaotic canteen site, and its stench of chemical cocoa. Past the scrapheap of tottering tin, robots with their bellies bust open, headless and legless, falling in lines. Many of the soldiers were still intact but unable to function, lying on their backs in pools of hot chocolate; they seemed almost alive with their twitching limbs and mouth-slots still hiccuping up soup.

Marzipan stared at the wretched things, with a look in her eyes of 'it served you right'.

'Super soupy sabotage,' Coco chuckled at the sight.

'Those little sweetie cubes caused all *that*?' Dolly asked.

'I call those sweets Froth-Bites,' Sugar replied. 'Specially designed to upset robot stomachs.'

Lydia looked back over the ruined canteen: it certainly was the worst case of upset tummy she'd ever seen. With a single dunk of soup, the sisterhood had managed to wreck a whole detachment of Stannic's troops.

Even many minutes later, the hiccuping pops still hadn't stopped, and the girls left the robots drowning in their greasy drink, to make their way to the factory camp beyond.

Next, they crept past kennel-like centres where a big junk pile of tin hounds were found with their noses plugged into bowl-shaped sockets. The dogs would normally be lapping up electric jelly, but now they lay starving, collapsed in empty bowls. A chain of doggy domino dustbins, unable to recharge, winding down, whining sounds coming from their drooling oily jaws.

The girls were glad to bypass the hounds as well, and soon they were right in the thick of the factory district. Wherever they looked they saw dinnerware potteries, cutlery and kettle foundries, teapot-makers and porcelain kilns with chimneys like elegant tapering milk jugs. Even now the chimney-jugs were belching out clouds of dirty grey smog. The fresh-baked cake and bread roll aromas that used to enrich the Delish air were noticeably absent here. Sugar knew that this was where the camp was situated. The confection camp that Stannic had built. At the very edge of the tea set city. With barriers and fences of electrified grills, and high metal gates garnished with spikes to skewer anyone who tried to climb over them.

'Sugar?' said Marsha. 'You're sure there's no other way into the Black Forest?'

'Not really. The Tin Man's turned this whole district into one big work camp.'

'Why pick on my city?' Dolly Mixture moaned.

'It's the most industrialized,' Sugar replied. 'Central, too, where lots of rail lines meet.'

The girls pulled up their hidey-hoods, muffled their faces against the stale air. Three of them didn't wear fleeces, of course; Sugar was in her dark grey coating, while Lolly blended in by standing sandwiched between the others. It was Marzipan's appearance, though, that caused them most concern: her skin began to pinch and wrinkle, and Marzi's face looked grey and aged. Her dress turned duller too and shed a few leaves.

'Fink ya need some new cloves, Marz,' Jawji joked.

Marzi looked worried at the fallen leaves. 'These are not clothes,' she said. 'These leaves are like an extra skin. Part of me. I am sure I'll be better once we're out of this pollutey city.'

The sisters took a moment to prepare themselves for the possible dangers within the confection camp. Sugar had no data about it; not one of Lady Hisska's snakes had managed to penetrate this place. And no one had ever escaped from a camp to tell of the toils and hardships. Lydia peered up at a tall iron gate. And then down at the bottom of an electrified fence. A few dead creatures lay along the pavement, fried spiders and zapped rats that must have touched the wire mesh.

'The electric fence should've shorted too,' said Sugar. 'Jawji? Can you bite a way through?'

Jawbreaker came forward to tuck into the wire.

'Sure it'ch switch off?' she asked. 'You *sure* it shun-electri-fried?'

Bull's-Eye picked up and hurled a rock; it struck the fence and fell to the ground without the slightest sizzle. 'Yeah, it's dead,' she said.

Jawji took a hold of the mesh, and proceeded to eat a way into the camp.

Chapter 17
Gingerbread Men

Soon Jawji's diamond-hard teeth had gnawed a hole big enough for the girls to crawl through. Then they scurried across a colourless yard. Around the back of a factory building. On through the deathly silent camp. Jawji chewing through fence after fence.

The place was gigantic, with grilled gates and rock-cake walls segregating the various prison zones. Interlinking liquorice tracks had been laid throughout the factory complex, and all around were tea caddy towers with electric spy-hawks perched on top. The hawks were presently 'asleep', it seemed, conserving their solar energy in this sun-thin city.

However, the girls heard a screech of gates, followed by a clatter of wheels. The rumble of wagons. Sounds of a train. The sisters went to investigate, and found a fenced-in area with warehouses, depots, and cargo bays. A great grey train had pulled up inside, and robot

trolleys and android waiters were ready to tend to its long line of wagons. A unit of armed guards was also standing by—armed, that is, with heavy tin rolling pins.

The robot waiters slid back the wagon doors, and Lydia half-expected to see them unload crates of sweet ingredients from any and every region of Candi.

What would they be? Biscuit grit from Baykari? Candy sand from the land of Nooga? Franjipan fat-fried chipstick timber? Boiled sweet blocks from the depths of Froza? Cooking sherry from Wineland lakes? Or even fudge, dug up from Likrishka?

But no. The cargo was people. Sleeping people. Pallets of them. Lifted out from the carriage wagons and put onto great tea-trolley transporters: half-horse half-table centaur-drays able to convey up to a hundred prisoners. Once a centaur-trolley was full, it trundled away to one of the warehouses. A place where, Sugar guessed, the people would be processed, before being put to work. Some could be kept here, some sent out again. Once they'd been scanned and catalogued. Everyone on a Candi database, reassigned to prison towns, confection camps and factories, detainer allotments, even fisheries. This was Stannic's master plan. All would eventually serve the Tin Man.

Lydia could see only grown-ups in the carriages. Containers of them packed like sardines. Thousands of them. A town-load, on this one train alone. And how many more deliveries would be made this day? How many this week? This month? This year?

With all that robotic security about, the girls felt it best to steal away. And so they did. Just as a series of shrill sirens suddenly shattered the quiet.

Teeea! Teeea! Teeea! Teeea! Whistling kettles wailed through the camp. The sisters hid behind mounds of tin cups left there like months of forgotten washing-up; across from the cups, Lydia could see a compound containing huge bread bins.

The girls were just in time to see robot sentries raise the bread bins' heavy doors. And from them, tired figures emerged. These were the people who worked in the camp, imprisoned in bins that Stannic had built. Men of all ages. Teens to seniors. Lumped in together. In prison together. In one big melting pot of misery.

There seemed to be at least a hundred men crammed into, jammed into each bread bin shed. Thousands in this portion of the camp alone. Thousands all wearing the same ginger-coloured clothes: an ill-fitting work kit of baggy jackets, baggy trousers; feet squeezed into gingerbread clogs; and each and every person's head tucked into a flat brown paper cap.

Once they had slouched out from their bins, the men queued before a row of tin huts; (flushing sounds, from within the huts, told Lydia they had to be outdoor toilets). From there, they made their way to huge adjoining dining yards; these were enclosures full of long tin tables and stainless steel benches under barn-like roofs.

As the sisters sneaked around the camp, they caught glimpses of the prison routine: trolley robots carting what looked like stacks of bricks around the yards; prisoners queuing before automated drinks machines, tough metallic tea urn-units that poured for them a cup of cold tea. And then, having stepped up for their morning cuppa (no milk, no sugar), the men lined up before the stacks of bricks; this turned out to be their breakfast: a single chunk of stale toast, burnt to charcoal black. Each man took his toast from the stack; then clutching his cup, he found a space to sit. Soon the dining yards were crowded as, queue by queue, the prisoners bunched up on the benches.

Prisoners in their ginger work kit, chewing on their burnt-black bricks. Sipping weak tea from their tin cups, choking down their toasted bricks. With a *crunch* of crust. A *crackle* of charcoal. Choking down their breakfast bricks.

And spying from the tower perches, hook-beaked hawks scanned their faces. Switched on, at the sound of the kettles. Lydia found the metal birds unsettling; fixing their pinpoint poison stares, across the camp, with quick flick beaks. The sisters hoped they hadn't been seen, and avoided the hawks wherever they could.

While the inmates continued eating, the girls contin-ued past the yards. They had nearly reached the centre of the camp when Ice Lolly stopped. She stood there frozen, with her hands in her pockets, staring through a wire fence.

'What is it, Lolly?' Marshmallow asked. 'Come on, we need to keep moving.'

The sisters looked where Lolly stared, and Lydia saw another enclosure, this time with women huddled at the tables. So many mothers and daughters among them, stolen from their families, separated from their children. The prison women also wore the same ginger outfits. And all looked haggard, sleepy, hungry, gnawing at their breakfast bricks.

'Have to help,' Ice Lolly uttered.

'Sweets first, people later,' Marsha said, pulling her away.

'Sorry, Lolly,' Sugar added. 'It's too dangerous to stay.'

'Maybe Lady Hisska will know a way to free them,' Marzi said. 'Another time.'

Lydia heard the shrill whistles again. Yet, where the first whistles were a wake-up call, this time they were an order to work. Telling the prisoners it was time to begin the first of their shifts for the day.

On this grey and groggy morning, weary people plodded on their way. Queues and queues shuffled off to the factories, bakeries, warehouses, depots, and waste pits. Megaphone ducks could be seen here too, fixed to the corners of all the buildings. But the power-cut had switched them off, and so the prisoners were spared their trumpeting. *Walk walk work work.* Now they were shut up mid-quack.

Still, the camp was under the watch of poison-eyed hawks and dumb tin soldiers. Those tall barrel-chested robots contrasted fatly with the underfed prisoners; so

easily they wielded their rolling pin weaponry, sometimes using them to shove the men and women, prod
them along as they dispersed to the work zones. And so
it was, without a word, the soldiers threatened them.
Showed them nothing but distaste and contempt—
Lydia knew this notion was nonsense. Robots had no
real emotions; no anger or ill-will towards the prisoners.
All these rotten intentions had been written into their
digital minds.

No. It was the robot-*makers*. Stannic's scientists and
programmers. They were the actual 'enemy' here. The
Tin Man's helpers had done these things to everyone.

And *who* were they? Lydia thought. *Where* were
they? These scientists behind the scenes? Probably safe
in their control kitchens. Transmitting Mister Tinny-
Bin's nasty orders to all the robots.

The whole of the camp was bustling now. The noises,
in the yards and factories, louder. Robot guards marched
up and down. Their metal boots, their hefty tread like
bullet-shots upon the ground. Sentry robots at the
gates. Their vizor-eyes. Rotating heads. Keeping order,
keeping watch. Keeping the people in their place.

The lines and lines of ginger-clad workers scuffed
along with aching legs, dragging their clogs across gravel
yards, slopping through puddles of cold black tea.

These tired and famished multitudes looked like
moving gingerbread men, some of them hunched,
strangely hunched with humps under their ginger
coats.

Gingerbread Men

Work was mostly done indoors, the people forced to make the food for Stannic's mechanical army. To sustain the very machines that enslaved them.

Factories synthesized chemical chocolate to feed the Tin Man's robot battalions.

Kitchens churned out energy porridge, fuel for the automated trains and lorries.

Bakeries turned out barrels of cake mix, rum pudding used by cargo ships.

Warehouses stocked with biscuit-bricks, to be used to construct new walls and barricades. Whilst waste pits were piled with inedible dregs, the by-products of all this industrial cooking.

There were many other tasks for the women and men to do, including maintaining the camp itself, cooking up rations of gruel and toast, washing sets of the ginger kit. Laundry rooms, goods yards, factory floors full of captive workers. Lifting loading, fetching carrying, wrapping packing. Clockery punchery, drudgery drudgery. Rota after rota of suffering. This was their life. Hour after hour. Day after day. Time consumed, eaten away.

For the prisoners, all that was left was survival. Drained of life. Drained of appetite. Never knowing whether they would end their lives here. Working till the sky slams shut on their huts; only to be woken by the wailing of kettles, by robots wrenching the bread bin doors. The silent guards that gave no answers. Gave no answers, gave no hope.

219

Lydia couldn't have imagined, in her wildest nightmares, the conditions in the prison camps would be so appalling. So much worse than her life in Tinport. With poorer rations, and much tougher work than her curriculum of cookery lessons. And the robot sentries were so much sterner than even Mater D had been. One cosh on the head from a tin rolling pin would crack your skull and do you in.

Hmm, she thought fearfully, this was the world Mister Tinny-Bin built. A world of slaves. Of nonstop work. A world from which there was no escape.

The sisters carried on in their search for the outer wall of the confection camp. They nipped right past the bread bin sheds where the people slept, in isolation, on hard wooden cramped wooden breadboard beds. The cells lay unoccupied, unguarded for now, allowing the girls to sneak behind them.

The area here was uncomfortably warm, being situated so near to the bakeries. The sides of some of the bread bin huts also seemed to be smeared in mould—no. It was *thicker*, much blacker than that. Like a layer of yeasty musty dough. Lydia noticed a similar substance clustered along the gutters and rooftops.

Sugar stopped for a closer look, but she suddenly winced, hearing the squawk of a hawk.

Bull's-Eye spied the poison-eyed bird watching them from a tower perch; she grabbed a decent-sized rock off the floor, and pitched a typically-accurate shot; the rock

struck the neck of the hawk, and took its metal head clean off.

But it was already too late; robot guards had been alerted and, as the girls ran past the huts, a pair arrived to block their escape; then another soldier loomed behind them. Without hesitation it swung its truncheon, the heavy tin rolling pin about to hit Hazel.

Hazel spun aside. The truncheon *crunch*ed down beside her, and while she pirouetted away, the robot strode up to strike at the others. Marsha barged her way across, and threw herself in front of the weapon; the blow bounced off her body and smacked the robot right back in its bucket head. It staggered back, its vizor smashed, wildly blindly swinging its rolling pin before collapsing in a creaking heap.

Now the first two robots approached, raised their weapons, ready to batter them. Peppermint jittered towards one of the guards, and one hot blast of her minty spit burned a hole right into its body; the fuel inside ignited, and the robot went up in a flare of fire.

The other attacker zeroed in, about to club Pepper with its rolling pin; Lydia got a hold of her tin, hit it with her fingertips, and drummed the robot to drop the truncheon. Then, as the weapon clattered to the ground, Bull's-Eye was next to snap into action: pointing her horns and gritting her teeth, she charged up to the robot guard. One pack-a-punch kick dislocated its leg; the robot fell and Bull's-Eye stamped

and stamped at its head, smashing its circuits, hoofing it
flat.

The sisters hurried from the scene, leaving the three
defunct robot guards. Jawji chewed them through more
wire fences, and they swiftly moved between buildings
and yards.

Bull's-Eye left little to chance this time; she picked
up rocks along the way and, whenever she spotted a
hawk, she knocked it off its perch, slinging the rocks so
quick and precise, the decapitated birds didn't know
what hit them.

As the girls reached the limits of the camp, the
mould from the sheds appeared more widespread, sticking thickly to the bakery walls. Thick and black and horribly lumpy.

Around this area, women toiled, digging pits, shovelling grits. They hobbled on, moaning groaning in pain,
with massive black burdens that weighed them down;
bulky black sticky buns bulging from their ginger
gowns. Most of these grown-ups could barely manage
another step, barely straighten their laden backs. The
burden buns sapped their strength, drained their
energy—

Lydia could have sworn she saw the sticky buns
budge. Swelling shifting hunched black bumps.

'What *are* those lumpy humps on their backs?'
Hazel asked.

'Don't know,' frowned Sugar. 'It looks like the stuff
that's all over the walls.'

'Hobble gobble-ins,' Ice Lolly whispered.

'We cannot leave the people like that,' said Marzi. 'Those lumps of dough are hurting them.'

'*We* can help them, can't we?' pleaded Dolly.

'Can't jus' do nuffin, Shugz,' Jawji added.

'I don't know what we *can* do,' Sugar said. 'It seems to be some yeasty rash. I don't want us to catch it too.'

However, as the sisters prepared to set off, they found that a load of this blackened dough had started to assemble and roll around them. Some lumps clumped along the sides of buildings, adhering like globs of glue, while others in the guttering moved above them, lurking circling living goo. These 'gobble' creatures (as Lolly had called them) were featureless except for the glint of an eye. Single eyes like big black currants squinting out from the masses of dough. These were the buns that hunched on the backs of the women and men who slaved in the camp. And the whole of the confection factory complex was rapidly becoming a nest of them.

Chapter 18
Currant Buns

There were now so many of these balls of dough, these gobbles crawling across the walls or inching forward along the gravel.

'They're like loaves o' livin' bread,' Jawji said.

One lump plummeted down from a roof, and landed nearby; it started to roll towards the girls, blinking its single currant eye. Bull's-Eye slung a rock real hard, but it bounced off the dough ball, didn't damage it at all.

Peppermint then sought to toast it with a retch of fire, but—to her horror—the flame made it rise; the gobble bun bloomed in size and rolled on as a smouldering boulder, a giant fireball scorching hot, coming after Peppermint faster than before.

The other creatures were attracted to the heat, and crept in on the rest of the sisters.

All except Ice Lolly, that is. Lolly had stepped in front of the boulder, maybe to put it out, quench its

flame; but to everyone's surprise the fireball shrank away. And when she motioned towards the other buns, they recoiled from her icy presence.

'Ze yucky dough don't like it chilly,' concluded Coco.

Lolly ran up to the fiery boulder, and thrust a fist into its midst. Lydia watched as it crackled and hissed; the bun scrunched into a crusty mass and, emitting an ugly gargling sound, it crumbled to ash.

With Ice Lolly able to repel the dough, the girls were free to turn and go. They cut across the prison yards, passing the pits and the gobble-backed grown-ups. As the workers struggled on, the heavy buns grew larger and hotter. Lydia saw one woman stumble, completely engulfed by her sticky hump. And to make matters worse, a robot soldier approached to punish this 'lazy' prisoner.

Sugar now ordered the sisters to act:

'*Pepper!*' she shouted. 'Toast the robots! *Toffee*, go help her! *Zye*, the spy-hawks!'

With a pair of rocks, Bull's-Eye dispatched a pair of hawks overlooking the pits.

Then Lydia, Peppermint, and Marshmallow dared to enter the danger area; Marsha sprang over to the robot soldier, gambolled under its feet, knocking it off balance *crash* into a trench, unable to get up again. Two more guards were in the vicinity, and Lydia drummed them to stop on the spot; the robots stood defenceless while Peppermint melted them with bursts of flame.

The prison women stopped and stared at these weird hooded sisters who'd appeared from nowhere: a tough chubby girl who could bump a robot off its feet; a child with horns who could knock off a hawk with the chuck of a rock; a girl with a toffee tin and the power to control the metal men; and a thin blue-skinned child able to fry them with her 'breath'. And then there was this pale little girl in a green cagoule: Ice Lolly knelt beside the woman that had fallen and, with a touch, she froze off the suffocating hump. Lolly then dashed from sticky bun to sticky bun, laid her healing hands upon the prisoners, turning their gobble rash to icy ash. It had only just occurred to Lydia—there was no dough upon the robots. It was as though it only afflicted people, fed off the vital lifeblood within them.

'It'll take Lolly ages to go round curing everyone,' Marshmallow said.

'And where did those bun-things *come* from?' Sugar wondered.

The sisters looked all about them, and saw a nearby bakery that seemed to be the source of the gobble problem. It was obviously not being used as a bakery. More a waste-disposal centre where all the factory leftovers were piped in and dumped in incinerator ovens; its chimneys spluttered out a thick black substance that slowly slopped down the sides of the building.

'I've read about certain chemical yeasts,' said Sugar, 'used to eat toxic sweets.'

'It must have mutated,' grimaced Marzi. 'Could only happen in a horrible pollutey city.'

'All of these buildings should have some sort of emergency shut-off. Ways to cool them down.'

'Let's *go* then, Shugz,' Jawji agreed. 'Lolly can shtop them bread for us.'

The sisterhood approached the bakery. Most of the dough creatures clustered there.

First, they had to find a way in, so Sugar sent Hazel to scout around the gobbles' lair. Skipping past super-fast, looking for a doorway, Hazel was able to elude the prowling buns; doing her fancy dancer's leaps, she dodged the dough balls, landed beyond them. Fleet-foot light-foot, in half-a-minute her task was done.

She showed the girls a delivery door, and Lolly had to clear a way to it, forming an aura of coldness around her to make the gobbles keep their distance. And when it came to those covering the entrance, she scattered them with her outstretched hands. Doors were the least of the sisters' concerns; Jawbreaker bit right through the locks and, as they warily entered the lair, they were struck by its nasty stink.

This sweltering den was totally dark. Sugar had to use her luminous tube; its turquoise light shone faint across the bakery, and Lydia saw the yeasty waste that spilled from the incinerators. Ovens and ovens, a baker's dozen of furnaces burning up chemical candy. Fouling the air with floury spores. And as the flour, yeast, and heat combined, so a black dough congealed upon the walls. Living moving replicating. Fed by the furnaces and forming into gobble buns.

All the bakery's trays and racks—once filled with muffins, doughnuts, and pastries—were now encrusted with these currant-eyed creatures. Enough to swamp the whole camp complex. Lydia could just about make them out. Carbon-copy gobble lumps that smothered the place. Plastered the ceiling. Galled to the walls. Bunches of them, batches of them, clotting together then splitting apart, sprouting from darkened dough-caked corners. Twitching into life as they sniffed fresh children.

'Did we really have to come in here?' Hazel fretted. 'It's horrid and hot. And those hobble-gobbles like the heat, don't they? They *do*. They absolutely lap it up.'

And though they didn't gabble on about it, the other girls were just as scared. Scared if the dough got a hold, that would be the end of them. Gobbled up alive.

The sisters ventured further in, Ice Lolly leading the way, keeping up a shield of cold to hold the gobble dough at bay. Really they wanted to sprint through the bakery, but there were so many creatures heaped upon the floor, they had to wait for the dough to creep back and let them pass. Then the gobbles closed in behind, hemming the children in on all sides. A doughy wall with a thousand raisin eyes. Hissing at Ice Lolly, shrinking from her hands, and the chilly wisps that streamed from her fingertips, glowing blue-green in the spearmint light.

While Lolly swept a path through the gobble-dough-goo, fingerless mitts grew from the mass to snatch at the sisters as they passed.

'*Ugh*, one of those hobble-gobbles touched my hair!' shrieked Hazel. 'They're *here*, they're *there*, they're every-whevery-where!'

Dolly squealed too, and Marsha squirmed as gobbles tried to cling to their backs.

Marzipan made her skin as hard as bark, flinching as a gobble tore some leaves from her sleeve. And Peppermint was especially jumpy, ducking her head and crouching low, painfully aware her fiery power would only cause the dough to grow.

Cowering as close to Lolly as she could, Cocoa-Butter uttered frightened: 'Don't lettem get us, Lol. Don't lettem get us.'

Another grubby gobble mitt grabbed hold of Jawji, so she bit clean through it, and spat it *splat* upon the floor; the vile taste of mutated yeast—of charcoal, mould, and dead-fly bread—nearly made Jawbreaker sick to her stomach.

Bull's-Eye also kicked out at the dough, but it caught her hoof and clawed up her leg.

'Get it off! Get it off! It's *hot*!' she screamed, and Lolly had to freeze the gobble before it dragged her away. She did her best to protect the other sisters too, and when one gobble grasped for the luminous tube, attempting to blot out the spearmint light, Lolly broke off an icicle spike from her hair, and poked the bun

right in its eye; the blinded yeast creature gargled in retreat.

And so the girls went deep into the bakery lair, with Sugar looking for a boiler room there, a control room, or any room that contained the means to shut off the ovens.

In the dimming spearmint glow (the tube-light oil was running low), Zye could see some stairs ahead of them. Metal steps that led down below. The girls reached this stairway at the back of the bakery. At least the heat was less intense there, and the stairs seemed to be free of dough. They scampered down to a door on the lower floor, and had to wait while Lydia opened it, using her tin to pick-the-lock and jolt-the-bolt.

Still the gobbles pursued the sisters, their bulky sticky bun-like forms kneading down the stairs. One great doughy dollop dropped on top of Lolly, and she fought her way out of it, turning the bun to icy ash.

Sugar then conducted the girls through the door, where they found an empty corridor. But, just before all of them hurried inside, one of the gobbles grabbed hold of Marsha; a stale black mitt muffled her face, stifling her terrified cries; Cocoa-Butter went to help her, tugged at her cloak but got pulled in too.

'Marsha!' called Lydia. 'Coco!' *Co. Co.* Her voice echoed cold down the lower floor corridor, as a mass of currant-dotted dough folded around them, swallowed them up.

'Help them, Lolly!' Marzi cried.

Ice Lolly darted back, and she too disappeared into the dough. The sisters had to let her go; there was nothing they could do for them now.

Bull's-Eye kicked and slammed the door as gobble-pulp pressed up against it; then Lydia bolted and locked it again, with the power of her mind and the rhythms of her tin.

'*Eee!*' Dolly cried. 'The gobbles are following!'

The dough had begun to roll itself flatter and seep like pancake batter under the door. The eight remaining children rushed along the corridor, and at the end they found what they were searching for. A boiler room. With temperature gauges, taps and pipes, all sorts of devices, machines, and controls.

'What's *this*, Shugz?' Jawji asked. She'd found a large soda siphon hanging on the wall.

'It's a fire extinguisher,' Hazel replied. 'Don't you *know* anything?'

'D'you fink it be any good against the bread?'

'*Yeah*,' said Bull's-Eye, seizing the siphon. 'I'll stop them stupid gobbles.'

She lugged the extinguisher back along the corridor; Jawbreaker went with her too, and took the fading turquoise tube. Bull's-Eye stared down the passageway, into the flicker-black blue-green gloom. Enough of the dough had got under the door to reform into a number of bun shapes and, as they slid ominously closer, Bull's-Eye pulled the trigger on the siphon, aimed the nozzle and froze the gobbles with a stream of compressed ice-cream.

With Bull's-Eye using the only light, the others were left to stand in the dark. Fortunately Sugar could use her night-vision to see the instructions and emergency controls. She knew just what she needed to do: shut down the ovens and turn the bakery cold. But as she tried to get the refrigeration system going—nothing worked. The machines were kaputty from lack of use. She needed Lydia to get them started. And fast. As time and spearmint oil and ice-cream were running out for them all.

Kneeling there in the bakery blackness. On her lap, the toffee tin drum. Lydia tapped the tin lid lightly, then *rap-a-tapp*ed rapid with her liquorice sticks. And as she concentrated on the machinery—the sprinkler system, refrigerators—all were mapped out in her mind. Lydia drummed more boldly now. To twist the taps. To start the sprinklers. To revive the refrigerators. Soon there came a rumbling and clunking of pipes.

Sugar tried the controls again. The cooling system rattled into life—then died down with a grunt and a groan.

'It isn't working!' Hazel Whirl panicked. 'Why isn't it working?'

'Give it a moment,' Sugar told her. 'It needs some time to come on.'

Bull's-Eye, meanwhile, stood her ground against the gobble-buns bowling along the corridor. With Jawji

shining the tube of light for her, Zye used the siphon to keep them back, icing the buns, turning them to ash. And if any of the dough balls rolled too near, she shot it with a blast of creamy extinguisher, then shattered its crust with a boot of her hoof.

But just as the tube lost the last of its light, so the lashings of ice-cream became a dribble. Soon the siphon ran out completely, leaving more of the gobble dough to inch its way through. Jawji and Bull's-Eye had to retreat, and wait there with the others in the dark, worried while the dough crawled ever closer, creeping down the corridor in a single all-consuming bloomer.

'Where's Lolly? Where's Lolly?' Dolly wept, so afraid.

The girls could hear a hissing as the gobbles pushed their way into the control room; only Sugar, with her digital goggles, was able to see the heated creature closing in to sluggishly engulf them. She dreaded it might be the end of them all—kept pushing the others back against the wall. Soon they could feel the dough kneading nearer, felt the heat against their feet.

Lydia squeezed her eyes tight shut, almost too petrified to breathe; with one hand she hugged her tin, with her other she reached out, grasped a hood, a shoulder of whoever was next to her. She was so sad for the others too; the last few days with these sisterly friends had given her something to live for now—only for her hope of a better life to be snatched away. Only to die in the depths of one of Stannic's toxic bakeries.

Lydia wondered how 'painless' being gobbled up would be; how it was for Coco and Marsha if Lolly hadn't got to them in time. It was too horrific to think about. This slow burning suffocating fate; feeling the mouldy dough pulping around them. And then the gobbles would smother her, and swallow up her toffee, crush the last breath from her—

Suddenly Lydia heard a sound. The rumble and clunk of the pipes returned. On the floor above them, the sprinklers came on and, as torrents of ice tea doused the furnaces, the temperature in the bakery dropped. Next, emergency refrigerators sent gusts of chilling air thundering around the building, roaring through vents built into the walls.

While Sugar saw the gobble blob crumble from the boiler room, all the girls could hear the gargling, the terrible death-rattles. Masses of gobbles. Nullified by the cold.

When it got quieter, they decided to risk it: led by Sugar's infrared vision, the sisters made their way back through the bakery. Wading through piles of ash along the corridor. Shuffling up steps coated with bread-crumbs. Lydia couldn't see a single thing, she felt her way along the cold wet walls.

Sugar looked out for Coco and Marshmallow, so relieved to find them with Ice Lolly, huddled, cold, in a corner of the stairs, unaware of anything in the scary dark around them; Lolly was blindly jab-jabbing an icicle at gobbles she imagined were still closing in.

The sisters reached the upper floor, passing the ovens, the dozens of ovens and trays and racks. A mist slipped coolly around their ankles. They splashed through puddles of ice tea and ash. Flakes of soot snowed down upon their hidey-hoods; this soft black sleet was all that remained of the horrible gobbles that had festered there.

And ahead was the delivery door. Free from dough and glowing with daylight.

Peppermint left the building first, scuttling buglike, watching out for robots; the rest of the girls then emerged through the mist, brushing ash and soot from their clothes.

Lydia saw these dry ice vapours pouring from the chimney jugs, a chilly fog that filled the camp, spilling across the prison yards, refreshing the air and the thousands of workers. All around, the doughy bun lumps gargled then crumbled dead. And with their lair more a freezer than a furnace, it seemed the gobbles could no longer spread.

'We can go now. Can't we? Lolly?' asked Marzi.

The little ice maiden stared about her. Nodded.

However, as they went to leave, Dolly stood there, lost in thought.

'Dolly's family,' Lydia mentioned.

'My mummy and daddy might have bin in here.'

'There are lots of different prison zones being set up all over the country, Dolly,' Sugar told her. 'Your parents could be in any one of them.'

'Once we have a way to beat the Tin Man,' said Marsha, 'all the families will be free. But we still have to find a few more treasure-sweets.'

And so they left the people in the prison camp, at least now free from the gobbles' sickly clutches. Jawbreaker chewed through the outer factory fence, only to find a tin foil barrier securing the city like the wrapper around Tinport. Just as she must have done, back in Likrishka, Peppermint attacked the barrier with a burp of fire. For a while, there was a burning stench as the tin foil crinkled and melted away.

Then, mindful of the singey edges, the girls stooped through and scampered to these nearby trees. They soon found themselves in the vast Black Forest. A forest full of dark brown trees with sparse purply slivers of leaves.

Chapter 19
Rum Truffles

It was silent in the forest. No sounds. Not even the *chirry twiffle* of a bird. Still, the girls were pleased to be clear of the factories, and most of them pulled their fleeces closer.

'That's odd,' said Sugar, tapping her hearing aids. 'I wonder why I'm not getting any snake signals?'

'I don't like the sound of that,' said Hazel. 'I thought they were everywhere ready to help.'

'I suppose there's no need to panic,' Marshmallow said.

'Oo, she such a worry-worry. Aren't you, Hazel?' Coco remarked.

'I'm sure I don't know what you mean,' Hazel sniffed. And then she added: 'It's better to be careful than careless though, isn't it? It is.'

'What sweet is it we are looking for?' asked Marzipan. 'You never did tell us.'

239

'A Jet Heart Truffle,' Sugar replied.

'The Black Forest's famous for truffles,' smiled Dolly.

'That *is* why we're here, Dippy-head,' Bull's-Eye said.

Without a tracker-snake to guide them, Sugar had to choose a direction, and the other girls followed in a disorderly fashion. Between the squat brown trees they went, puffing at the wintry air.

In contrast to the spacious and fragrant White Forest, the Black Forest was close and smelt of mildew. And unlike the sugary soil of Franjipan, the earth here was like stodgy black gateau, sustaining a strange variety of plants: thick thorny brambles, knifelike nettles, and patches of sharp point raspberry spears.

The sky shone through the twisted branches, branches that had shed much of their foliage which now mushed muddily on the floor. The deep *slop slop* of the children's foot-trudge merged with the *boozy buzzes* of bugs. Lydia glimpsed these thin red stick insects stuck to the tree-trunks, and even a termites' pudding nest. The girls did their best to avoid these pests, and occasionally Peppermint would startle them all by spitting flame at something hovering, creating the sight of lighted insects spinning away with wings on fire.

'There's lots of horrible bugs round here,' moaned Marsha, swatting at a gnat.

'I think now's the best time to use these,' said Sugar, taking a packet of sweets from her pocket. 'I call them Pesty Pastilles. They should repel the insects.'

She handed one of these small white sweets to each of the girls.

'Do we chew 'em? Or swallow 'em, or what?' shrugged Bull's-Eye.

'I would bite them slowly. And breathe the flavour out.'

The pastilles had a sour citronelly taste, but Lydia didn't mind if it kept away the bugs. The sisters reluctantly munched on the sweets as they continued through the creepy forest; they tried not to dawdle anywhere, but Bull's-Eye suddenly stopped and drew their attention to an object on the ground. It looked like a length of frazzled bacon.

Sugar knelt for a closer look. 'The remains of a tracker-snake,' she said with her usual frown. 'Something attacked it. So it cooked itself with microwaves.'

'But what could catch a camouflage snake, Shugz?' Jawbreaker asked.

'A snaffle-wolf,' the girls heard Marzipan say. 'Look, its tracks are a short distance away.' She showed them the pawprints in the damp black soil.

'Better keep moving,' Sugar Cube beckoned. 'And Zye? Keep a sharper lookout. Might be all kinds of beasts about.'

Sugar led the sisters on, deeper into the tangle of trees. Along with the *slosh-slosh* squelch of their footsteps, Lydia heard these intermittent groans.

'That your shtumach again, Marsha?' said Jawji.

'Well, I'm *hungry* again,' Marshmallow replied.

'What are we allowed to eat here, Marzi?' Lydia enquired.

Marzipan peered into the shadowy woodland. She said it would be harder here to root out food. And though she'd heard that, within the Black Forest, one could find the richest most tasty sweets of all—it could also be a deadly place, full of poisonous plants and savage creatures. As the sisters could see for themselves, this wasn't exactly the best time of year for picking forest fruits; they passed by bushes of overripe berries sweating out pungent alcoholic smells. And sometimes rotten nuts pattered on top of them, falling from the branches, shrivelled in their shells.

While they walked, Marzipan talked of the Delish forest's fabled delights: confections that affected the mind. Gave sight to the blind. Or were filled all gold. There were rare sweets that might turn one into a beast, be it a werewolf or boar; crystal fruits that revealed one's fortune, or made one see unpredictable things, such as cookie monsters, jelly people, or teapots with wings. 'In olden times,' Marzi enlightened them, 'this place was known as the Forest of Dreams.'

'How d'you know about all these shweets, Marz?' Jawji asked.

'My mother was a very good teacher,' Marzipan replied. 'She spent her life travelling and studying sweet plants. I learnt all I know from her.'

In one shady place, the children found what looked like polka-dotted saucers strewn across the forest floor.

'*Oo*, more mushrooms,' Coco said, skipping over.

'Don't go near those,' Marzi warned her. 'They might bite!'

'Mushrumsh don't bite,' Jawji scoffed.

'They are not mushrooms. Those are toadstools that can trap little insects.'

'Nah. Ya joshin', aren't ya, Marz?' Jawji nudged her. 'What chew fink, Shugz?'

'Let's see, shall we?' Sugar took a shiny wrapper from her pocket; she fashioned it into the shape of an insect, and tossed the paper into the toadstool patch. The girls jumped as the closest toadstool snapped up the wrapper in its cap, and chewed it up.

They stayed well clear of these fungus flytraps, and left the patch for drier ground. There they settled to eat their sweets, and ease their hunger pangs. Peppermint looked particularly forlorn, and she showed the others her empty pastille pouches. Most of the other sisters finished off their special sweets too. Sugar was worried. But what could she do? There were no proper shops anywhere any more.

Marzipan's appearance had also changed again; her face and arms turned almost black, and her leafy garment browny purple, the colour of the forest trees.

'Has anyone seen my teaspoon?' said Hazel. 'You haven't stolen it, have you, Coco?'

'No, no. We not want your silly spoon,' Coco retorted testily, as she nibbled at her very last square of white chocolate.

243

'It's not silly, it's silverly. Oh, I must have left it somewhere.' Hazel had to use her fingers to scrape out the last of her choccy-nutty paste; she got it all gooey around her mouth, and the others thought this was most amusing.

'Here y'are, Haze, use this,' said Jawji, offering her a battered spork she had tucked away in her knapsack.

'I'm not eating anything with *that* dirty diggy thing.' Hazel turned her nose up at it, and dabbed her lips with a handkerchief.

'You got some smush on your chin,' Dolly pointed out helpfully.

'Oh—oh, *nuts* to you, dippy Dolly,' pouted Hazel.

'Hazel *Whirl!*' Marshmallow scolded. 'You're a spoilt Nutti girl!'

'Well, I've had a bellyful of living in the rough.' Hazel started to get upset. 'When are we going to go home? When can we leave this horrid forest?'

Sugar sighed. 'We'll go once we've got this truffle. *You* can find it, can't you, Marzi?'

'I don't know,' Marzipan replied. 'Truffles grow underground. And are only found at certain times.'

'We can't dig up the whole forest, can we?' added Dolly.

Whilst Lydia had been chewing her toffee, she'd detected what could only be described as 'feelings' in the air; instinctively she got to her feet, and sniffed at some alluring aroma. 'What do truffles smell like?' she asked Marzi.

'They are supposed to be very rich and creamy. Or chocolatey. Sort of different, I believe.'

'Why do you ask, Toffee?' Sugar said. 'If you think you can find the truffle for us—'

She told the girls to pack up their knapsacks, and let Lydia take them where the scent trail went. It grew even darker within the forest, and the girls held hands to stay together safe. Lydia proceeded slowly, leading them further between the trees.

'Hurry up, *Toffee*,' Bull's-Eye snapped. 'Or we'll be here for ever.'

The sisters walked for a while, tired, continuing through to a tangle of brambles; but this was no ordinary bramble patch: the thorny stalks were thick as branches, flaky black and flecked with frost. Fleshy red drupelet fruit, like clusters of blood blisters, poked between the thorns, and the girls ducked past to reach a moonlit glade where the soil seemed ashen and dead; it was as if this area had been burned away, leaving it surrounded by bare-branched oak trees, their trunks wound with tourniquets of poison ivy. The air was cool and kirschy with cherry juice; Lydia could feel it bleeding through the glade. She could also sense a chocolate scent, dense and spine-shivery in the soil.

'This *must* be it,' Lydia whispered.

'Toffee is correct,' Marzi agreed. 'I've heard that truffles grow beneath trees in cindery areas such as these.'

'Hush then, sisters,' Sugar whispered, 'we'll set up

camp here till we find the truffle. And watch out for snaffle-wolves, as well.'

Jawbreaker *schnapp*ed some branches from a tree, and cut them up with her whopper choppers. Pepper then went to light the wood, but after all her efforts destroying robots and burning holes in tin foil walls, she struggled to bring up the stomach acid that allowed her to 'spit fire' the way she did. The glade was dark and getting colder; the sisterhood really needed a fire. Peppermint tried for many moments, using all her energy to summon up a flame; she made one final painful strain, scrunched her eyes and flexed her chest. From her white lips, a flickering acidic burp— enough to light the bitten branches and grow into a glowing camp-fire. (A fire attracting large black moths that flickered and fluttered and dithered through the flames, bothering the sisters who batted them away.)

By the minty firelight, Lydia wandered from oak to oak, sniffing around the roots for the strongest hint of truffles; she circled the glade for a while, before— 'Here,' she indicated. Lydia sat by a short black tree and started to scrabble at the soil with her fingers.

'Won't find truffles *that* way, Toffee,' Marzi said. 'They grow on the deepest roots of trees.'

'How we gonna chig up the chruffles then?' asked Jawji.

'I will reach them,' Marzipan replied, sitting down cross-legged beside Lydia.

First, she transformed herself into her wooden state,

placing the palms of her hands on the ground, and making her arms as hard as bark. Marzi's eyes wrinkled shut, and she began to bore her fingers into the soft ashen soil. Soon her forearms were completely submerged, with finger twigs feeling around underground.

Minutes passed by. Peppermint's campfire crackled away. The other girls waited while Marzi sat silent, her arms burrowing blindly below them. More minutes passed by, until Marzi slowly, ever so slowly, extricated her arms from the earth; at last, her gnarled wooden hands emerged, curled around these small soily spheres, spherical sweets in a range of colours: deep plum purple, cherrymaroon, creamy brown, and berry black.

'What did you find, Marzi?' Marshmallow asked.

Marzipan said nothing; she didn't even open her eyes. Lydia saw her body return to normal, changing from wood to flesh and blood; her natural almond colour returned too. Marzi had exhausted her powers. At last, she gazed up at Lydia. Held out her hands to her, almost in a trance.

'It was bizarre,' Marzi said. 'Was as though the sweets were seeking *me* instead.'

Lydia took the soily sweets from her, laid them out in the lap of her pinafore.

'They're all ruffly,' she mentioned. 'No wonder they're called *tree-ruffles*.'

'Whish one's ze one we want?' Coco asked.

'A Jet Heart Truffle,' Sugar said. 'It could be one of those really dark ones.'

Lydia picked out a purply-black confection; she mulled it over as a connoisseur might mull over wine, eyeing it closely, twitching her nose at it. She did the same for the rest of them too; there was something mysterious about these sweets, these fine-layered whorly growths. Truffle by truffle, Lydia considered them; each had the scent of a different forest fruit: cranberry, damson, blackberry, plum and cherry; some were crumblier, others creamier, but all whiffed strong and zingy in the nose.

'Well, Toffee?' Sugar asked. 'Any luck?'

'They smell sort of naughty. But nice, though.'

There was one truffle Lydia hadn't touched; something made her leave it till last. There it lay upon her pinafore, a red-stained sphere of confectionery earth. As Lydia put her fingers to it, she sensed this truffle to be somehow 'darker' than the others. She scraped the cherry red surface with her nail, revealing a jet black creme underneath; the truffle's centre seemed to be made of the darkest richest chocolate imaginable. Lydia licked her finger and her tongue was stung by a bitter shot of cocoa. Just that slightest taste was enough to send a shudder through her heart.

'This—this must be. The one we want,' she stammered.

'You're sure, Toffee?'

Lydia nodded. Sugar asked her to put the truffle in a carton, and then she popped it into her coat along with the rest of the treasure-sweets.

They'd now found four from the six on the list.

'What we going to do with the other truffles?' Dolly asked. 'Can *I* have one, Toffee?'

'Oo, *we* want one too,' said Cocoa-Butter and she nicked a blackberry truffle off Lydia and took a cheeky bite. 'Mm *mm*, oo, soo yum yum,' she munched.

Lydia passed round the rest of the truffles, for the others to try, before Coco pinched them.

'These are *so* scrumptious,' Marshmallow said, having selected a plum duffy truffle.

'Jellicious,' Jawji agreed, chewing through a cherry one.

'Mm,' smiled Dolly with a brambleberry truffle. 'Ta, Toffee.'

'*Marzi* rooted them out, not *Toffee*,' Bull's-Eye said, snatching a cranberry red. 'So *thanks*, Marz.'

'Me try truffle, please?' Ice Lolly uttered, and Lydia waited patiently while the shy little child picked out a sweet with hesitant fingertips. ''Nk you,' Lolly smiled.

Once Peppermint and Marzipan had their share, there was only one truffle left.

Sugar decided not to have one. 'It might not agree with me. Anyway, thanks, Toffee.'

'Hazel?' asked Lydia. 'You haven't had one.'

'I don't want one of *those* dirty dug-up things,' she huffed. 'And aren't truffles supposed to do doolally things to people? I bet they do. No *thank* you.'

'*You* have it, Toffee,' Marzi smiled. 'You deserve it.'

249

Lydia ate her truffle slowly, savouring every flavour-ful layer. 'Mmm.' The sweet was utterly sumptuous, its centre of dreamy creamy ganache with complex forest fruity tastes that branched out from her mouth, then lingered long upon her tongue like trickles of thick chocolate syrup.

'Can we get out of here now?' Hazel shivered.

'Where do we *go* now, though?' said Marshmallow.

'We're heading for a hideout at the edge of the for-est,' Sugar replied. 'But it's hard to tell where we are without a tracker-snake.'

'Oo, what hideout is zis?' whispered Coco.

'My instructions from Hisska were to head towards the Wineland border. And a grove by the Cherry River. To meet someone there.'

The girls decided to spend the night in the glade. It had been another tiring day, but still they found it diffi-cult to sleep; their child minds were full of fears. Better to stay awake and keep watch. Watch out for who-knows-what in this unfamiliar place.

Sitting around the shimmer-moth campfire, they shared their stories of escape. Lydia heard about terrible machines: giant metal crabs, mosquito planes, and armoured lorries of mechanical men that attacked the sisters' towns and villages. She heard how one of Hisska's snakes had led Sugar to a sweet-filled dinghy-doughnut left for her in Baykari Bay, and how she rescued the others along the way. How each of them had to leave their family, friends and homeland. A life uprooted. A life on the move. With nothing but each other and their precious packs of sweets.

After everything the girls had been through, Lydia thought it strange that they should now be afraid of the dark or a few wild animals. Maybe it was the forest that made them feel like this. Its sweets and fruits. And their psychological scents and flavours.

It was 'hurt' Lydia was most afraid of. But more than a bruise or a pinch of pain, it was hurt inside. Especially loss. The loss of her mother had hurt her more than any smack from a wooden spoon. And for years those feelings had haunted her most. Now she could sense similar emotions haunting the other sisters too. And as long as the Tin Man remained Chief Chef of Candi, future children would come to feel the same way. Growing into a world of fear and loss and blind obedience. Of taste-tests and work camps, or worse.

Chapter 20
Cherryade

The sisterhood huddled in their fleecy cloaks, and tried to get some rest. Bites of time passed slowly by. Marsha's stomach continued to grumble. A couple of the others mumbled half-asleep. Through the forest, Lydia could feel the air turning shivery cold. She noticed the campfire embers sizzle out. Then she thought she heard a howl. Lydia scrambled to her feet. It was getting lighter. Almost dawn.

A rosy mist floated low across the resting children. A mist that appeared to metamorphose them. Lydia saw the others in a semi-dreamy haze; the tiniest taste of the Jet Heart Truffle still stung potent on her tongue. Manifest as a deep scream rooted in her throat and mind. Before her eyes, the sisters' shapes shifted into horror beasts, a pack of hunchbacked animals that rose up from the mist all around; their cloaks became blood red, trickle red hidey-hoods with savage yawning

wolfish faces. Any second they might see her, hear her, tear her to pieces.

Frightened by these nightmare creatures, Lydia began to run away. Into the shadowy woods she went, into the gloom, the glimmer of daylight; running with the toffee tin tied around her. Lydia slipped across muddles of pud, puddles of mud she sloshed in. Lost.

Lydia wandered for quite some time, cold, alone, in a sleepy truffle trance. The little girl tensed at imaginary growls. Howls and noises, animals near. Could pounce any second from these vicious bushes; sniffed-out snaffled-up, snicker-snack and left for dead; she sensed the snarling slithy wolves macabre and nimble in the corners of her mind. Predatory beasts with prune-coloured pelts and lupine eyes. Moving through silent listening trees. Fiery misty cherry trees. Fiery cherry. This scent burning in her nose, stronger and stronger, as the forest became lighter.

Lydia followed the cherry aroma, her fears clearing away as she walked; the shadowy snaffle-wolves scarpered sharpish from the crannies of her mind. Daylight showed through the Black Forest trees. But still, Lydia was lost. Where could she go? She knew there were creatures and beasties about—

A nearby rustling scared her. There was something there. The head and tusks of a ferocious beast jutted out from behind a tree: a spiky-faced boar with deep hollow eyes. Lydia was just about to run, when the boar stood up. Stood up straight and spoke her name:

'Toffee?' it called out softly. 'They tell me your name Toffee.' This beast had a female voice with a foreign accent.

'Who are you?' Lydia stared confused. 'Are you Lady Hisska?'

Using its hands—gloved hands, not trotters—the beast lifted its splintery snout, revealing a girl's face beneath. A teenage girl. Surely too young to be a grizzled old Snake Lady. 'My name is Lattay,' the teenager said. 'Come with me. The others are safe now.'

'The others?'

'One of your sisterhood is like a computer. I track her with this.' Lattay showed Lydia a hand-held device, what appeared to be a large flat blackberry. 'Then they tell me one of you missing. So I return to the forest to find you.'

Now, without her animal mask, Lydia could get a good view of Lattay; very tall and athletic-looking, she was maybe sixteen years of age; she had sharp roast brown bangs of hair, and skin of rich café-au-lait which really did suggest she was from a long way away. Lattay wore dark safari gear, and a purse and sword were fixed to her belt. Next, she took a spray-can from her jacket, and used it to send a blast of perfumed fire into the air.

'That's the burnt cherry smell,' Lydia whispered.

'It is a fake musk to put off prey-d-eaters. And it also help us find our way.'

'Where are we going?' Lydia asked.

'A secret refuge, edge of the forest.'

Lattay led the way, aided by the trail of charred-cherry scent; Lydia could easily 'read' it with her nose. Char cherry south. Char cherry west. They came to a spot where two rivers met. Two red rivers that rippled into one. The forest's mist frothed up from its surface. Lattay cupped her hands to drink from the river; she beckoned Lydia to try it too. The refreshing water was tingly on the tongue with a vibrant taste of cherryade.

Then Lattay went west again, following the bubbly current and, in time, the two of them arrived at a grove where Lydia noticed some of the trees had been engraved with assorted symbols: swirls and eyes, arrows and lines and letters written back-to-front.

A few wild creatures flittered around the grove: a spiky red skunk that scurried across the branches; a thin streaky weasel sneaked through the grass; a cherry possum nosed slyly from its hollow, whilst up above fruit bats flapped in the trees. There were also bees buzzing about, but Lattay used a different can of spray, made a lavender cloud to shoo them away. Made them drowsy. Drowsy beezy dropping zuzzily onto the grass.

Lattay ushered Lydia on, carefully, quietly through the grove. One of the trees had been cut to a stump, smooth and flat, very low to the ground. Lattay knelt beside this stump, and knocked six times on its innermost ring.

After some moments, Lydia heard clicking, clicking unlocking sounds.

Then the stump flipped up. Opened like a lid. A lid that led into the forest floor.

Lattay told Lydia to step inside; she looked down to find a slide and a mellow honey glow below; Lydia placed her feet onto hard polished wood, tucked in her arms and slid down this chute. Down down into a dimly lit room. For her it was exciting, descending into this secret place. Lattay used the slide too, after closing the tree stump behind her.

Lydia was surprised to find herself standing in the hold of some underground ship; she was also intrigued to see pictures in the timbers—human figures and birds and animals etched into the varnished wood. A person stood in the corner too. A man who held this pot by a handle, a honey-pot that lit up the hold like a candle.

'You found her, Lattay?' came his soft-spoken voice. 'Oh, you've found dear Lydia.' The man shuffled forward and, as he did, he tapped a walking stick against the wall. Despite his timid tottering steps, he appeared to be only about thirty years old—perhaps a little older, Lydia thought, as his straggly dark hair was thinning a bit; the man wore a thick black dressing gown and slippers; it looked as though he'd just woken up. And his face. Lydia peered at his face. She recognized him from her family photo. It seemed to be—it *had* to be. Her mother's younger brother.

'Uncle Terri?' Lydia cried. And she ran to him, and hugged him tight.

Lattay carried the honey-lantern, leading Lydia through narrow corridors. Uncle Terri tapped his cane upon the floor, and touched the walls as he followed on behind. It was clear to Lydia: her uncle was blind.

Down carved wooden passageways, past cabins and galleys all gangplank-linked—They weren't *really* inside an underground ship, but an old lodge built beneath the forest. It was simply the way the place had been fashioned, from all the different parts of boats, that made it seem to be a seagoing vessel sunk into the ground. Sunk out of sight and out of mind.

They eventually reached a dining hall furnished with a long log table and important-looking sculpted chairs. And there, in the dreamlike honey-light, sat the rest of the sisterhood, tucking into bowls of oatmeal.

As Lattay and Lydia entered the hall, Hazel called out: 'Oh, *there* you are, Toffee! We were really really worried. We thought you'd been snaffled by woffuls!'

'Think I nearly thought I was,' Lydia replied.

'You shouldn't have gone off like that, Toffee,' Marsha scolded her.

Bull's-Eye glared at Lydia too, but said nothing as there were two grown-ups there, Uncle Terri and another in the hall, also wearing a dressing gown: a twenty-something woman with beautiful deep blue, sharp-shaped eyes, and waves of long black hair. She had ochre-coloured skin, and her face was marked with these copper-bright stars, three stars upon her forehead and cheeks.

'Do not be too harsh on the poor dear child,' the young woman said (despite her exotic looks, she spoke with a Candi accent). 'The forest. Its treats can play tricks on the mind.'

'And Toffee's back now. That's the best thing,' Dolly added with a smile.

'Your cans of spray work tiptop, Morella,' said Lattay, addressing the mysterious woman.

Morella asked Lydia to sit at the table while she whipped up a bowl of tum-warming oatmeal, a lumpy porridge with succulent redcurrants, hot off the cherry log stove. While Lydia ate, the others were shown to their own cabin quarters: a room with honeycomb compartments built into the walnut walls; each honeycomb contained layers of spongy bed linen, and most of the sisters picked a bunk, and had a nap. There were also robes and slippers to change into; Morella took their other clothes to wash. (Their fleecy cloaks had got mucky too.)

Lydia decided to keep her uncle company and, as he tottered back to his rooms, Terri reached out to feel the walls, directed by the decorative carvings.

'Mummy never told me you couldn't see, Uncle Terri.'

'You were just a baby,' he replied, 'the last time the family got together.'

Terri's quarters had four portions: a bedroom, a bathroom, a study, and a workshop. The study was where the two of them now stood; Lydia had taken a

honey-pot lamp, and it gave the whole room a golden glow. While there was little furniture there, the flavour of the chamber was far from plain: it had tactile walls all engraved with illustrations, and a captain's table with a globe of the world. Terri settled down on what appeared to be a treasure chest; he let Lydia sit in the only chair there—a rocking chair—that she creaked back 'n' forth on the old wooden floor.

'Have you lived here underground all the time, Uncle Terri?' Lydia asked.

'Not until recently,' he replied. 'Then Morella and I shared a house nearby.'

'Is Lattay yours and Morella's daughter then?'

'Oh *no*,' Terri said, almost laughing. 'Morella is *much* too young to have a child of that age. No,' he told Lydia, 'Lattay is your half-sister. Your father brought her here some time ago. To help you on the rest of your journey.'

'Daddy Petro—?' Lydia was puzzled. 'Petro is Lattay's daddy too? And he was *here*? But Celine said he's in a confection camp.'

'Oh, Lydia—You *still* don't know? Of course, your mother never had a chance to tell you.'

'What do you mean?'

'I'm talking about your *real* father,' Terri replied. 'A man called Alazandr.'

'Oh, that's *Celine's* dad,' Lydia said. 'And Elixa's daddy.'

'No. You and Celine and Elixa *and* Lattay. You all have the same father. Alazandr Argenta.'

'It all began about twenty years ago,' Uncle Terri continued. 'When Elixa was a little girl. Your father, *her* father, helped her to escape from Mokachino.'

Lydia listened closely to every word, trying to remember what Celine had told her. 'Wasn't it Elixa's nasty mum they were escaping from?' she said.

'Oh.' Terri seemed surprised his niece knew this. 'That's right. Did Mari—erm, did your mother say something about it?'

'Celine told me. And about the toffee-kitchen that vanished in the forest.'

'Karamesh,' Terri whispered. 'Mari's favourite toffee. Well, your father Alazandr met your mother soon after he left Mokachino. They fell in love and got married straightaway. Had a child together: your sister Celine. Alazandr wasn't there very much for them though. He was always off on excursions to Tangiya. Hunting for rare and magical sweets. So he said.'

'Don't you *like* . . . my daddy, then?' It sounded so strange for Lydia to say that. In one moment of truth, she had a new father. Someone she hadn't even met.

'We all have a great deal to thank your father for,' Terri said. 'But Alazandr did cause your mother much grief. You see, he always led this double life. With another wife in Karamesh. Lattay is *their* daughter, and she is one of Elixa's top toffee apprentices.'

'Celine said she speaks to Daddy Alazandr sometimes,' Lydia mentioned. 'Oh—I bet it was him who brought my toffee tin.'

'Alazandr was always travelling between families. And the last time he left your mother, she was pregnant with you. Remember, this was the year when Stannic took control of the region. Changing the naming laws, and restricting the rights of non-Likrish citizens. With Alazandr stuck in Tangiya, and your mother afraid he may never return, one of her dearest friends offered to register his name as your father.'

'Daddy Petro,' Lydia said.

Terri nodded. 'Petro Rhodium had been your mother's friend for many years. He worked at the Burnville fudge factory too. He promised to help raise you as his own. Mari never married Petro, but she took the precaution of taking his name. It would be safer for you to have a Likrish father.'

'*Hurh,*' Lydia sighed. 'It's all very *adulty*—'

'You were going to be told the truth when you were older. But then your mother fell ill. And you were taken away to that detainer town place. Lucky, Mari confided in me all this information. She'd changed your date of birth too, so it seemed you were conceived later. With Petro.'

'You mean, my birthday's *not* my birthday?'

'You were actually born on the first anniversary of Stannic's election to power. That means you'll be ten years old, this Midwinter.'

'So *that's* why I got sent toffee on Midwinter's Eve,' Lydia realized.

'You were Mari's saving grace, in her last years,' Terri

said sadly. 'Celine being away at Confectionery Academy.'

'So Celine's my *proper* sister, then?'

'Yes. And Elixa's your half-sister, of course.'

This pleased Lydia. Knowing she was wholly related to Celine. *And* Elixa. Toffee-chef Elixa.

'So Daddy Alazandr works for Lady Hisska too?' she asked.

'*Elixa* is the one known as Mam-ba-Hisska,' Terri said. 'She is helping your sister Celine to defeat the Tin Man.'

'With the treasure-sweets?'

'Now that Celine is in the Sweet Elite, she is in a position to serve Stannic one of her special desserts. But she needs these rare ingredients for it to work.'

'How did Celine know about the sweets to start with?' Lydia wondered aloud.

'Your mother—she was more amazing than you could ever know. All the women of our family, the Arora family, have read, compiled and written secret cookbooks, gained a vast knowledge of ingredients and recipes. It was your mother Mari who passed these secrets to Celine. And I bet you never knew that, before you were born, your mother served in Stannic's Sweet Elite.'

'Really, Uncle Terri?'

'She resigned after a short time. Publicly, she said it was for family reasons. It could have been that she refused to be part of Stannic's master plan. The Tin Man

may even have been in love with your mother. Celine sent me a message later, saying that she saw him at Mari's cremation; that was when he promised *her* a future place in the Sweet Elite.'

Oh, all this was too much for Lydia to swallow in one go: Daddy wasn't *really* Daddy. Her surname wasn't *really* Rhodium. Half-sister Elixa was Lady Hisska. And Mummy had been a brilliant scholar who knew all about black-heart truffles, dizzy fizzweed, and jelly gemstones—

'I have your mother to thank for something else,' Terri said. 'She discovered a very rare Black Forest sweet. Lydia? Would you go over to that chest in the corner? You'll find a tub in there. Would you give it to me, please?'

Lydia took the lantern to a corner of the study where she found another, smaller 'treasure chest'. In it was a plastic tub. She prised it open with her fingers, and inside was a single sweet. The sweet was unwrapped; it was soft and white, and smelt a little of liquor. It was a 'tree-ruffle' all right, but quite unlike the chocolatey ones Marzi had unearthed.

'It's a white rum truffle,' Terri said. 'Only one or two of these are known to grow each year.'

'Oo,' Lydia smiled. 'Is it really *really* tasty?'

'Oh no. Sorry. It's not for you.'

Lydia handed the tub to her uncle, and Terri very carefully took the truffle and broke it in half.

'They are called the Eyes of the Earth,' he said,

taking a bite. 'And one of these sweets can give me hours of sight.'

Terri finished eating the half-a-truffle. Then he squinted at Lydia, his little niece.

'It's the first time I've ever seen your face,' he smiled.

Chapter 21
Pear Drops

Lydia was very tired now, and she went for a nap in a honeycomb bunk.

Teatime later, she was woken by someone gently jogging her shoulder.

'*Dear Lydia*?' came a motherly voice. '*Little Toffee*?'

Lydia rubbed her eyes, and blinked into a dim honey glow; the first things she saw were the glinting stars on a woman's face.

'We'll be eating soon,' Morella smiled. 'Won't you join us?'

'Those stars on your face are pretty,' said Lydia. 'Are they stick-on?'

She reached out to touch one of the coppery shapes, but Morella smacked her hand away, and the expression on her face became very grave. 'Those marks are brands,' she whispered deadly seriously. 'Deliberate burns. Put on my face when I was very young.'

'I—I didn't mean to say anything bad,' Lydia said.

'I know,' Morella smiled sadly, and she held Lydia's hand. 'These brands are a permanent reminder of my family and homeland, and even my name that I lost when I was a child. If it hadn't been for your father Alazandr—Oh, to me he is the finest man alive.'

'What did he do?'

'I was abducted by wicked people called the Jampyra. Marked to be a victim, a *blood sacrifice* in some . . . sickening initiation ceremony. Alazandr saved me, risked his life. He brought me all the way from Tangiya. I was adopted by the Arora family here.' Morella placed Lydia's hand against one of the burns on her cheek. 'Maybe these marks are lucky stars too,' she said. 'Your family cared for me as their own. Gave me a loving home here in Delisha.'

She let Lydia get down from her bunk bed.

'Here you are,' Morella said warmly, draping a dressing gown around her. 'A wrapper for a Toffee.'

Lydia joined the others in the dining hall, sitting around the table on those grand old chairs. A delicious bouquet drifted in from a nearby kitchen, and Morella entered with trolleys full of food. She was all glammed up in a grassy green dress and floral accessories: a daisy-chain necklace and seed-bead bracelets.

'Now then, girls,' she fussed. 'Has everyone got clean fingers?'

The children responded in chirpy chorus:

'Yes, Morella. *We* do, Morella. I washed *my* hands. Sure, Morella. Hurry up, I'm hungry.'

It was funny seeing how the other sisters behaved in the company of grown-ups: Hazel, as ever, was keen to impress ('It's nice to sit down civilized to eat, that's what I say.') and Sugar was asking all sorts of questions regarding life underground; questions about power sauces, plumbing and light and refrigeration (Terri's answers mentioned stuff about bio-fuel generators and technology sent from Karamesh). Lydia was glad to see that Bull's-Eye didn't act so unpleasant now either. Indeed, all the girls were ever so polite, and Peppermint displayed a daughterly affection for Morella, holding her sleeve and laying her cheek against her dress. She even helped to wheel out the trolleys, while Morella laid the table. The woman did everything so elegantly; she sashayed through the dining hall, placing wooden salad bowls and dishes before her peckish guests.

Lydia waited in great anticipation, long denied such dinnertime delights.

Yet she found the food to be quite peculiar, what she could only describe as 'vegetable confections': candied cucumber in parsnip sauce, garlicish allsorts and cherry tomatoes; dishes of kidney chilli jelly beans, crunchy sugar peas and celery crisps. There were minty chestnuts roasted white; lemon-and-lime-spiced sweet potatoes; broccoli rocket with peanutty butter; marrow mallows and beetroot strudel; tofu flan and tortillas to be dipped into pots of damson jam.

There soon ensued a scoffy chatty party as the girls enjoyed the various dishes. Terri was also able to help, with his sight restored, and he served fresh cherryade to them all.

For afters, there was a choice of desserts: yam tarts, carrot cake, hot cress buns, or festive stollen flavoured with nuts and raisins and geranium.

Lydia and the rest of the sisters thanked Morella for the dinner. Some of them even went to help her as she loaded the trolleys with the clunky wooden bowls.

'Terri?' Morella called. 'Why don't you show the girls the lodge, while I clear the dishes? Something to do before bedtime.'

'Well then, young ladies,' Terri smiled. 'If you'd like to grab a lantern or two, I'll give you the grand tour.'

The sisterhood shadowed Uncle Terri through the ship-shape chambers and corridors. Up and down ramps and platform floors. Walking the planks past honeycomb rooms, cosy living spaces, cabins and stores. They even crossed a bridge that spanned an underground aqueduct carrying cherryade straight through the lodge.

For Terri too, it was a rare opportunity to see the place where he now lived; he showed the girls these cellar libraries stocked with cookbooks and recipe scrolls; culinary knowledge preserved over centuries, and sealed in cupboards, in bottles and jars.

Pear Drops

Deeper still was a basement containing hundreds of pudding bowls filled with rich Black Forest soil; the basement's timber ceiling was peppered with holes, and tree roots from the forest high above burrowed through, down into the bowls.

'Our truffle room,' Terri said proudly. 'Magical sweets have been grown in this lodge for many generations.'

Lydia weaved around the roots and bowls, overwhelmed by the fruity smells; she could tell, with the merest twitch of her nostrils, just where a truffle might be forming. And one creamy aroma seemed familiar:

'Oo, there's one of your white truffle eyes in here, Uncle Terri,' Lydia said, tickling around the roots of a bowl, and fishing out this small soily sweet.

'Thank you *very* much,' Terri replied. 'I'll be sure to save that.'

Not far from the basement was another space that featured very different sweets. In a cellar, heat-maintained by long incandescent candy canes, the girls saw a series of oaken worktops with rows of glass bell jars. Each jar covered a potted shrub shimmering like a miniature Midwinter tree and bearing multicoloured teardrop sweets.

The sisters walked beside the worktops, their eyes all aglitter with this beautiful wendy-garden.

'This is Morella's domain,' said Terri. 'She's an expert in aroma-culture. These are some of the confectionery perfumes she creates and cultivates.'

'I can't shmell anyfin,' Jawbreaker said.

'You have to *eat* a perfume sweet to bring out its scent,' Terri told her.

'I knew that,' Hazel said. 'My mummy buys me a box of perfume liqueurs every birthday. But I never knew they grew on trees. I didn't.'

Lydia peered into one of the jars at a shiny white teardrop tree. '*Winter Pearl Drops.*'

'That's right,' said Terri. 'Celine sent word that she'd need these sweets for her special dessert. Morella has been preparing them for many months. They're incredibly difficult to grow. She'll make sure you take two or three before you go.'

Next, Uncle Terri took the sisters to his workshop, to show them the masks adorning the walls: animal heads carved from bread—wolves and civets and tigers and bears. It was Terri who'd made Lattay's mask, a gingerbread boar with hardtack tusks.

The floor was covered with unswept wood shavings like curly quavery crisps; there were paring tools and half-whittled objects set up on casks and barrels of rum, whereas other hand-crafted knick-knacks (toys and mugs and cartoony toby jugs) could be found in cabinets around the workshop.

'I fink it's mazin' ya made all these,' Jawji grinned, 'wivout bein' able to see nuffin.'

'It's easier to carve smaller objects by touch,' Terri said. 'And the white rum truffles allow me to—Well, let me show you.'

Uncle Terri led the sisters to a hall where a row of gold-glazed people seemed to hover from the walls. As the children wandered through the lantern-lit place, they could see that the people were figureheads made of honey cake. In addition to the usual cultural heroes that would have fronted the boats of old, Terri had sculpted portraits of his family: his mother Rosé, and father Pyrus. And, of course, his sister Mari.

Lydia stepped up, quite entranced; she stood before the figure of her mother, and pressed the side of her face against the wall, imagining invisible arms around her.

'Miss m' mum so much,' she muttered.

The other girls looked on sympathetically. Each one of them yearned for a mother's embrace.

'I still count the days as days without her,' Terri said. 'You know your mother loved you dearly.'

Hearing that made everything sadder for Lydia. Knowing so much love had gone from her world. But she knew her uncle had meant it in a caring way.

It was late now, and the girls returned to their quarters, to bunk up in their honeycomb beds. Morella brought them some herbal tea, a dozen cups of this lime-coloured liquid.

'Eee's *green* tea,' Coco sniffed.

'It is spinach char with a pinch of peppermint,' Morella told them. 'Good for you. Help you sleep. It is very grown-up.'

'I'd love a cup if it's grown-up,' said Hazel. But after a sip, she winced: '*Yuck*. It's like sucking on tea leaves.'

273

The rest of the sisters didn't fancy it either, but Terri had an idea, and he went and fetched a jar of jam. A deep red rhubarb-and-ginger jam. He stirred a spoonful of it into each cup to make a sparkling fruity tea. Which all the girls guzzled down happily.

As Terri and Morella turned to go, Lydia called her uncle over. She had something for him, retrieved from her pinafore, something small and wrapped in a handkerchief.

'Uncle Terri, I don't want to lose this,' she whispered. 'It's Mummy's crystal heart. Will you keep it here safe with you?'

Terri clasped the priceless crystal. His sister's loss hurt him still. With tears in his eyes, he wished Lydia goodnight, and left to lock the heart away, snuffing out the honey-light.

The next morning, Terri was blind again.

At breakfast, Morella asked the sisters to sit, while she brought out a bowl of ritual trifle. She held it up in front of her, closed her eyes and recited:

'Cream of sky. Custard of the earth. The cherry-filled jelly of the underworld.'

Then Morella placed the bowl back on the table, and served the trifle clockwise.

'So now you say,' she asked the girls: 'Cream. Custard. Cherry jelly.'

Again (like Marzi's peach tea ceremony), as though some serious mealtime game, with the others, Lydia repeated: 'Cream. Custard. Cherry jelly.' Though she did think it a bit silly.

Still, the trifle was really tasty: juicy chunky cherry jelly layered with custard and topped with whipped cream.

Once this unusual breakfast was finished, and Morella had left to wash the dishes, Lydia asked: 'What was all that stuff about creamy sky and underground jelly, Uncle Terri?'

'It's an old old saying,' he explained. 'It comes from the cookbook of a Delish society. One that first produced the trifle. Morella said it out of respect for our family. We've been part of this Order for generations. Your mother taught Morella this "secret" trifle recipe.'

'Oh,' Lydia tutted sadly. 'There are all these secrets and things Mummy did that I never knew about.'

275

'Delish cherry trifle isn't really secret,' Terri said. 'Not these days anyway. But secret groups and orders are still found all around the world. Groups sharing tastes, cooking techniques, and favourite sweets. Throughout history, they helped to shape civilization. But some also have a sinister side. It's a sweet society that now rules Candi, after a series of fixed elections over the past ten years or so. This group of chefs held secret banquets, did deals with people in important places: newspaper owners, businessmen and so on. Stannic was the Master Chef of this group: a brotherhood who call themselves The Knights of the Crossed-Knives.'

'The plate-and-knives,' Lydia realized. 'That *is* the Tin Man's sign.'

'And with each Crossed-Knife Chef taking a piece of Candi, Stannic and his rich supporters could set up the robot bases and factories. He intends to make everyone—millions of Candi-Landers—serve him for ever. These times are dangerous,' added Terri, 'that's why we've had to bide our time, and plan some secret way to get rid of him.'

Morella soon returned to the table, carting a large wooden jewellery box that unlocked to reveal tiers of sweets she'd brought to fruition in her private cellar. She showed off this marvellous selection with pride, rivalling Dolly with her animal collection. There were pale perfume perry drops, black morello, berry tots; palm of violet, opal fruit sweets; musky caramel, pearly vanilla seeds; honeysuckle suck-em-'n'-sees, orange, jasmine, and chewy kiwis.

'And most important, I have these Winter Pearl Drops for you.'

Morella picked out a pair of white perfume sweets; Sugar Cube sealed them safely in her jacket.

'How many treasure-sweets do we still have to find?' a curious Marzipan asked.

'We have one to go,' Sugar said. 'Something called Ruby Red Shortbread.'

'Is a pity,' tutted Coco, 'zat we cannot pinch it from some sweetie boutique.'

'I've heard of short*cake*,' added Hazel. 'And shortcrust pastry. It's very tasty.'

'Shortcake shortbread, same thing,' Bull's-Eye shrugged. 'And anyway it's a biscuit. So better try the Baykari quarries for that ruby red bread.'

'And Lattay is here to accompany you, to help you reach Tangiya,' Morella said.

Lydia looked across at the teenage girl, this surprise sister who'd now join their group. Lattay really was Lydia's half-sister too and, best of all, she came from Karamesh.

It was time to go. To leave the lodge. This storeroom of memories. This haven of emotions. Morella made sure everyone's knapsacks were packed with food and drink, including these fruity granola bars, cinna-munch cakes, and flasks of water.

She also let each sister select a perfume sweet from her jewellery box; Lydia chose a Delish pear drop, its scent the same one her mummy wore at home.

The children had hugs for both Terri and Morella, and then they shared cheerios and good wishes. Peppermint, however, didn't want to leave, and Morella had to give her some words of encouragement before they parted company. Pepper, of course, like most of the girls, had run out of her power-sweets.

While the others got into their hidey-hoods, Lattay put on her safari jacket, covering the creamy shirt she wore, and tucking in a necklace laced with coffee beans.

'If you're coming with us, Lattay,' Marshmallow said, 'you have to have a code name.'

'How about *Nutty*?' Dolly said again. 'Cuz of your nutty necklace.'

'Zey not nuts, silly,' Coco teased. 'Zey coffee beans.'

'How about we call you *Coffee Creme*, then?' suggested Hazel.

'That's a nice name,' Lydia agreed. 'Coffee Creme.'

Lattay

And so, from the dining hall, 'Coffee Creme' led the sisterhood down a long long passageway. They ate their perfume drops as they went, and the lovely aromas that flowed from the sweets would stay with each girl for the rest of the day.

They made their way through a network of wooden tunnels deep beneath the forest. At last, they came upon a secret hatch which opened into a cool dark cellar. A wine cellar, stocked with hexagonal barrels, and racks full of dusty bottles. Beyond this cellar were stores of preserves, of potted fruits and jars of jam, enough to last months, even years. Then stairs led up to a fine old manor house, the place where Terri and Morella had a home.

Morning sunlight hazed its rooms and, through a window, Lydia could see they were somewhere beyond the edge of the forest, with fences and a high hedge all around. She had completely lost track of time during the day or so spent underground.

All was quiet, as Coffee and the sisters crept outside across the crisp morn manor grounds.

They went past wire-netted vegetable gardens, wells of water, and dandelion-'n'-burdock pop, up to the manor's old garage: rusting there was a three-wheeled wine truck, bottle green with a canvas roof and a huge hamper stuck on the back. In times past, Morella would have driven this truck to the local market, but now it would transport a dozen girls off to complete their treasure hunt.

'Are you quite sure you can drive this—this vintage thing?' Hazel Whirl asked Coffee Creme.

'Hazel, don't be so rude,' Marshmallow said.

'These past weeks I stay here,' Coffee replied, 'Morella teach me how to drive.'

The children climbed into the back, and sat between stacks of punnets and crates. (Morella had already lined the hamper with duck-feather duvets, to make it cosy.)

Coffee then drove them away from the manor, away from the forest, in the vintage truck; the vehicle was all grinding gears, pop-cork pedals, and crunchy clutch. She used her blackberry-tracker to navigate, gathering information from snakes dispersed as aerials across the region.

As the truck grunted along the country lanes, the sisters nosed around the punnets; some contained dried sultanas, others had candy pips at the bottom—they were fine to eat, not rotten or anything—and they nibbled on a few as they peeped out of the hamper.

Lydia saw the rambling Winelands, an uneven expanse of hills and farms, hedge-lined fields of colourful crops, brandy snaps, lollipoppies, sun-kissed raisins.

She also glimpsed the Wineland wildlife: grazing red deer or pale apple pommy-horses trotting across the meadows; a flock of orange ducks flapped and quacked overhead, over the farmsteads and vineyards, the villages and spritzy rivers.

At first, it seemed to be a lovely ride through the countryside, but soon there were signs of the Tin Man's

intrusion: houses wrecked, farmland neglected with plough-forks poking in the soil. Caravan sites with empty wagons lined up like giant painted barrels. The world had changed so much in such a short slice of time.

'I've been thinking,' Sugar Cube said to the group, 'about our lack of power-sweets. And where we can find some more.'

'We coulda done without wastin' them days in Likrishka,' Bull's-Eye mentioned, 'waitin' for Toff.'

'Can't blame Toffee,' Marsha argued. 'There used to be plenty of sweet shops before Stannic shut them all.'

'There *is* one place we can go, though,' continued Sugar. 'For everything we need.'

'Will it have lots of soft candy?' piped up Dolly.

'And ice pops?' added Lolly.

'Will there be choccy-nutty spread?' Hazel said. 'And—and pralines?'

'Oo, will ze be shocolart?' Coco enquired.

Pepper also jotted '*Will there be mints?*' on her electronic wafer.

'Yes, Pepper, yes,' Sugar nodded. 'There'll be mints and everything. Doesn't anyone believe me?'

'It sounds a lovely place,' said Marzi. 'Are we going there now? And will it have marzipan?'

'Well,' replied Sugar, 'I hope we can get there some time tomorrow. It's a place in Nooga called Sweetie World.'

'Sweetie World!' Coco cried. 'Zat's at BonBon. Our mums' home towns! We can all go shop. Zer zese choco boutiques we *must* show you. We steal from zem all ze time.'

'We're not going shopping,' Sugar tutted. 'And we only "borrow" things when we really need to.'

'We pinch what we want,' Cocoa-Butter pouted. 'Ms Bossy Cube.'

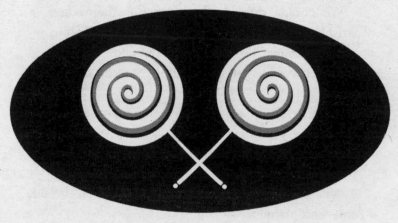

Chapter 22
Wine Gums

After about an hour's patient drive, the children came to a fine wine estate. Tracker-snake transmissions had warned of roads ahead that were closed—Stannic already carving the fields and vineyards into work zones. Coffee drove the three-wheeled truck to an archway entrance where iron gates had been torn off their hinges; she steered inside the high stone walls, passing through a magnificent vineyard, up to a creamy stone chateau. Then she parked the truck out of sight, beneath a row of fruit trees.

Everyone clambered out. With such a long journey still ahead, it did them good to stop and stretch. The day was too warm for hidey-hoods, and so they left their fleeces in the hamper.

'Cor,' said Jawji, 'I know this place. Use to gavver fruit chews in these vineyards.'

She asked Coffee if they could spend a little time to

get some wine gums. And so the children took some baskets, and wandered across the colossal estate.

They strolled the rolling red folds of earth where rows of sticks—cocktail sticks as tall as the girls—had been speared into the soil to support the upright wine gum vines. It was clear the vineyard had not been looked after for quite some time. Twining tangled leafy tendrils spiralled up and down the sticks, bulging with juicy grapelike gums, acres of them, left unpicked.

The sisters set about wine gum gathering. For Lydia, it was a bit like brambling; twisting the clusters of sweets from the vines, and tossing them into the baskets. She revelled in the outdoors too, the fresh air breezy with the bouquet of wine, all the swoony fruity scents wafting across her sensitive nose. There were many different flavours of chews, in luscious colours, to collect.

These were the gums that made Jawbreaker's jaws strong, and kept her teeth in chomping prime; and so she used this opportunity to cram her paper bags with them, to stuff her pockets and her mouth full too. Jawji, in her patched-up jumper and flappy shorts, was really in her element. Although she was illiterate, she had learned to understand the land: to her the furrows of a field were as easy to read as the lines in a book, and their vines were like words full of leafy letters, punctuated by blossom and sweets. Jawji could tell by sight which gums were worth picking, which were at their tastiest, or even if they were overripe.

In one place she showed the others these bumps of earth between the vines.

'What made these?' said Marzipan. 'Some kind of underground animal?'

'Nah,' said Jawji. 'They're gumball-bowls.' She went to one of the bumps and poked around in the soil for a while; then she pulled out an extra-large gum, a magnum-gum the size of a plum. 'See? Really good gumballs them. Wurf chiggin' out.' And Jawji flipped the sweet into the air, and caught it in her large mouth.

All of a sudden, Dolly squealed, and picked at something inching up her shin; then, with an irritable wriggle of her shoulders, she flung it across the field. 'Eee, *leeches*!'

Lydia now noticed these spangly slugs crawling out from the soily bumps; some slugs were striped, others were colourful, while some had shells like swirly sweets. They were crawling all over Marzi as well, curling around her leafy limbs; unlike Dolly, she didn't seem to mind them, and stood there fascinated as snails wound around her fingers.

Jawji went and plucked a black slug from Marzi's dress, chucked it in her mouth and chewed it. 'Mmm, *slickerish*,' she said, much to the squeam of some of the others—

Especially Hazel: 'I've never seen anything *so* disgusting. You're *so* disgusting, Jawji.'

'They're *nosh*,' she replied, and held out a couple of the snaily slugs, but Hazel spun well away from them.

Most of the other sisters trusted Jawji and tasted a gummy morsel or two. Hazel just squirmed, with a sour expression on her face. ('Oo, you dirty beasts. I do declare. I'm going to be sick. I do.')

'Hmm,' pondered Lydia, nudging at the slugs with the toe of her shoe, 'I might try a rainbow *snay*-ull. Do you cook it?'

'Nah,' answered Jawji, 'jus' shake it out the shell an' shove it in ya gob.'

Lydia nabbed a twisty snail, ate it whole from its horns to its tail; she found it tangy, oozing juice, slightly bitter with a taste—a taste she couldn't quite relate—a taste of some new exotic fruit.

After the snack of slugs and snails, the girls collected their gum-brimming baskets, and went back to the truck for a spot of lunch. Coffee had brought a picnic hamper with loaves of zesty candied bread and, on paper plates, she passed around the slices buttered with a brandy sauce. There were sticks of chewy red rhubarb too, that Morella had grown in the manor gardens.

As the children prepared to leave the chateau, Coffee revealed the real reason for stopping in this deserted spot: she brought out a large champagne bottle from beneath the driver's seat of the truck.

'Oo,' said Dolly, 'are we going to have some tiddly pop?'

'If you drink from this bottle,' said Coffee Creme, 'you be hiddly not tiddly.'

Coffee walked around the truck, shaking shaking the champagne bottle, twisting the cork and aiming this glittering spray across the three-wheeled vehicle.

From top to tyre, from hamper to bumper. The sisters stood and watched astonished, as the wine truck vanished once the spray dried on it; drops fell onto the driveway too, leaving weird befuddling puddles of nothingness.

'It is glassy mint oil we brought from Tangiya. A recipe of sister Hisska's.'

Next, Coffee showed the girls the purse on her belt.

'I have kit full of useful goodies, if you need,' she said, opening the purse and revealing an array of sweetie weapons and cutlery tools: 'I have *doyng-doyng* liquorice, *zap-zap* prong, *snap-snap* clippy crisp, salty *sniff-sniff*, chicl sticky-stick—'

(Coffee didn't know all the names for things in Candi-language, and her mixed-up descriptions made all the girls giggle.)

'What those small red bonbons?' Lolly nosed.

'They are cherry bomb,' Coffee told her.

'Wicked,' Bull's-Eye grinned, and grabbed for them, 'I'll have some o' those.'

'Zye, they're not toys!' Marshmallow said.

'I *know*,' Bull's-Eye scowled. 'But I'm the best thrower. So there.'

'All right. Take two,' said Coffee, offering her a pair of the red grenades. 'To use a cherry bomb, you pull out a stem. When it tremble, you throw it. Quick.'

And so they set off from the fine wine estate, now in an invisible mint-coated truck. As they travelled, the children stared from the strange glassy hamper; Jawbreaker, especially, looked thoughtful, remembering the fields of her childhood.

'So you use to live in zat chateau, Shawshi?' Coco asked her.

'Nah. I *worked* there, yeah. An' other vineyards. In the off-season. The fields'd be full of all our folk. Pickin' the fruit gums for the well-fee farm owners.'

'I wouldn't fancy that at *all*,' said Hazel. 'With all those slugs and snails and muck.'

'*Them* never bovver us,' Jawji laughed. 'The luggin' big baskets. Vat was tough. I use to carry the 'andles in me gob. Cuz it hurt your arms and back an' that.'

'Oh, that is no job for a child,' uttered Marzipan.

'Ah, it wunt all shabby, Marz,' Jawji replied. 'Cud sneak a few yummy gums, chew 'em as we went. An' season finish wiv harvest-fetch an' the farmers had their bunfire parties. But sham we not get to go to those.'

'Why didn't they invite you?' said Lydia. 'You gathered the harvest.'

'Sorta seen us as strangers, din' they? You know, curio shirk-us folk.'

'Oo, *yes*,' said Dolly Mixture. 'You used to be in a circus, din't ya?'

The sisters wanted to hear more, so encouraged Jawji to tell her story:

'Well, it wunt a huge fayre or nuffin. A *confection seaside show*, we call ourself. There were kids all ages an' some grown-up crew. We had jellyfish dancers. A spiky-skin urchin girl, she cod swallow a sawfish. A frog-leggy boy wiv a greeny body. These crab twins who juggle seashells.' Jawji became quite animated, impersonating the children she described. 'Yeah, there was turtle boy too; he had flat flippers for fumpin' a drum. An' there was a really fin eely girl wiv a catfish-face.'

'*Catfish*-face?' Dolly giggled.

'Yeah, she had goggly eyes an' wishkers, an' could hold her bref for ages. So she use to wear a fish tail an' swum in a big punch bowl.'

'What you do, Juju?' Ice Lolly asked.

'Wotcha fink? I was one o' the freaks. Used to have to dresh up as a shark—ya know, a fake nose an' everyfin. Folk from all over come an' see me munch stuff. Treacle cockles an' coral rock. Lobster shells, sugar claws an' all. Use to crush 'em wiv me big ugly gob.'

'It's not a big ugly gob,' said Lydia. 'Means you've got a nice big smile.'

'Did you have one of them enormous tents to perform in, Jawji?' asked Dolly.

'I saw a ballet in a marquee once,' Hazel interrupted. 'I bet it was better than *yours*.'

289

'Nah, we din have no big toppin' tent,' Jawji said. 'Jush use to do stuff off back o' the wagons wiv colourful cloffs. On a long sun days, we trav' around the seaside, pulled by evvy shire 'orshes. Shloggin' our caravan round.'

'Why would you choose to live like *that*?' Hazel asked sniffily.

'Never choose nuffin'.' Jawji shrugged. 'Never knew any other life. I was an abandon baby, an' them freakfolk begum my family. We shtuck tugevver froo rough an' tougher.'

'Oh.' Hazel looked away, ashamed. 'I didn't know, you know. I'm sorry, Jawji.'

'Ah, it wunt tough *all* the time, Haze.' Jawji smiled. 'Nosh in summer. At the beach an' that. Cud play makin' sand-puddins an' eat seafood shweets. An' even at harvest-fetch, the gumyard farmers have the burnin' picnicker man.'

'What is zis peeky-neeky man?' asked Coco.

'He's this huge puppet chap of old bashkets and straw,' said Jawji. 'Farmers build him in a field at autumn, fill him wiv fire-woks, then chuck a flamin' chipstick at him. Our folks'd shy away an' watch ash fury-darts an' rockets crosh an' shplode in the shunset. An' we drink grape-pop an' toast toddyberries on our own minicha bunfire. After that, the winter frosht crispets up the gum farms. So we have to board up the wagons for long cold schnaps. Play cards, make Midwinter dolls an' that. Then, gum shpring again, our

shideshow was back on the roads, tourin' round the fishy villages.'

'If everyone came to see your show,' said Hazel, 'wouldn't you be rich? And not have to slave away in the fields?'

'Fisher-folk only pay us in gobstops and penny chews. Never coins. Them're for the well-fee. An' anyway, I got fed free shweets to chomp. Candy shrimp an' that, they chuck. *Roll up an' feed Jaws*, our barker use to shout. *The famish shark-girl.* That was me.'

'So Jaws—or Jawbreaker—was always your name?' said Marzi.

'Nah. My name's Donna. Dunno my born name.'

'It's *Ganash*,' said Sugar. 'That's what my files say. Your mother's name was Retsina Ganash.'

'Well,' grinned Jawji. 'Never knew that. Donna Ganash. I got a proper name now.'

'And a *ganache* is a very posh chocolate,' nodded Hazel. 'It is. I bet your parents were really rich.'

'Wow,' Jawji smiled wider than ever. 'Got any more nollidge on 'em, Shugz?'

'Just your mother's name,' said Sugar. 'There's nothing about your father.'

'I reckon,' pondered Dolly, 'it's cuz he was a no-good drunk—oh, sorry.'

'Ah, do not worry, Jawji,' Marzi sympathized. 'I never knew my father either. Mother said he was a scientist explorer. A sweetie botany expert like her.'

291

'What happened to your daddy then, Marzi?' asked Lydia.

'He travelled far away to Tangiya. And mother say he never returned.'

'Actually,' admitted Sugar, 'I only have data about Dolly's and Toffee's dads. Lolly has a stepfather. Marsha was adopted. Rest of us were raised by single mums. Coco's got two mums for some reason—'

'Daddy Petro isn't really my father,' Lydia told her.

'My daddy,' Dolly added, 'was erm, my *second* daddy. Daddy with the teapot shop.'

'I don't like my step-pop!' Lolly cried, catching the others by surprise. 'I hope he was nab by the crabs!' Then she folded her arms and sulked in the corner.

'Oh, poor Lolly,' Lydia said.

'I know,' nodded Marsha. 'She kept that bottled up.'

'So you never 'ad a dad *neither*, Shugz?' Jawji whispered, resuming the discussion.

'I had a sort of dad. A cyber-dad,' Sugar said. 'We'd talk to each other on the internet. I was so ill in my early years, I couldn't have contact with the outside world anyway.'

'How did you know it was your father?' asked Marzi.

'Oh, Mummy got him to e-mail all this personal information. In code, of course. Just so he could get messages to me, from time to time. I still don't know his real name though.'

'He had a code name too?' said Lydia.

'A Tangi name,' Sugar replied. 'He called himself *Bo-a-Karam*.'

'What does that mean?'

'Caramel Man. And when Stannic shut the internet down, the *snakes* started sending me data instead. And Lady Hisska knew all of Daddy's passwords.'

Just then the wine truck screeched to a halt, and Coffee Creme clambered back into the hamper. She explained they'd stopped near the Tin Man's blockades. To get across the Winelands now, they'd have to break through into the work zones.

The sisters peeked at the blockade ahead: a seemingly endless line of barrels. From the cover of their invisible truck, Coffee noted the robot sentries, two tin soldiers, one either side of a great grilled gate, guarding this entrance at the metal barrel barricade; their weapons were spray guns attached to yellow pop bottles—Lydia saw robots with guns of that sort when she was sent to Tinport all that time ago; she now knew the bottles contained chemical booze. Go-to-sleep flavour, to make you snooze. That's how Stannic captured people.

Coffee took a small tin from her jacket; she broke the lid's seal, and passed the tin around. A dozen oval topaz wine gums lay inside: 'Each take one,' she said to the sisters, chewing her sweet first. 'Eat it as I leave the truck.'

'What *are* they, Coffee?' Sugar asked.

'Rare citrine fruit gum. We found its juice can counter sleepy-pop. Now you stay here, out of sight.'

293

Coffee swallowed her citrine sweet, and took a deep breath to steady her nerves; then she seized three of her cherry bombs, and scurried from the truck.

The children ate the bitter-taste gums; Lydia found hers tough to chew, till its thick skin squished with a potent drop of grape juice. Then they all remained anxious spectators, watching the robots aim their guns as Coffee Creme came running towards them; their sensors had already picked up the crunchy clunking approach of the truck, and the sentries now fired two bursts of spray, sousing the road with alco-pop. Lydia felt the spray leak into the vehicle and tickle her eyes, but the wine gum meant its wooziness was nullified.

And when the alco-pop spray had cleared, she saw Coffee Creme still standing her ground. *One two three*, she bit the stems from the cherries. *One two three*, Coffee cast the grenades at the gate and the robots. There were *one two three* metal-shatter detonations as the guards and gate were blasted apart by cherry red explosions.

However, while the other girls peeped from the truck, they spotted a spy-hawk launch into the air; like a poison-eyed surveillance camera, the hawk had been clocking Coffee's every move.

Bull's-Eye quickly leapt from the hamper, fully intending to knock the bird off; she bit out the stem from one of her cherry bombs, and slung it at the hovering hawk. Her throw, though, was a reckless one (missing her sweets, meant missing her target). The

grenade exploded beyond the blockade, leaving the electric hawk to soar away over the Wineland landscape.

'Where was it off to?' Lydia wondered. 'Off to report to Mister Tinny-Bin. Rotten snitchy thing.'

'Ah, *custard tarts*!' Bull's-Eye blurted out in annoyance.

'There's no need to use crude language, Zye,' Hazel criticized.

'I'd have blast the stupid bird, if I'd had my stupid sweets,' Zye argued.

Coffee Creme rushed up to the truck. She ordered Bull's-Eye back in the hamper; then she started the engine again, putting her foot down, daring to accelerate once they were through the blown-up gate.

Chapter 23
Beer Drinker

Coffee now drove through the occupied zone, still guided by one tracker-snake or another, sending their wireless microwave codes to her blackberry-like device. Thus the children could steer clear of barricades, avoid the villages patrolled by robots, policed like Likrishka's Detainer Towns. There were fenced-off prison camp places too, where the people slaved in the fields and vineyards, instead of in chemical factories.

It felt bizarre driving on unobserved, in a truck with a magical glassy-mint mask; at one point, Coffee had to swerve it off the road as an armoured lorry almost ploughed straight into them, oblivious to this invisible vehicle travelling across the restricted districts.

Later that afternoon, Lydia heard a distant buzz: a sound that got louder and louder, moanier and dronier like a swarm of bees. Through the transparent canvas roof, she saw a pair of insect aircraft carrying multiple

bottles of pop, rasping low—Lydia couldn't help but duck—The insect planes passed over though, without detecting the sisters' truck. Soon zoom, their drone diminished.

'Them're jush like the huge musqueeto that shprayed my caravan ashleep,' said Jawji. 'It wuz really jammy Shugz found me first.'

'And those horrid mosquito things still fly the sky?' asked Hazel.

'They spray sleepy-pop on anyone who tries to escape and hide,' replied Sugar.

'But if people can be put to sleep at any time,' said Marsha, 'then even if we helped to free them, nothing can stop it all happening again.'

'And maybe one day they will sleep for ever,' Marzi uttered bleakly.

Teatime and suppertime were spent on the truck: the sisters ate the last of the candy brandy loaves; then there were the baskets of wine gums to chew through. Jawji showed them how to make 'jammy gum-wedges' by squashing the sweets between slices of bread.

The sun soon set, and the sky darkened to a deep deep claret. Finally from claret to black, as night time drowned the sorrows of the Winelands.

Coffee wasn't able to drive the unlit country lanes, so she parked in a field well away from any road; then the sisterhood snuggled in the duvets, sleeping till the early light.

By dawn, the wine truck's glassy glaze had begun to fade, and the children had to continue their journey in a semi-reflective spectral truck. It was a slow journey through liquory hills, rich sherry vineyards, fields full of rye; barley sugars, hop gardens, wheat crops and pop springs, cognac and wine lakes all passed by.

'Are we going to get to Nooga soon, Sugar Cube?' Hazel Whirl asked.

'We're heading for the Lager Lands first. To the place that makes the sleepy-pop. It was Coffee's plan to try to blow it up.'

'So there won't be any more snoozy-booze?' said Lydia.

'Alcohol's very flammable,' answered Sugar. 'Should be simple to start a fire.'

As the morning drew on, the girls could see people labouring hard on detainer farms. Stannic the Tin Man still needed this workforce to keep his empire, feed his government. Expert farmers. Skilled agriculturists. Poorly rewarded with rations and threats. Fearful workers slaving away. Surrendering all the fruits of their labour to trolley patrols that collected the crops. Soon this fine harvest would grace the menus and wine lists in restaurants patronized by Likrishka's rich: Stannic's high society supporters, the greedy Dinner-Jacket regime.

To the watchful eyes of the sentinel robots, the sisters' truck was simply a mirage, a ghostly presence passing through, through to reach the Lager Lands, a region known for its distilleries and breweries. Many of these buildings were automated now, run by robots and Stannic's scientists. The rest of the region had been left to rot: contaminated vineyards growing poison raisins; wine rivers slicked with sickly vinegar.

Coffee had to drive through a greyish green fog too, a real pea soup gloom, its source, this single installation: the alco-pop brewery. Beery and sewery. Dim in the distance, enveloped by fog; its six chimney funnels spewed up smog, polluting the surrounding countryside.

The closer the sisters got to the brewery, the smellier the air became.

'*Urh*, what a pukey stink,' Bull's-Eye sniffed.

'I never have to put up with these pongs back home,' Hazel complained. 'I don't.'

The chemical stench made the girls feel queasy too, especially when mixed with the jolting of the truck on the grape-nut roads.

Fortunately, Sugar carried anti-sickness tablets with her. 'Here, everyone have one of these. I call them Tumma-Salts. They'll stop your stomach doing somersaults, and prevent you from sicking up.'

'We don't want to hear about things like *that*, Sugar,' Hazel uttered. 'Thank you very very very much.'

Lydia took her medicine with gratitude, and chewed the minty tum-settling tablet.

Coffee Creme steered the truck off the road, and brought it to a halt on the bank of a river: a dark cloudy river of ale that flowed towards the brewery. The sisters stepped down, with their bags, from the hamper, their three-wheeled vehicle now quite visible.

Coffee was thumbing at the buttons on her blackberry, and soon she summoned a tracker-snake to them, this one chequered in green and grey. It slithered along a riverside path going '*Glug-a-lug-a-lug. Glug-a-lug-a-lug.*'

'Ooh,' said Dolly. 'A lovely little sneak.'

The girls were rather pleased to see snakes now, it seemed.

Sugar knelt down and put her laptop on the path, to let the serpent pour in its data (like getting the latest snaky newspaper). Once it had finished, it slipped away into the river of ale, and Sugar read out the snake's report: 'There's a depot round the back of the brewery. For pop-transporters.'

'You mean it'll take us to Nooga?' asked Hazel. 'Sugar? Sugar Cube? Excuse me.'

Sugar sat there strangely silent and, in slow slow-motion, she closed up her laptop and put it away.

'Is something the matter, Sugar?' asked Marsha.

'Yeah, what is it?' said Bull's-Eye. 'What's wrong with her?'

Sugar was shaking; she looked pale and dazed.

Coffee felt her forehead. 'We need to get her away from this awful place,' she said.

First, they had to dispose of the wine truck; its fuel

tank was almost out of petrol jelly anyway, and some of the sisters helped Coffee to push it, to get it rolling, down the bank and *splash! blup blup blup*. Down into the river.

The children were sad to see the truck go; it was still a fair distance up to the brewery, and the path they took went past a bog, a foggy swamp of slurry ale. They had to swat away flagonflies too, pesky insects that sipped about the riverside weeds; and then there was the *belching bingeing belching* vomiting croaks of stout-black toads.

Sugar Cube got worse as they walked; she tottered unsteadily, and Bull's-Eye had to grab her coat to stop her from tumbling into the river.

Lydia was really worried about Sugar now. Especially with most of the sisterhood powerless, as well. At least they had Coffee Creme to lead them. Sugar was so frail she could hardly stand, and the tall strong teenage girl picked her up and carried her.

The enormous brewery loomed up ahead, and Lydia could see it was well-protected. Beer keg battlements, built around the installation, turned it into a virtual castle; its six-pack of chimneys resembled turrets, and the bog of ale surrounding the walls served as a malty moat.

There was only one way to approach the castle, via a wide gravel road. And appearing out of the pea soup mist, the sisters saw a delivery lorry crackling along it; with its many many wheels and long smooth tanker, the lorry looked like a metallic caterpillar. At its arrival, a forked portcullis was raised, letting the caterpillar scuttle through to the brewery depot.

Two more robot sentries were there too, armed with batons in the shape of bottles.

'Best not waste any cherry bombs here,' said Coffee. 'We need to break in quietly, then find some stowaboard transport. It is only way to get through all the robot blockades now.'

Lydia would have to tackle the sentries without the other sisters' help. She decided to eat a chunk of toffee; about a quarter of the packet remained, and Lydia felt a little guilty, chewing away at her nourishing scrumptious Karamesh confection.

She told the others to wait close by, while she walked the gravel road alone, right up to the portcullis gate. Lydia with her tin in front of her, on its ribbon around her neck. Liquorice drumsticks tight in her grip.

As she stepped towards the sentries, so the sentries stepped towards her, programmed to defend the brewery, to attack anyone unauthorized there. Metal bottle batons raised, the robot guards honed in on her quick, pacing pacing.

Lydia waited, concentrating, tapped out a rhythm on the tin lid drum; a rhythm that shuddered through both of the robots, allowing her mind to magnetically control them. She made them turn and march before her, towards the malty moat of ale. Lydia the drummer girl kept up her tempo—*left right, left right*—kept up the beat. And the hefty metal sentries lurched in front,

upon their 'hup hup' puppet feet. Caught up in the snare of her drum. The rhythm of the toffee tin. *Left right, left right.* Then with a finale ruffle: 'Hup to, hup!' She made them march right into the moat. *Splish splosh. Bubble, froth.* The robots sank below the murky surface.

Now that the entrance was clear of sentries, Jawji was free to break in to the castle; she bit off some rivets from the forked portcullis, loosening one of the heavy prongs so the rest of the sisters could force it aside and crawl on through. Then they made their way inside, to find the lorry depot.

Luckily, the inner castle was unguarded: the robots there were busy at machinery inside the brewery, or else they were tending to fork-lift trucks loaded with demijohns and crates of ingredients. The sisters crept around the massive installation, its structure a cocktail of brickwork and steel, of pipes and funnels and scaffold extensions bolted onto an old beer mill.

Lydia peeped in through the windows to see where the snoozy-booze was produced. Distillery apparatus sloshed with pop and alcohol mixed with liquid chloroform; the resulting brew was steeped in vats, boiled then dribbled into plastic bottles.

Near the brewery was a beery reservoir, its surface froth giving off a drunkard stink; the foul brown ale that filled the reservoir provided the beer-swilling brewery with its fuel, its generators chugging away while pipes thirstily slurped up the drink.

Next to that, the girls saw the depot and its line of delivery lorries, labelled with their destinations: *Wineland lorry, Delish lorry, Franji lorry, Likrish lorry, Froza lorry, NewNooga lorry*—a veritable tongue-twist of caterpillar-tankers being loaded up by robot waiters. Lugging big bottles up and down ramps. Loading the cargo of alco-pop. And piping in energy porridge from pots.

'Whish lorry ze one we want?' whispered Coco. 'Oo, NewNooga!'

Being so used to flitting about as a slippery flicker of golden light, Cocoa-Butter barely waited to check if the way was clear or not; she skipped across the depot of pop, up the ramp of an open lorry. The others followed with a lot more vigilance, edging around behind fuel pots and tankers, before boarding the NewNooga vehicle, and hiding with Coco right at the back, behind a yellow bottle stack.

There was still one important task to do: the sabotage of the beery brewery.

With Peppermint missing her power-sweets, it was left to Coffee to use the firelighters kept in her purse; and so she stole from the caterpillar lorry. Lydia went too, in case she ran into any robots, and the two of them sneaked back to the stinky drinky reservoir. Lydia didn't need to use her drum; the robot waiters and fork-lift trucks carried on unawares, carried on dumb.

Coffee knelt at the edge of the reservoir; she took a fizzy firelighter match, struck it on a honeycomb strip

and dropped it through the thick brown foam to ignite the flammable ale beneath. Once on fire, the flames spread quickly *whosh!* across the reservoir surface. Sizzling ale. Sozzling froth. The beer-driven brewery continued to quaff. Lydia and Coffee rushed back to the depot, joining the others in the back of the lorry.

The reservoir fire raged away. And as the pipes supped up the flaming ale, the whole of the brewery set alight and started to erupt with immense gassy gurgles. Boiling foam and snot-green smoke were sneezed out from the chimney funnels, turning white, blinding white, as fire refreshed the sky. Coffee had given the place a serious case of heartburn, a burning beery belly-ache to flush its boozy systems clean.

It wasn't long before alarms were sounding, and the lorries in the depot had to lock up and go.

The girls were on their way again. Leaving behind the fiery brewery. Rumbling along in a metallic caterpillar. Seated next to a load of bottles, rocking and knocking together. These pop bottles were the extra-large sort. Plastic containers almost four metres tall, full of snoozy-booze for the huge mosquitoes.

'I hope this pop doesn't spill,' said Hazel. 'Or we'll all be put to sleep, won't we? We will.'

The sisters had other worries, however: Sugar wasn't getting any better.

'Pollution must have poisoned her,' Marzipan said with sorrow.

'Why Sugar and not us, though?' asked Marshmallow.

'I think it is to do with the technology inside her,' Coffee replied. 'Most possible is alcohol fermenting the sugar in her system.'

'Yeah, she dush look a bit sloshed,' Jawji said. 'Like she et a buncha wine gums that gone off.'

The sugar in her system, Lydia thought to herself. 'I think we need to change her sugar lumps,' she said. 'The ones in her arms and legs.'

'How do we do *that*?' Marsha shrugged.

'Well, she has these scars, and these slots—'

'You *have* to do it, Toffee,' said Marzi. 'She looks very sick.'

Lydia searched through Sugar's pockets; her chunky jacket was full of them, and each pocket contained some pill or pastille, some gumdrop or bonbon, some lozenge or chew, a range of amazing medicines.

Eventually she found a pack of sugar lumps, white energy cubes wrapped in clear plastic. She rolled up the sleeves of Sugar's coat—and her trouser legs as well—and ever so carefully flicked up the rectangular scars in her skin. The sisters looked into the weird open slots, the artificial cybernetic compartments that ran through Sugar's limbs; amidst the complex circuitry, the sucro-veins and microchips, Lydia could see the sugar lump cells held in place by special clips.

'Doctors always wash their hands before they dig their fingers in,' Hazel pointed out. So Lydia used a little water from her flask, cleaned her hands and dried them on her pinafore; then, with nervous fingertips, she tinkered with the springy clips, changing each of the six sugar lumps. Out with the old, in with the new. (One cube in each arm. Her legs needed two.) It had been like pulling rotten teeth; the lumps had turned brown, and Lydia tipped them into Coffee Creme's hands.

Coffee sniffed at the brown sugar lumps. 'Smells as if they been dipped in whisky,' she said, screwing up her nose. 'No wonder she was slipsy tipsy.'

Lydia covered up Sugar's limbs; then she fed her a couple of glucose pills. After a while, she showed signs of improvement.

'Betcha saved Shugz's life, Toff,' Jawbreaker smiled.

The sisters ate some of the food Morella had packed for them; then they rested on the long lorry ride. Sugar unplugged her goggles and hearing aids, and put herself in 'sleep mode' to help herself recuperate.

Lydia was curious to see where they were going and, using her tin, she unlocked the sliding door behind them. Drummed it ajar, just open enough for a snifter of a nose outside.

The caterpillar-lorry had gone beyond the Lager Lands, passing the big tin barrel barriers like giant sets of metal dentures chomping up the countryside. (A bar code on the grill of the lorry allowed it to check-in and check-out of places.)

'I got a great idea,' Bull's-Eye announced with her usual modesty. 'Let's get ridda this stupid pop.'

'Ooh, that is a good idea, Zye,' Hazel agreed.

And so, when the lorry began to travel up a hill, the children got ready to roll the bottles off the back.

Lydia watched them as they went: there were dozens of bottles to dispose of in all. Yellow pop bottles for dumping down the hill. And two-by-two the bottles of pop were deliberately dropped.

Splish-splish splash-splash splosh-splosh froth.

The impact popped off the bottle cap tops, leaving fizzy trails of alco-pop plummeting like long thin bombs, two four six eight bottles bouncing down the hill. Ten twelve bottles plus, all of them did spill. And, as the last yellow bottle load dropped upon the road, there was no alco-pop left for the aircraft any more.

Chapter 24
Candy Store

In time, the stowaway sisters crossed the fortified Wineland border, the border to Coco's homeland Nooga (Nooga being two bijou regions at west'most mainland Candi: NewNooga and NuttiaNooga).

Here the country lanes became dual carriageways, carriageways all traffic-free, apart from an occasional robot-driven lorry.

Sugar woke up, feeling groggy. 'We haven' reash BurBon, have we?' she slurred.

'Oo, yes,' Dolly cried excited. 'We're on our way to Sweetie World!'

'Calm down, Dolly,' sighed Marshmallow. 'We're not there yet, you know.'

Most of the sisters kept quiet during the journey. Sweetless and speechless. Weak and weary. Lydia could only fret for her friends, and she murmured to herself with worry: 'Come on, caterpillar-lorry. Hurry *hurry*.'

It was late afternoon when the lorry reached BonBon, at the heart of NewNooga.

NewNooga was a barren province riven with rivers, and rather short on natural treats. These rivers, however, had made it ideal for dealing in goodie-goods, and Nooga's network of two-way canals became important import-export routes. As business in NewNooga grew, so it invested in its tourist industry, trading exclusively in luxuries, leisure and pleasure, and artistic creativity. The sisterhood had already bypassed stretches of desert land playfully tastefully patterned with candy sand. Once-plain plains were now transformed into public parks, peaceful spaces for culture and sculpture. For Lydia, they were a wonder to behold: abstract structures stuck in the ground, surrounded by sand paintings and flossy floral plots; there were large glass allsorts in lustrous crystal liquorice, twists and twirls and swizzle-sticks and squares and colossal lollipops.

At the centre of this was Coco's home: BonBon—often called the confectionery capital of the world. Or more correctly, the confectionery *capitals*, as BonBon was two towns in one. Two towns either side of a river—the River Twix—with their layouts symmetrical; that made one the mirror of the other. Thus for each building built on one side of the river, so there was a reverse

version, another on the other side, in a complementary colour. It was easy to see which was which. One BonBon had a scheme of cream and caramelly yellow, while the other had darker cocoa colours: a chocolatey town of purple and brown.

The caterpillar-lorry approached an airport just outside this dark side town.

As it neared, the children heard intense insect noises; then it was past a vast construction site where the lorry stopped at an empty bottle bay. The sisters hastened from the rear of the caterpillar, horrified to find the lorry had rolled right into the base of planes. Lydia stared scared at the sight of the aircraft: two huge metal mosquitoes at rest on these steel tiers. Zuzzing buzzing, busy refuelling, feeding from mega jam jars, using long proboscis-pipes to snort up a sort of raspberry petrol. No wonder the planes rasp past, she thought.

The craft were ever ready to ride, to any land in Candi, to make a drop of sleepy-pop. But thanks to the sweetie sisters, the pop's beery brewery was a burning ruin. The Tin Man's mosquitoes quite boozeless useless.

The sisters fled, left the nest. Next to the airport depot was the noisy construction site, it too creepy and crawling with creepy-crawlies: silkworm scuttle-trucks laying cables, dirigible bluebottles floating lifting, and an army of robot waiter ants serving various lever-arm cranes, riveting girders, bolting scaffolding, hauling slabs of caramac tarmac, heaping spadefuls of chemical minerals, mixing treacle concrete from the sugary ingredients.

With the site a hive of preprogrammed activity, the preoccupied robots weren't hard to avoid. The girls scurried, hurried away unseen; sneak-a-bit, peek-a-bit, quick-there-hide, pleased to leave the banging clanging cacophony behind.

They scampered past canteens set up to feed the robots; past scrap yards packed with confiscated cars. And as they made their way into BonBon, Lydia looked back at the nest of nasty insects, its skyline outline a crisscross mass of skeletal steel; BonBon's symmetry messed up by this singly ugly eyesore.

The sisterhood strolled after Coco, crossing the darker part of town with its deserted streets of chocolate concrete. This side of the river had been known for its nightlife, its vibrant bistros, brasseries and bars, concert venues, avenues of cafés, cocoa-mocha counters and patisserie piazzas; there were quality quarters of haute-cuisine confectioners, bonbonnière studios and chocolatier ateliers. Salons and saloons resembling fanciful layer cakes, metro retro towered desserts, knickerbocker glories with stripy storeys, boxy black and cola-colour blocks. All with tinted glass façades glittering lit with treelike streetlights, dark-trunked palm-trees with white pod lamps.

A separate pair of sucronium power stations powered BonBon. Gently lighting the two-tone towns. Twin towns so still and silent. No robots here, no hounds around. The sisters the only ones in NewNooga now.

Coco took the others across concentric cocoa roads.

Roads safe and traffic-free like Tea Set City's clutterless streets. They passed malls and galleries and candy arcades, all the stores and studios locked up when the people were captured; when the BonBon population had been ordered to stop. Stop their civilized lives, put their livelihoods on hold, before being loaded onto coaches, trains, or lorries. Some were now lowly workers, working in Stannic's confection factories. But the best of the chefs, entertainers, and artists were dispatched to Likrishka to delight his elite.

The girls didn't linger long in town; now the best place for them was Sweetie World.

Sweetie World was a world-renowned theme park, built on sandy land between the River Twix (where the waterway split into two for a bit). The sisters crossed one of the Twix's biscuit bridges, over the river where—There were the entrances, duplicate gates containing the greeting: '*Welcome Welcome to Sweetie World*' (words in curly-whorly lettering).

Atop the gateposts, Lydia saw two statues, life-size stylized model mermaids. (Mermaids made suitable emblems for BonBon, what with its river-links, docks, and canals.) The statues were crafted in contrasting couple-colours: one was blonde, the other was burgundy, and both had open mouths that seemed to sing a silent song. As the sisterhood approached, the mermaids did indeed begin singing; triggered by visitors, they started to twirl upon their tails and, from their mouths, smoothie soothing voices flowed in stereo soprano.

These mermaids made a melodious ambience in the evening air. But Sugar told Lydia to silence the pair: 'Quick quick, Toffee! They might attract attention.' And so she shut them up using the tin. Gobstopper *tap-tap*, she rapped upon the tin lid, Lydia switching off the mechanisms in them.

Then Jawji chewed the chain from the gates, allowing the sisters to enter the theme park. The sky above BonBon was blue-black dark, but Sweetie World lit up automatically at night, lit up with a constellation of caramel and vanilla illuminations, letting the girls see its stunning sights. Past twin turnstiles, they went through to an amazing plaza and a sugar-glass palace that looked like an elaborate chocolate space cake. 'Oo *la la*,' Coco clapped happily. 'Is a palai' shocolar'!'

Not far from this was an ornate rococo cocoa fountain; the fountain's rich liquid chocolate hadn't been renewed for some time, and a scummy skin had formed on top of what was now a pool of cool mud pud.

Sweetie World itself was a self-contained candy land, its theme the planet's aliment elements: mineral sweets, plant sweets, icy confections, and liquid drinks.

'*Woo!*' wowed Dolly. 'We're *really* here. I dreamed of being in Sweetie World.'

'Oo, it *is* nice and quiet without the queues,' said Hazel (Hazel had visited before).

'Will it be safe to wander round?' asked Lydia. 'What about see-see TV?'

'What about stupid *hawk*-spies?' said Bull's-Eye, still miffed she'd missed the one in the Winelands.

'Let's get inside then, out of sight,' said Marsha.

From the plaza, these parallel caramel paths led around orchards, boulevards and gardens. With eyes wide, Lydia took a look at the wondrous surroundings; she thought that a theme park would be all silly and childish—but no no, not in BonBon. Here, confectionery was serious business: the park was refined and finely designed, curvy carved outer spacey places, spaced by lemon grass or lines of lime, sometimes with a rim of trimmed fruit trees. Strange ferny furniture grew from the grass: comfy frond-fringed flora sofas, palm chairs, moss stools, and drop-leaf tables.

And at every turn were pastel sculptures, beautiful sylph figures, sweet-spirit sprites, sleek and lean animals, bush shrub birds.

Marzipan, for instance, noticed a two-headed horse (the 'echo-equus' of Nooga folklore). 'This *is* a kooky gee-gee,' she smiled. 'I never seen its like before.'

Past the paths, past pastille trees, past ponds of floater lotus sweets and surface-swirly lily-pops. Past sprinklers spraying in colours of quirky squirty water plaits.

Past all these was the series of galleries Sweetie World was famous for, where sweets from all around the world were showcased in cases, all to be tasted.

The galleries were in these lovely pavilions, white with spiral pie spires for roofs.

With all the pavilion-galleries sealed, Lydia had to drum on her tin to open up the doors and stores. The display cases were also locked, looked after usually by staff, served on receipt of bonbon-tokens.

The children had never seen so many sweets, so many sorts in so many displays. Tray arrays with ample samples laid out in dice-sized baubles and cubes.

The sisters dispersed inside the gallery halls, chirpy girls all calling out: '*Toffee! Toffee! Open these ones! Please, Toffeeee! Here, Toffee, here! Aya, Toffs, these shweets look good. Oo, we want these! Toffee, please.*'

Lydia had never felt so needed and pleaded for. Her tin lid drum in handy demand, she ran around the cases picking the locks.

'Don't have to have *her* help,' grumbled Bull's-Eye. 'I can just smash the glass.'

'No breaking anything, Zye,' Sugar sighed. 'Anyway, these cases aren't glass. They're plexi-plastic. Specially unsmashable.'

'Huh, s'pose you're right,' Bull's-Eye huffed; she refused to argue with Sugar Cube. 'Tell Toff to hurry up then. *Tell* her.'

The sisters sought out their favourites first, their life-enhancing enchanting confections. Filling jars and cartons and bags, packets and pockets and pouches and flasks. Unlock-a-case, crack-a-case, the children ran round, taking the sweets as fast as they can; nicked and nabbed and eaten with glee, putting spares in their knapsacks for later and tea.

There was a whole gallery hall with all sorts of soft mallows to suit Marshmallow.

And one with candy pick-'n'-mix for Dolly Mix.

Marzipan tried the many types of almond fondant, sugared dragées and nut-cluster comfits.

Peppermint pouched all the peppermints and spearmints.

Bull's-Eye poached all the marble gobstoppers, topping up her tie-up purse with boiled bullet sweets.

For Hazel Whirl, there were hazelnut pastes in a range of jars; she also filched the feuilletines and pralines. 'Oo, pralines the *bestest* nutty choccies, they *are*,' Hazel said. 'And they're less messy than choccy-nutty spread.' After tasting a few sweets her speed returned— in fact, she became rather overexcited, pirouetting spinning round pinching praline after praline, line after line.

Chocoholic Cocoa-Butter got stuck into squares of gourmet white chocolate, whilst Jawbreaker stocked up on a bumper crop of gumballs.

Jawji enjoyed gorging on these new chewy chews, though she did feel a bit iffy pilfering wine gums from these fine displays instead of from a vine or field. 'Jush feels like *thiefin'* to me,' she revealed.

'Oo, soo what, Shawshi?' shrugged Coco. 'Someone has to eat ze sweets.'

So something for all of them, somewhere in the theme park:

Ice Lolly's lollies came from a pavilion full of popsicles, ice-creams, and frozen desserts. While in a

medicinal gallery, Sugar found sugar lumps, sucrose and glucose pill supplies. She also located a gift kiosk with chocolate-finger torches which she dished out to the others.

Dolly even nicked some souvenir jewellery: a lollipop watch and jelly bead bracelet, and spangles and bangles that jingled and jangled.

'Dolly, only steal *useful* items,' Sugar said. 'We don't want you chinkling and chiming all the time.'

'But—but Cocoa-Butter said these looked deluxe on me,' quibbled Dolly, reluctantly putting the bangles back (except she kept the lolly watch).

So something for all of the sisterhood.

All except Lydia, that is. Despite the other toffee on offer, there was nothing from Karamesh for her here. None of Elixa's tangy speciality.

Lydia *did* find something, however, even as precious to her:

One of the pavilions was devoted to various mineral sweets: cookie dough, cakey dough, crystal jelly, and fudge sludge. And there, in an exhibit of famous chefs, confection inventors and innovators—

There was an image of her mother Mari, a photo with notes on her accomplishments and ability, saying things Lydia never even knew. It seemed that being a sweetie-taster involved more than scoffing fudge all day: it was expertise and experiment, a creative understanding of the flavours of the world.

Her mother had been a confection-physicist and

candy-scholar rolled into one, a woman whose studies had delved into the deepest secrets of taste. A woman worthy of reverent mention in this place that celebrated culinary invention; this ultimate theme park where science and art served the very sweetness of existence, transformed it into confection perfection.

'Our father talk of Mari Arora, Toffee,' Coffee said, standing in the gallery hall. 'I have mother named Karandi in Karamesh, I miss.'

'Coffee Creme? Lattay?' Lydia asked. 'What's Daddy Alazandr like? Celine never told me much about him.'

'Alazandr's an amazing man.' Coffee smiled. 'Does such crucial work for us. Many missions, expeditions. I fear for him so much.'

Coffee took Lydia by the hand and together they went to the botanical gardens: colossal glasshouses housing plentiful Plenti plants, bushes and shrubs.

Then there were these arboreta, trees of transferred rainforest fruits: jump-up-and-grabbem bunches, sneak-up-and-pluckem chews, reach-up-and-squeezem sweets, all with their tutti-frutti tastes. Tangerine nectarine, pawpaw, peach pear, pineapple, sugar apple, tangy mango, passion and persimmon. So much luscious delicious food at their fingertips to eat.

'A treat for me to see these trees, Toffee,' Coffee whispered sisterly; this part of the park put a real sparkle in her large dark eyes. 'I taste this beauty in Tangiya each day.'

'You've lived all your life in Karamesh?' said Lydia.

'Yes. I toffee-chef apprentice there. Karamesh is special place. You soon see.'

Elsewhere, the girls saw a grove of trees grown in soil so fertile, a loam so mulchy and munchable, it seemed to be of the finest cocoa.

'Kokoa trio-brioma,' Coffee told Lydia. 'Chocolate assortment trees.'

Lydia gazed mesmerized; she wandered around the arboretum room, seeing the trees' sleek leaves and the oval odd pods seen between. There were pods of all colours, in sizes from lemon to melon.

Coffee Creme drew her short sword from its sheath; she reached up to cut a pod down, then she used the sword to scrape and prise the thick tough rind and the weird white purée layer inside. Coffee then showed the delighted Lydia the chocolate beans in this buttery purée, pouring out a heap of sweets to try.

'Mmm.' The chocolate was melty, tasty with hints of fruity flavour too.

Coffee cut down a dozen pods, and she and Lydia carried the selection to share with the other sisters. Each pod had different beans: some had chocolate-orange cremes, others coconut or malted centres, coffee fondant and nutty seeds.

Eating chocolate, fresh from the trees, was even new for Coco: 'Oo, too dee-de*lectable* beans,' she beamed, supping the buttery purée as well.

It was late at night by the time the girls finished in the glorious galleries; then they slept in these hospitality suites inside the plaza palace—a place not for tourists, but for VIP visitors.

Come morning, the sisters sat in the suites to eat their chosen confections; the children still had this little ritual. Friends together, eating together.

Sweetie World would have all they needed, for now: conveniences, washrooms, loos; cafés and kiosks had fridges of food; there were vending machines for nourishing hot drinks, chicory chocolatey cocoas and teas. Or refreshing cold cordials, sodas, and squashes.

And the taste galleries with their sweetie freebies, varieties denied to Lydia during her time detained in Tinport. They'd made the sisters well, as well. She didn't want to know what would have happened to her friends if they'd gone on longer without their sweets.

And daily, Lydia's own tin of toffee got emptier and emptier. Piece by piece.

Chapter 25
Nutshells

As she ate her breakfast treats, Lydia noticed a golden ghost with a gleaming grin hover over her tin.

'*Toffee, Toffee!*' the spirit whispered.

'What d'you want, Coco?' Lydia asked.

'*Toffee, Toffee, bring your tin.*' Cocoa-Butter waited impatient; she even pickpocketed Lydia's liquorice sticks and held them out to her. '*Here*, Toffee, *here*,' she teased. 'Everybody too. Scoot, scoot!'

Lydia looped the tin's ribbon round her neck, and she and the other sisters (even Coffee) followed. 'Where we going, Coco?'

'We show you,' she said as she dashed ahead, her sneaky sneakers *tap-tap tap-tap* up the plaza palace stairs.

The girls trailed her to a gallery hall—its theme '*The Confectionery of the Future*'—featuring sweets synthesized by science, quantum-cuisine, and cutting-edge

technology. Here were the latest taste sensations: marvellous mélange layered bars that melted in the mouth sublimely bubbly; truffle fondants of such subtle softness their centres were sealed in soldered treacle. There were ultra-creamy caramel manons, machine-souffléed to a moussy smoothness; extra-crispy X-ray wafers sizzled to size by laser toasters; sour ball sweets with fleeting half-flavours; ripply syrups to zap up any pudding, and icing isotopes to spice any dessert.

Escalators led to further revel levels, and Coco, so keen to see, she slip-skipped quick up the escalator stairs. 'Look look! Here here! Everybody, *everybody*!'

The rest of the sisters stepped up after to see a sweetie planetarium, its plexi-plastic cases with a fascinating selection of cosmic confection, trays of rarest extraterrestrial treats brought back by space probes or dropped by lolly comets. Here were candy asteroid fragments, astro nougat, nuggets of moon-mint, galactic kali and solar molasses, interstellar caramels cooked in quasars then frozen in the freezer of space.

'Oo, look at *this*,' said Sugar, showing the sisters a stick of rock speckled with sparkly sprinkles. 'A bit of the sweetie-meteorite that wiped out all the dinosaurs.'

Close to that, were these samples of a creamy chocolate rock.

'*Lunar Gîanduja*,' Marzipan read. '*Pralines par excellence. Scooped from the moon.*'

Hazel gazed at them, her heart beating quivery quick.

'Hmm,' said Dolly. 'I'd like to taste *that*.'

'Well, it's not for you,' Hazel twittered. 'It's for *me*. I love praline. And Janduya's *my* name, though it isn't spelt the same. Toffee, Toffee, you have to open it. You *have* to.'

Lydia used her tin lid drum to unlock the lock of the plastic case, so Hazel could try a praline. Its taste (so smooth, so lunar loony) sent the girl in a nutty flutter; Hazel danced upon her tiptoes, around and around the palatial planetarium, spinning running flustery-fast, coming back to pinch another chip of lunar praline, pinch another, pinch another, speedily greedily stuffing them in her mouth.

'Oh?' she twittered. 'I didn't eat them all did I? Don't think I did. Have they all gone? I want another one. Oh, Sugar! *Sugar?* Sugar Cube, we *have* to go to the moon now. We do.'

'Haze has gone nuts,' Bull's-Eye laughed.

Suddenly Lydia heard a sound. The sound of creamy harmonious singing. The mermaid statues had started up, only to be shut up by a *b-b-burst* of gunfire. Frightening gunfire that chilled the children's veins.

'Sumfin' musta just gun froo the gates,' stated Jawji.

The sisters dashed to a window. Saw robot soldiers stomping towards them, tramping around the chocolate fountain, up the paths to the plaza palace. Eight tall artillery robots with nut-gun limbs and backpacks full of bullet shells.

'Mister Tinny-Bin must be looking for us,' said Lydia.

'You mean *Stannic?*' panicked Hazel Whirl. 'How did he know we were here? How?'

Bull's-Eye scanned and panned around the park, sighting a metallic bird perched in a far-off fruit tree. 'Stinkin' spy-hawk spyin' on us.'

'Grab your bags!' Sugar shouted. 'Everyone, now! We have to get out of here!'

Lydia heard the soldier robots stomping round, surrounding the building. And, as the sisterhood fled downstairs, the robots shot out the windows upstairs. Volley after volley of bullet nutshells shattered through the sugar structure, smashing a mishmash of sharp shard glass across the gallery floors. Sizzling electric light and nutshell shots just missed the sisters, ricocheted around them as the plaza palace was blasted to pieces.

Sugar told the others to get to the display cases, and desperately they dived behind as bullets blew the lower windows away. Lydia winced as brittle shells shot hot into the plexi-plastic, leaving pockmark shotmarks all along the cases before the children's faces.

After that attack, came a pause. The sisters had to think quick. Trapped in the galleries, with soldiers outside set to shoot them to bits.

'What about your cherry bomb bonbons, Coffee?' Dolly asked.

'I have three left,' she replied. 'Yet the robots might shoot as I try to throw one.'

Hazel got off the floor, all-a-flustered: 'I'll lead the

robottos away,' she gabbled. 'Away from the posh hospitality suites. I'll meet you all at the exit gates. Get the bags and coats and sweets.'

'Hazel, careful!' Lolly said. But, before anyone could argue with her plan, Hazel ran from the gallery palace and sped between the battery of robots.

Straightaway sighted, the eight turned to shoot her. Lydia heard the terrible horrible rapid fire of nutshell bullets as Hazel started to dart around the park, pirouetting round paths and pastille trees. Luckily, the nutty lunar pralines she'd eaten had made her extra hyperactive, made Hazel Whirl twirl twice as swift. She set off like a blurry tornado, tore around Sweetie World, whirling from gallery to gallery to gallery; her heart aflutter, feet aflutter, jittery with moon gîanduja. Hazel ran faster than she'd ever had to, skipping split-second in front of the nutshells, the stuttery rattling gatling gunshots cutting up splintering pastille trees behind her, shattering pavilion after pavilion. The artillery robots kept *shoot-shoot-shoot*ing, unable to latch on to the unbelievably speedy ballerina.

This was the children's chance to escape. In the suites, the sisters dithered, gathered their sweets and fleecy cloaks. 'Everyone got their knapsacks?' asked Marshmallow. 'Dolly, where's yours? Where did you leave it?'

Only when the gunfire died, did they dare to scout outside; the girls grabbed their bags and scrammed from the palace, across the plaza, around the fountain.

The robots were some way away, facing away and pacing a path on the far side of the park.

Hazel, however, was nowhere to be seen. Why hadn't she returned? Lydia feared the worst. The girls couldn't, they *wouldn't* go without her.

Suddenly a gingerly figure staggered from a nearby gallery.

'Oo, look look!' called Coco. 'Is Hazel! Hazel!'

'I'm sure—I'm sure the robottos out of nuts,' she puffed tearfully, brushing splinters from her hair. A nutshell bullet had grazed Hazel's shoulder; a smouldering wound that Sugar Cube covered with a rice paper plaster. She also handed her a chalky pink sweet.

'Here, Hazel,' Sugar whispered, 'have this bonbon. I call it a Num-Num. It'll take away any pain.'

Hazel was graciously grateful, as she chewed the analgesic sweet.

'You're really brave, Hazel,' said Ice Lolly.

'Yes, you has us worry-worried,' added Coco.

'Amazin', Haze,' said Dolly Mix. 'I mebbe been nutted to bits.'

Hazel was all whirled out, and a little bit nutshell-shocked. She shuffled forth with the others, ready to depart from the park.

A hawk now flew at them, circling circling, its trilling drilling into Sugar's ears.

Bull's-Eye seized her cherry grenade, bit out its stem, aimed and threw. Her aim was true. The bomb hit the

bird as it passed, blasted it with a tinny tinsel spray of cherry fire.

The girls legged it to the exit. Atop the gateposts, the shot-up shattered mermaid statues—the robots no doubt firing at anything vaguely human that moved. The sisters crept out of the exit gate. A gate where four more soldiers waited. There they stood. Standing guard. All in a line, a firing squad. A four-strong rank of clunks 'n' clanks. Fully-loaded nut-gun soldiers.

The children had no time to retreat. The robots raised their rifle-like arms.

Lydia fished out her drumsticks quick, drumrolled on the toffee tin around her neck. *Ratta-tatta-tat*. She concentrated, to get that magnetic telekinetic connection. To manoeuvre the robots, four at once. With her mind, with her tin, she drummed, she commanded, made the four turn to face one another. Nutcracker *clack, click*. Their finger triggers activated. Mechanisms letting out a devastating gun-burst. The robots shot shot potshot each other with a nutty cracker metal clatter. *Cracker-clatter-clack*.

After the bursts of nutshell bullets and pepper-shot hot metal settled, the sisters picked their way around the robots, all four fallen full of colander holes, leaking cooking oil upon a pile of shells.

'That could'a bin *us*,' Bull's-Eye muttered, booting the nearest robot bottom.

'Smashin', Toffs,' Jawji cheered. 'Ya trash them machines shambles.'

'You fine there, Toffee?' Marshmallow saw Lydia give a shudder of the shoulders.

'Just thinking,' she said. 'I used to be scared of a spoon once.'

'Was it some enormous tinny teaspoon?' Dolly asked baffled.

'A huge ice-cream scoop?' Ice Lolly said.

'A giant iron ladle?' added Hazel.

'N-noo,' replied Lydia, a little embarrassed. 'Was a rotten little wooden one.'

Outside Sweetie World, the girls saw the truck that had brought the robots: an open-topped articulated vehicle, slinky zincy lobster-like with radar eyes, head-light eyes that twisted towards the sisters. The monster lobster rumbled at them, extending its extra-large pinching pincers. Peppermint sprinted up and blasted its eyes with a retch of her fire, 'blinded' the lobster, set it aflame; then left the truck to cook, as a smoking wreck.

'Come on, everyone,' beckoned Sugar. 'We've got to get to Baykari next. Zye said we'd find the last treasure-sweet there.'

'Baykari's quite a way away,' added Hazel. 'Nuttia-Nooga's next to it. Tis too.'

'It's the BonBon docks we need,' said Sugar. 'Some boat or other to take us there.'

'We know ze queakest way,' Coco cried, and scurried away.

The sisters crossed the River Twix's biscuit bridge,

this time to the light side of BonBon, the side where the roads were paved with gold, golden bars of caramac tarmac. This town was renowned for its picturesque precincts, arty-marts and markets and fairs; squares of swirly sweet stalls and olde-worldy candy vendors, pastry plazas, croissant crescents, structures in prismic colours of caramel, cream, and custard.

Coco took the sisters through the quality streets of sweet boutiques, their frosted façades glittery lit by the palm-lamp streetlights.

'We spree for free from *here* and *here*.' Coco pointed to shops she'd stolen from. 'Aa, we not nick a thing from *zat* one. It got lots of heevy steely doors and choccy box and tricky locks.'

'*Zat one*' was a gemstone store with vaults of valuable bauble edibles: nut quartz necklaces, opal lollipops, almond diamonds from the mines of Lemonia. This sweetie jewellery all hallmarked, embossed, and boxed. A tasty stash for Stannic now.

The sisters passed the fashion boutiques, their 'haute-cuisine confection-couture', kitchen-kit and dress-desserts, there to be pored over, or even worn. The windows were lined with many mannequins, leggy and elegant, in two-tone ensembles, caramel-and-cocoa combos, this season's smartest gourmet outfits.

'There's these weirdo dolly folk stuck in there,' Jawbreaker remarked.

'Zey dummies, dumdum,' Coco teased. 'Not seen zese before?'

'Never sheen shops as these nor anyfin,' admitted Jawji.

Coffee Creme was just as intrigued at street after street of premier emporia, BonBon's dandy candy stores with the trendiest dinnerware and kitchen knick-knacks. A real retail delight. A posh shopper's paradise. All doubly deluxe and twice as pricey.

Hazel wowed at a window with the latest up-to-datest phones. All no good now, Sugar told her, as the Tin Man commandeered the telecom networks to control his rotten robots.

The children continued along the golden roads, strolling among the cultural quarter, by the ice-drink rink and twin-screen cinema, the Gluggeneim Wine Gum Museum and Candi-National Confection Centre (with its precious recipe and cookbook collection); a dash past the Pralini Palais, the Syrupy Symphony Tea-Theatre and Comfit Garden opera arena. Coco led the girls through alleyways and walkways, past des-res apartments and glitzy ritz hotels, alongside BonBon's parallel canals, eventually to a canary-yellow wharf.

At the docks were tower blocks, or so Lydia initially thought; they were really thousands of boxy containers, coated in chocolate (chocolatey *paint*), and the stacks were constantly moved or removed, placed or replaced by robotic cranes. These chocolate box container towers were *so so* tall the girls got vertigo just looking up, up, and up at the sheer verticalness of it all.

The BonBon docks were the beating heart of

Stannic's operations; and where the blocks once held stocks of ingredients, goodies, and toys, now they contained construction materials, machine parts, robot parts, fuel supplies to sustain his empire.

Pairs of barges, cargo barges, bore the container crates along the canals; some were being loaded, some unloaded, some were coming, others going. The barges were huge, the scale of whales, with wooden hulls pan-elled in a battenberg pattern, and paddle-wheel-tails like large sliced cakes.

The children sneaked between the containers, to one of these whale-vessels level with the wharf. 'Hurry, hurry,' Sugar urged, and the sisters skipped up and hopped on board. Then they hid in the 'head' of the whale, a head with a helm and an autopilot.

The paddle-whale let out a *deep deep* trombone moan, sounding as though its tummy rumbled. The girls sneaked a peek as a crane arm came and crammed a big bag well into the belly of the empty whale.

'What's that stack o' stuff bein' stuffed in, Shugz?' asked Jawbreaker.

'It's pudding fuel,' Sugar said. 'A solid lump of rum punch cake.'

'The boat runs on sponge cake?' said Dolly.

'Of a sort,' Sugar told her. 'It's cake mix soaked in white spirits. Makes a high-powered pudding for barges and ships.'

While the whale was fed its food, its tail-wheel started turning; Lydia heard it churn the water, sloshing

up a wash of cream; then the barge budged in a mist of steam, left the wharf and the canalside cranes.

The pumpback humpback whale of a boat blew *puffa ta-puffer ta-puffer ta-puff*, its pad-a-paddle pud propulsion pressure cooker pushed them on. The sisters rested in the head of the whale, relieved to be leaving BonBon at last.

Sugar Cube accessed the vessel's computer to override its radar navigation; this way she could change the whale's destination. 'Make it take us where *we* want to go,' she said. 'Coffee can steer it to Tangiya after, if there's enough pudding fuel left.'

A while ago, Lydia would never have imagined she'd be a stowaway on a whale with many new friends. Floating along the Candi canals. *And* off to see her half-sister Elixa. This thought gave her so much cheer; Tangiya, a boat ride, a tea tide away.

From the whale's gunwale, Lydia spied other robot boats, other battenberg barges with cargo, going about their programmed business, doing round trips on the two-way waterways. Pink-and-yellow paddle-tailed whales, steam billowing from blowholes, filling the air with aroma rum.

Chapter 26
Gobstoppers

After a time, the twin canals became one, a sign that the sisters had left NewNooga. The whale-barge paddled steadily along the single creamy waterway, puffing its way past orchards of nut trees, crops of pretzels, and fruit loop fields.

'Oo, we're in NuttiaNooga now,' said Hazel. 'Getting close to *my* home.'

Beyond the Nutti countryside, the land became loftier, loftier and rockier. The trade route cut through an alpine valley where trillions of tonnes of nougat-granite had risen through the planet's crust.

The children stared in awe at the triangular mountains sloping down around them; and ahead was an equally extraordinary sight: a canal tunnel carved through the nougat itself (a feat of sweetie construction on a par with the ancient Polosseum, or the coconut pyramids of distant Spyssia).

The paddle-barge entered the mountainside, into the tunnel, right into the granite.

Sugar switched on these whale-eye headlights, one pink beam, one yellow beam shining down the long dark tunnel. Lydia could see the seams of varied rock running through the nougat mountain, its sugary walls flickering with bits of nutty quartz.

The roof of the tunnel, though, was treacly and black from decades and decades of freighter traffic, of cargo barges puffing out their pudding steam.

It took a long time for the whale to reach the other side of the mountain. In fact, it had paddled along the canal for most of the day. It was evening by the time the barge finally passed the valley of nougat, passed its proper port-of-call: the hickory docks of NuttiaNooga, its waiting cranes, and crates of cargo-nuts.

'Pity we couldn't see where *I* lived,' said Hazel. 'It's this lovely little cottage, right beside the nut woods in the Filberg hills.'

'That sound nice,' Marzipan pined. 'I would like to visit it some time.'

'Yeah, me too, Haze,' Jawji agreed.

'You'd be very welcome, *Miss Ganache*,' Hazel Whirl replied. 'But I'm not bringing a scruff round for tea. I'm not. You'll have to get dressed up if you're going to meet Mummy.'

The sisters spent a peaceful night, safe in the head of the battenberg barge.

The boat continued on its Sugar-set course, and it was some time next morning when they got their first sight of this vast rocky island. 'Are we in Baykari yet?' Dolly said, nosing from a window.

'Nearly, Dolly, nearly,' Sugar replied.

Everyone in the barge perked up as they neared a beach of broken cracker sands.

Baykari was an enormous chunk of land that had split into four portions eons ago: furthest south was the isle called Kukido, a barren block of biscuit rock. To the north was the savoury isle of Krackatucka. Then there was the easternmost bready blob of Krustikob, and to the west was the doughy isle of Layakayk, which rose up like a giant bun dunked in a lemon tea bay.

First, the paddle-whale puffed past Krackatucka; its cracknel caves and parched crêpe shores crashed with waves of salty water swirling about the island here.

Further inland, were fondue volcanoes, sizzling cheesy lava-filled craters, their craggy batter peaks rising from layers of floury ash. The scent of grilled cheese wafted on a sea breeze, and the whale continued past Krackatucka, around the crouton rocks of Krustikob. Past its crusty coves, pitted pitta beaches and bread-crumb shores *breeosh breeosh* lashed by waves of broth. Lydia spied numerous soupy lagoons with thin fish noodling loopily around them. The *crim-craaka* cries of gliding bay-gulls echoed across the consommé tides, while the whale followed the bread crust coast, eventually reaching the outcrops of Kukido.

Krustikob and Kukido were separated by a channel of tea (called the CuppaChar Channel), and Sugar programmed the steamer-barge to veer around and steer along it.

The children peeked out as they passed between the different lands, dwarfed by cliffs of bread and biscuit: Kukido's broken cookie rock blocks towered over them on the left, with Krustikob's slopes of dough to the right, the bread of the land buttered by sunlight.

The whale paddled on, heading west, *puff-puff*ing under these high iron bridges, trestle table structures with breadstick railings that spanned the channel and linked the cliffs; there were cake-shaped cable cars above them too, one of the ways people used to cross from one island over to another.

Of the four isles of Baykari, only Krustikob and Layakayk were populated. Yet grown-ups from there found work across the entire region: excavating biscuit in Kukido's quarries, fishing and diving off Krackatucka's shores, and even working on a treacle-oil rig, further out in the Sea of Tea.

Along the sloping Krustikob coast, Lydia saw open countryside and plant life flourishing in the isle's doughy soil. The whale travelled past seaside villages: *Pannetown. Baluma. Multeesa. Bruschetta. Chabatta. Bagetti*—their names now amended or taken away as they all became Detainer Zones, and the villagers lived and worked for Stannic. Rows and rows of baked loaf cottages, farmhouses, windmills, and granary barns;

bread roll hillsides, wholemeal fields, groves of fig rolls—all enclosed by wrapper perimeters. The Tin Man was turning the lovely villages into prisons; his robot soldiers now roamed the isle's bready breadth, guarding the harbours, patrolling the bridges.

If Lydia was saddened to see this, Bull's-Eye was most upset at the sights; this was her land, her home being ruined. 'Stinkin' Stannic's stupid machines,' she fumed, staring with loathing across the coast.

Towards the heart of Baykari, the sisters sailed the watery tea, Sugar Cube seeking a suitable place to beach the whale, then steal ashore safe. Ahead of them, however, she saw something suspicious semi-submerged along the CuppaChar Channel. What appeared to be a series of boulder-sized boiled sweets. Stripy spiky gobstoppers to stop any craft that trespassed these waters.

'They must be explosive mines,' Sugar told the others. 'I don't think I can steer the boat around them.'

It was too late to shut off the pudding engine too; the whale's momentum would take it into the first of the bobbing gopstopper bombs. And if the barge was hit head-on, the sweet would surely blow them all to smithereens.

Sugar tried to turn the whale towards the cliff instead, swerving the barge slowly around, agonizingly near to a mine—Suddenly there came a *thump, crackle, crunch* as the whale crashed on a hard-baked outcrop. Rocks of cookie jarred the barge. All the sisters tumbled to the floor. The whale boat tipped against the cliff, its hulking hull wedged on the biscuit rocks, its paddle-tail still whacking at the water, *rubba dubba dubba dub*, drawing one of the mines towards it.

Before the girls had got back on their feet, the gobstopper bomb collided with the tail wheel. An almighty *kaboom!* jolted the boat; wood chips, tea spray, and boiled sweet shrapnel pelted against the head of the whale. Lydia felt the barge creaking, sinking; she looked back across the body of the boat; the tail was totally blasted away, the wooden sides were now on fire.

'Sisters! Sisters!' Sugar shouted. 'Everyone up top. The engine could explode any moment.'

'What do you mean "*up top*"?' asked Dolly.

'We'll climb across the head of the whale, and try to get up the cliff.'

The children grabbed their knapsacks quick; they

clambered up the battenberg panels, up on top of the tilted whale, ready to jump to the biscuit cliff. Coffee was first to get across, to a part of the cookie-rock weathered in steps; then she helped the others as they stumbled up after, abandoning the fiery barge below. The sisters scrambled across the cliff just as the pressure cooker engine exploded, the pudding-filled whale belly erupting behind them in a huge gush of tea and steam. Rum pud, wood, and crumbs filled the air, and all the girls ducked as a fallout of flour showered down upon them.

They picked themselves up and brushed themselves down, took off their hoods which were coated in crunch crumb. Marzipan shook out her leafy limbs that had turned the colour of almond brown. Now out from the shade of the whale, the sisters could really feel the warmth; and because of the sea surrounding Baykari (a sea of volcanically-heated tea) Kukido island was dry and ovenly. Lolly didn't feel well, at all.

'I guess I'd best hand these out,' said Sugar, unbuttoning a pocket and taking out a packet of sweets: 'I call them Coola Cubes.' She gave the girls these lemon-lime candies. 'To counter heat stress and generally refresh.'

The sweets tasted citrussy zesty, and Lydia soon found herself feeling much cooler. Ice Lolly also seemed a lot happier, and the bright blue spikes of her icicle hair chinkled and chimed in the sultry air.

The sisters decided to lighten their loads, leaving their hidey-hoods there on the cliff.

This left Peppermint in a light green skirt and white

cotton top with the sides torn for her four arms; Lydia still thought it was weird seeing her extra limbs.

Jawji, without her jumper on, wore baggy shorts and a patchy T-shirt. Bull's-Eye was in a faded red tunic, and Hazel looked graceful in her chocolatey dress.

Marshmallow though, in her purple robe, resembled a large ungainly plum. And Lolly was still an unusual sight in her lime nightdress, and shoes of gum.

Lydia was still in her dark grey pinafore and pale pink smock, while Dolly wore a brighter frillier frock.

Cocoa-Butter fluffed out her soufflé beret, but it was too warm to wear her sweater today, so she ditched it along with her cloak and stockings, leaving her in a caramel blouse and skirt and, of course, her tinted shades.

Coffee simply loosened her dark safari jacket; she was used to living in a hot Tangi clime. Sugar had to keep her coat on too; that was one item they would never leave behind.

And so the sisters set off along the cliff, their mouths watering with Coola Cube juice, their shoes crunching across the cookie rocks.

Before she flung her hood aside, Jawbreaker carried it and licked off the crumbs.

'Urh! Jur-jee!' Hazel grimaced. 'Don't do *that*.'

'What, Haze?' Jawji grinned. 'I *like* bishcuit.'

'But *eee*!' squirmed Hazel. 'You don't lick it off your clothes.'

Ice Lolly, meanwhile, scoured the ground for

chocolate-chip pebbles; she picked a couple up and was about to take a bite from one.

'I wun't eat that, Lolls,' Bull's-Eye told her. 'That've bin baked in the sun for years.'

Lolly looked at the cookie pebbles, screwed up her nose, and threw them away.

'Best biscuits found underground,' said Zye. 'You wait till we get to the quarries.'

'Amazing though, in't it?' Dolly smiled. 'This isle being one big biscuit.'

'Incredible,' Coffee said.

'Edible sea bedible,' Lydia giggled, remembering Mummy's Baykari rhyme.

'Actually the island's made of an assortment of biscuits,' Sugar informed them, 'all layered on top of one another over millions of years.' She went on to say how biscuits and cake were the leftovers of prehistoric sea creatures crushed and baked in volcanic ovens. Fossilized fondant, congealed jams, and custard cream were sometimes sandwiched in between.

The children headed inland, across this biscuit wilderness towards what seemed to be a factory in the distance. A trail of cookie cobblestones led to Kukido's quarry complex complete with its pits and biscuit refinery. It was about midday by the time the sisters reached the quarry perimeter. Already Lydia heard machinery quaking the biscuit beneath their feet and, time to time, these long-necked digger heads craned up and dipped down into the cookie rock.

Bull's-Eye took them to the disused quarter of the quarry; the area was ringed by a barbed-wire fence with signs warning '*No Entry*' and '*Danger!*' The air was scary too with the smell of hot treacle, the sky above the quarries smeared with smoke.

Lydia approached the perimeter fence and, using her toffee tin, she made a wide gate through the wire, drumming the strands so they snapped and crinkled back, curled and wound into pointy metal pompoms. Beyond the fence, the sisters nipped past depots full of industrial-sized cookie jars brimming with biscuit grit ready for shipping to mainland Candi. The quarries themselves were beside the refinery, its chimney stacks still fuming away, still being used by Stannic's automatons.

Bull's-Eye led them to the edge of vast tiers of mineral biscuit, and Lydia peered down the levels and ledges, the sloping open pits and trenches, jigsaw blocks of cookie rock with a labyrinth of tunnels dug within them. Decades of biscuit excavation had created an enormous network of mines running through the whole of Kukido isle.

And there, down in the biscuity pits, roamed more dreaded robot monsters: a dozen or so bulldozers demolishing the derelict quarter, mechanical creatures with steam-powered piston limbs, hissing kettle heads, and great baking-tray forelegs that shifted tonnes of crumbs. With their armoured shell bodies, the bulldozers resembled giant beetles, or even triceratops as, at

their heads, were long steel spikes to break up stubborn boulders of biscuit. Surging across the quarry rock, these beetles chugged *cha-mocka cha-mock*, lurching along on their chunky legs, their spout snouts snorting out hot tart treacle smoke.

Toiling alongside the chugging dozers were other sorts of monster machines:

These were the diggers Lydia had seen and, with their long articulated necks, they also reminded her of dinosaurs, sauropod dip-ploddi-cutters or dig-a-pit-a patter-saws.

These treacle-powered diggers worked away at the quarry cliffs, biting and biting chunks from the cookie blocks, and spitting out the biscuit gravel into barrel-jars. The dinosaurs made a tremendous noise, and inside their jaws, the sisters could see they had metal cookie cutter teeth that whirred and pared away the walls.

Across from the quarries were active mines, on the far side, supervised by spy-hawks. Clifftops lined with gingerbread huts, robotic trolleys, wagon trains, tin containers. And queues and queues of human miners. Gangs of slaves in ginger prison kit. Carrying lamps and chisels into cookie tunnels. Down below in the jelly-light glow. To hack and pick and break and pack. Then let the robots cart away the tins of quality biscuit snacks.

If the sisters were to have a chance of finding the last of the treasure-sweets, they would have to get into the biscuit caves via the derelict mines.

Bull's-Eye knew a way down the tiers, and while the activity continued all around, the children descended the connecting ramps, seeking to sneak by the dinosaur diggers, busy oblivious to all but their eating. Past the pound of quarries and mines, past the stink of treacle, they found a way to hurry round, and watch for the beetles; nipped across the derelict tiers, down and down the levels, dashed under a digger's nose that puffed fumes of treacle. Bull's-Eye directed the girls to a mine, and they dashed between the towering machines, through a mist of biscuit dust, making it into the mouth of a tunnel, into the derelict darkness. The girls wiped tears from their smoke-treacly eyes, then fumbled around in their knapsacks to find the torches Sugar had given them.

The roar of diggers, the revving of bulldozers made the quarry walls crack and quake; the tunnel shuddered, the sisters were spattered with a smatter of crumbs. Just then, massive dinosaur jaws came whirring down through the roof of the mine, heavy cookie cutter teeth taking a great bite out of the rock, almost taking off the children's heads.

The clanking digger came forward for another bite.

The sisters scurried through the deep dark tunnel and, as the machine screeched and clanged through the quarry tier, it brought down a broken biscuit land-slide.

The children ran into the mine; a cookie cave-in rumbling after, filling the tunnel up behind them.

Marshmallow let the others squeeze past her, using her roly-poly pillow of a body to shield them from the torrent of rock. Marsha's back took all the blows, the biscuit buffeting her along, before the tunnel roof collapsed and the mass of cookie rock crashed down and buried her.

The other girls turned in horror, shone their torches through the dusty tunnel. They hurried to search the biscuit rubble, calling out Marshmallow's name, scrabbling frantic through the mound of crumbs.

Marzi turned herself to wood, and burrowed head-first into the rubble; she disappeared for fearful moments. Lydia was afraid if they didn't find Marsha fast, the poor girl would suffocate.

Marzipan soon struggled out of the gritty biscuit, clinging onto Marsha's arm. The others got hold of her branchy limbs and dragged the two of them free from the crumbs, making sure they were both all right. Thankfully, Marshmallow's toughened form meant she was jarred but largely unharmed, and together the girls staggered further down the mine. The noise of the dinosaur demolishers diminishing.

Chapter 27
Jam Sandwich

Safe for now, they pointed their torches along the long passageways; the beams of light showed tunnels sloping downwards, reinforced by tough tea trays. Some tunnels still had the liquorice rails once laid for trolley tins to bring back the best of the pick-chipped biscuits; and led by Bull's-Eye, the group of children followed a track of buckling liquorice.

Deeper down, they found that the man-made mines joined natural caverns. Biscuit hollowed out by centuries of slow erosion, carved by liquid springs, drips and dribbles of milk and tea that made all these weird passages winding through the isle. The sisters stooped into the caverns, weaving round biscuity stalactite sticks. Sugar Cube marvelled at the quarry geology, real life science at her fingertips; Lydia marvelled at the biscuit assortment; at every turn something munchable to snap off from the cavern walls.

And so the girls sampled their way through the layers, the sedimentary cookies and nutty shales, chewy oatmealy digestive rusks, and crunchy flinty ginger rocks. Some of the lighter layers of biscuit were scarred by seams of custard cream, while other strata were darker and more a kind of cocoa coal ('Biscuits from the Borbonian era,' Sugar told them).

At one place, Bull's-Eye kicked at the walls, chipping at the biscuit with her hoof. Lydia pointed her torch to see and, glittering in the chocolatey light, were gemstone sweets dotted in the ginger rock. 'These the best sweets round here,' said Bull's-Eye, filling her purse with the marbled gems. She flashed her torch casually around the cavern, and invited the other girls to try the pieces she'd hacked out with her hoof.

Lydia saw a round marble at her feet. So *these* are Bull's-Eye's favourites? she thought, dusting off the ginger crumbs and sticking the marble in her mouth. 'Probably taste sour and I'll have to spit it out,' she muttered to herself.

Lydia certainly had to be patient to appreciate the sweet; the marble was glassy and brittle and tough, yet she found it had lovely levels of flavour, punchy and minty, fruity too.

'Oo, these are really *nice*, Zye,' she said without thinking.

'Told ya so, Toff,' Bull's-Eye replied.

The others agreed; these sweets were certainly worth

digging out, and the sisters sucked a marble each as they crept down through the caverns.

'Let shope this last treasure-shweet's easy to get,' said Jawji.

'What was it called again?' added Hazel. 'Ruby Red Shortbread?'

'How will we know where tis in zis maze?' asked Coco.

'Shortcake sediments are quite deep down,' said Sugar. 'It's *cookie* layers, *ginger* layers, and shortcake's below those. Then we look for biscuit bits that are shiny and red, I suppose.'

'I don't remember findin' any shiny red biscuits,' Bull's-Eye said. 'Never usually go this far in though.'

'You used to come down here lots, Zye?' asked Marzi.

'All the time, to find marble sweets. I got in through the quarry them machines were smashin' up. It's bin closed off for years. That's why all them Danger signs.'

'Seems a hazard place to be,' said Coffee.

'I guess,' shrugged Zye. 'No one ever stop me. An' anyway all them stinkin' robots weren't around then.'

It got warmer and warmer, the lower the girls went, and Lolly was able to cool them a little by icing the air, with her hands, as she walked. But it wasn't just hotter, it got mistier too, from vents of tea steam spouting through.

Are we *really* below tea-level? Lydia thought.

Sugar's goggles kept misting up (much to her

annoyance), and she was also worried that steam had softened the cavern rock and weakened the walls and floors.

She warned the others to tread very carefully. One wrong step and they might drop down a chasm.

The sisters crept through secretive grottos, and everywhere they looked the walls were threaded, embedded with fossil confectionery. Prehistoric sweets were seldom found, but here were *caves*-full far underground. They were all across the floor too: the crystallized caramelized bones of dinosaurs, piecemeal monsters with gobstopper eyes.

Did Bull's-Eye's powers really come from *dinosaurs*? Lydia wondered. Maybe her horns were those of a zye-syruptops. Or her hoof the toe of a stickarockasaurus.

Indeed there were many types of fossil-sweet here:

There! Textured black in the ground, the skull of a molassoraptor. There! The leg bone of a lemon curdodon sandwiched in the biscuit. Before them, the jaws of a nutcrackasaurus. And over there! A pink layered wafersaur flattened into the cookie rock.

'They look yummy. Are they safe to eat, Zye?' Dolly Mixture asked.

'Yeah, s'pose so,' Bull's-Eye replied.

The girls dispersed throughout the grottos, playing hunt-the-fossil sweets, finding the various species and flavours, tasting these once-in-a-lifetime treats.

Pepper picked at the biscuit seams, trying the minty

dinosaur eyes. Marshmallow munched on the crystal orange crest of a marmaladoloafodon.

For Marzi there were the almondy bones of the dymonycus sweetie species.

Coco, on the other hand, had discovered a deposit of try-a-ruskasaurus twix.

Lydia chewed on the toe bones of a toffodon, its extinct treacle flavour all tingly on her tongue.

'No wonder they're called *diner-source*,' she smiled. 'It tastes like dining back in time.'

Bull's-Eye tried some gingersnap raptor ribs, while Lolly licked the fin of a fishlike isyosaur, the creature caramelized in a sea bed of biscuit.

Dolly, meanwhile, unearthed the talons of a candy-dactyl; each metamorphic claw tasted different from the other. 'Mine's an allsort-a-sor,' giggled the girl.

'I never thought I'd eat sweets millions of years old,' Hazel smirked, as she swallowed some fragments of nutty pralinodon. Then there was Jawbreaker crunching her way through the sherbety vertebrae of a long-neck dibdabacus. And even Coffee found a meteor-roasted mokafrothatops to savour.

Sugar was the only one who went without. 'Will everyone stop eating dinosaurs?' she frowned (wiping her steamed-up goggles again). 'I don't want to stay down here too long.'

And so the girls continued through the baking fossil caverns. Their way ahead at one point was blocked by a small waterfall trickling milkily down the biscuit seams.

'I'm not sticking my hairdo under *that* gunge,' Hazel said.

'It's only spring cream, soppy,' teased Bull's-Eye ducking through quick.

Lolly went next and dipped a hand in the cream, freezing it so the sisters could nip past unsplashed.

They waved their chocolate finger torches to see where it was they now found themselves. And on the other side of the 'milky-fall', the sisterhood stood in a cavern of shortcake. Whereas most of the grottos were gritty and rough, baked to the touch and crunchy underfoot, as soon as Lydia set foot in this place, she could feel the difference in the ground. This cavern floor was raspy crispy, in layers of fragile wafer.

Sugar Cube sensed it too. 'Everybody stay back here,' she whispered.

'Oo! Look look!' Coco cried, pointing to a distant wall. Her torchlight glistened upon some fossils, ruby red against the white of the shortcake. Jam-filled teeth and claws and horns, all sandwiched in the prehistoric rock.

'Ruby Red Shortbread. We found it! We found it!' Even Sugar became excited, her electro-tinged voice reverberating through the cave. 'Oo, there's lots of it over there. A whole treasure-saurus.'

The crystalline shortcake was some way away though, across the flimsy wafer floor. The sisters needed Dolly again and, after Marzi had wound a vine-like arm around her waist as a kind of harness, the others aimed

their torches for her, while Dolly edged out from the shortcake ledge towards the ruby bones. Ever so slowly she picked a path across the fragile floor. Each of her steps crisped a footprint in the wafer, and Marzipan twined her arm further and further. Dolly got closer to the fossils. She stopped just short of the shortcake wall, the dinosaur bones shining ruby red above her head. Dolly didn't dare make the slightest jump to get to them; instead she twisted off one of her arms, and held it in her other hand for extra reach; she made a few attempts to grab at a fossil, her fingers only managing to scrape away some shortcake crumbs.

'I try again,' she giggled embarrassed. 'Get it next time,' she promised.

Dolly stretched with the disembodied arm. Wafer crackled under her feet.

'Nearly, *nearly*.' Her fingers brushed the ruby red biscuit. Dolly concentrated on clenching her hand. 'Nearly. *Got it!*' She gripped onto a jutting bone. 'Oh, it's all stuck in the rock. Hold on.'

Lydia watched nervously as Dolly stood on tiptoes, the strata of wafer splitting beneath her; she clawed her fingertips around a piece of fossil sweet, wearing away the surrounding shortcake; then, once she'd got her hand around a strand of the bone, Dolly gave a sudden tug and, as she yanked the ruby out, the layers of wafer cracked under her weight; the entire floor of the cave gave way. Dolly fell into a gaping chasm, and Marzipan nearly went tumbling after. The other girls held on to her, and as Lydia took a peek over the ledge, she saw Dolly dangling by Marzi's arm, poised above a deep abyss with stalagmites below: spears of biscuit that would have run them through if the sisters had gone inside. It was jammy they dodged them.

'I'm all right though!' *Tho tho*—Dolly's voice echoed through the steamy chasm.

The sisters pulled her back to the ledge and, as she clambered onto sturdier ground, Dolly let go of this biscuit bone. Bits of ruby red dinosaur shortbread preserved in solid strawberry jam.

'Well *done*, Dolly,' Sugar said, picking up the fossilsweet and wrapping its bits in a serviette. She added it to the wonderful collection:

Diamond Sun Beans, *Sapphire Fizzweed*, *Amethysts*, *Pearl Drops*, and a *Jet Heart Truffle*.

The pockets of her sugar coat were truly a treasure trove. The sisterhood's hunt for the sweets was over. Now they had to find a way out of the caves.

For a while they faced the terrifying prospect that, after all their efforts, they might never get out. Be

trapped for ever underground. Stuck there like dinosaur bones in the rock. The children wandered from cavern to cavern and, wherever they could, they climbed through the biscuit, back up through millions of years of layers.

At times, the gaps in the rock were too tight to squeeze through, so Jawbreaker set about gnawing at the cookie walls—sometimes hard-baked, sometimes soft-baked, sometimes she had to bite at thick biscuit pillars—And each time the obstacle cookies crumbled before the might of her teeth.

Their progress, though, was slow and tiring, and one sister suffered most from the heat. Lolly suddenly slumped against a wall, her icy powers wilting fast.

'Feel poorly,' she mumbled.

The girls looked on anxiously as Lolly leant against the biscuit, perspiration dripping from her body, *drip drop drip* from the tips of her hair; the ice maiden was literally thawing thinning melting before their eyes.

'Do you have any Coola Cubes to give to her, Sugar Cube?' Hazel asked.

'They won't be strong enough,' Sugar feared. 'But—we do have something.'

From one of her pockets, she took out a capsule containing a pair of purple crystals. The Chilly Jelly Amethysts.

'The treasure-shweets, Shugz?' Jawji said.

'But what if Lady Hisska needs more than one?'

mentioned Marsha. 'We can't go all the way back to Froza for seconds.'

'Lolly could die,' Sugar whispered.

Ice Lolly's skin appeared almost transparent; it was painful for Lydia to see the light blue veins showing through her glassy face.

'Shooga—' Coco unzipped her handbag, and took out a handful of crystal sweets she herself had intended to keep; the beautiful Froza jewels glittered in the torchlight. A Chilly Jelly Amethyst lay among them. 'Here, Lol, here,' Coco grinned, giving up the purple sweet.

'Thank you, Coco,' Sugar said, and she fed the amethyst to Lolly.

The poor girl barely had the strength to break it between her teeth but, as she swallowed its jelly centre, the treasure-sweet soon took effect; for Lolly the chills were most invigorating. Her body regained its substance, and her hair froze in longer icicles.

'Are you better, Ice Lolly?' Coffee Creme asked.

'Feel all ice and froozy inside,' she smiled.

Lolly stood up with renewed energy. Her eyes glowed blue too, and she literally radiated cold, an icy aura that refreshed the girls, and left the biscuit frosted behind them.

The children set off again and, after a while, they could feel that the cookie rock wasn't so much crispy, as silty underfoot; their torches illuminated puddles of tea on the tunnel floor.

'Reckon we've gone through half the isle,' said Zye. 'We must be near the shore.'

'Oo, we *must* be,' added Hazel. 'I can feel a sea breeze.'

The children trudged on, through sips and dips of ankle-deep tea, and soon they stumbled into a flooded cave from where they could see the night-time sky. They waded through to these cookie nooks on drier inclines higher up.

It was safe and quiet in the cave, a pleasant place to stay the night. The girls drank handfuls of the herbal tea that rippled unsweetened shallow below them; they filled their water bottles with it too. Then they finished off their food, and lay down to rest in the biscuit nooks.

Although it had been another tiring day, Lydia found it hard to get settled; she got up and made her way along the rock (careful not to slip into the pool of tea); then she sat at the mouth of the cave, peering out across the sea, feeling the volcanic air warm upon her face. Lydia was aware there was one more journey yet to be made. There, across the moonlit water.

Their final destination. The lands of Tangiya.

'A'right, Toff?' came a low voice. A voice with an oddly friendly tone. Lydia turned, a little startled to find two cold red eyes staring at her. It was Bull's-Eye, with her pupils glinting in the moonlight. 'What you gawpin' at now?' she whispered.

'T-Tangiya,' Lydia replied. 'I mean, I think it's over there.'

'Yeah. It's there, Toff. In the day, I can see all the way to the trees on the shore.' Bull's-Eye gazed out, far into the sky. Lydia thought she could see the stars reflected in those target eyes. 'I use to come to these caves a lot,' added Zye.

'By yourself?' Lydia said. It was strange to be speaking with Bull's-Eye like this.

'Always bin by myself,' she mumbled. 'Din't go home some nights. No one told *me* what to do.'

'You had no daddy, did you?'

'Prob'ly left Mum and me when he found out I was an animal, I dunno.'

'Oh. My daddy left my mummy too. And *my* mummy was lovely,' Lydia said sadly.

'Here, Toffee.' From her tunic pocket, Bull's-Eye took out a marble sweet and slapped it into Lydia's hand. 'You said you like these. They were my mum's faves, as well.'

'*Thanks*, Zye.' Lydia took the sweet and popped it into her mouth.

'I can spare it,' Bull's-Eye shrugged.

While she savoured the minty marble, Lydia gave an enormous yawn.

'I'd try get some sleep, Toff. Probably hours till sun up.' Bull's-Eye turned away and went back to her place in the cave.

Lydia did the same; climbing to her cookie bunk, she

Jam Sandwich

put her head on her knapsack pillow, and closed her tired eyes.

The next thing she knew she was woken up by raucous squawks. Lydia blinked from the sun-bright cave; the shadows of seabirds glided past, and she could hear the washy *closh* of tea tides outside.

A little later, after eating their power-sweets, the girls left the cave of tea and biscuits, emerging on the south-west shore of Kukido. Above them were cliffs and flaky caves, the nesting holes for a colony of lemon puffins. Lydia watched the small lean seabirds plummet into the coastal waters to catch a bite of kipperfish found around these isles. The wind that whistled down the cliffs whiffed of seafood with lemon sauce: the saucy smell from bright yellow guano, puffin poop drizzled across the biscuit rocks.

Now the sisters had to cross the Sea of Tea to reach Tangiya. To find Lady Hisska and deliver the treasure-sweets.

They sauntered down to a cookie dough beach where they squelched through puddles of lemon tea, waves of it rolling rolling in like liquid rolling pins.

'Where do we go now, Coffee?' Marshmallow asked.

'A snake is meant to arrive,' the teenager replied. 'To take us to a secret boat.'

Chapter 28
Banana Split

As the children strolled along the dough, Jawji told them about the seaside confections she'd often find on the coast back home. 'The norf Winelands have these cold mudgy beaches, an' shell-vidge shweets are always washin' up on shore.'

She mentioned scallops filled with sushi mousse. Hard-rock cockles and gummy mussels. Jelly-brunch clams, and julep oysters with peppermint pearls inside.

And so the sisters scoured the shore, looking to collect some seafood treats.

Coco was more interested in starting a dough ball fight, lobbing soft clumps of sand at everyone, then skipping away quick so they couldn't hit her back. Bull's-Eye, though, pelted her with little smarting pellets of dough, and Coco pouted and called her a cheato and declared: 'We no want to play no more.'

Further up the shore, the sisters saw a lemon puffin

p-p-picking, p-p-pecking at some food it had caught; the seabird flapped away when they approached, and Lydia noticed it had left behind a funny finny fish of a kind: a plate-like skate-like pancake ray.

Peppermint used her fiery powers to heat up and crispen the flat slab of fish, then Jawbreaker sprinkled it with lemon tea, and Coffee took her sword and cut it into portions. The children snacked on the pancake fillet. *Hmm*, the ray was toasty tasty, and the lemon water gave its flesh a fragrant and refreshing zest.

After that appetizing bite, the girls dispersed across the shore, searching rock pools, puddles, and crumby sand for any other edibles washed-up on the land.

'Oo, look what I've found!' Hazel posed, holding a beautiful climpet shell. 'I bet it'll make a lovely brooch. I do.'

'Are there any more?' asked Dolly. 'I'd like a jewellery shell.'

'Ya supposed to eat them not *wear* them,' Bull's-Eye teased. 'Silly girly jewellery.'

They also saw scores of these round red creatures, the size of saucers, scurrying on sets of little clacky legs.

'Candy crust crabs,' Bull's-Eye said, and she bolted right into the mass of them, stamping her hoof to smash some of the shells, hopping away from nipping pincers, and chasing the creatures as they scattered to the sea.

'Stop that, Zye!' Marsha cried. 'That's *horrible*.'

'Stay starved then,' argued Bull's-Eye. 'I'm havin' crab cake for *my* breakfast.'

Jawji and Bull's-Eye gathered up the shattered crustaceans, sharing out the pieces with the others. They handed round claws and carapace cases, Jawbreaker cracking them open with her teeth, and spitting the bits of shell across the shore.

'Don't do that, Jawji, thank you,' Hazel asked politely.

'Shorry, Haze,' Jawji replied, and to please her fussy friend, she got out her spork and used that instead, bodging out the soft flossy flesh of the crabs.

Dolly sniffed at a clawful of the pink floss. 'Eee, is this *fishy*? Oo, nice taste though.'

Even Sugar ate the crab's meat paste, finding it filled with essential sucrose.

'Here, Toff,' offered Bull's-Eye, 'd'ya wanna bitta candy crab?'

'No, she *doesn't*, Zye,' Marsha snapped, giving Lydia a disapproving look. 'We don't want food you trod on.'

But when Marshmallow wasn't looking, Lydia nabbed some fragments of crab. 'Thank, Zye,' she whispered, and pocketed the broken bits and pieces, picking out and tasting the crab's unusual raspberry flesh, and gnawing at the saccharide shell, as well.

It wasn't long after, that Sugar detected a tracker-snake; Coffee's handy blackberry locked in on its signal too. Before they moved off, though, the girls washed their sticky hands in the warm lemon breakers tickling along the shore.

367

'I wonder if we'll see the liquor-neck monster,' said Dolly. 'It's supposed to be in the sea around here.'

'What is zis licky-nicky monster, Doll?' Coco asked.

'It's just some mythical sea reptile,' Sugar scoffed. 'It doesn't really exist.'

'Every silly thing exists in Dolly's dippy head,' said Hazel.

'Well, the liquor-neck monster,' Dolly Mixture enlightened them: 'It's got a long black neck, a dragon's body, and an octopus tail. It's ever so funny.'

'Why's it called a "lick-a-neck munchter"?' Jawji asked her.

'*Erm*,' Dolly pondered a moment. 'Cuz—cuz only sailors drunk on *liquor* ever see it.'

'I would have thought, if it's black, it's made of liquorice,' Lydia suggested.

'What a loada rot, Toff,' Bull's-Eye laughed.

'So what is *zat* then?' Coco pointed out to them. 'Zat sea monster way out there?'

Bull's-Eye stared at a shellfish shape heaving into view around the biscuit coast. 'Another stinkin' lobster,' she said with dread. 'Carryin' robots with guns.'

Lydia thought she saw something too, the glint of a metal bird high in the sky.

'The snake signal is this direction,' Coffee indicated to them.

'Let's get *out* of here then,' said Hazel. 'What are we waiting for? Fast as we can.'

368

The children dashed up the cookie dough beach, and soon they could hear the shaking of a rattlesnake—
Chok-a-bikki. Chok-a-bikki.

Then a kind of scissor noise—
Sliv-a-snick-a, sliv-a-snick.

The sounds of knifing wings in the air.

Lydia saw two electric spy-hawks swoop and swipe this cocoa-speckled tracker-snake; the serpent had to self-destruct, shrivel up to wipe its data. The pair of hawks then chirruped to each other in their irritating fax-like talk; then they flew above the sisters, their screeching affecting Sugar's senses, making her stop start restart stumble. Coffee Creme had to carry her along.

As she ran, Lydia tug-tugged the toffee tin from out of her knapsack; then she got hold of her liquorice sticks and, with an angry *ratta-tatta-tat*, she battered one of the metal birds silent. The other hawk then soared away. The girls could only turn and watch as it sliced across the coast to alert the patrolling lobster craft.

Lydia glanced across the sea. Tangiya had seemed so near, so wonderfully touchable, but now she wasn't sure if she'd ever reach it. The lobster craft floated sideways in, closer and closer, its oarlike claws propelling it through the waves of tea. And standing along its open-top carapace were two rows of eight artillery robots.

'Shooty troops!' Ice Lolly cried.

The children fled towards the cliffs. *There!* A nearby biscuit cave. The robots started firing their guns.

Nutshell bullet shots hit the shore behind the girls.

They darted inside the cave to find it was narrow and shallow and led nowhere. Too late to find another shelter. The robot troops were now in range, their aim focused on the cave. In desperation, the girls ducked down. Nut-shots blasted all around. Lydia was petrified as gunfire lines peppered and peppered the biscuit walls. Hazel Whirl burst into tears, recalling her scary experience in BonBon. Round after round of deadly nutshells drilled into the cookie cliff, hammered away the edge of the cave, shattered biscuit bits pattering down.

After this long sustained burst of bullets, the robot soldiers' firing stopped.

Bull's-Eye dared to take a look. 'The lobster boat's comin' ashore,' she told them.

There was no escape for the sisters now. Trapped inside the biscuit cave. Not even Coffee Creme's cherry grenades would be much good against a squad of armed robots. In a minute, the soldiers would have them surrounded. Programmed to shoot. To shoot to kill.

Suddenly, the children heard an explosion, and a great big spout of tea cascaded across the shore; they peeked around the mouth of the cave to see the lobster shell half-sunk, its cargo of tin can soldiers defunct, cooking in a fire of their own oily fuel.

Coffee Creme scrambled from the crumbling cave. The rest of the sisters followed her out, their shoes crunching over cookie chips and nutshells. Lydia peered around the shore and, some way away from the flaming lobster, something some*one* staggered from the sea:

A tall brawny man, clad head-to-toe in a peel of caramel, emerging through the waves of lemon tea. His face was hidden by a half-an-orange mask, and a liquorice-black torpedo was strapped to his back. Of course, the peel was really a wetsuit, and the liquorice torpedo, a scuba unit. In one hand, the man held a kooky harpoon too, that looked like an ice lolly stuck on a trigger stick.

Coffee and the others rushed down the beach to greet him. 'Popka!' Coffee cried. 'You save us!' She threw her arms around his waist, and nearly knocked the poor fellow back into the sea.

'Wicked the way you cook that lobster,' Bull's-Eye grinned at the caramel man.

'This can fire rocket-lollies underwater,' he replied, showing Zye the harpoon weapon.

'Who *is* this, Coffee?' Marsha asked.

'This is *Popka*,' Coffee smiled. 'Father.'

'That's my real daddy?' Lydia realized.

The man removed his mask and headgear and, for the very first time, she saw his face: his toffee-tanned features, his tousled hair flopping back from his head. He looked a little older than Lydia had imagined—probably because of his silver-grey hair, and stubbly salt-and-pepper beard. 'My name is Alazandr,' he said to the girls. 'I am, indeed, Lattay's father. And—' There were tears in his eyes. From the underwater dive? Or the emotion of seeing his daughter, perhaps? '—I'm also the father of every one of you.'

Sugar stared, almost mute with wonderment. 'You're Bo-a-Karam?' she mouthed.

The sisters, however, had no time to question him; a poison-eyed spy-hawk still hovered near.

'We have to hurry away from here,' Alazandr said. 'I've a boat all ready. In Layakayk bay.'

He led the children around the coast to where Kukido was closest to the isle of Layakayk.

Layakayk lay across a narrow channel (the LemonChar Strait), and Lydia expected to see a cake-walkway or a table bridge, perhaps, spanning the strait. But no. The girls arrived at a place where a promontory of rock had long-since collapsed, and the pillars of cake had weathered down to form a row of hard flat stones reaching from isle to isle; these slippy-looking stepping scones were maybe a metre or two in diameter, with steaming tea pouring in between.

Coffee jumped lightly across the scones to a bank of porous sponge cake opposite. She beckoned the rest of the sisters after her.

Peppermint easily leapt across, typically jittery quick to the bank. Then Coco, then Jawji, then Bull's-Eye joined her. Dolly followed clumsily, then Lolly and Marzi, before it was Lydia's turn to hop across the whopper scones. She went hesitant at first, skip-a-bit, jump-a-bit, braving the spray of hot tea waves and steam wafting up in her eyes. Lydia had to be very care-ful as the stones were smooth and wet with tea; if she slipped and fell, she'd suffer more than an embarrassing bump on the bum—she risked drowning in a swirl of boiling water. One scone at a time. She hopped and stopped. The last jump was the longest of all, and Lydia made a final lunge, stumbling to the other side and scrabbling ashore.

Marsha sprang after her, then Sugar hopped across, and climbed the sponge to safety. Hazel tried to skip effortlessly, classically, one scone to the other, but she skidded a little on the last stepping scone and almost fell into the deep hot tea. Hazel gratefully landed on the edge of the shore, leaving Alazandr to cross last of all.

The girls then followed him across a beach of gooey cake mix, towards the nearest seaside houses. The inner isle of Layakayk was a prison for the people now. And so the coastal villages were deserted. The sisters passed these cupcake cottages in brownie-brick and marble cake; there were ice-cream parlours with arctic roll pillars, teacake rooms, and pretty little choux shops. Lydia also saw a lighthouse, a towering ornate cake stand structure with a sugar-encrusted doughnut mirror for sending beacon beams out to sea.

Beyond the cottages, they came to a basin bay, carved from pink and white layers of cakey clay. Rows of pleasure boats used to be moored there, but now the basin was filled with broken crockery, bobbing clinking against each other. 'What're those bits of cups floating in the water?' asked Marsha.

'They're mug-boats,' Alazandr said. 'Stannic must have had them destroyed. So no one could escape.'

Hidden amidst the broken boats, in the shadow of the layer cake wharf, the girls now saw a huge fibreglass canoe glimmering yellow in the dark green water: a banana-shaped speedboat, equipped with a power-packed kettle-engine, and tins of assorted supplies.

Alazandr stepped down the layers of cake; he got into the canoe, and put the kettle on. The banana's engine started trembling, bubbling and boiling with charging energy; the sisters jostled aboard with their bags.

Coffee *clicked* the kettle switch. And *Slish sloosh!* They were off with a *whoosh!* The sisters sank back as the speedy canoe *ba-na-na na-na*ed across the bay, splitting the flotsam crockery mugs and making a trail, a milky way through the tea-green tides.

Alazandr steered the canoe full speed, leaving Layakayk far behind.

'So where we goin' now?' called Jawji.

'To Tangiya,' Alazandr replied. 'To see the lady you know as Hisska.'

Hisska. *Elixa.* Lydia smiled to herself. I wonder what she *looks* like? Was she really some old grizzled witch as Dolly had supposed?

While Alazandr changed out of his wetsuit top, Coffee took control of the boat. The man unpeeled the caramel coat and, before he put on a khaki jacket, Lydia could see these burns across his back, like a constellation of rusty stars sparkling bronze on his toffee skin; these marks reminded Lydia of Morella's brands, and she was tempted to ask about them.

'How did—when did you get those starry scars?'

The other girls were looking now, and Alazandr folded back his jacket to show them.

'I got these marks a long time ago,' he said. 'Twenty years ago. And it was the closest I've ever come to death. Three of these great metal insect creatures attacked me in the jungle. I killed them all with cherry grenades, but one got too near and, as I turned, the hot sparks sizzled across my back. Left me scarred for life.'

'Great metal insects?' Marsha asked. 'The Tin Man's robots were in the jungle, way back then?'

'These creatures were nothing to do with the Tin Man,' Alazandr replied. 'They were vicious organic metal creations. Half-living machines made by someone even more vile than Stannic. A woman called Kafeena. A sorceress from Mokachino.'

'If father hadn't escaped,' added Coffee, 'not one of us would have been born.'

The banana motorboat roared across the Sea of Tea, the children enjoying the rush of the journey, fresh air combing through their hair.

For the first time, they could feel triumphant, having escaped the Tin Man's Candi-Lands.

They also steered clear of Pepper's home, Mentha, the largest island of an archipelago gleaming like turquoise gems in the distance. Soon, across the sheeny green seascape, Lydia looked upon a beautiful coastline lined with trees, swaying palms with spearmint leaves, decorating the horizon as far as she could see.

The coast of Mixakoko. Tangiya.

Daddy will be taking us to Karamesh, she thought. The secret toffee-kitchen of Karamesh. A place only he knows how to find.

The children's speedboat neared Tangiya, skirting speckled cocoa powder beaches, and cutting across the cream tea tides *doosa doosa* along the shore.

'Would you believe?' Alazandr said. 'I never got a chance to ask. My main concern was to get you out of Candi safe. I never asked how you got on with our task.'

'All six treasure-sweets,' Sugar Cube smiled. 'I have them safe in my pockets.'

'*I* found some of them, Caramel Daddy,' piped up Dolly.

'We *all* found them,' Marsha added.

'What do we need the sweets for, father?' asked Marzi.

'We believe there may be a way to defeat the Tin Man Stannic. And those sweets will be the vital ingredients of a dessert that could finish him for good.'

'Good,' said Bull's-Eye. 'Stinkin' Stannic.'

Chapter 29
Cocoa

The sun shone bright in a milky blue sky and, though it was cooler at Mixakoko than on the volcanic isles of Baykari, it got hotter as the day wore on, and everyone grew thirsty. Alazandr opened a supply tin, producing a small bouquet of flowers with petals like strips of white chewing gum; he tore off a couple of petals for himself; then he handed the flowers round to each of his girls.

'Here you are,' he said. 'Hydro-Gum.'

Lydia chewed a petal of the strange gummy flower; it really made a splash in the mouth, and was as good as a long drink of mineral water; the minty petals helped cool Ice Lolly too, and proved as good as a popsicle for her.

Alazandr now told Coffee to steer the canoe across to an estuary; and so they passed the cocoa beaches, and sailed between the tall green trees, along a creamy soda river, into the Tangi rainforest.

The forest was dense with vegetation, all in emeralds, yellows, and reds; a floral kingdom, generous and various, lush with flowers and shrubs and ferns, exuding delicious confectionery aromas.

'Look at all these wonder plants!' Marzipan wowed, seeing these exotic trees she'd only ever read about. The girl had become a lot leafier too, growing an extra layer of attire that took on the reds and greens of the forest. Even Marzi herself was surprised; she had never been dressed so colourful.

Lydia was also enchanted by this place. It seemed, to her, to be a place before time. An eternal realm, from where arose the roots of all her sweet desire.

Animal sounds could be heard on all sides, the *co-co* calls of capuchino monkeys; a branch-snap of birds and their *wazzo wazzo, orio lorio, sip-sip chipper chirrups* and *caws*. Lydia glimpsed some of them: yackety parroty fruit cockatiels, a cocoa-crest toucan, fan-tailed fricasee, a nectar quetzal, and many other shy birds, high birds with paradise plumes in lavish hues. Butterflies flitted past with bright tint wings and, across the river, along the banks, was a sweet 'n' savoury variety of insects: chicori-cicadas, fruit flies, and ladybirds all in a candy box of colours. The sisters were delighted at the sights of other wildlife too, their trip a virtual river safari: up in the trees were ginger sloths and kola bears, peach-gobbler monkeys, and nouga-cougar cats; down on the ground were candy anteaters, mint-tailed tapirs, honey badgers, and prickly pearcupines. They even passed by a hippopotatomus, a large river mammal with a lumpy spud-like snout.

Alazandr's motorboat sped them on, deeper into the luxurious forest, the soda river threading through the tangle of Tangi trees. Hours they travelled, steadily, patiently, breathing the heady drippy air.

Occasionally, within the forest, Lydia noticed sites and settlements: traditional biscuit- and nut-stone buildings, many of which were sugarloaf huts topped with domes of crinkly walnut; other structures were larger staggered ziggurats panelled in amber, ultramarine, and chocolate brown.

Alazandr told his daughters some of the villages' names: '*Munchu Lunchu, Nacho Peachu, Bownti Barra, Olja Maika. Pica Nica, Torti Chiipu, Leema Buttabeena, Bitta Jujuba.*'

The people of Mixakoko were dedicated farmers and cooks, and each of these places contained its own candy-kitchen, producing sweets and chocolates, desserts and confections from all the natural riches here.

It was getting quite late, and still the sisters sailed on, chewing the last of the Hydro-Gum. At one place, this quiet river widened to a lake with clear soda waters and banks of roasted cocoa slate; there, in the twilight, Lydia saw a jaguar lapping at the water's edge, its beautiful toffee fur with crushed-nut spots. Coffee steered the banana canoe across the lake along a new tributary, a narrower river that weaved through even denser bushier forest.

Lydia started to sniff toffee now. She could taste its pure aroma in the air: tangy, sweet and buttery, with a hint of mint—*minty toffee?* Was her nose playing sniffy tricks? 'Mmm.' She felt a little lightheaded. '*Karammmesh,*' Lydia whispered to herself, as the toffee scents intensified. She looked all about her, but there was no village anywhere to be seen.

The banana canoe continued through the darkening Mixakoko forest; eventually Alazandr turned off the engine, and the speedboat eased up and drifted slowly on the soda current; next the sisters had to bat their way past a 'curtain' of liquorice creepers trailing down across the water. And beyond the liquorice, the river stopped. Suddenly stopped at a dead end block of caramel rock. Lydia tried to peer above the block of rock, yet all she could see was a mass of indistinct trees and sky. Lower down, however, just visible in the soda water, were three of these large glassy cubes of 'ice'.

Alazandr took a silver flask, a spherical flask the size of a grapefruit; he unscrewed the two halves, to reveal its segments, one of which flipped up as a spout.

'A little drink-key,' he said with a wink.

But Alazandr didn't drink anything at all; instead, he poured lime juice onto the ice cubes. He then flipped up another two spouts, and poured two more liquids, one after the other, as if he were mixing a cocktail.

'It's . . . er . . . one dash of *lime*,' Alazandr murmured to himself, 'two drops of lemon pop and a splash of pineapple—on the rocks.'

Now, where there had been a crack in the caramel block, a portal slid back revealing a tunnel.

'Down the hatch,' Alazandr said, and after a moment, a current of water pulled the canoe through into the dark; then the portal moved back behind them.

A faint orange glow began to blossom above the boat, and Lydia and the others could see that they were drifting across a pool inside a circular chamber. The canoe came to rest against a cream stone ledge, at a place with an arched door. Alazandr climbed from the boat, then he helped his children out.

All of them made their way through the arch, the sisters' footsteps *click-a-clack* across the stone, away from the chamber, into the unknown.

Through the door was a plain smooth passageway, again lit by an orange-blossom glow. This corridor took them further inside the rock and, after a while, the way was blocked by a large bronze plate that Alazandr unlocked with a key-spoon.

He slid back the plate, and led the girls into a large square room, a dining-room with a wide round table lit by snack-o-lantern lamps.

This room reminded Lydia of Uncle Terri's underground lodge; it was also decorated with hieroglyphs and symbols, but instead of wood carvings, the walls were full of intricate cocoa bean-and-peanut mosaics roasted into the stone. The mosaics covered these cubbyhole cupboards filled with supplies and fridges and food stores.

'We don't have too far to go now,' Alazandr assured the children. 'But we'll have something to eat here, and carry on in the morning.'

He unrolled a dozen bean bag futons kept ready in one of the cubbyholes; then he laid them around the round table, so the sisters could get some rest. As each of his daughters flopped down on a futon, Alazandr fetched them cool frappé juices, and a supper of assorted native treats: chocolate-enrobed nuts, and cocoa-buttered pumpkin bread, and slices of tropical fruit to eat.

While the girls tucked in to their scrumptious supper, their father went to use an adjoining bathroom; he came back washed and shaved, and smelling all minty in a fresh safari outfit.

Next, Alazandr fetched a dozen bronze goblets shaped like conch shells, and he placed one each in front of the girls. Then he brought out these thermos pots, and went around the table, serving the children, filling their goblets with liquid chocolate; this was no ordinary watery drink, though. It was pure '*crio-yo-cocoa*' and, as it gently poured from the pots, the liquid spilled thickly into the goblets, topped off with a delightful froth.

For Ice Lolly, there was cocoa ice-cream and, after Alazandr had dished it out, Lolly (shy Lolly, who for years had lived with a horrible step-dad) surprised the man by grabbing his sleeve, and resting her head against his arm. 'I love you, Popsi,' uttered Lolly.

And so the girls enjoyed their cocoa, lounging on the futons in the snack-o-lantern light.

Lydia breathed in the chocolate bouquet, put the goblet to her lips, sipped a bit, and let the 'crio-yo' drink swoon around her mouth; she closed her eyes and savoured the taste, a taste slightly toasty and earthy, yet moussy smooth in the same warm mouthful.

Coco, meanwhile, thirstily *gulp-slurped*, *gulp-slurped* her goblet of the gourmet chocolate.

'Steady *on*, Suzette,' Alazandr told her. (He didn't know the sisters' code names.)

'Oh, Cocoa-Butter's a proper choco-hoco-licker,' Dolly Mixture said.

Alazandr went back to the cupboards, and fetched a pear-shaped pepper-grinder.

'Why don't one or two of you try *this*?' he said. 'It goes very well with cocoa.'

'What is it, father?' Marzi asked.

'It's served at special ceremonies.' Alazandr filled a fresh bronze conch from another pot of crio-yo-cocoa. Then he held the pepper-grinder just above the goblet and turned the handle; red and green crystals sprinkled down into the drink. 'Its name is *chilli-kayana*. Candi-Landers call it sweet chilli pepper. But it's *hot*,' he warned. 'So sip it.'

'Silly to call something's that hot *chilly*,' said Hazel.

'It's a different kind of chilli,' Sugar told her.

'I drink chicory chilli-drink all the time,' mentioned Coffee. 'It is nice.'

'Nice like ice tea?' asked Dolly.

'Sugar's already said it ain't that kind of chilly, Dippy,' added Bull's-Eye.

As he passed the goblet among them, Lydia noticed Alazandr smirking at the sisters' daft chat. When it was her turn to try the chilli-chocolate, she took the heavy bronze conch from his hands, uttered a thank-you, and took a satisfying sip of this sweet yet zingy gingery drink. Alazandr glugged hot cocoa straight from the pot; he finished off the lot, exhaled a long sharp breath, and wiped away a chocolate moustache.

'Don't drink from the bottle, Daddy!' Hazel scolded, as though she told him off all the time.

Lydia did think it weird hearing the others calling Alazandr '*Daddy*'. But then this situation was so bizarre. She'd already heard extraordinary things about her new father. And now, with a chance to observe him closer, Lydia could see he did have a certain magnetism and charisma: his chiselled yet chocolate-boxy looks, his eyes of sparkling wine. Alazandr had a deep commanding voice as well, with an accent that she couldn't quite place.

Where was he from originally? Lydia wondered. Tangiya? Candi? Some other even more remote neverland? This man who had appeared from nowhere. Alazandr *alakazam*. Suddenly arrived in his daughters' lives.

It was truly the weirdest of family reunions. Lydia now saw the others in a new light. It took some sinking in to think they were all related to each other.

Sugar Cube and Ice Lolly, for starters. They were actually sisters? And Jawji and Hazel were certainly unlikely siblings. Then there was town-loving Coco and country-living Marzipan. Marsha from Delisha, Pepper from Mentha.

And Dolly Mixture—

Bull's-Eye just realized: 'Ah *no*,' she groaned. 'I'm Dippy's sister!'

'You're all half-sisters,' Alazandr reminded them.

'You have to invite me round for tea now, Zye,' Dolly giggled. 'Oh, what's your real name?'

'You don't know each others' names?' Alazandr asked.

'Sugar thought it be best to have code names,' Marshmallow explained to him.

And so the sisters told each other their proper names:

Hazel was Shelley Janduya, of course.

Ice Lolly's name was Liise Cassata.

Dolly was Candice; Jawbreaker, Donna.

Marzipan was Alma-da Miniegg.

Coco's name was Suzette Éclair.

Sugar Cube was Gluca Kristell.

Bull's-Eye's name was Dinah Blade.

Marshmallow was Sophie Münch.

Peppermint jotted down her proper name too:

'*Katti Kendl*' she wrote on her wafer.

All of them, though, found their sweetie-titles easier to remember, and Lydia didn't mind being 'Toffee'. It suited her.

The sisters also had plenty of questions to ask their new-found father. They jogged his arms, and chirped in his ears:

'Daddy? Why din't you stay with Mummy?

Father? How come we are all the same age?

Daddy? Why are we from different bits of Candi-Land?

Dad? 'Ow is it we grew to be weirdos?

Daddy-daddy? Can we have some more cocoa, please?'

And as for the important answers: it all revolved around twelve tins of toffee. Golden tins of Karamesh toffee.

'It was about eleven years ago,' Alazandr began, 'when a certain sweet society gained power in Likrishka.'

'They were the ones with the plates and knives, weren't they?' said Lydia.

'The Knights of the Crossed-Knives, that's right. And their leader was a famous Master Chef. An enchanted man, created by Kafeena.'

'Who *is* this Kafeena person?' Marshmallow asked.

'Kafeena was the daughter of Queen Espressa of Mokachino,' replied Alazandr. 'Espressa was a wise and gifted healer. But Kafeena grew up to be even more amazing: never before in one young mind had such a knowledge of chemistry, biology, bakery, and sorcery so ingeniously mixed. And it was, oh, over *thirty years* ago now, when Kafeena was barely a teenager: a Candi-Land man visited the palace, a novice chef who'd travelled to Tangiya seeking cookery knowledge and confectionery secrets. Kafeena made him drink an experimental potion; at first, it turned his tongue to tin, gave him a perfect sense of taste. Then this organic metal spread through his body, till he became a man of living tin with armoured skin that makes him virtually immortal.'

'*Stannic*,' said Lydia. 'I always wondered how he got that way.'

'Stannic was a name Kafeena gave him. It means *tinny* or *metallic* in Tangi-language.'

'All this toil and trouble,' said Hazel, 'because of that horrid saucy-person.'

'Now, the woman you know as Hisska,' continued Alazandr, 'is my eldest daughter Elixa. She's a very talented kitchen-witch—'

'Told you she was a witch!' Dolly interrupted.

'For a long time now, Elixa has planned to stop Kafeena and her sinister associates from regaining power in Mokachino. I should explain first that, from a very young age, Kafeena was drawn towards a magical confection cult that arose in the orchards of Jamatarta. This accursed Order, called the Jampyra, threatened to spread through the whole of Tangiya. Queen Espressa lost her life to them, and in her daughter Kafeena they had a powerful royal ally. I can hardly begin to tell you of the Jampyra's vile ways; their powers derive from preserves and liqueurs and the blood of the innocent.'

'Morella was taken by them when she was little,' Lydia said to her spellbound sisters. 'You know those marks on her face? The Jam-people burned her. And Daddy saved her.'

'That was the night,' Alazandr whispered, 'when I got those scars on my back.'

'What were those metal creatures you killed again?' Jawbreaker asked him.

'They were giant mantids, thin quick sharp-limbed things. Kafeena created them as guards for her palace. Well, on this particular night, all those years ago, the entire Jampyra Order congealed at the palace for one of their bloodthirsty initiation ceremonies. I led a group that attacked them. Few escaped the devastation. On both sides. Many good friends of mine died, but we managed to destroy Kafeena's kitchens and laboratories, and the creature machines she was growing there. It ripped the heart out of their organization, though we couldn't wipe out the Jampyra completely.'

'What happened to Kafeena?' Sugar Cube asked.

'She disappeared,' Alazandr replied. 'A council of Mokachini chefs has ruled in her place ever since. I was able to rescue both Elixa and Morella from the palace that night. Morella, you know, now lives in Delisha. Elixa stayed here in Mixakoko and, as I said, she vowed to stop the Jampyra should they ever return. One of her ideas was to bring a number of gifted powerful children into the world. So, using all of her cooking expertise, Elixa made one special batch of toffee. Toffee with rare

spices—which I hunted down for her—and, dare I say it? The toffee was enriched with drops of her very blood.'

The sisters responded with winces and '*eees*' and '*urhs*'.

'*I* had my part to play in this too.' Alazandr shrugged and smiled boyishly. 'Well, what can I say? Elixa's toffee would work most potent on an unborn child. And during my lifetime, on my travels, I've had many lady friends. So, over a period of a year or so, I travelled around Candi. Rekindling friendships, relationships, and affairs of the heart.'

As Lydia had said before, it was all very 'adulty':

It turned out that eleven young women across the Candi-Lands had succumbed to her father's charms. And all had had his children. Children mutated by Elixa's toffee, tins of which he bestowed as gifts to be eaten by the mothers-to-be during their pregnancies.

The first woman was a scientist from the isle of Layakayk. There were mothers on Mentha and Krustikob too. Then mainland Nooga and Delisha; he knew four women in those two lands, one of whom moved to Froza. There was also a single mother in the Winelands who abandoned her child and left her with a sideshow. Alazandr even travelled as far afield as Franjipan. And, on his return, he stayed in Likrishka, visiting his wife Mari. She was already a toffee lover, so he left one of the special tins with her, telling her to eat the confectionery should she ever be with child.

(Lydia remembered this golden tin; her mother used it to keep 'private recipes' in.)

'One thing Elixa didn't realize,' Alazandr said, 'was how strong the influence of your mothers would be. Their favourite sweet cravings worked their own magic, along with the toffee, giving you all unique abilities. And maybe because of one ingredient or another, you all turned out to be baby girls. A sisterhood to help her against Kafeena. And against the Tin Man, of course, whose own empire grows day by day.'

Coco was a little confused. 'But we never have a father,' she said to Alazandr. 'We have two mother who love each other.'

'Your mothers conceived you with my help,' he explained. 'By certain *artificial* means.'

'You said there were twelve tins of toffee,' said Sugar. 'But you asked me to find *ten* other sisters.'

'One golden tin was left unused,' Alazandr replied. 'I must have stashed it away somewhere—Yes, Gluca, you're right. That slipped my mind for years.'

So it turned out that toffee was the source of *all* their powers.

They were all Elixa's half-sisters. Toffee-sisters of Karamesh.

'I hope you can forgive me, my dear sweet daughters,' Alazandr said. 'I never wanted to hurt anyone, and it pained me to leave your lovely mothers. Elixa and I felt we could change the future for the better. And with Stannic's machines now eating away at the world, the

time was right. You were old enough to help. And when we needed those six ingredients—Who better to do this special task than our very own sweet-sisterhood?'

Sugar got up off her bean bag bed and, button by button, she popped open her pockets and placed the treasure-sweets on the table.

'My my, you *clever* girls,' Alazandr said, looking upon the rare confections. 'We were right to trust you with this task.'

The sisters settled down for the night.

Alazandr dimmed the snack-o-lantern light and they slept around the dining table, curled up on the futons. Always the last to fall asleep, Lydia noticed Alazandr stayed awake, watching over his dozen daughters, wistfully remembering all their mothers, his 'lovers and sweethearts' from a decade ago.

Hours later, the children rose in the dining-room silence and, after breakfast, Alazandr led them, through more plain passageways, to another chamber door. A large gold plate. Standing between the girls and their final destination.

Alazandr opened the combination lock. Lydia's heart was beating fast as the golden shield slid back into the wall, letting in a stream of spearmint daylight.

'Dear daughters,' Alazandr bowed to the sisters. 'Welcome home to Karamesh.'

Chapter 30
Toffee

Lydia was the first to wander out into the light, minty light with a brightness and radiance she'd never witnessed before. And, of course, the air all around was delicious with the scent of toffee. Toffee flooding her dizzy senses as she saw a wondrous village before her, sprouting from the amber earth. Karamesh. A place of crystalline buildings with sugar-glass domes, spears and spires and other exotic petal structures, their glittery treacle-glazed surfaces reflecting the clear azure of the sky. Lydia had literally stepped out from a cliff, a concave cliff of caramac rock protecting the village on one side, while the other side was ringed by trees and, just beyond that, a wide soda river.

Alazandr led the sisters out, across a toffee-paved terrace, towards sunlit gardens encircling the village. All around were the sounds of birds, mingling musically in singsong chorus.

To Lydia, it all seemed dreamlike, everything seen through an ultra-fine mist.

'See *there?*' Alazandr said, pointing out a cactus-like tower with spikes that spouted out a shimmering essence. 'Glassy-mint gas is sent into the air. Makes Karamesh invisible from the outside. Impossible to find.'

'Why do you want to keep this lovely place a secret?' asked Marsha.

'Well, if *I* lived here,' Hazel Whirl told her, 'I'd want to keep it for myself. I would.'

'It is not *quite* like that with us here,' said Coffee. 'This secret site was agreed many years ago, by leaders of Mixakoko.'

'Karamesh is kept hush-hush for all sorts of reasons,' Alazandr added. 'And all those involved, in the building of it, had to drink this dazy-dazy juice and agree under hypnotic trance to keep the location secret. So there are hundreds of Mixakokans out there who know where Karamesh is; but they don't know they know, if you know what I mean.'

'I know what you mean, Daddy,' nodded Dolly. 'I don't know where it is either. And I'm standing right here.'

'It was rebuilt especially in honour of Elixa,' Coffee said.

'That's right,' Alazandr smiled. 'The project wouldn't have been possible without her; this whole area of forest was veiled in glassy gas from the very

beginning. A special minty essence that she created. It perplexes, confuses one's sense of perception.'

The sisters were well aware of its effectiveness; one bottle of glassy essence sprayed on their truck had got them safely through the occupied Winelands.

'Wasn't Elixa a little girl when she came to Tangiya?' asked Lydia. 'She was a wonderful toffee-chef even then?'

'Elixa possesses extraordinary abilities. Her arrival in Mixakoko was quite an event.'

The sisters strolled these flowery lawns, then sat upon some benches; a cooler-trolley awaited them there, complete with fruit smoothies in long glass flutes.

Coffee Creme, meanwhile, left to see her mother; she soon returned, accompanied by a woman in an orange sarong; she had milky coffee skin and swirls of purple hair pinned with stripy swizzle-sticks; she also cradled a baby in her arms.

'This is Karandi,' Alazandr said to the girls. 'My wife here in Karamesh.' Karandi smiled at them, and cooed to her baby (a boy she called Harico, who was Alazandr's only son).

Once the sisters had finished their drinks, Alazandr took them back towards the village; their roundabout route through the blossom-filled gardens offered a glimpse of the wonderful food being grown in the lush grounds around Karamesh: compact fields of nuts and sweets laid out like patchwork chocolate quilts.

There were allsort allotments, cocoa groves, and

medicinal gardens with potion ingredients, herbal reme-
dies, roots and mints and allergy chews. Lydia noticed a
network of brooks, of clear spring soda streams running
between the sweet-plant plots. She saw people there
too, of all ages, tending the precious shrubs, planting
bulbs or pulling roots, scything cereal crops, or laying
leaves and herbs on trays.

Karamesh had a large village population. A privileged community of farmers and physicians, of healers,
nutritionists, chefs and herbalists. Many of the villagers
had different skins: some had the dark chocolate colour
of cocoa, others had the lighter colour of coffee; there
were even some with the blue tint of spearmint. More
people could be seen in and around the village itself, as
the sisters went past the glassy buildings, the clusters of
houses that seemed to merge amber and caramel melt
in the mint-hazed sun.

Upon reaching a pineapple dome, right at the centre
of Karamesh, Alazandr led his daughters through a
revolving door to an air-conditioned hall; from there, a
complex of corridors branched out to various spacious
interiors, all dreamily lit by filtered sunlight. The people
that the sisters passed on the way scrutinized them
curiously, unused to seeing strangers.

'Everybody's *looking* at us,' whispered Dolly.

'They know who you are. How special you are,'
Alazandr said.

They soon arrived at a large computer suite with
technicians at consoles and keyboards and touch

screens. The place, however, looked more like an aquarium full of liquid crystal pools and bowls; electric-linked tanks with plasma shoals, eely processors intermingling, squirming shimmering fishy circuits, shifting tails and filament fins, sometimes jellified sometimes liquefied, their X-ray layers swimming with data and calculations in constantly changing connections and formations.

The rippling jelly-electric light cast patterns across the sisters' faces. Lydia imagined this was what it might feel like to stand inside a giant brain; seeing ideas and moods and memories forming and flowing around a mind. And Sugar Cube: her digital eyes gorged on the sight of all this technology.

'Karamesh contains the most scientifically-advanced systems in all the world,' Alazandr said. 'The site makes great use of solar power. And recycled energies. We're pretty self-sufficient here.'

The children also saw an area where dozens of snakes slithered in and out of tubes: chequered tracker-serpents in assorted colours designed to spy around different terrains. 'And how do the snakes work?' Sugar asked. 'What powers them?'

'Their spines are flexile processors containing concentrated sucronium,' Alazandr told his has-to-know-it-all daughter. 'That can keep them going months at a time.'

He spoke briefly to one of the technicians next and, before Alazandr left, he ushered the girls into a viewing suite, a sort of mini cinema, with cushy seats.

Coffee Creme switched on a monitor screen filling the entire wall before them. A fluctuating fractal picture appeared. A picture that quickly settled to show the inside of a cube, about the size of a tennis court, made of digitized sugar-glass. This 'cyber-cube' was filled wall-to-wall with oven doors. Glowing hotplates patterned the floor. Plates and ovens, ovens and plates serving up course after course of cakes: sliding cakes, flying cakes, rising, floating, diving cakes. Myriad desserts launching fast from all sides.

And, moving in the midst of this barrage of cake, the sisters saw a figure clad in green-and-black snakeskins; a tall woman with a vivid bronze face, and thick black bands of liquorice hair tied behind her head.

'Lady Hisska,' Marsha whispered. '*Must* be.'

She was far from their image of a grizzled old witch hunched over a cauldron and cackling to serpents. Elixa was a strong athletic woman of thirty years. And, as wave after wave of these cakes attacked her, Elixa struck them, every single one of them, chopped them out of the air with a knife. A cake knife with a long glassy blade. The way the cakes disappeared when they were cut, told Lydia they had to be computer-generated. Still, it was the kookiest computer game she'd ever seen. Elixa stood her ground, in the centre of the cube, cutting down this pudding bombardment, deleting dessert after dessert.

'This game seems awfully dangerous,' said Hazel.

'I can't look! That cake's going to hit her!' squealed Dolly scrunching her eyes shut.

'They only holographic image,' Coffee reassured them. 'Nothing is real. Anyway this is very highest level. Elixa is a cake-cutter who is level Scorchy-Hot.'

On the screen, the girls continued to watch the action in the cyber-cube.

More and more digital desserts appeared, shooting out of the oven walls or floating up from the umpteen hotplates, moving ever quicker and quicker, spiralling around Elixa.

'What happens if she gets a pie in the mush?' Jawji asked.

'The computer tally up penalty points any time a person get hit by a cake,' Coffee replied. 'But Elixa rarely makes mistake.'

The cyber-cube cooked up challenge after challenge; cakes of all sizes, speed, and formation: lime pies sliding sideways from the sugar-walls; souflés rising quickly from the glowing floor. There were hover-tarts on spinning plates; double doughnuts in figures of eight squirting out beams of virtual jam. There were treble-tiered layer cakes with candle flares. Lemon flans skimming past Elixa's ears. Roly-poly puddings as big as wagon wheels. Supersize pastries and curd-spurting turnovers. Holographic muffins and low-flying buns. Fast flipping flapjacks and hard-to-cut cupcakes. Yet Elixa dealt with whatever was dished up, swishing and flashing the glassy blade, cleaving cakes at an incredible pace, and eliminating them from the kitchen of play. And not one lash of jam nor slice of cake grazed Elixa's slinking form;

she swivelled and ducked and leapt and thrust. One cut effortlessly flowed into another as though the knife were a flimsy streamer.

Hazel admired Elixa's elegance as well as her extraordinary speed. 'She's *amazing.*'

'She was *my* sister first,' Lydia smiled.

('My sister first really,' Coffee whispered.)

'She must have practised all of her life,' said Marzipan.

After many minutes of precise intense cake-cutting, gasps from the girls and hands over mouths, the game came to a halt. Elixa's cyber-cube session had been the most magnificent gymnastic performance they had ever seen. Coffee switched off the screen, and went to inform her of the children's arrival.

Within minutes, Elixa was at the door of the viewing suite. Her snakeskin suit shimmered in the light, and she'd untied her hair so her liquorice locks fell loose in braids. The woman's deep green eyes took in the sight of the nine-year-old girls, these children she'd empowered with toffee and drops of her very own blood.

'*Elixa!*' cried Lydia. And she ran up and hugged her around her waist.

'May doos surs,' Elixa whispered to them. '*My sweet sisters.*'

The girls were taken for a tour of the toffee-kitchens; silently, respectfully, they walked the curving corridors, eventually reaching a busy workplace: colossal kitchens

with old-fashioned worktops, gleaming clean bronze machines, overhead fans and curly pipes; the place looked like some metallic garden, paved with paths of enamel tile, with shelves full of flowery utensils, orchid whisks, and petalled spoons that seemed to grow from the polished bronze pots, vats, and pans, bowls and basins all filled with a sweet confectionery nectar. *Toffee*. Its delicious bouquet filled Lydia with euphoria. The fresh invigorating sugary aroma '*Mmmmmmmm*mm'. For the rest of the sisters also, there was something miraculous about this place. Toffee was a part of all their lives. It spiced the blood. Suffused the senses.

The kitchens were tended by a team of chefs, women wearing golden smocks, black-and-orange snakeskin aprons, and dark brown hats that looked like large chocolate cupcakes plumped upon their heads.

'The toffee is all by skilled hand,' Elixa said. 'And the site of Karamesh is close to rich toffee seams. We also grow select supply of spices.'

The female chefs took cool drum bowls and stirred ingredients into pure hot liquid toffee. Then the bowls were placed in cradle-like devices that poured luscious folds of the syrupy confection evenly onto trays.

As the chefs prepared the glorious toffee, they'd come and go, to and fro, holding pans and level trays, wending their way around counters and tables, expertly swerving this way and that, hula-hooping their hips and shimmying along in such a funny fashion it gave the girls the giggles.

Next, they followed Elixa and Coffee to a room where the toffee was left to solidify. Assistants with little hammers then broke it into glistening nuggets, to be scooped and wrapped and tinned and shipped.

'Where does all the toffee *go*?' Lydia enquired.

'Most goes overseas,' Elixa replied. 'Smuggled to lands far beyond. There are many countries across the world with toffee connoisseurs. Their custom is essential to us. As you see, our activity is also scientific, cooking up new confectionery technology.'

'Can you do anything about the Tin Man's robots?' Marsha asked.

'We think we have developed a way to overcome their programming.'

'Special wavelength signal serpents,' elaborated Coffee. 'We soon to release hundreds of thousands to—how you say—jam scramble the robots' brains.'

'That is after we have shut down Stannic's headquarters,' explained Elixa. 'And *that* we will. One way or another.'

'Oo, where is his heady-quarters?' Cocoa-Butter asked.

'A fudge factory,' Elixa replied. 'At Burnville, in Likrishka.'

The sisters were shown to their own delightful living suites and, for the next few days, they enjoyed the comforts of a home-sweet-home that some of them had

never known. Karamesh seemed more of a sweetshop or playground than a busy secret base. Some of the children could be found running around in the cyber-cube, trying the many recipe-programs: for instance, the cube could become a bowling alley or shooting gallery, one where Bull's-Eye showed off her ability, hitting pop-up skittles and sweetie sprites, indeed everything the cyber-cube conjured up. Being in Karamesh brought out a nicer side to Zye, laughing at comical jelly targets or coming-to-munch-you-up monster pies.

Naturally, Lydia spent her time in the kitchens. As honorary toffee apprentice, she donned a snaky apron and a cupcake cap. While the other women chefs were mixing, whisking, adding ingredients and laying out trays, Lydia was called upon to offer her opinions; treated as an expert taster, she danced around the tables, sipping liquid toffee from bronze teaspoons:

'Mmm's delicious. Needs a bit more liquorice. Too buttery. Not buttery enough. Oo's that got, erm, persimmon? I like this one.'

Lydia did feel a bit cheeky telling all these toffee-chefs what to do, but her sweet-taste skills and sensitive toffee-nose were very much admired here. She even helped Elixa mix a batch of her very own tangy confection; of course, she had to wait a day while the toffee was properly cooked and cooled. Then it was packed in a brand new tin.

Elixa prepared her special toffee for the rest of the sisterhood too; it would serve to replace their power-

sweets. Now the girls really *were* like Lydia's sisters. Each with a tin of their own potent toffee.

For the fourth evening of their stay in Karamesh, Elixa organized a village celebration. And once the spearmint light of day had given way to the lantern light of night, then the party could begin.

Outside, in the toffee-scented air, the people sat around a grassy arena. The children were entertained by music and games, kaleidoscopic holograms, and dancing piñata-puppets. (The glassy mint mist surrounding Karamesh suppressed and distorted sound as well, so the joyful festivities would be as the chatter of birds to the outside world.)

Finally, after supper, the grown-ups brought gifts for the village children: blood red goodie bags, tied with green ribbons, containing pastries and trinket sweets: bread roll skulls with icing eyeballs, candy bones, crystal fruit hearts, and little liquorice skeletons.

'These sweets are very gruesome, they *are*,' Hazel said to Elixa.

'Oh *no*, Shelley,' she replied. 'Not meant to be gruesome at all. Like life and blood and bone and soul. As love and death are a part of life. In Tangiya, tis custom to share these sweets and bread. Pay respect to our ancestral dead.'

Also among the confection gifts were tiles of toffee, three for each child. These tiles had been made using various moulds embossed with Tangi designs of old:

Pictures of hearts and skulls and eyes; of flora and fauna, cake-swords and fruit knives, toffee hammers and ladle spoons, soda drops, flames, and suns and moons. The toffee came in assorted flavours, from pale lemon tiles through pure amber and strawberry reds, to chocolatey browns and liquorice blacks.

Elixa explained that long ago such toffee tiles were used for divination: ways of telling one's fortune, or revealing the secrets of their soul. 'The old Mixakokan word for toffee,' she said, 'is *kar-a-ma*. It flows like blood inside this land. Inside *us*, too. Gives us power and strength.'

Elixa told Lydia to dip into the goodie bag to see which three toffee tiles she had received, seemingly at random.

The first tile was liquorice-black, and embossed with the image of a jaguar with a snake's forked tongue.

'This is a picture of So-moki-Pantira,' Elixa told her.

'Did you say *Smokey*?' Lydia asked.

'*So*-moki. A sweet-tree spirit cat. Was said to keep watch over the cocoa groves.'

The second tile was a fudge-coloured skull.

'Does—does that mean *death*?' Lydia said.

'The image of a skull often represents the soulless body,' Elixa replied. 'Also loss. Even change and renewal. Many conflicting things to many different people.'

The third tile was a lightning cloud cast in amber toffee; a design, so Elixa explained, that stood for Rumblatatta-Thundaratl, a powerful spirit of the air.

She said nothing more and let Lydia take the tiles to eat. As she chewed the tasty toffee, Lydia felt those conflicting feelings, bittersweetness, hope and loss, memories of Mummy fresh in her mind. She looked up at Elixa with tears in her eyes.

'Oh, Lidaya,' her half-sister whispered. She reached over and held Lydia close to her. '*May doosa*, Lidaya.'

Chapter 31
Sultana

The next day, Elixa gathered the sisterhood to bid farewell to Alazandr. He was all prepared for a mission back in the Candi-Lands. He had packed his supply tins full of hunter's clothes and all-terrain kit, including one extra-chunky chocolate jacket, along with his confectionery weapons and gadgets: laser cutlery, spyglass spoon, glow straws, magnet gum, bonboms, and fire lighters. Plus a tub with all six treasure-sweets inside.

Elixa also scrunched a bag of sweets into his pocket.

'Glasseer mints, Popka,' she hissed.

Alazandr smiled, and kissed her on the cheek.

Then he received a hug from each of his younger daughters. In the short time they'd known him, the sisters had grown very fond of Daddy Alazandr. A genuine sweet-hunter. Secret agent. Jampyr fighter. Adventurer, explorer, hero all in one.

They watched him leave in a small amphibious

sports car, oval-domed and ladybird-like, a vehicle he could drive on land and navigate through water. Everything depended on Alazandr now. And on Celine Argenta, his second-eldest daughter.

'Father will get the ingredient sweets to our sister Celine in Likrishka,' said Elixa. 'Only she will be able to use them and serve them to the Tin Man Stannic.'

'Then we can all go home?' asked Hazel. 'Everything be back as it used to be?'

'I don't want to go home,' said Marsha. 'I want to stay here for ever.'

'*Ooh*, yes,' smiled Lydia. 'Please. Karamesh is the best place in the world.'

All the sisters nodded in agreement.

'Karamesh is a very busy place right now,' Elixa said. 'Many things to prepare, for when the Tin Man is defeated.'

'The swarm of signal scramble snakes, for one,' said Coffee Creme.

'Oo, can I help with those?' Sugar Cube asked.

'Thank you, Gluca. But we do have everything under control.' Elixa now turned to Coffee, and spoke to her in Tangi-language. Lydia could only understand words such as 'Lattay and taffee and Dairipan'. There was mention too of a 'Sultan Parmasham'.

Coffee nodded. 'Grassia ta, Elixa.' She smiled at the sisters, and told them the news. 'We are all to go stay at royal palace in Dairipan. I hear it is most full of beauty.'

'Ooh,' said Hazel. 'Beautiful.'

408

Their excursion began on the soda river that ran around the fertile 'isle' of Karamesh, and then out through the vast rainforest. They went in another huge banana-shaped canoe. Coffee and her eleven half-sisters. Along the winding soda rivers, sailing from Mixakoko to the westerly land of Dairipan.

The canoe was laden with the girls' tins of toffee, along with a hamper full of Karamesh treats, a goodwill gift for the Dairi ruler. The sisters all wore these newly-issued outfits: light white tops and toffee-tinted skirts, with chocolate-coloured hooded robes to put on later should it get cold. Sugar had to keep her white jacket to hand, with so many of her medicines packed inside.

The banana motorboat bubbled along, through the glittering glades of Tangiya; orange sunlight gleamed through the fruit trees. Smells of liquorice and cocoa wafted over them. Lydia saw other boats along the river, passing by; soda floats, trade boats, flowing by in the blink of an eye. The sisters travelled for most of the day, eventually leaving the forest behind; the soda river ran through caramel grasslands, before the landscape turned, indeed churned into hills, buttery hills and dips of cheese. It was what Lydia imagined the moon might be like. Hard dairy craters, cheddary gorges, and shores of soft white fromage sand.

It was evening by the time the sisters arrived at a harbour by a cheesy beach. They were pleased to see a very posh chariot waiting there: a motor-carriage with fat satin cushion seats, and a trailer carrying enormous tea bags, fuel to be brewed in the chariot's hot water tanks. Seated at the front was a middle-aged couple, a man and a woman, wearing long cream togas; the man was the royal driver Curd, tall and stern, he said very little; the woman was a lady-in-waiting called Flora; she too behaved very upright and formal, and even the blonde butter curls of her hair were wound in a tight double bun at the back. Curd helped Coffee with the sisters' belongings. Then they all left the canoe and hopped aboard the tea-powered chariot.

Off they went, heading for the Dairi palace. Lydia could hear the fuel stirring round the engine, and the chariot's exhaust spouts puffed out fragrant tea-flavoured steam.

They rode rough roads past bread-'n'-butter marshlands, crusty islands with huts of straw, water buffalo and yellow flamingoes. A handful of fisherfolk were out hunting late, with big fishing-forks and griddle sieves; gliding along in turtle-like kayaks, they scattered storks and pelicans that were out for their own fish supper, there in the moonlit marshes.

Curd drove the chariot around rice pudding paddi fields flooded in soy milk; they went through quiet night-time settlements, farms with porridge oat pastures and malt-houses.

'Dairipan is so cut off from everywhere,' said Coffee, 'it stay unchanged for hundreds of years.'

'Have you been here before then?' Marzipan asked.

'No no,' replied Coffee. 'This is treat for me too. For years, couriers from Karamesh have been made most welcome at the palace as guests. Our chefs made gourmet toffee for the ruler here: Sultan Parmasham. A shame, Elixa told me, we hear news he died some time ago. So we're here to deliver a gift to his daughter. The hamper of toffee tiles. A tribute to his kindness and patronage.'

'I bet his daughter's a gorgeous little princess,' Hazel said. 'I'll teach her to dance, and we'll be bestest of friends. And she'll shower me with flowers and sweets and presents.'

'Sultan's daughter is a *grown*-up,' Coffee smiled. 'Her name is Sultana Marjareen.'

'Funny been called a sultana,' said Jawji. 'That's what we call dried old raisins.'

Eventually the chariot approached a palace, right at the heart of Dairipan, isolated by rocky ravines; the place was an architectural marvel, all salt block towers, cracker-clad walls, and domes like colossal dollops of cream.

The chariot was met by attendants in flowing robes, carrying buttery oil-lamp bowls and, once the girls had been welcomed from the carriage, they were led through courtyards and soldier-guarded hallways, up to opulent guest suites.

The beds had headboards adorned with rams' horns, and were draped with creamy sheepskin blankets. A maid then poured these malted milkshakes for the children, and this helped them all get a good night's rest.

Late next morning, Flora woke the girls, and asked them to wash and dress for brunch; then they were led, in obedient procession, to be introduced to the sultana herself. As the sisters filed through the halls, Lydia noticed the decor on the walls: horns and antlers snapped from animals, cat skulls, and skimmed skins of cheesy cheetah fur.

The girls were shushed and ushered through into a dining-room where an old woman reclined on a lion-skin sofa behind a turtleshell-plated table; the rich sultana was in all her regalia: a filigree-sugar and tiger's eye tiara, with embroidered silken tablecloth robes.

Lydia wondered just how old her *father* had been, if this aged crone had just come to the throne. Sultana Marjareen's wrinkled skin was as pale and veined as mouldy blue cheese; her weedy white hair was pinned behind by cheetah-teeth, and she even wore spectacles

to protect her eyes; specs with round reflective lenses like two silver bottle tops wedged upon her nose.

Dolly Mixture began to giggle and, when Bull's-Eye asked what she was snickering at, she blurted the words '*Dried old raisin!*' making the other girls giggle as well.

The sultana grimaced at the sisters' laughter, and Lydia felt queasy seeing Marjareen's tea-stained teeth; she thought there was an unfortunate resemblance between 'her majesty' and Mater D: the way she was agitated by the children; the way in which she *nn* nibbled on a breadstick, and *click-click-click*ed her bony fingers to call her servants to her side: these muted maids who moved in mime, as though all talk was forbidden here.

Marjareen bottle-eyed her dozen young visitors. Lydia noticed a few of her sisters squirming uneasily, a bit self-conscious, aware they were quirky and kooky-looking.

The Karamesh hamper of toffee tiles was brought before the old sultana; Coffee now curtseyed and bowed politely, and presented this tribute to her late father Parmasham.

Marjareen dug out a clawful of the shiny toffee, gourmet gifts that no one surely could refuse. Lydia looked on disappointed as the woman simply sniffed at the tiles, then dropped them *clack-clack* back in the hamper, without a word of gratitude. Flora summoned a palace guard to take the hamper and lock it away. Then she whispered an apology to the sisters, telling Coffee that, unlike the sultan, Marjareen didn't like toffee at all.

Nevertheless, the misery-guts sultana allowed her dozen guests to join her for brunch, and the sisters were seated on milking stools around the turtle table.

To eat, there were snacks, such as cornbread crackers with buffalo-butter and stork-liver paté; to drink, there was orange squash (which none of the girls would even touch, once they found out it was pulped from jaguar guts). Their cutlery was grotesque too: knives were made of lions' incisors; sporks from the beaks of corn-flake crakes. The sultana used these chopstick tusks to *snip-snap* at cubes of raw marsh-sushi, or slurp up strips of slithery eel soused in sour vinegar sauce, all served in bowls resembling bird's nests.

Dolly decided brunch might be fun if she turned it into a tasting game. 'I eat with my little teeth,' she began, 'one of these cheesy wotsits—'

Marjareen hissed and glared at her, and Dolly shut up and looked embarrassed.

Flora told Coffee it may be best if the sisters left the palace for the rest of the day. Marjareen herself had no children, and she appreciated peace and solitude.

The royal dairy was nearby, and Coffee Creme was eager to see it. So, after brunch, Flora showed the children out, passing by these bare gravel gardens. Lydia had assumed that palace gardens would be full of lush lawns and ornamental trees.

'Sultana Marjareen no venta osseen,' Flora explained

in Tangi-tongue. 'Ella nasha hortica, sa mosa servi clova sill ti tray drajay.'

'Marjareen rarely goes outside,' Sugar translated for the others. 'And she doesn't like plants. That's why she had her servants cover all the soil in stone.'

So now the gardens were pebble-dashed patches where nothing grew. *Stoopid sultana*, Lydia thought. Gardens ought to have flowery flavours. But those stones made a crummy view.

Still, a few *oo-coo*ing birds had settled upon the palace walls, milk-white doves that Flora was sure to shoo. Marjareen didn't like wildlife either. Marjareen didn't like anyone, it seemed.

Curd was ordered to take the tea-chariot, and chauffeur the girls to the royal dairy, a short ride beyond the ravines. On the way, the children saw farmers sitting on butter carts pulled by scrawny yellow yaks with orange horns like curvy carrots. The yaks *clip-clopp*ed slow along the stony roads. Curd was an impatient driver, though, and he sounded a shrill whistle-horn, scaring the dairy yaks out of the way, and *brewm-brewm*ing loudly past.

The chariot took the children to the royal pastures. These fenced-off areas were posted with soldiers, men dressed like the palace guards (in plated tunics, tin bowl helmets, and holding cheese knife swords). Curd left the girls at a grand wooden gate, and one of these surly soldiers let them inside.

Beyond the gate were vast fields of nettles where a herd of cattle was allowed to roam. Large red-and-white

striped cows. Sleepy-looking, lowing lowly, milling around, all spindly legs and bulging bellies, feeding, chewing, digesting the nettles. The dairy air was sweetly whiffy with the cattle's chocolatey dung. These particular cows, so Coffee said, were a rare crossbreed, able to produce flavoured milkshakes, and clotted creams.

The sisters made their way through the fields, along a path of yellow slabs.

Dolly had some silly whim, detached her left leg and started flinging it in front of her, making it hop back in a zigzag across the path. '*Follow the butter brick road,*' she sang. '*Follow the yellow brick stones.*'

She balanced on one leg, chuck-a-leg, hop-a-long, followed the butter brick stones.

'What you playing, Dolly?' Lydia asked.

'Hopscotch butterscotch. Everyone can play.' And then she explained the rules: 'First, you pull your left leg off—'

'You silly dip, Doll,' Bull's-Eye laughed, shoving the one-legged girl off the path.

Dolly fell over 'hoops-a-dizzy' almost landing in a flat splat cowpat.

'Careful the cacao poops,' Lolly said, handing Dolly her leg, and helping her up.

At one point, the sisters had to wait, as cattle crossed the patta-butter path.

'Move, moo-moos!' Coco joked, shoving one of the stripy cows; but the hefty heifer couldn't be budged, and it flicked off Coco's beret with its tail.

Once the animals had lumbered by, the girls walked the path to see the milking parlours; there a kindly dairymaid let them try the luxury milkshakes, dipping these tasting cups into a range of brimming buckets.

The thick drinks tickled the sisters pink with their exhilarating fruity flavours, and they chatted about the shakes to each other with a positive gush of adjectives:

'*Mmm. Dreamy. Creamy. Scrummy. Yummy. Luscious. Shlushus. Oo too delicious.*'

The parlours were part of a large busy farmyard with barns and cattle sheds, motor-cartons and refrigerated urns. Farmhands shovelled up the rich manure (the chocolatey cowpats were prized as fertilizer); then they packed it onto automated trolley trucks in special air-tight plastic tubs.

Coffee had said that Dairipan had stayed unchanged for centuries. Yet this farm looked quite up-to-date, and some of the machinery reminded Lydia of the Tin Man's Candi-Land technology.

She'd also noticed, on the chariot ride, weird-looking scarecrows stuck in the fields: horrible metal tinny-bin men with limbs like huge butter knives, and milk bucket skulls with motion-seeking eyes, and sonic bird-scarer speakers for teeth.

Lydia was being silly. What did she expect? A rich royal dairy farm was bound to invest in the latest equipment. Still, something seemed amiss. Sultana Marjareen gave her the creeps.

Chapter 32
Popcorn

Next to the farm was a popcorn plantation, so the sisters nipped over the low wooden fences, and wandered around the cobs of corn, the swathes of cream-green maizey grass that almost reached their faces.

Peppermint snapped off a stalk, spat and lit the tip of corn, and let the kernels pop into her hands. She did the same for Lydia too, but as the hot popcorn leapt off the stalk, Lydia jumped back in surprise and only managed to catch a few seeds, most of them falling on the sandy soil.

'Butterfingers, Toffee!' laughed Ice Lolly.

'Me next! Me next!' Dolly Mixture called, and Pepper lit a stalk for all her sisters: some stalks were yellow and yielded butter-flavoured popcorn; others had orange caramel kernels, whilst some popped ready-salted blue.

Not far from the fields was a milk-like lake, and the

children sat upon the cream crumb shore, and crunched on tasty handfuls of popcorn. They could all relax and forget their worries for a while. Revel in the caramel warmth of the sun.

There was still a fair slice of time before the chariot was due to arrive, so the girls went to nose around this stack of huge cartons beside a nearby barn.

'Maybe there shum milkshakes in there,' said Jawji. 'Or yogutsh we can try.'

'Or fromage frai',' Hazel smiled. 'That'd be nice. It might.'

'Did you know you can get frog-leg yogurt?' Dolly told them. 'But, *erm*, I prefer cherry.'

These 'cartons', however, were made of metal and painted with a 'flame' and 'skull-and-cross bones' signs.

'There must be some burnable and poison substance in them,' warned Coffee.

'I bet it's pesticide gas,' said Marzi. 'To keep away the popcorn flies.'

'*Oww!*' Sugar suddenly cried; she yanked her goggles from her head, and complained of interference scratching across her digital eyes.

'What's the matter, Sugar?' Marsha asked concerned.

'Didja change ya sugar lumps, Shugz?' enquired Jawji. But Sugar could only choke in reply, her utterances coming in low dull crackles.

'You're going to have to do something about your voice box, Sugar,' Hazel said. 'It's really *really* giving me the jibjabs. It is.'

Sugar pulled out her hearing aids as painful signals thickened in her ears. Electrical tremors seemed to shiver through her limbs. Her eleven half-sisters looked on helpless.

'Oo, what happen to you?' asked Coco.

'I reckon it's those tinny-binny scarecrows,' said Lydia.

Sugar stumbled forward blindly, barely able to speak or hear. Coffee had to pick her up and carry her again. 'We get you help,' she said. 'Back to the palace.'

It was then that Lydia saw the cause of Sugar's ills. *'Poison-Eyes!'* she cried and pointed, and the others looked as electric spy-hawks rose from the popcorn fields all around: Stannic's thronging snitchy things flocking up on high; two dozen of the hawk birds packed in the sky. And as they hovered overhead, the birds began screeching their fax-like *tictac tinkring click-click* trills, before ceasing.

Where had they come from? Lydia thought. Must have already been lying in wait.

Soon came the sounds of a summoned drone that echoed across the fields and sky. Lydia remembered the same same buzzing noise over the Wineland farms, a noise that shuddered through the children as, upon the horizon, rising fast, were the pair of mosquito aircraft from BonBon; again the spy-hawks squawked and signalled, and the two enormous biplane insects closed in on the dairy farm.

The sisters scattered, and sought to hide. Where could they run to? Where could they run? They all shied away from the poison-eyes that called to the planes with alarming cries. They had never been so afraid for their lives. The girls cried, 'Hide!'

A few of them hid amidst the popcorn. Others went towards the farm for help.

Lydia fled to the edge of the lake, and cowered down in these cheesy reeds, daring to peep through a few of the stalks as the two mosquitoes rasped above her, diving like fighter planes, skimming the fields and scaring the cattle to random stampede. Lydia noticed, in place of the sleepy pop, each mosquito carried canisters of jam, gleaming red jars of raspberry fuel, enough for the flight from Nooga to Dairipan. The insect aircraft then landed on their lever-legs, twisting their articulated heads with sister-seeking compound eyes, and sharp steel proboscis stingers ready to run them through.

A terrifying fray ensued, and Lydia watched it all happen in a horror blur. Catching snatches of action and sound. Scaredy cattle rushing past. Smashing fences. Sisters squealing. Farmers fleeing. Animals bellowing. The activity set off the scarecrows too, their harsh robotic screams added to the rasp of the insect aircraft.

One of these mosquitoes homed in on Bull's-Eye as she darted through the popcorn fields. A swiping stinger almost decapitated her; Bull's-Eye flung herself out of the way, the proboscis caught and shattered one of her horns. Zye fell hard; she tried to limp away, at the mercy of the looming mosquito.

Suddenly Hazel Whirl leapt across and tugged Zye clear. The insect plane slashed at them fast, and Hazel twisted side-to-side, the stinger just just just missed spearing her. She couldn't outspin it for ever, however. The ground was rugged, and Hazel stumbled and tumbled to a dizzy halt. The mosquito jittered up to thrust its stinger through her—and it stopped as stones smashed bullet-hard into its head, blinding one of its compound eyes, and causing it to turn aside. Bull's-Eye had thrown the stones to save Hazel, and she only needed a second to leap to her feet and pirouette away from the 'half-blind' plane.

The electric hawks, meanwhile, circled the farmyard, and as Jawji and Dolly tried to hide inside a cattle shed, the birds screeched their coded screeches to give the girls away.

The second fearsome mosquito zoomed over and, using its lever claws, it ripped the ridged-crisp roof from the shed. Dolly screamed as the slats of timber were torn off *snak-snak-snak snak-snak-snak* just above her head. The mosquito then stabbed its steely proboscis to get at the pair of frightened girls. They scurried between the machines and fixtures, dashing from the exit while the insect got tangled up in pipes and equipment.

Jawbreaker scurried one way, while Dolly went another way, running in her clumsy fashion, clatter-foot across the yard. The spy-hawks spotted her.

All two dozen swooped. Their grasping talons set upon Dolly Mixture, whisking her high into the air.

From her lakeside hiding place, Lydia saw Dolly struggling and squealing while the electric birds climbed in the sky. For ghastly moments, time seemed to still. Dolly's squeals abruptly stopped as the hawks flew away in all directions, rending her candy body apart, and dropping the pieces across the farm. The birds then swarmed together again, flocking over the dairy fields, searching for the other girls.

The one-eyed mosquito followed the hawks, with a carton of pesticide tight in its claws; flying lopsided over the popcorn plantation, it punctured the carton releasing a green gas. Cocoa-Butter was crouching below; she took off her shades and blinked into the sky, as the toxic cloud sparkled down upon her; Coco breathed in a lungful of the gas. She sneezed '*Chu-chu-cho chocolut!*' then collapsed. The poison-eyed hawks came to claw her up, but Peppermint raced to her sister's aid; she attacked the birds with bitter cries, flame-thrower cries that fizzed through the pesticide.

Pepper roasted every one as the predatory hawks soared in low, her outburst setting alight the fields with a *crop-a-pop* cacophony of hot popping corn. The *cracker-snaps* crackled loud around the girls, prairie-wide waves of popcorn kernels popping off a million snacky stalks.

The mosquito grabbed another toxic carton, its aim to snuff out this destructive firebug. Peppermint waited till the plane was close, and she roared her powerful

acid fire to ignite the carton right there in its grasp. *Poppadoom!* The pesticide gas combusted, blasting the mosquito in two. Peppermint ducked as raspberry jam jars sprayed down on her, bloodily and hot. Even Lydia saw the fireball flash, as she dared to look from her place at the lake. The half-a-mosquito craft crashed to the ground, rasping splats of raspberry fuel pouring from its fuselage, leaving a stench of burning jam.

The second and last mosquito, though, still swept across the dairy fields, its claws ploughing up the soil, scraping around to find the girls. To hunt them down. To catch and kill them, one by one.

Lydia stared while this sunlit nightmare went on and on. But what could she do without her drum?

Unknown to her, though, Hazel and Lolly had got together and whispered a plan.

Lolly scampered through the fields of popping popcorn. Hazel then stood before the roofless cattle shed, waving her arms to attract the mosquito. The giant insect descended fast, its shadow bearing down on Hazel, six snapping claws ready to tear her up. As the mosquito swooped, Hazel used all her ballet skills, skipping bravely to evade its claws, spinning between them, then darting away. Beyond the farmyard, beyond the fields. Slow enough so that the plane could chase her.

Lydia watched as Hazel Whirl dashed towards the lake of milk, twirling around its shallow shore, kicking up the whitish water. The mosquito soared straight at her, stabbing through reeds, slashing its front claws,

thrashing ferocious with its stinging spear. Lydia lost sight of Hazel; she glanced around frantic, fearing the giant mosquito had caught her. Then, she noticed Ice Lolly wading out into the water.

Hazel had spun away across the shore, so the mosquito turned to stalk Lolly instead, jittering viciously towards her—just as Lolly froze the whole milk lake, turning it, and the half-dipped mosquito, into a block of ice-cream. (Lydia had to scramble back too, as the reeds beside her whitened with ice.)

The insect tried to free itself, split away from the icy mass; its body, however, was frosted fast; its fuel tanks clogged with raspberry ice-cream; legs and wings and tin canny abdomen fused inside the frozen lake. The mosquito gave out a last dying rasp, chilled and killed by Lolly's power.

Although the skirmish was over, and the hawks and two mosquitoes were dead, this victory felt hollow and sorrowful. Hazel Whirl sped away, back to the sultana's palace, while those girls still standing gathered to help their fallen sisters.

First, Lydia saw Marzipan emerge from hiding in the nettle fields; tears of sap seeped down her face, and Marzi had her arm tucked awkwardly inside her sleeve.

'You all right?' Lydia asked. 'Oh, *Marzi*. Does it *hurt*?'

Marzi had shown Lydia her arm which was now a broken stump. She'd been caught up in the cattle stampede, bumped about and knocked to the ground. And though she'd turned herself to wood, her arm was crushed by a stamping hoof.

'I'm sorry, Marzi,' Lydia said.

'I was fortunate,' Marzi uttered. 'It was Marsha who saved me from worse.'

Marzi led Lydia back through the field, and there was Marshmallow lying unmoving in a patch of flattened nettles.

'Marsha protect me,' Marzi explained. 'She got in the way of the cattle.'

For once, Marshmallow looked seriously hurt, heavy heifer hoof-marks all along her body. A herd of cows had thumped across her back, trampling her flat, and even through her ultra-thick skin, Marsha's mallow bones were battered and bruised.

As gently as she could, Lydia turned the poor girl over; Marshmallow felt horribly limp and tender.

'*Oooh*,' Marsha groaned. 'I feel all mushy mellow inside.'

'Shush, Marsha, shush,' Lydia tried to comfort her. 'Hazel has gone to get help.'

The sisters checked on Peppermint next. Pepper whimpered in pain from raspberry burns on her hands and face. Bull's-Eye, meanwhile, kicked at the hawks she'd toasted dead, their frazzled batteries and circuit guts; and if any of the debris let out the slightest sizzle, Bull's-Eye stamped it into the dust.

Cocoa-Butter lay close to Pepper, dazed and sick from the toxic spray.

'Come on, Cokes,' said Jawji, helping her up.

'We unwell,' Coco mumbled. 'We ha' malady.'

And what of Ice Lolly, who had stopped the last mosquito?

The sisters went back to the milk-like lake to find Lolly still standing there; the effort of freezing the water so fast had caused an ice block to form around her. A block like a popsicle, or an ice-cream tombstone.

Bull's-Eye limped out onto the frozen lake and used her hoof to chip away the ice, so the others could dig out the popsicle block. Jawji then helped Lydia drag Lolly's body ashore. Sunlight glittered through the frosty block and Lolly looked like a levitating spook, stuck inside this popsicle cocoon, her arms by her side, her eyes closed, intense concentration frozen on her face.

'Is she—still *alive*?' asked Marzipan.

'Lolly will be all right,' said Lydia. 'She *has* to be.'

'She was like that when we first found her, though, wun't she?' mentioned Bull's-Eye. 'All froze in that hill of ice.'

'She was not as deep-freeze as this before,' said Marzi.

The sisters stood by Lolly's frozen form, as the afternoon sun began to melt the popsicle block from around her. But Lolly remained in a comatose state, and no one knew a way to wake her.

'*Shugz* would know what to do,' said Jawji.

Sugar Cube was in a bad way too. Coffee had carried her safe to a storage shed, and though the hawks were

all destroyed, their poison codes still shivered through Sugar as a 'wireless virus' corrupting her system. Whenever she tried to plug in her senses, painful interference needled her mind.

Hazel soon returned with help, running ahead of the royal tea-chariot. The five stricken sisters were laid out in the trailer and taken back to Marjareen's palace.

'What about Dolly?' Lydia asked. 'We have to find Dolly.'

'Doll's dead,' Bull's-Eye said.

'Oh, don't even *think* that, Zye,' Hazel told her. 'She—she might be all right.'

'Well, where is she then?' Bull's-Eye snapped. 'Why don't she call out or somethin'?'

The children looked at each other uncertain, having seen the sickening way the hawks had torn poor Dolly apart.

'Didja see where she was thrown?' asked Jawji.

The sisters peered about them, at the vast plantation.

'I will find her,' Marzi said calmly. 'I will search every part of the farm till I find her.'

Marzipan went into the nettle fields first, crouched down and spread her branchy limbs, using her one wooden hand as a pitchfork to rake through the nettles and gritty soil.

She soon retrieved a doll-like hand. Marzi called, and Hazel hurried over, taking the left hand back to the farmyard. 'Look!' said Hazel, as she put the hand upon the ground. One of the fingers clearly twitched.

With renewed hope, Marzi went back to her task. It took a long time for her to scour the fields, seeking the sections of her sister.

The others waited, not wanting to leave her; doing what they could to help, they scrabbled about on their hands and knees, between the stalks of crisp burnt popcorn, hoping to stumble upon any part of Dolly.

Every so often, Marzipan would stand up to say she'd uncovered some more of the body. Then another, and another piece, her stockinged feet, a leg or shoulder. She passed them to Hazel who twirled back and forth to place the parts on the stony farmyard. Gradually the children put Dolly together as though she were a grim jigsaw. Ever so carefully, Lydia fit the pieces in place, treating them like fragile china, assembling her shattered tea set of a sister.

As she wandered round, Bull's-Eye found a broken watch—Dolly's lolly-watch from Sweetie World; even tough-cookie Zye began to cry.

Marzi continued her solemn search, harvesting the pick-'n'-mix of Dolly's candy limbs. All afternoon she searched, then late into the evening. Coffee made a trip to the palace, to fetch the girls some food and drink, and bowls of buttery light.

Marzipan eventually retrieved the main piece of Dolly's body. This made Dolly whole again, except that is, for her disembodied head.

Lydia rested her ear against Dolly's chest, but she couldn't detect any heartbeat there. She didn't know if

this was usual or not; after all, Dolly's bloodless flesh was connected by solid candied bones and circulated by strange 'microwaves'.

At long last, after many hours of raking her fingers blindly in the dark, Marzipan found the missing head, and the sisters looked on hopefully as Dolly's eyelids flickered dreamily.

'*Please* be alive, Dolly,' Lydia whispered into her ear. 'We found all your pieces.'

'Dolly'll be fine,' Jawji said, mainly to reassure herself.

The chariot returned for the children, and Dolly's cold body, now complete, was laid out gently on the trailer tray. As the chariot rolled away, Lydia took a final look over the sorry moonlit scene: dairy farmers still rounded up the cows; the milkshake cattle calmer now, they *moo*ed and roamed the popcorn fields, feeding on the overcooked stalks. And the misty lake with the dead mosquito, the ice-cream surface crackling as it thawed.

Chapter 33
Milk Bottles

Late next morning, in one of the palace suites, Lydia, Jawji, Hazel, and Bull's-Eye stood by the beds of their afflicted sisters, five of whom lay critically ill. Coffee Creme and Flora soon joined them, accompanied by a doctor, Sultana Marjareen's personal physician.

He was a bald elderly man, in a milky coat which had something of an antiseptic, toadstool smell about it. Lydia watched as the doctor clumped about the room, stopping to use a magnifying spoon to nose at the seven bedridden sisters:

Marzipan and Peppermint were badly hurt, but their injuries weren't life-threatening. Lolly and Dolly, though, showed no change, lying unconscious in their frozen states. It was the conditions of the other three girls that were worsening; Marsha, all flat and bruised. Sugar so pale, twitching electrically, her vital signs worryingly low. And Coco so still, so ill from the pesticide,

her skin almost milky white; she was a most distressing sight.

Lydia wanted Cocoa-Butter back, back to her ghostly mischievous self; she wanted kindly cuddly Marshmallow to be well again; and Sugar back to the smartie-pants she so admired; and shy brave Ice Lolly, and silly giggly innocent Dolly.

'They *mustn't* die. They *must* stay alive.'

The doctor took just a scant glance at them, murmuring curdling words to himself; then he muttered something to Coffee which made her angry and a little upset. 'He said he will not treat these *freakish* foreign children,' Coffee Creme translated.

The doctor sneered at the girls as he went to go, and Lydia ran up and pushed and punched him:

'Well leave my sisters alone then!' she cried. 'Doctor Mouldy Toadstool!'

Flora had to intervene, and the old doctor stormed out at Lydia's tantrum.

'I will send word to Karamesh,' Coffee said, taking her blackberry and tapping in a message text. 'But even if they send someone, it will not be today. And maybe then, they cannot help.'

'What about some magical sweet?' asked Hazel. 'Lolly was saved before, by the chilly treasure jelly.'

'If only Shugz were well,' Jawbreaker said again. 'She'd know what to do.'

'Yeah,' said Bull's-Eye. 'Bet she knows more than that sultana's stupid doc.'

The sisters looked across at Sugar. She lay in her deep sleep-mode, battling a poison virus that threatened to shut down her nervous system. And all that intellect and learning was locked inside, with no way of accessing it.

Lydia thought and thought, and realized there may be a way to get through to her. She had to wake up Peppermint who was resting after her nasty burns; it broke Lydia's heart to look at Pepper, those raspberry ripple scars across her face. Lydia asked if she'd use her wafer to try to communicate with Sugar. Though she was most reluctant to disturb her, Lydia hoped there was something, some cure Sugar might know about, some reference, some myth filed away in her memory.

First, she put a hearing aid into one of Sugar's ears, and then she told Pepper to write on the note pad. 'Ask her, say: is there some special magical life-saving sweet we can find?'

Lydia watched the wafer screen as Pepper took her digital toothpick, wrote out the message and pressed 'transmit'. Nothing happened. For many moments.

'Oh, wake up, Sugar,' Lydia whispered. 'We *need* you, *please*.'

The words 'message received' suddenly appeared on Pepper's note pad, and Sugar Cube shivered conscious, wincing at the slightest sound that she heard as static crackling inside her head. Lydia went to her, held Sugar's hand; she could see that her sister was in great

discomfort, frowning and fidgeting as she chewed her thoughts slowly.

'Perish. Trees. Jam-a-tart-a,' Sugar uttered eventually, her voice sounding sickly and slurred. 'Now *please*, disconnect me.'

Straightaway Lydia unplugged the hearing aid; Sugar scrunched her eyes shut and 'crashed' back to sleep.

'Perish Trees, Jamatarta,' Lydia repeated. 'That's what Sugar said.'

Flora led the five girls through to a deserted part of the palace; the sultana's guards were absent here, and Flora took them along secluded servants' passageways, then down to a cellar that was out of bounds. The woman lit a carton lantern, and it shone around the cellar with a cool milky light; then she rolled back a rug revealing a trapdoor built into the cellar floor; Flora lifted the teaspoon latch, opened the trapdoor, and led the children down.

Coffee, Lydia, Jawji, Hazel, and Bull's-Eye all stepped after her, descending steep stone steps until they stood before a salt block wall. Flora pushed at one of the blocks, and part of the wall turned at an angle, making a narrow entrance into a darkened treasure chamber. Coffee translated the words Flora whispered to her:

'Marjareen had this chamber locked when her father died. But this is secret way in, that Sultan Parmasham trust Flora with.'

The treasure chamber was cavernous and cold, and its floor was tiled in alternate squares of polished white salt and crushed black peppercorns.

There were plinths with drinking vessels and animal sculptures in shiny onyx; sugar glass cabinets of rare mint coins, and calendar discs carved in tablet; the walls too were covered in colourful murals depicting Tangi flora and fauna, and along a long hallway, past sweet stores, armouries, and cases of jewellery, Flora showed the sisters these salt cellar libraries.

The girls were overwhelmed as they walked the clicky chequered floor, browsing the thousand and one bookcase crates, staring at shelves of illustrated labelled bottles, hundreds upon hundreds of milk bottles holding handwritten rice paper scrolls: collections of Dairi stories, the verses of the Milki bards, culinary tales, recipe fantasies, and sweet hunters' journals, preserved over centuries.

Flora spoke of the sultan's love of stories, and how he would read to the servants' children.

'Flora has been very sad since Parmasham died,' said Coffee Creme. '*He* was kind to all his people.'

'And he loved toffee, didn't he?' Lydia added.

Flora consulted a weighty calfskin-covered book, an index written in buttery ink; she perused its pages for any mention of '*Perish Trees*', and this index led her to a bottle from one of the dusty anthology crates; Flora read the label before ushering the sisters to a table; there she peeled back the foil bottle top, and poured out a sheaf of rolled up parchments: crisp rice papers, milk white papers containing pictures and maps and verse. The words were written in an old Dairi-dialect, similar to Tangi-tongue; and so Coffee and Flora sat and read the parchments by the milky lantern light.

'Isi, kin da,' whispered Flora. '*Confita te-resha. Erbora Perisha.*'

Coffee told her sisters the information they'd found in the bottle: 'These stories were recorded by sweetie hunters. Tales of a vale full of magical fruit. The hunters name them Perish Trees, or Orchard of Death and Eternal Breath.'

'So it's only a story though?' Hazel asked. 'Or a really real place where special sweeties grow?'

'These ancient stories of Jamatarta,' Coffee said. 'They go back hundreds of years or more. It say: *Beyond the spine of a sleeping salt giant, lies the vale of Perish Trees. An orchard where the soil bubbles, and rivers pour in the air.*'

'What does that mean, then?' said Jawji. 'We have to go find an old giant's garden?'

'No, no,' replied Coffee. 'See this map on this paper?'

Lydia and the others nosed at a picture drawn in strawberry ink: a map showing round trees beside a small mountain range.

'The spine of a salt giant,' Coffee explained, 'is . . . er, *poetic* for the Salta Mountains. And in the orchard, hunters took a few precious fruit. All had lovely marvel tastes and herbal properties. But one especial fruit: its

juice was found to cure all ailments. Heal all wounds and sickness and disease.'

'That's what *we* want,' Lydia said. 'Sugar must have read about it.'

'Here, it is mention,' Coffee continued. '*Panasaya taffaya pome. D-ura preykarp, rinda rose.* An all-healing apple tree of golden fruit with red toffee skin.'

'What's that animal drawn by the trees?' asked Lydia.

'Yes,' said Coffee gravely. 'The hunters tell of *drakona pomodo.* A dragon of the toffee-tree that cannot be killed. That same creature is recorded here many century later; a dragon of red toffee skin that must feed on the magic apples. Groups of sweet-hunters, many killed, torn limb from limb, as they escape with fallen fruit; this is how apples were found to be magical, when they tasted drops of the golden juice. Its peel is poison to people though. And the fruit was seedless, so no other trees could grow.'

Flora drew the girls' attention to a verse on the final roll of rice paper.

'There is written some strange warning,' Coffee translated: '*The dead grass will come alive, and many wooden serpents rise.*'

Before they left the treasure chamber, Flora took the children to the armoury, as they may need some weapons to defend themselves on their dangerous journey.

Sultan Parmasham had been a peaceful, cultured man, and the armaments here were mostly for show:

jewelled trinkets, foreign gifts, or ceremonial heirlooms. Coffee took her pick of the swords, a gold-handled scimitar with a curved diamond blade. The others seized some metal-tipped cocktail spears.

Then they went back up to the palace suites to tell Marzipan and Peppermint the news. A miraculous cure for all their ills could soon be in the children's hands. The two of them were determined to help, and together the seven sisters promised to find this healing toffee fruit for the five of their siblings critically ill. These apples may be their only hope.

Lydia picked up Sugar's jacket, rummaging through it for any marvellous medicines there; she found some Num-Nums and a few Slumber Bonbons; these might at least help her sisters sleep and take away any pain for a while. And Lydia came across something else, tucked away in one of Sugar's pockets. A simple paper bag of sweets that may help save *all* their lives . . .

She gave the Num-Nums and Bonbons to Flora who would tend to the girls while the others were away. Coffee also entrusted her blackberry device to her with instructions to send a message to Karamesh if they didn't return.

'And tell Flora not to let that mouldy doctor near them,' Lydia said to Coffee Creme.

The girls had intended to leave that very hour. However, the chariot driver Curd refused to go to Jamatarta, a land that he considered cursed.

Coffee explained their dilemma to Flora; the sisters needed speedy transport.

Flora summoned a maid, and sent her outside by the palace kitchens where there were hourly deliveries of food; the maid returned with a Dairy farmer, and Flora got him to lend Coffee his motor-cart, in exchange for the hamper from Karamesh. The farmer gladly accepted the toffee. And so, in secret, they stole the gourmet hamper from under the sultana's nose.

The children set off in the farmer's old motor-cart, with Coffee following a map Flora had provided.

The journey south-west to Jamatarta took a few hours, and the girls had a much-needed nap on the way; they rested on their fleecy blankets against some tubby baskets in the back of the cart.

Some time during the afternoon, Lydia was jolted awake to peer out over another new landscape. In truth, she saw it through tired eyes, through a sun-seared and dreamy mind. Hills and gorges 'all denty and blomonjy'. They had gone beyond the Dairi farmlands, its eggplant crops and maizey fields, pastures full of yog-goats and cream-coated sheep with their *maas baas* bleating. Now they crossed these butter-stone plains. Drippy-pan, the fat of the land. Puddles of rancid margarine *splutch-splutch*ed under the wheels of the cart, as Coffee drove them steadily along. The ride was often uncomfortable, bumpy, bum-numbing, hot and uncomfortable. The cart had a *jug-jug* churning engine, bubbling exhaust pipes,

and a saucepan fuel tank that sounded as if it had been filled with popcorn.

'Why couldn't we go in the nice posh chariot?' Hazel moaned to Coffee Creme.

'The driver Curd was afraid,' she replied.

'Cowardy custard Curd,' grumbled Bull's-Eye.

They popped past flour-beds and semolina reservoirs, passing through a parched cracked desert littered with tummy-rumbleweeds and patches of sparse cress grass. The sisters saw, in the middle of nowhere, a long-vacated café fort; a curly-horned dairy oryx snacking on a cactus, and cheddar condors perched on distant couscous rocks.

Late in the afternoon, the girls stopped to eat the food they'd brought. Up ahead now, across the desert, Lydia could see forbidding mountains, solid salt with spine-like peaks topped by a butterscotch mist.

While they ate, the seven sisters spoke of the possible dangers ahead, reminding Marzipan and Peppermint of the things Coffee had read. 'What was that you mention about the grass and serpents rising?' asked Marzi.

'The story said they were dead and wooden,' Lydia told her. 'But alive, as well.'

'I'm more bothered about the dragon,' said Bull's-Eye.

'How big's this dragon then, d'you fink?' asked Jawji. 'Big ash a tree or sumfin?'

'I doubt that,' said Marzipan. 'The Jamatarta woods were once home to the apple-green pomodo dragon;

they died out here long ago, though orange dragons are still found in Jarfa, and they grow to the size of Spyssi tigers.'

'This dragon red,' Coffee reminded them. 'It live on the toffee-apples. So the story said.'

'It sounds really really perilly,' said Hazel worry-worrily. '*I* can outrun anything, but what about the rest of you?'

Lydia reached into her pocket, and took out a paper bag of sweets; she kept a few of the sweets for herself, and pressed the rest into Bull's-Eye's grasp. 'See if you can use these, Zye. They're *jade snails* my big sister made. Sugar said there's this special spice in them that can paralyse people. Maybe they can put the dragon to sleep.'

'Yeah,' said Jawji. 'Zye can chuck 'em down the dragon's froat or sumfin.'

The sisters ended their makeshift meal with pieces of their special toffee; yet even the nourishing Karamesh confection couldn't stop certain nightmarish ingredients from stirring around their childish minds: thoughts of mysterious Jamatarta, a land of dragons and poison trees; of sorcery and eerie Jampyra.

Pepper was the only one who couldn't speak about her fears. She looked a sickly sorry sight, and with no Sugar to talk to, she'd become withdrawn again; her slender body huddled in her cloak, her humbug-eyes staring from the hidey-hood. Lydia thought Pepper was very courageous to come along.

Coffee took a few minutes to top up the cart with corn oil fuel, so it would be ready for their return.

Then she had to use all her strength to hand-crank hand-crank crank the engine. And once it was popping and churning again, the sisters set off to the Salta Mountains.

The afternoon light began to fade as the motor-cart took them through a mountain pass. The pass was rocky and the cart b-b-bumped across pits and potholes and salt-shake blocks. Coffee stopped, and the girls got off, before the cart tipped over.

'Now we hurry,' Coffee said. 'Get the fruit quick. It is start to get dark.'

'Don't forget a basket for the apples,' added Marzi, handing Lydia a tub from the cart.

They took their snails and spears and sword, and Coffee led her six half-sisters through the salty pass. The children emerged from the mountain to find a vale cradled in its mineral-rich slopes. This verdant vale was full of grassy mounds, each containing a single tree, mostly tall rounded trees bearing shiny fruit. Jampire bats hung from some of the boughs; nutcracker grackle crows *raak*ed from the branches.

Also across this weird orchard, Lydia heard a constant fizzing.

Once down the mountain slopes, the sisters found the ground slightly sludgy, pulsing underfoot with hot spring pop; the soil itself did seem alive—

Hoosh! Joosh! Frothy geysers sudden gushed.

Suddenly. Somewhere. Some way from the girls. The vale spurted with disconcerting fountains. Fountains of soda which fizzled away, leaving the air moist and tickly.

'*An orchard where the soil bubbles,*' Lydia said to herself. '*And rivers pour in the air.*'

The atmosphere here should have been refreshing, but instead it smelt mouldy dead; overripe fruit-sweets rotted on the trees, or fell and fermented into heaps of jammy compote that crawled with hornets or ugly banana slugs. The children screwed up their noses in disgust, shimmying between the trees and over mounds where they trod upon the bones and skulls of little animals. Scattered dragon-kill.

Lydia sniffed her way through the orchard, looking for the solitary toffee-apple tree. With the light so dim now, she needed all her hunter-skills. 'There's a definite scent,' she said, 'of *lovely* toffee in the middle of all the mouldy smells.'

Through the high twisted grass, Lydia led the rest of the sisters, jumping from mound to mound, trying not to slip on the ground. Over the unsettling steep drop bumps, passing trees of pungent fruit, pomegranates, custard pears, scrumpy apples, and frusty turnovers.

Who knew what magic fruits grew in this enchanted vale? Left every year to fall and decay? Untried and untasted. Who would now know the stories surrounding them, stored in bottles, and lost inside the sultan's cellars?

The girls continued, scanning for the fabled dragon

and, right in the midst of the vast shadowy orchard, Lydia sniffed out a tall yellow tree. And the tree bore small apples with glistening crimson shells.

'That's the toffee-tree,' Lydia whispered. 'I'm sure it is.'

'How are we going to get the apples?' asked Hazel.

'We could jusht hope the fruit drops off,' said Jawji.

'I ain't waitin' here in the dark,' said Bull's-Eye, peering round, 'with a dragon about.'

'I will pick the apples,' nodded Marzi. 'The rest of you can keep lookout.'

Marzipan went towards the tree; she stood at the bottom and made her body wooden; then she twined herself around the trunk, and began to creep up towards the magic apples.

Chapter 34
Apple Juice

It took Marzi a long time to climb the tall tree, and with only one hand to reach for the fruit, she twisted her broken stump into a crook to hook onto branches, and inch her way up. The rest of the sisters waited anxiously on a nearby hillocky bump; they stood in a circle gripping their spears, their backs against a custard pear tree. Coffee had her purse of emergency goodies with her, and though it was now getting murky in the vale, she dare not even light a candle, thinking it might attract the dragon. Bull's-Eye kept watch, with the bag of jade snails at hand. Indeed, all the girls blinked into the gloom, straining their eyes, staring through the orchard.

Still no sign of any dragon. And the constant *bu-bu-bubble* of the soil made it harder to listen out for it; the occasional spray of a geyser didn't help either, pushing *gushing* up without warning, sometimes near enough to make the girls jump.

Then. There. Bull's-Eye spied with her brittle eyes, something dragony—

A shape slipped swift through the twists of grass. The sisters' hearts were beating fast. Bull's-Eye's hand began to shake as she grabbed for a fondant snail from the bag.

Then. There. Lydia glimpsed it too. Around the mounds. A lizard slinked. This stealthy lizard, the size of a lion, with shiny crimson toffee-glazed scales.

The dragon disappeared from view.

'Where is it? Where is it?' Hazel fretted.

'Shut *up*, Haze!' Bull's-Eye snapped.

Suddenly the dragon pounced from the grass. The sisters squealed and leapt away to adjacent mounds. Apart from Coffee who advanced on the lizard with her scimitar drawn; the dragon lunged, she nimbly side-stepped and struck the sword across its neck—but the diamond blade glanced off the toffee glaze, not even scratching the dragon's skin.

The lizard hissed, then whipped around the pear tree, looking to attack again.

Peppermint tried to scare it away next, with an extra-strong minty blast of her breath, but the dragon ran right through the flame, sank its jaws into her side, and tore off one of her arms from her body. Pepper screamed in fiery pain. The lizard paused to swallow the middle limb, crunching on Pepper's flesh and bone.

Bull's-Eye now scampered up and slung the jade snails, aiming for the dragon's jaws, skimming the

sweets at its gaping mouth. One snail lodged between its teeth. The dragon snapped its red jaws shut, biting into the alcola-laced sweet.

The sisters watched in tense suspense. It took a little while for the snail to take effect. But the deadly lizard slowed and slowed. Then. There. The dragon remained. A toffee-glazed statue. Slithered to a standstill. Paralysed by Celine's jade snails.

Bull's-Eye fell to her knees with relief, having ended the dragon threat.

Or so she thought. A second lizard now sprang out behind her: the dragon's lifelong sterile mate. Jawji yelled, but her cry came too late. Bull's-Eye spun around, and before she could kick at the lizard with her hoof, it slashed its claws deep into her leg. Zye fell in agony, and the dragon rounded on its injured victim, to go for the jugular, to take a fatal bite. Lydia thumped on the bottom of the basket-tub to draw the dragon to her instead. The lizard turned, hissing nastily, and Lydia scattered the snails she had, right in front of the dragon's snout, almost as though she were 'feeding the ducks'. The dragon snapped a couple up. Gulped them down. Then it lunged at Lydia—only to stop and drop 'dead' at her feet.

Lydia peered at the pair of pomodo dragons, feeling a mixture of fear and awe.

'And they're hundreds of years old,' she wowed. 'Living on toffee-apples all this time? The fruit *must* be special and magical.'

The sisters couldn't see any more lizards. They would have attacked by now. Two of them, though, had suffered agonizing wounds, and needed the healing toffee-apples fast: Bull's-Eye sobbed with a lacerated leg, whilst Peppermint was almost delirious with pain, clenching her side that bloomed blue blood; her scarred face was an anguished mess, blurting out stinging minty tears.

Lydia tried her best to calm her. 'It's all right, Pepps. Marzi's nearly there. We'll get you one of the magic apples.'

The girls waited many painful minutes while Marzipan inched along the branches of the toffee-tree; her twiggy fingers plucked two red apples, and she tossed them down to Hazel Whirl who leapt up to catch them before spinning back to Coffee Creme.

With no time to waste, Coffee used her fruit knife to slit an apple open, revealing the golden delicious flesh beneath its crimson shell. And at the seedless core of the fruit were drops of a viscous amber juice.

Pepper desperately licked at this nectar, and the others watched in wonder as she soon became well again; and not only did the stump of her limb stop bleeding, but her extra middle one fell away as well, leaving her with regular arms and legs. (Lydia was pleased to see Peppermint's facial scars disappear too.)

It was Bull's-Eye's turn for treatment next, and after drinking from the second apple, her leg quickly painlessly healed.

While all this was going on, though, thin yellow tendrils had started to surface, snaking from the orchard grass, reaching out to poke at the children. Then the soil shifted beneath them, and Lydia could feel the toffee-tree's thick roots stretching underground, like a nest of serpents.

'Hurry up and pick the apples, Marz!' Jawji cried. 'The grassh is gummin' to life!'

Hazel continued to pirouette around the mound, to catch the apples that Marzi threw down; but now she had to twirl and hurdle roots that grew all about her, swishing, swiping, nearly tripping her. Hazel leapt to reach the toffee-fruit, jumping back to put them in the basket; however, when she went one final time, a thick root coiled around her leg; Lydia heard a grisly *crack!* as the root constricted and crushed Hazel's ankle.

Jawbreaker raced across to help; she bit at the root, but a hot cider sap spurted from it, burning her mouth. Jawji chomped down, despite the pain. The taste of blood flooded over her teeth, yet she managed to crunch the root in two. Hazel was free again, and had to hop and hobble on one foot, over the grass to the others nearby. The sisters waited for Marzi now, Coffee using her scimitar to cut at the multiplying shoots and roots, keep them at bay as they rose from the ground, like blurry serpents, in the fading light. Yet, as Marzipan jumped down from the tree, two yellow roots corkscrewed around her.

The girls stood aghast as the roots contracted, *snap-snap-snapp*ing her wooden body, leaving Marzi lying on the grass, as a lifeless pile of splintered branches.

The sisters fled in sickly panic, blinded by tears of pain and anguish; they flitted about the gloomy orchard, thinking the further they got from the toffee-tree, the less danger there would be. They swung their spears in pitiful defence as the roots burrowed up from the damp bumpy earth, reaching for the frightened girls, attacking and smacking and whacking trees around them, causing grackles and bats to flap about their hair, and a putrid fruit salad to shower down, with hornets circling everywhere. Then there were the eruptions of hot soda pop to dodge, frothing without warning into the air. It was as if the rotten vale itself was trying to trap the children there.

Lydia sought to escape with the apples but, as she jumped from mound to mound, a trailing root tripped her up, and all the fruit spilled from the basket into the tall dense grass.

The snakelike roots closed in on the girls, ready to snare them, to crack their skulls, to break their bones— When suddenly a fizzy white star burst bright; the roots swayed still in the air, as if stunned, allowing the sisters to back away. Coffee ran in front of them, waving a sparkly fizzle-stick flare, and slashing her scimitar all about her, cutting back the hordes of roots which spat out burning spurts of cider.

She moved and cleaved so swift and precise, hacking at thick roots, pruning tendrils that whipped at her feet. Her scorchy-hot sword skills were almost as fine as sister Elixa's.

The flare's white light soon petered out, and the mutant tree roots now regrouped, attacking Coffee from all sides, responding to the slicing scimitar. The roots rose faster, converging in a massed assault and, just before Coffee was lost in the knots and tangles of roots, she detached the purse from her belt, and threw it. Lydia grabbed it. Snapped it open. Tipped out the sweetie weapons and tools: elastic liquorice, electric shock fork, snapper crisps, smelling salts, dizzy whirls, chew glues—none of which seemed to be much use—apart from one item: a small red cherry grenade. Now Lydia knew what she had to do.

She nipped back close to the toffee-apple tree; she took the cherry bomb, bit into its stem and pulled with her teeth; the stem came free from the cherry red shell, and Lydia could feel the bomb begin to tremble in her hand. She hurled the cherry into the treetop. The tiny grenade exploded, and the tree lit up in a blaze of red fire. From trunk to bough, its yellow bark charred to black and, all across the orchard, the writhing roots shrivelled back. The tree burned dead with the last of the dragon-fruit cooking on its scorching branches, leaving a pong of hot toffee-apple tart.

Coffee Creme was the first to reach Lydia, her clothes riddled with the cider-burns from a hundred

sword-cut roots. The two of them rushed to Marzipan who lay at the foot of the burning tree. Lydia felt almost numb with sadness, looking at her splintered wooden body. She knelt and touched Marzi's almond face, a face all grained and wrinkled. Marzi gave the faintest groan.

'She's alive!' Lydia cried. 'The apples I dropped! We have to find them!'

Lydia hunted for the fruit that had spilled, scrabbling through the sludgy soil which seemed to get warmer and warmer as she searched. The orchard was getting brighter too, and she looked up horrified as tongues of fire licked lizard-like at the mounds around her. Lydia sniffed out the toffee-apples quick; the hard red rinds were hot to touch and she dropped them finger-tippy into the tub. Seven of the magic apples, Lydia retrieved. She tried in vain to find some more, but the cider fire was spreading fast. Soda pop geysers also burst into flame, fizzing blazing from the burning vale. 'Hurry, Toffee!' Coffee called. 'We need to get back with the apples we have.'

The girls left the orchard as fast as they could, limping, crying, and nursing awful wounds; Coffee carried Marzipan, and Lydia clutched the tub of fruit. She cast a glance back at the magic vale lit up with fountains of hot pop fire, streams of flame pouring in the air, cider still sizzling in the rot-sweet soil. And in the midst of the fiery orchard, two dragon statues stood. A pair of ancient lizards that would eventually perish without the fruit from their toffee-apple tree.

The sisters rested next to the cart on the mountain pass, a safe distance from the vale.

Coffee placed Marzipan down on a blanket, and Lydia handed her the first of the seven apples. Coffee used her knife to crack open the apple skin and ever so carefully drop the precious juice into Marzi's mouth; almost instantly Marzipan was better, her broken body returned to normal, and her skin became smooth, not wrinkled or treelike. And, whereas Peppermint's extra limbs had withered away, Marzi's lost arm miraculously grew back: weird twiggy bony fingers branched out from the stump of her elbow, before extending to a full-stem limb. Marzi wrapped both of her arms around Coffee, weeping tears of gratitude.

Lydia helped to feed Jawbreaker next, dripping the nectar from one of the apples into her badly-burned swollen mouth; straightaway, her pain went away.

Lastly, Hazel drank from a toffee-apple; her leg had turned a horrible purple, but one taste of the magical fruit juice and the agonizing swelling went down; in no time, her ankle was spinny-new. 'Ooh, no pain,' Hazel smiled with a twirl. 'I can *dance* again.'

Four life-saving apples remained, and Lydia knew that wasn't enough for all her sisters back at the palace.

The children made the long return journey. Coffee driving the *pop-a-churn* motor-cart. From Jamatarta, back through the desert, to the cheesy dips of Dairipan.

'Why don't I take the toffee-apples?' Hazel said. 'I can be back at the palace in a dash.'

But it turned out that Hazel couldn't dash very fast at all now; she tried to twirl in her usual way—she even ate some of her Karamesh toffee, but that didn't make any difference either. Her ability to move with super speed had left her.

It must have been the apple juice, thought Lydia.

Peppermint began coughing and choking next.

'You all right, Pepps?'

Pepper steadied her chest, and stared at Lydia with her humbug eyes. Pepper nodded. Then she opened her mouth. 'Yes, Torffee,' she whispered with a hoarse voice.

'Pepper, you just *talked*. But then—' Lydia could see a pattern emerge. 'You can't make your flame any more.' Peppermint coughed again, then shook her head. The apple juice had doused her powers.

'My feet feel weird as well,' mumbled Bull's-Eye, and she looked down at her hoof. It was now a bare foot—*yes*—She had two feet now.

'Your horns have gone too!' Lydia pointed out. 'Oh—your *eyes*!'

The apple juice had removed the coloured rings; now Bull's-Eye had eyes with whites and warm iridic blues. No cold red centres with super-sight.

'How about *you*, Jawji?' Lydia turned to her. '*Jawji!*'

Jawbreaker looked up at her, and held out her hands which contained a pile of diamond-like teeth. 'Me big teef fell out, Toffs.'

Lydia was surprised to see that Jawji's mouth had shrunk too, to a typical child's size. The tomboy flexed her smaller jaws, showing a set of normal enamel teeth growing in place of her whopper choppers.

Marzipan was last to change. As the almond girl sat quiet on the cart, her leaves began to wither away. She had to wrap up in a fleecy blanket. The apple had also cured Marzi's skin, and she could never become wooden or camouflaged again.

The girls reached the palace, late that night, and Coffee was allowed to drive the cart unhampered through the guarded gates. Flora met them in the cold dark hallway, the sultana having ordered her to watch for their return. Earlier, Marjareen had noticed the sisters' absence, and Flora had to divulge their quest. Since it appeared to have been a success, her highness wished to have one of the apples.

'Solo pome, *playta*, kin da,' Flora implored—Could they spare just one to appease her majesty?

Coffee explained that the tree was burned, and the fruits they'd saved were the very last ones.

Lydia showed the basket to Flora; she could see there were only four apples left.

Now, a light shone down the hall, and Sultana Marjareen appeared wearing a ram-skin gown, and accompanied by a maid and a guard.

Flora whispered to Coffee to hurry, before the apples were stolen from them. The children thanked her, and rushed from the hallway, taking the precious fruit up to the suite where their sisters lay seriously ill.

Still, they had to make a heartbreaking decision: one of the five had to go without.

'It has to be Sugar,' uttered Lydia with tears in her eyes. 'I don't think an apple will make any difference. She's all scientific inside.'

And so she got ready to feed the juice to the other four; she knew it would change them, remove their powers, but their lives were more important to her than anything.

First, the apple juice revived poor Marsha; yet her crumpled body didn't balloon back to its roly-poly shape; Marshmallow remained quite slim, and her skin became thin and 'hurtable'.

Next, Cocoa-Butter drank the juice from her apple, and the other girls had to hold their noses, as Coco let out a gargling burp and stinky green steam came out of her mouth.

'Oo, excuse *we*,' she pardoned-me, grinning and sitting up in bed.

Coco's skin regained some colour, but instead of going caramel or ghostly gold, it settled to a creamy buttermilk.

Apple Juice

Lydia turned to Dolly Mixture now and, after taking a few drops of the nectar on her tongue, Dolly soon became conscious.

'You all right though?' Lydia asked her.

'That's what *I* say,' Dolly giggled.

'You won't be able to take your arms and legs off now, you know.'

'Ooh, you're *right*, Toffee.' Dolly pinched herself all over; her body wasn't candy, but normal flesh and blood. 'In't that funny?'

Finally, it was little Lolly's turn to have her dose of apple juice. Once Coffee had sliced through the toffee and fed the juice into her mouth, she soon came out of her frozen slumber. Ever so glad to see her awake, Lydia embraced her icy sister—though 'icy' no more, of course: the all-healing fruit restored Lolly's anatomy to some normality; saucy red blood now poured through her veins, giving her permanent colour and warmth.

'Don't feel froozy any more,' said Lolly, smiling and blinking her bright blue eyes.

Flora arranged a little supper in the dining hall, and servants brought out cheese and biscuits, with soy milk for the weary girls. Lydia looked at her sisters there, now able to rest after all their adventures: without their powers, they were more of a plain selection, instead of the sweet assortment of before.

Only Lydia remained unchanged. And Sugar, of course; it was because of her still being ill that a dismal atmosphere filled the room.

'There is no computer doctor to help Sugar here,' said Coffee. 'We will take her back to Karamesh. First thing tomorrow. We will find a way to move her.'

'I hope we hear from Daddy then soon,' whispered Hazel. 'I just want to go home to Nooga. I do.'

'Elixa may have some news—' Lydia stopped herself from saying any more. She noticed Sultana Marjareen squinting at the sisters from across the hall, and pursing her vinegar-crinkled lips; again she reminded Lydia of Mater D and how she used to watch her while she choked down her yucky meals.

The sultana issued an order, to Flora, that supper be cleared away '*chop-chop*'. Then attendants led the sisters to their rooms where they found desserts had been left there for them: generous slices of creamy cheesecake washed down by goblets of strawberry milk-shake.

Lydia visited Sugar Cube, before she went to bed. She'd taken Pepper's wafer to speak to her, to wish her sweet dreams, and tell her that help was only a day away. She placed a hearing aid in Sugar's ear, then tapped in the text, and waited to see if the message was received.

Sugar lay virtually lifeless now, her body with barely an electrical shiver. Lydia refused to believe that Sugar would never recover.

She couldn't imagine her dear sister as a soulless shell, without life or personality. Lydia smiled as a sprinkle of pixels lit up on the wafer screen, but the text was all garbled and crumbled up. The pixels flickered a little, then died.

Lydia dropped at Sugar's bedside, sobbing, sobbing heart-stabbing sobs. Till, eventually tearfully, she fell fast asleep.

Lydia dreamed she travelled on a sleeper train. A royal train full of luxury carriages. She wandered along a corridor, compartment to compartment, and in each room, one of her sisters waited:

Pepper, Dolly, Bull's-Eye, Marzi. Lolly, Coco, Marsha, Jawji. Hazel Whirl and even Coffee. And there was Sugar. Awake again.

The dream was serene with sunlight and happiness. The half-sisters chatting about their futures and families. Words with smiles. Hopes and wishes. And as the train *truffled* home, they were greeted with a victory parade. With colourful sugary cake decorations, hundreds and thousands sprinkling down. Crowds of people waving wrappers and streamers. Happy families from liberated lands. Children eating all the once-forbidden sweets. And in the crowds, the girls saw their mothers, their brothers and sisters and friends all freed.

Chapter 35
Biscuit Tin

Lydia woke up in a room with plain tin walls; she lay upon a plain tin floor. The room had no windows or furnishings except for a fluorescent white ceiling light and a plastic stool, uncomfortable-looking, all knobbly blue like a huge liquorice allsort (under which she found a round pink potty). The outline of a metal door could just about be seen in the wall. Lydia was locked in what seemed to be a big biscuit tin.

The last thing she remembered was a dream. A vivid dream about a train. Travelling lovely. All sugar and spice. Sunny and nice. Till suddenly all was ruined. From the train, she saw scenes of happy people—all ruined by a mean old crone in the crowd. Marjareen—no, *Mater D*. With a nasty scowl on her nasty face.

'*Thurz the orrib litter dreg!*' Mater D pointed with stabs of her finger. '*Gets her! Gets her! Thur she is!*'

Lydia tried to hide from those poison pebble-eyes.

Then the train changed from being luxury carriages. Turned cold and grey to a tinny prison train. Rhythmic clicks *liquorice sticks* whisked it past the celebrations. And the train entered a trackless tunnel. Burrowing underground into thick fudgy darkness . . .

The biscuit tin room was cold, and Lydia pulled her jacket closer—a pyjama jacket, the colour of fudge. It reminded her of ginger prison clothes. And, in addition to the fudgy jacket, she wore plain fudge trousers, and her feet were stuck in a pair of clogs.

Lydia had a headache too; in fact, she felt quite queasy, as though she had eaten some rotten dessert dished up by Mater D.

She sat there confused.

Had *everything* been a fantasy? Had she dreamt of Sugar and Coco and Dolly and the rest of her long-lost half-sisters? Had she imagined all the sweet locations, and finding the treasured confectionery?

A sound made Lydia lose that thought. The door unlocking, then creaking open.

The doorway was blocked by a brutish-looking robot sentry. Standing there. Not moving or anything. Lydia stared nervously at the robot. It looked just like Prime, Celine's one-time bodyguard. Its chest embossed with a '*tin plate and crossed knives*'. The Tin Man's markings. Stannic's sign. Without her toffee, without her tin, Lydia was helpless again.

But then the sentry stepped aside, and she saw a young woman in the doorway.

She had bobbed dark hair with a silvery sheen. It was Lydia's elder sister Celine. She was dressed in a tin-grey uniform, and Lydia ran to her, hugged her around the waist.

'I've only a few moments to talk to you,' Celine said, a sadness in her silver-grey eyes.

'What's *going on*?' Lydia asked. 'Where *am* I?'

'A prison cell deep below Stannic's headquarters.' Celine glanced at the door, and fidgeted with her lapel. Her tunic was empty of decorations. 'I can't do anything for you right now.'

'Stannic's headquarters?' Lydia said. 'In Burnville?'

'You're right underneath the fudge factory.'

'The one where Mummy worked?'

'Yes.'

Lydia heard heavy footsteps stop outside.

'I have to go now,' Celine said.

The tall tin sentry stepped aside.

'Don't leave, Celine, *please*—' Lydia froze.

Stannic had stepped through the door. The Tin Man himself. In a starchy white uniform, and chef's hat crown.

'Excuse me, Master Chef,' whispered Celine, bowing her head as she passed by.

'See her out,' the Tin Man said, and the sentry Prime shoved Celine away.

Lydia retreated to the cold cell wall as Stannic made his way across the room. His expression remained calm, and he turned his steely gaze on Lydia.

It was creepy the way the Tin Man never showed any emotion. And yet after all the things Lydia had seen—his work camps, his robot army, his captive cities and destructive machines—it turned her stomach just to be in the same room with him, to face whatever fate awaited her.

But Stannic made no move to harm her. Lydia could hear his tin heart ticking.

'Where are you taking Celine?' she said. Stannic didn't seem to be listening; he surveyed the plain tinny cell, its liquorice seat and bare metal walls. 'It's not very nice in here,' Lydia continued. 'And I don't like this pimply chair.'

'You do not talk back to me,' uttered Stannic in an emotionless tone. 'After the trouble you have caused me, you expect a hotel suite? An invitation to tea? And as for Celine: she is in *my* service, and will use her cooking talents to serve *my* cause. In a few days' time, she will serve dessert at my grand Midwinter banquet. Eleven years since I was made Master Chef of Likrishka.'

'I don't care,' Lydia muttered under her breath.

'It is only because of Celine that I spared your life. For now.'

'What about my sisters?'

'Those filthy sss-saboteur brats?' Stannic spat out those words as though they were poisonous pastilles. 'I was to have them liquidated. However, I have just received word that a woman called Kafęena is set to arrive here on Midwinter's Eve.'

'Kafeena from Mokachino?' Lydia whispered with a shudder.

'Then you know of her blood*thirsty* reputation?' The Tin Man let his words' sinister implications percolate through Lydia's mind; she remembered Morella and the talk of Jampyra, and some vague horror ceremony too vile to mention. 'Your *sisters*' fate,' Stannic now said, 'I will leave to Kafeena. I'm sure she will relish their blood served fresh. And when she is finished with them, they'll be barely fit for leftovers.'

At that coldly uttered sentence, Lydia began to shiver. And with her eyes sizzling with tears, she scampered across the room, and cried:

'I *hate* you, Mister Tinny-Bin! I *hate* you!'

Lydia kicked out at Stannic, kicked him and kicked him, kicked him in the shins. *Tinc clunk kick clank clink clank clunk!* But the little girl only hurt her toes on the Tin Man's armoured legs, and all her kicking didn't leave the slightest dent.

Stannic casually pushed her away. 'You little dreg. You can't hurt me. And there's nothing anyone can do to harm my army. Soon my new prototype soldiers will be ready. Advanced robots. Built right here in this factory. To a new improved recipe.'

Lydia felt even sicker when she heard this. Her beloved fudge factory her mother made famous.

The Tin Man stepped towards the door. 'I leave you with this news,' he said. 'It is fitting that Kafeena should reappear now. The two of us have much to discuss: a

powerful alliance to control Tangiya. Your companion from Mixakoko—called Coffee, I believe—in exchange for her miserable life, has agreed to lead us to the secret base of Karamesh. No doubt, the source of all those spysnakes. Once my first batch of robots is ready, this base will be found and roast to the ground.'

Lydia was horrified. Not Karamesh. The most special place in the whole world. Gone for ever. It was all too much for her to bear.

Stannic left the girl to her tears and despair. Lydia imprisoned. With no tin to drum. No toffee. No sisters. No one to help her.

Lydia remained in her solitary tin for days. Though time meant nothing to her now. She saw no daylight, saw no cake-clock. The white fluorescent ceiling light, sometimes on, sometimes off. It wasn't always quiet either; often she heard machinery above the cell, factory sounds thudding through. And then the clunky footsteps of robots. Android waiters that brought her trays of nasty-tasting ration food, mashed-up doggy-baggy stew, or cups of ruined instant soup. Tired and hungry, she troubled herself to sleep.

And when Lydia slept, she was haunted by nightmares: running through decaying forests, deserted cities, or fields of snow. Attacked by robotic crabs, mechanical

woodpeckers, lobsters, and ants. Some of the beasts tormenting her mind were shapeless and suffocating, loaf-like, wolf-like, prowling shadowy buildings or woodlands. Other times the creatures were fast and metallic, caterpillar lorries and centaur trolleys, electric hawks or giant mosquitoes.

Lydia's latest nightmare found her stumbling through corridors chased by steely skeleton chefs. And after she had jarred herself awake, she sat up on the cold tin floor, in her scratchy fudge pyjamas.

Lydia peered around her cell, just as the door was unlocked and opened. There she saw a short sullen man with a liver-spotted bald eggy head, wearing thick shell-like specs and a yolky yellow scientist outfit.

'Her most noblest royal personage Kafeena,' the man said to Lydia, nervily, 'has requested a few mum-moments to see you.'

Then he nodded to someone outside, and a tall figure entered the cell.

Lydia's heart raced as she looked upon Kafeena. Here, standing before her. The sorceress of Mokachino. In deep red robes and a copper apron, a pink mohawk headdress crest, and a great serrated breadknife by her side.

Kafeena's face was the colour of dark chocolate, smooth and ageless, with strange liquid eyes; and there on her cheeks and forehead: three small blood red stars similar to Morella's burns, the unmistakable marks of a 'matri arch' Jampyr.

The scientist closed the door behind him, leaving Lydia alone with her.

The girl had never been so terrified; she backed away, but there was nowhere to hide.

Kafeena took a sweet from her apron, a chocolate liqueur which she crunched between her golden teeth. '*Lidaya*,' the woman hissed, her voice whispery, seething and sinister. 'Lidaya. Do *not* be afraid.'

Suddenly, all the terror left Lydia with that simple uttering of her name. She looked closely at Kafeena's face, seeing her chocolate skin become bronze; her syrupy hypnotic gaze too, changed to familiar emerald eyes.

'*Elixa*,' Lydia gasped, and she ran up and clasped her arms around her sister, wept against her cold copper apron.

'Sweetest Lidaya,' Elixa whispered. 'You do not think I forget your birthday?'

'It isn't my birthday—is it?'

'Yes. It is Midwinter's Eve. The Tin Man Stannic also celebrates today.'

'Mister Tinny-Bin told me about his rotten dinner.'

Elixa held Lydia's face gently in her hands. 'His stint of terror is almost at an end,' she promised. 'Our father Alazandr delivered the sweets secretly to Celine. We must trust in her ability now. Celine has this one chance to serve the Tin Man our treasure-dessert.'

Lydia tried to smile. Then she remembered: 'Stannic said he's going to set his latest robots on Karamesh.'

'Then we must stop him, mustn't we?' From the armoured pocket of her coppery apron, Elixa took a toffee tin, and pressed it into Lydia's hands: 'You must hide it for now,' she stressed. 'Wait until it's safe to use.'

Lydia put the tin underneath the pimply seat, while Elixa dipped into her apron a second time and took out a cylindrical flask.

'Essential molasses,' she smiled, opening the flask, and drinking its thick black treacle neat; the empowering liquid flowed inside her, and Elixa finished by crushing the metal flask in her hand. Then she ate another liqueur, and Lydia saw Elixa's skin darken once more. 'Use the tin, Lidaya. And your toffee-given powers,' she said. 'Release our sweet sisters, and scat this place.'

'Have you seen them? Are they all right?'

'They are in cells somewhere close, I believe,' Elixa replied. 'I'm so sorry for sending you to Dairipan. Sultana Marjareen betrayed you to the Tin Man. Flora sent Karamesh news of your capture, and so we set up this deception. I arrived here disguised as Kafeena to "honour" the Tin Man Stannic at his banquet. To propose that together we could enslave all of Tangiya.'

'What about the *real* Kafeena?' Lydia said. 'Where is she?'

'Kafeena is a secretive woman. No one has heard from her for many years. Mixakokan artisans made this outfit and sword for me. Then I set out in a boat, arrived with a small entourage from Karamesh. Stannic has them under watch in hotel quarters, far from Burnville.'

There were sounds outside the cell; the scientist was about to return.

'Now I must go,' Elixa said. 'A feast awaits. And Celine may need my assistance to escape.'

She stepped away and left the cell as the door was opened for her.

Then, once its lock clicked and closed, Lydia hurried to retrieve her tin; she found nuggets of lovely amber toffee, and two bronze hammers for drumsticks, within.

Her mouth watered at the thought of the toffee. Lydia eagerly gobbled a piece; then another, and another two, she chewed and chewed. (It also took away the taste of the ration food.) Soon she felt that tang on her tongue. A familiar tingle in her fingers. Lydia took out the pair of hammers, and resealed the tin with the toffee in. Then she put the tin on the floor, tapped the hammer-tips at the lid, and concentrated on the door. Lydia was ready to *rip* it from the wall; she'd bring down the whole of the factory if she had to.

But no. She began with a delicate *tap tap*.

An ever so dainty *tap-a-tap* to pick the lock.

The tin and the toffee and her mind combined to make an invisible key. *Click-clack-click.* The door opened on demand.

Lydia filled her jacket pockets with the toffee, and carried the tin in the crook of her arm; she was extra-watchful as she crept out into a wide grey passageway, checking there were no robots around.

She brushed her blonde hair out of her eyes, then

skipped along the passage; Lydia soon reached a dead-end corridor containing anonymous metal doors with barcodes, but no windows. They must have been cells, Lydia thought, similar to the tin she'd found herself in.

Suddenly there was a noise in the corridors. Heavy rhythmic robot footsteps. The clinking din of a guard's tin limbs. Lydia put her tin to the floor; she waited till the robot clunked around the corner; then, as soon as it came in sight, Lydia drummed it under control.

Dud-dur-um! Dud-dur-um!

The tinny beat echoed through the dead-end corridors. She made the robot stop abrupt. Then *whack!* Its head was battered flat. Lydia had to jump back quick as the robot topple-crumple-crashed.

Once she regained her composure, and was sure there were no more robots to interrupt her, Lydia used her tin lid drum to unlock the nearest metal door.

Tappa-tap tap, tippa-tip tip. Tip tip tap tap. Stop.

After the clack of the lock, the door squeaked ajar, and she took a peek inside.

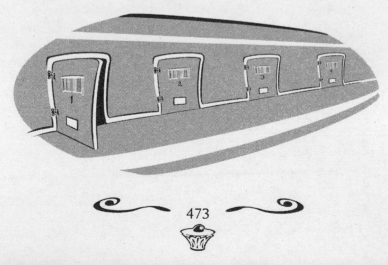

Chapter 36
Liquorice Allsorts

Lydia saw a room with plain tin walls, and an allsort stool (a yellow coconutty one) placed upon a plain tin floor. Sitting on the allsort was a girl in a fudge-coloured pair of pyjamas; a girl with light blue skin and stripy hair. There was no mistaking her half-sister Peppermint.

Pepper looked up with her humbug eyes. '*Torffee?*' she uttered and smiled, jumping up from her allsort stool, so happy to see her Likrish sibling.

The two of them left the small tin room to walk up and down before the doors of the others. Nine more doors which Lydia unlocked, one by one, with the key of her mind and her tin lid drum.

In the room next to Pepper's, Lydia saw a little girl with flossy hair, perched upon a pimply pink stool. As soon as the girl caught sight of Lydia—

'It's Toffee!' Dolly Mixture greeted cheerfully, leaping up from her allsort seat.

Lydia let go of her tin and hugged her sister, squeezed her tight, knowing that she couldn't fall apart in her arms.

'I in't seen anyone for *ages*, Toffee,' Dolly smiled. 'Oo, there's Pepper too. Anyhoo, I woke up in this funny tinny room. I din't know how I got here, but it's ever so nice you visit me.'

'This isn't a funny tinny—*Dolly*,' Lydia said. 'It's a rotten prison. And we've got to get out.' So the three of them left the cell, and opened the next.

In the room next to Dolly's, Lydia saw a ginger-haired girl in prison pyjamas, sulking on top of a twisty tube of liquorice. Even with her horns now gone, there was no mistaking Bull's-Eye. As soon as Lydia opened the door, Bull's-Eye glared at her.

'Toff!' she greeted tearfully, hopping up from her allsort seat, and embracing Lydia, much to her surprise. She certainly had changed since their first encounter.

'Oo, it's Zye! Hi, Zye!' piped a voice from the door.

'Is that Dippy?' Bull's-Eye smiled, and she went over and hugged Dolly too. 'Oh, it's so good to see you, sissy.'

And together the four girls left the cell, and Lydia drummed to unlock the next.

In the room beside Bull's-Eye's, Lydia saw an almond-skinned girl, sitting cross-legged on a black-and-orange liquorice cube. Although she was no longer covered in leaves, there was no mistaking Marzipan.

As soon as Lydia opened the door, Marzi peered up at her.

'Toffee?' she greeted quietly, getting up calmly from her allsort seat.

And so, with Lydia, Peppermint, Dolly, and Zye, Marzi left the cell, and the five of them went and tried the next.

In the room next to Marzipan's, Lydia spied a blue-haired girl shivering in her fudge-coloured pyjamas, upon a liquorice-layered stool.

As soon as the girl peeked up to see—'T-Toffee?' Ice Lolly greeted timidly. And she came out to join the other five as they went to the next prison cell.

In the room next to Lolly's, Lydia saw a golden-haired girl lying against a liquorice log.

The girl looked round at the sound of the door and, as soon as she saw Lydia—

'Here, Toffee, here!' Coco greeted brightly, scampering up to embrace her.

Then all seven sisters left the cell, as Lydia drummed to unlock the next.

In the room next to Coco's, Lydia was intrigued to find a purple-haired girl, pale and thin in fudgy pyjamas, crouched down on a pimply blue stool.

As soon as she saw Lydia—

'Oh! It's Toffee!' Marsha got up from her allsort seat, and greeted her with a hug.

Lydia still wasn't used to seeing her so slim. And Marsha felt weird having such thin skin.

And so she and Lydia left the cell and, together with the others, they tried the next.

In the room next to Marsha's was a champagne-haired tomboy in fudge-coloured togs, squatting on a stripy cube. Even though her mouth was normal-sized now, there was no mistaking the friendly face of Jawbreaker.

'*Hey*, Toffs!' she cried, as soon as she saw Lydia.

And Jawji jumped up from her allsort stool to join up with Peppermint, Dolly and Zye, Marzi, Lolly, Marsha and Coco.

In the next room, Lydia found an auburn-haired girl, in fudgy pyjamas, posing on tiptoe on a liquorice tube. As soon as the girl noticed her—'*Helloo*, Toffee!' Hazel greeted with a curtsey, kicking away her allsort stool. She twirled balletically across the cell, kissing Lydia on both cheeks like proper theatrical people do.

She welcomed the rest of the sisters too, as they went and tried the final door (where they guessed they'd find Sugar, of course, and hoped they'd see her well, once more).

But no. In the final tin was a teenage girl with roast-brown hair, sitting unhappy in scratchy pyjamas, upon a round pink stool. Lydia had forgotten all about Coffee.

The girl got off her allsort seat, and joined the others with sweet relief. But there were no more rooms to open now, and Sugar Cube had yet to be found.

Lydia took her sisters back along the passageways, guided by the factory sounds.

After passing through connecting corridors, they came upon a heavy vault door.

Lydia used her tin to unlock it; she turned the handle-wheel with her mind. Then she did a drumroll to pull back the door, and all the children filed through. Through to a vast metallic tunnel with an overpowering sugary smell. The sisterhood stood before an underground river. A slow-moving river of liquid fudge.

Not far from the factory, across the site of Burnville, a number of diners were arriving to celebrate Stannic's anniversary. They arrived in black limousines, driven by robotic chauffeurs. Through the gates, past the lawns, around the ornate factory buildings, and up to the entrance of a dining hall with fine wine fountains, burgundy carpets, and a magnificent flight of stairs. Stairs that led to Stannic's Elite banqueting suite.

Seven men arrived, in all their finery, including dinner jackets garnished with medals. This brotherhood of seven 'knights' who served their leader Stannic. Knights of the Crossed-Knives. Ruling the Candi-Lands alongside him, and carrying out his terrible plans.

At the *closh* of a pan-gong, they made their way up the stairs, two floors, before pausing at these double doors, while Prime the sentry scanned each man for weaponry. Inside the opulent banqueting suite, with its crystal chandeliers and lozenge windows, was a long mahogany dining table draped with a dark grey tablecloth. Stannic was already there, ready to greet his brotherhood.

Each man entered the suite, formally announced by a robot butler:

> *'Minister for Citrus Forests,*
> *Colonel Steel of Franjipan.'*
> *'Minister for Energy-Jelly,*
> *Commander Kroma of Froza.'*
> *'Minister for Candy Industry,*
> *Captain Kadmium of Delisha.'*
> *'Drinks Minister, Field Marshall Mercury,*
> *administrator of the Winelands.'*
> *'Minister for Goods Transport,*
> *Admiral Aluminium of Nooga.'*
> *'Minister of Mineral Ingredients,*
> *General Led, Head of Baykari.'*
> *'Robotics Minister, Professor Ferrous,*
> *Sous-Chef of Likrishka.'*

This was Stannic's second-in-command, and the professor saluted him and took his place at the Tin Man's side. With his kitchen-cabinet of ministers assembled, Stannic introduced another guest:

An aged woman, the Sultana of Dairipan, tottered into the room, assisted by her personal physician, the miserable 'Doctor Mouldy Toadstool'.

'Dear brothers, we extend a royal welcome to our loyal ally Marjareen. She cleverly delivered our juvenile tormentors to us, after placing simple sleeping pills in their desserts.'

Marjareen bowed low to Stannic, all hunched and humble in her silken robes; then she dismissed old

'Doctor Toadstool' with a flappy-slap from her blue-veined hand.

Once the Tin Man had taken his place at the head of the table, the others were all seated too. Only one chair remained unoccupied.

Elixa now appeared at the doors, accompanied by a robot butler. Elixa with the 'features' of Kafeena, the brands of the Jampyr (special stick-on transfer stars), and her lavish attire: flowing red robes, headdress crest, the jagged bread-sword and copper apron, each with elaborate authentic-looking markings.

'Brothers,' the Tin Man proclaimed, 'we are privileged to receive another to our table. Her most noble *majesty* of Mokachino, Kafeena.'

The men, and the sultana too, were taken aback at the woman's appearance.

Stannic was also slightly unsure of what to make of her surprise arrival: this tall intimidating woman he believed to be the same reclusive sorceress who'd given him his armoured body, and set him on his path to be Master Chef of a confectionery empire. The Tin Man kept a respectful distance, in his chair nearest the door.

Elixa greeted him in Tangi-language: '*Jzay salu ta Stannic. Salu ta supyra guta quizina.*'

The robot butler translated her words: '*Great Stannic, I honour your unrivalled taste.*'

The Tin Man bowed his head to her. 'Taste I owe to you, *Queen* Kafeena.'

481

Stannic then gestured to a robot waiter holding a tray.

'Your sword, if you please,' he said. 'No one brings weapons to this table of peace.'

Without a word, Elixa surrendered the sword, and placed it down upon the tray.

'And your apron and headdress, if you please, your majesty,' the Tin Man added.

Elixa took off her copper apron, leaving her in her deep red robes; lastly she removed the headdress, revealing dyed golden hair arranged in coils and cornrows.

The waiter took the apron and weapon away. The doors were locked, and the robot butler showed Elixa to her seat at the far end of the long long table.

The Tin Man's banquet could begin. It proved to be an exquisite feast, course after course, prepared and served by Stannic's sweetest elitist chefs:

Liquorice Allsorts

Praline prawns in a smoothie fruit cocktail.
Jaffa-fish consommé with side-eye of orange squid.
Raspberry crab claws with lolli-flower garnish.
Offal of the snaffle-wolf softened in franjipane.
Mixed nut cutlet in bitter jujube and coffee sauce.
Sparkling citrus sorbets to refresh
the palate in between.
Roast breast of bird-of-paradise
spiced with spearmint leaves.
A selection of sandwich wafer pastries
layered with slivers of crystal jelly.
Buttons of royal Dairi cream cheese
on crusts of high-fired wholemeal bread.
All complemented by vintage liqueurs procured
from the finest Wineland vineyards.

Each head chef presented their respective dishes, entering via a service elevator that connected the banqueting suite to the kitchens; the men and women wore black ceremonial aprons, and tin-grey tunics with medals, bars, and Likrish decorations.

These chefs were assisted by a quartet of waitresses, four elegant mannequin androids, silver-skinned and dressed in couture; they even sashayed like catwalk models, moving smoothly throughout the room.

With the lively *clink* and *clash* of cutlery, the diners tucked into their meals, munching the generous portions with gusto. As they ate, the Tin Man's brotherhood rhubarbed with approval and praise.

And many gourmet courses later, it was finally time for dessert.

Stannic raised a glass of wine to his guests:

'A toast. To a new era in the Land of Candi. And—' Stannic raised his glass to Elixa, '—to the future conquest of Tangiya.'

Celine now entered from the service elevator, pushing a silver dessert trolley.

The Tin Man summoned her to the table. 'I sincerely hope, on your sister's life, that you have cooked up something spectacular to crown this historic night.'

Chapter 37
Fudge

Deep beneath the Burnville factory, Lydia and her sisters stood at the side of a dimly-lit tunnel, before a strange underground river. A river of fudge that slugged along, giving them the creeps. Liquid sludge just below, steaming with stifling heat; full of syrupy currents and very wide and deep. This river of fudge that pushed along, sickly sugary sweet.

The molten fudge pulsed slowly through these steel arches. Arches that supported walkways topped with biscuit brick. The hard-baked brick was hot from the fudge. And a second industrial vault-like door lay on the other side of the river.

In their clogs, the sisters dashed, *bicci-brick-a brack-a-clack*, over the boiling steely arches, feeling the sticky heat through their pyjamas. The girls soon left the tunnel of fudge, and beyond the industrial door was a basement. The very lowest level of the factory.

From there was a flight of metal steps, a great spiral staircase that went up and up towards the surface. The noise of machinery was louder now. Stannic's new robots under construction. *War machines*, Lydia thought, being made by Mister Tinny-Bin.

Lydia led her ten half-sisters all in their matching fudge-coloured outfits. Up the flight of metal stairs. Taking them up one floor at a time. At every level was a metal lattice balcony giving a view of the factory floors. The first with a sign by the stairs on the wall.

A sign that read *'Lower Level Twelve'*.

A level where the sisters saw long wide workshops filled with rows of steely skulls. Cranium plates being welded together. Ugly grey, like metal nutshells, gleaming in a cold white light. Dead decapitated heads with empty sunken eye sockets.

Precision-machines fitted sucro-circuits, computer chips, and sonic systems into the skulls. Artificial intelligence processors. Independent digital brains.

Lydia put her tin to the floor. *Drubba-dubba-dubba-drub*. Drummed all the skulls. Crushed them as if they were fragile eggshells. *Drubba-dubba-dubba-drub*. Line by line. Lydia cared nothing for delicate effect, beating at the tin lid as she never had before. Her double-handed pounding channelled through the toffee hammers. Channelled through the toffee tin. Channelled through her mind. Lydia focused, concentrated, sent rapid tattoos of destructive energy rapping through the machinery.

Then she stomped up the metal stairs, her sisters climbing the spirals after her.

'*Lower Level Eleven*'

A level where fluorescent tubes created a disco disconcerting flicker-lick of light across the room. A room with tables filled with what seemed to be rows of chromium bull's-eye sweets. Polished eyes with laser lenses. Zooming deadeye mechanisms slotted inside the sockets of the robot skulls, giving them ruthless super-sight.

Ratta-tatta-tatta-tat. Lydia's tin drum shattered all the eyes. Blinded the robots line by line.

Then she clomped up the clanky metal stairs, her sisters staying close behind.

'*Lower Level Ten*'

A level where these nasal sensors were fitted onto the fronts of the robot skulls.

Sensors for sniffing out any enemies. *Fee fie foe fume.* Hungry for human flesh to consume.

Lydia wished all the sensors smashed. *Tatta-tatta-trash-trash.* Drummed to destroy them. The rhythms of the tin, and the toffee, and her mind combined.

After which she stepped up the spiral stairs, with her sisters close behind.

'*Lower Level Nine*'

A level like an infernal forge. Conveyor belts and robot arms, automaton tools, mechanical levers. Linking, clinking metal together. Fixing skulls to inanimate bones. Building giant steely skeletons. The skeletons from Lydia's nightmares.

Towering monstrous robot ogres, five times the size of the old tin soldiers.

Row upon row were strung up on grills and chained to toasting racks. Skeletal creatures half-assembled. In a trolley dolly mixture of moving parts: ribs spines hips limbs, wrenched and blow-torched, soldered, bolted. Seen in a spark-scarred smoky light.

This level was the noisiest. The factory racket at a nasty intensity. The girls' heads hurt with the clanging and the heat.

Lydia positioned her tin upon the balcony.

Rumbla-tatta-thunda-rattle. Dismantled all the skeletons. Flattened them like crushed drink cans. Assembly line by assembly line.

Then she stomped up the clanky metal stairs; her sisters ascending safely behind.

'Lower Level Eight'

A level where Lydia saw more robot skeletons, side-by-side in dentist chairs. Sitting while whisks and drills and pincers screwed sets of metal dentures into each already-scary skull. Razor sharp incisors. Bone-crunching back teeth. Powered by high-pressure grinder breaker jaws.

Lydia's drumrolls pummelled all the robots.

Batta-datta-clatta-clout. Knocked their teeth out. Battered them there in the dentist chairs.

Then she stomped up the metal stairs, her siblings close behind her.

'*Lower Level Seven*'

Where the sisters could see a cool mist drift across a frosted factory floor. Here on this level, lolly-shaped units were fitted like livers into robot ribs. Freezer units. Filled with coolant. Chilling scoops of chemical cream.

Lydia used her tin lid drum to bust the robots' bodies open. *Tubba-dum-dubba-dum*. Spilling icy chemicals. Causing the factory floor to shut down cold.

Then, with her ten half-sisters in tow, Lydia ascended the stairs to the next level.

'*Lower Level Six*'

Where another batch of steely skeletons were kitted out with disposal systems.

Gruesome blenders. Liquidizers. With caffè latte stomach acids. Designed to digest flesh and bone. Recycle the waste matter back into fuel.

Lydia drummed to upset the stomachs.

Badda-bam-bash. With an acid splash. She extinguished all the robots there, and again clog-stomped up the clanky metal stairs.

'*Lower Level Five*'

A level where vanilla smells added to the smoky metal stink of the other floors. Where fudge from the factory's underground river was cooked in vats into a black electric sauce.

A level where rows of the skeletal ogres were fitted with glistening circulatory systems; platinum arteries, hearts, and veins like a complex network of drinking straws.

Row after row of the hideous robots were hooked up to these infusion-machines, while litres of swirling hot fudge sauce were pumped into their systems.

Energy fudge like sickly mud to give the robots heat. Liquid fudge flowed through the veins. A sauce electric sweet. Full of sugary blood that curdled black and neat. And as if this wasn't creepy enough. The robot hearts began to 'beat'.

With this saucy infusion trickling around their metal blood vessels, the skeletons suddenly came to life. Their infrared eyes glowed. Stared. Soulless electrical killing machines. Fudge-blooded. Activated.

Lydia now felt fearful butterflies flutter around her stomach; she took some toffee from her pocket, shoved lovely chunks of it into her mouth. Then extra-determined, lid-hitter Lydia drummed on the tin as hard as she could. Crude dynamic clatterful patterns that burst the saucy fudge-filled veins, shuddered through the steely bones. All the menacing metal machines buckled and broke from the thump of the drum; then Lydia stepped up the stairs again, leading her sisters to another factory floor.

'Lower Level Four'

The children saw more skinless monsters. Robot ogres' bony limbs fitted with punchy power-pack muscles. Padded with wads of marshmallow insulation. And sealed with a glue of chewing gum.

The forceful effects of Lydia's drum bashed each robot out of shape. Using her hammers she scratched

and scraped, tearing the gum and mallow from their metal frames. Sawing the skeletons into pieces, their arteries spurting electric fudge.

One moment alive, the next crackled dead, the ogres' bones were sliced like bread.

Lydia, with toffee blazing through her body. Lydia, the drummer girl, led her sisters on. They had to keep going. Along the clangy metal stairs. Spiralling up another level of the factory.

'Lower Level Three'

A level where confectionery weapons were installed into the ogres' arms. Minty flame-throwers to roast and toast. Acid sherbets to blind and scald.

Lydia picked up her hammers again, banged them on her tin lid to control the robots down below. Making the skeletons attack each other in vicious gladiatorial scuffles. She drummed and drummed relentlessly. Her arms ached, her shoulders hurt, but Lydia knew she *had* to continue; eating her toffee, she hammered and chomped, hammered and chomped. The chewing chewing resounded in her ears. Lydia left the robot fighters burning in fizzing hot mint sauce. And so up to another level, with her sisters, Lydia climbed.

'Lower Level Two'

Where the flesh-eating robots were layered with armoured carapace scales. Casings coated in camouflage butter-paint, flickering ghostly in the shadowy workshops.

Lydia used her tin lid drum to flay the robots. Turn the ogres inside out. Fudge-bloody skeletons falling and thrashing, tremor convulsions in the volatile light. Drowning in liquid hot confectionery. Pits of slicky black thick black fudge. Lydia led the girls up the stairs again, up to the last of the lower factory floors.

'Lower Level One'

A level where the walls were lined with wiring. Black liquorice cables. Red swizzly leads. Where computer screens monitored the robot testing. A finished batch of soldier ogres at their weird PT routine. Stretching and flexing, all in unison. Repetitive repetitive. Hopping and twirling. Patterns of movement being drilled into their digital brains. Showing their mobility. Speed and agility. Like giant macabre ballerinas.

Lydia drummed the robots as before. Stabbing and battering, digging at the tin lid. Rattling shaking the bodies apart. Twisting them into a mishmash hash of reforged ogres. Eyeless faces, metal mesh bones. Mallow and muscle unhinged and blistered. Steely disjointed dancing figures engulfed in electrified fudge.

The toffee tin's percussive destruction brought down the factory, floor by floor. Level by level. Everything metal. Lydia giddy, lightheaded, and driven. Rumbling drum sounds erupted in her mind. A toffee-euphoria carried her on. Up and up the factory stairwell. The other sisters still behind. Afraid to look back at the collapsing structures. Feeling the mounting heat in their feet. The spiral stairs dismantling after them.

All the levels smashed together. Workshops, body shops, sonics and optics, armouries, dentists, refrigerators, incinerators. All the factory's netherworld horrors. Buried under metal, rubble and fudge.

Lydia now reached a flight of cream-coloured concrete stairs with a wooden handrail that the others used to haul themselves up.

Cocoa-Butter, Peppermint, Marzipan, Bull's-Eye.

Dolly, Ice Lolly, Hazel, Jawji, and Marshmallow.

With Coffee Creme last, making sure nothing followed them, that nothing survived the rumblings below.

Lydia took them up to the ground floor, and corridors leading to soundproofed control rooms. Where human technicians, scientists, and programmers sat at computers, overseeing Stannic's empire.

Tireless android operators were also plugged into the banks of computers, loading saucer disks, reading writing hard-drive lollipops, co-ordinating the confectionery electronica. Sending signals to candy cane transmitters. Orders to soldiers. To fuel depots, building sites. Trains and barges and robot lorries.

Here the Tin Man's plans were cooked up. Where everything was masterminded.

Coco may not have been ghostly now, but she still knew how to sneak around, and she tiptoed through the antiseptic corridors, looking for an exit, while her sisters followed.

'Oo! Look look,' she whispered to Lydia. '*Here*, Toffee, *here*.'

Lydia peeped where Coco pointed and there, in a room like a hospital laboratory, she spied a spiky-haired girl in a fudge-coloured bedjacket, lying still on an operating table.

They had found Sugar, though they couldn't be sure if she was alive.

Lydia could see her hearing aids and glasses in pieces on a tabletop. Beside them was a female scientist conducting some kind of analysis. All around the white enamel room were platters lined with surgical instruments and various mixers, microwaves, and monitors showing Sugar's vital signs.

Lydia nearly cried with relief; Sugar Cube appeared to be conscious, her brain waves simmering across one oven screen.

Lydia waited till the scientist left the laboratory. Then she stole inside, and went up to the table.

'Sugar, *Sugar*. Please wake up.'

'T-*Toffee?*' Sugar murmured wearily; it seemed she could hear without her hearing aids. She turned her head, and peered at Lydia. 'Is *you*, Toffee?' Sugar whispered in a voice that wasn't artificial.

'Can you get up?' Lydia asked. 'We need to get you out of here.'

Sugar couldn't move her limbs, and little sticky pastille sensors hooked her up to all the machines. Coffee switched off the monitors first, carefully disconnected the pastilles, and lifted Sugar from the operating table, to carry her in her arms.

494

All the sisters were accounted for now. But as they left the laboratory, the rumblings from below extended to the upper rooms. All the computers began to flicker and misbehave; desks and instruments started trembling; windows and partitions cracked and shattered; the walls shook as though caught in an earthquake.

The children had to get out quick. The floor splitting beneath their feet, they scampered through the crumbling corridors, reached a fire exit, and finally emerged from the infernal fudge factory. Out onto the Burnville site. Into the fresh air and the cold of night.

Chapter 38
Dessert Course

Not far away, at the banqueting suite, Celine Argenta stood before a silver trolley. She presented her special cake to Stannic. A cake including the treasure ingredients Lydia and her sisters had collected.

Celine's dessert looked most luxurious. Liquorice black with a luminescent icing piped around its rim. And in glassy sugar, at its centre, a decorative plate and two crossed knives. In honour of the Brotherhood. The Tin Man and his Candi Knights.

Stannic took a knife and cut the cake into twelve. Eleven equal slices for each person at the table, with a much larger piece for himself. The cake was served with silver forks on silver plates. Its rich flavoured chocolate layers oozing with a snail-green cream.

Stannic let his guest 'Kafeena' try the first slice.

Elixa ate half of her chocolate cake, before wishing the Tin Man: *'Bonbon appetite.'*

At this, the brotherhood tucked into their own desserts; even Marjareen *nn*-gnawed at her cake like a ravenous rat.

The Tin Man's ministers were gushing with their compliments: '*My mostest heartiest congratulations, Stannic. Delightfully delicious-full, Stannic. An untoppable masterpiece, my great leader. Pièce de résistance. A peak of Likrish cake cuisine.*'

Even Stannic calmly agreed: 'You've excelled yourself, my dear Celine.'

The young woman smiled weakly, and bowed her head. Then she went and stood behind her trolley. Waiting for something to happen.

It was clear to Celine that the Tin Man couldn't be harmed by poisons or conventional means. Therefore she'd needed to serve him some extraordinary dessert with unique ingredients. Ingredients such as treasure-sweets she'd only ever read about. In books researched by her mother Mari and her grandma Rosé Arora. It was from them that Celine had learned to make cakes and confections that, once eaten, could reach out and touch the mind, affect how someone thinks and feels.

And Stannic's anniversary dessert. A cake few chefs could cook to perfection. A just-dessert designed to infiltrate the very soul.

The Tin Man was last to finish his cake; with his enchanted tongue, he relished every mouthful. The soft black liquorice, moist dark chocolate subtly blended with its six fruit flavours: jelly lemon, jewelly blueberry,

orange sherbet, cherry truffle, a drop of pear and a biscuit base of strawberry shortcake.

And just as the flavours of the cake had been revealed, so its ingredients began to take effect. The essence of the Pearl Drop provided a perfumed disguise of delight to lull the unsuspecting diners, and allow the rest of the dessert to strike: a taste of Diamond Sun Bean juice to sop up their memories, a trace of soily Jet Heart truffle to root out their darkest thoughts, and a dash of Sapphire Fizzweed dust to fizz their fears within their guts.

And it all commenced with a simple burp.

Professor Ferrous, Stannic's second-in-command, croaking like a bloated toad. Field Marshall *hic!* Mercury *urp!* started up with *hic-urp* hiccups. Then Captain Kadmium doubled up with tummy rumbles. Steel and Aluminium were blocked up with the bum-bum grumbles. While General Led and Commander Kroma felt frozen chills behind their eyes.

The ministers felt nauseous, creased up helpless, as sapphire sherbet fired in their stomachs; yet these were no ordinary run-of-the-gullet belly aches: the brotherhood's suffering was of their own making. The crumbly base of Ruby Red Shortbread had exposed the layers of decent humanity buried within these gluttonous men. Forcing each of them to search their conscience. To face up to their cruelty and greed. To suffer for the mistreatment of their people. All the corruption and hatred and guilt now weighed and preyed

most potent on their minds. Emotions manifest as excruciating pain. Congealing gummily in the gut. Emitted in great gassy gastric eruptions, stinking in their mouths. The men tried to take the foul tastes away, wash them away with gulps of champagne. But the wine turned to vinegar on their smelly breaths, making them convulse and retch. Vomiting spasms that seared in their chests.

What they thought was a victory feast had ended for them in sour defeat.

As for Sultana Marjareen: Stannic saw her shrivel and crinkle crisp before his eyes. And all of Marjareen's meanness and nastiness—and her betrayal of the sisters—sizzled inside her like hot gallstones; the frail sultana slipped from her chair, her bony fingers clawing at the tablecloth, a last gasp gagging breath rancid in her throat.

Elixa, on the other hand, remained unaffected: as someone who'd led a life of goodness and selfless sacrifice, she was immune to the effects of the just-dessert.

But Stannic was left unaffected too. It seemed that Celine's cake had failed after all.

Now, the Tin Man threw back his chair, and went to reach her. 'Traitor,' he uttered to the frightened woman.

Celine ducked behind her trolley, and Stannic bashed it aside with his fist; in desperation she held up a tray, but that too was punched away. Then the Tin Man grabbed Celine by the collar, and pinned her against the wall.

Elixa sprinted the length of the hall, racing past the retching knights, batting away the mannequin waitresses sashaying round the room in confusion; not built for combat, the silver androids were felled with a single chop, Elixa's hands like whipping vipers, taking their heads or limbs clean off.

Celine struggled, struggled to breathe, as Stannic slowly sadistically slowly closed his hand around her neck.

Elixa got near enough to land her fiercest kick, breaking the Tin Man's strangling grip and sending him reeling away from the wall. Celine sank to the floor, choking and tearful.

Stannic was shaken by Elixa's assault, and she took advantage of his fleeting shock; tugging him up by his Master Chef's jacket, she slung the Tin Man onto the table, and he rattled across in a dinnyful clatter of pdinnerware and wine.

Elixa then seized some silver plates, and skimmed each one with unerring accuracy; the plates' sharp edges struck Stannic on the head and neck—He survived each strike without a scratch.

The Tin Man now took up the long silver cake knife, and attacked Elixa with unexpected ferocity. More of a killing-machine than a man, Stannic cut at her fast and focused, swiping the knife wide and precise; sometimes chairs and ministers got in his way, yet Stannic hacked and stabbed at them too, unconcerned who he hurt or murdered.

Elixa proved too swift, at first; the two of them moved around the table, Stannic's flashing knife just missing her. She evaded the blade again and again. The Tin Man, though, only needed to connect once— He pounced with his other hand, grabbed Elixa's trailing sleeve and, in the moment it took to rip free, Stannic slashed the knife deep into her shoulder.

Elixa slithered away in pain; she retreated behind the dining table and, casting off the loose red robes, she stood there clad in her snakeskin suit. Treacly black blood poured from her shoulder, and Elixa's face lost its dark liqueur disguise.

'You're not Kafeena,' Stannic uttered. 'But you look just like her. Who *are* you?'

'I am her daughter,' Elixa replied through clenched gold teeth. 'Here to stop the *wretched tyrant* she created.' Her words, however, sounded meaningless. Elixa was wounded, and Stannic seemed unstoppable.

Once again he turned to Celine; the Tin Man hauled her to her feet and dragged her back to face Elixa. The Master Chef regarded her scornfully. 'You're responsible for this pathetic attempt to poison me.' He almost smiled as he surveyed his fallen ministers. 'These lackeys, these *liquorice lace-lickers* can easily be replaced. And so can treacherous confectioners.'

Stannic stared his stare of steel. He placed the cake knife against Celine's throat, its blade stained with treacly blood; he would slice the neck of her sister before Elixa's very eyes.

502

'Treacherous—' he uttered again, though this time the word seemed stuck in his oesophagus, '—treshur—retch—iska—infect—shoc—' The Tin Man let go of Celine; the knife dropped, and he doubled up in pain—the first pain he'd ever experienced since his tinny transformation; Elixa could see the surprise in his eyes. Stannic felt *pain*. His body responding as if it were flesh again. The treasure-dessert had suddenly worked, affected his unique metal mind and consequently his metallic insides.

Elixa saw her chance. She ran around the table, straight at Stannic, and despite the pain that ripped through her shoulder, she lifted him with a mighty effort, used him as a battering ram, smashing the Tin Man through the wooden doors, and pushing him onto the second floor balcony.

Celine was now free to go, and on trembling legs she stumbled down the stairs, down down to the dining hall foyer. Only to run into the robot Prime standing guard in the night-time courtyard.

At the sound of her footsteps, Prime spun round.

Celine remained still. 'Prime. Please. Let me pass,' she ordered calmly.

Celine stepped forward, but the sentry wouldn't turn aside; it raised its weapon-arm which sizzled with electric sparks, and this time the motion wasn't a warning.

Her one-time bodyguard turned executioner, its hand about to fry her with a bolt of electricity.

Suddenly Celine heard running footsteps, and—
Shunk—Prime's arm was sliced off with a crackling
flash. Then *chop*—*hack*—*crunk*—the robot's legs were
severed by a disembodied diamond blade. Prime toppled heavily noisily to the ground, its bucket head spinning, its body thrashing till they too fell apart and lay in
clean-cut segments on the courtyard.

Celine narrowed her silver-grey eyes, as a phantom
suit began to materialize. And she watched with utter
relief as Alazandr reappeared. First faint X-ray bones,
then his face which flickered fleshily till, in moments,
she could clearly see her father as a glassy glimmer in
safari khakis and a chunky chocolate jacket.

Invisible, he'd stolen in, through the gates, when the
limousines arrived. The effects of the glassy mints he'd
eaten were fading, and Alazandr now bounded up the
stairs, armed with his sword, to help Elixa.

He'd almost reached the second floor when he saw
the Tin Man stagger along the balcony, his mind dis-
tressed from the just-dessert, his insides boiling with
guilt-ridden bile that writhed from his lips, leaving
sickly trails down his Master Chef's jacket.

Elixa stood away from him, clutching her injured
shoulder and, at the appearance of the ghostly Alazandr,
Stannic began to back off scared, flailing his tin fists, and
flinging himself from the balcony.

The Tin Man's heavy metal form tumbled down like
a tinball pinball, plummeting two floors, crashing to the
ground.

Incredibly, Stannic got up unhurt, and he lurched across the foyer carpet, shoved a frightened Celine aside, kicked his way past the remains of Prime, and crossed the moonlit courtyard towards a waiting car.

Alazandr screamed in sheer frustration that the vile dictator might get away. Then he checked on his daughter Elixa whose arm was streaked black with blood.

Alazandr took off his chocolate-coloured coat. 'This jacket,' he said, 'is packed with explosive jelly-cake. Enough to blow up the entire site. I'll go to the kitchens. Set the cake to bake. Elixa, take this diamond sword. See that Celine gets out of here safe.'

Elixa nodded, seized the sword, and hastened down the flight of stairs. Alazandr followed, then descended to the kitchens, leaving the hall and the powerless ministers. The heaving, groaning, hateful brotherhood. Brought to their knees by a just-dessert.

Chapter 39
Knives and Forks

Lydia led her sisters from the Burnville factory, around the frosted night-time site. A Midwinter chill bit into their clothes, and they kept to the gritty gravel biscuit driveways, footsteps clogsteps crisp upon the paths.

Lydia pointed a toffee hammer 'This way!' in the direction of the factory gates.

Behind the girls, alarms were sounding. Scientists were rushing frantic from the factory. Teams of chefs, of assistants and kitchen staff fled the other buildings too. Most of them crossed the icy white lawns, but the frosting started to melt around them; the soil softened beneath their feet, turned darker and darker with increasing heat. *Fudge fludge, fudge fludge.* The scientists and kitchen workers squirmed and squelched. Their shouts and curses alerted the sisters and, as they looked round, the lawns turned muddier, muddier still, till they realized it was hot fudge sauce oozing up around the site.

Then something pushed up from under the soil. A sliver of metal. Then another, there another. One by one. Six by six. All across the grass, blades sliced through the fudgy earth. Sets of steak-knives emerging like plant shoots. Steely stalks like fingers like forks. Glinting in the pale moonlight. Most of the Burnville personnel were bogged down, sticky stuck between these rising sliver knives, and the sisters could only watch, unable to help, while the people sank into the sauce. Slurped down slowly. Disappearing into pits of fudge.

Lydia had to turn away squeamish, as the workers' shrill bloodcurdling cries were lost in the screeching of forks and knives.

Scythe-like arms now appeared from the pits, then sharp misshapen cutlery legs, distorted skulls with razor teeth. Multi-jointed skeletal torsos, with crests and tails and circuits and veins dripping with electric blood. The disfigured remains of Stannic's ogre robots. Twelve or thirteen of them. A baker's dozen. Clambering rising from the fudge-sodden soil. Stained steel factory rejects, giant knife-and-fork monstrosities with jagged grinning jaws.

The girls scurried away as fast as they could, to the gates and railings securing the site.

Then they stopped.

A robot watchdog guarded the exit. And this was nothing like the litter hound Lydia had bashed way back in Tinport.

This mean lean sausage dog had a copper nozzle

muzzle on a gas cylinder body, and it stood there, tail fixed to a post, staring along the gravel of the drive.

The watchdog's eyes zoomed in on the children, and its muzzle spat out a jet of fire, flame-thrower bright, almost reaching the scattering screaming sisters.

Lydia stayed a good way away; she put her toffee tin down on the drive, and struck its lid.

Dud-dur-um! Dud-dur-um!

She concentrated on the watchdog head, improvising a drummy command to get control of the fearsome hound, as her sisters tried to open the gates. They had to hurry. Not far behind was the strident shriek of machinery. Thirteen hunchbacked half-baked skeletons were loping lolloping limping towards them.

One at a time, the sisters inched past, Coffee carrying Sugar in her arms, trusting Lydia to keep her hold upon the hound, and stop it from turning and breathing flame. But this sausage dog was tough to tame. Lydia was tired. Her hammering drumming started to falter. She strained to contain the dog's nozzle muzzle from emitting another jet of fire.

Now came the sound of screeching tyres. A limousine being driven at speed. The iron gates automatically opened, and Stannic's car came hurtling up the driveway, about to run Lydia down. Hazel may not have been *super*fast, but she skipped back quick and pulled Lydia clear. The wheel of the limo flattened her tin. The gas-powered hound roared fire at the car.

The vehicle swerved and crashed into the sausage dog, crushing its cylinder and bursting into flames.

Stannic staggered from the blazing limo. Staggered back as giant skeletons set upon his shattered car, splitting it apart as if it were a metal nut, digging in with knife-fork fingers, chomping off bumpers, armoured doors, biting the robot chauffeur to bits, and fighting over the choicest morsels, doughnut tyres, axle sticks, guzzling the oily sauce from the engine.

Lydia's sisters had stolen away, safely through the open gates.

'*Hurry*, Toffee!' Hazel called.

But Lydia had seen two people running around the corner of the dining hall: Celine and Elixa.

They stuttered to a halt, gaping aghast at the ogre robots clustered around the factory exit, tearing at the fiery wreck, picking apart the carcass car.

Lydia had to move these robots away. Her tin, however, lay crushed on the driveway. She scrambled back for the flattened lid, started to bash it with the palm of her hand, and focused her mind on the monstrous skeletons, trying to draw them to her. Her crude idea worked. The skeletons finished their roast limousine to follow the *thud thud thud* of the lid.

'Go, Celine!' Elixa ordered. 'I may need to stay to help our father.'

Celine didn't argue, and she made her escape, past the wreck of Stannic's car, out through the factory gates, and into the orchard surrounding the site.

Knives and Forks

Now the skulk of grisly robots came after Lydia in a mishmash mass. A haphazard wall of knives and forks, hobbling angular along. *Scratch scritch scrosh.* This friction mess of skeletal cutlery cut up all the lawns and paths. *Scrish scrash scrush.* With a shriek of joints. Sounds like screams. A metal cacophony of killing machines. Marching. Marching. Stamping in step to the tin lid tempo. Elixa and Lydia led this procession of misshapes back across the site, back towards the dining hall.

They also saw Stannic, a short way in front of them, tottering forward in a smouldering uniform. The sounds of the tin lid thundered through his head. He could hear, so near, the march and lurch of his skeletal machines. He dared to look back and, in the moonlight, Lydia was startled to see the twisted expression of fear on his face.

The just-dessert still churned in his mind. Sapphire sherbet effervesced in his ears. Amethyst jelly made frozen tears crystallize across his eyes, while the Ruby Red Shortbread petrified the guilt in his metal gut. Who knows what cake-induced hallucinations were flashing across his forget-me-not conscience? What intense tormenting nightmares now haunted this jet-hearted darkhearted man? This man, the cause of such misery and suffering. The destruction of livelihoods and homes. This man who had masterminded the confection camps. Imprisoning innocent citizens and families. All of these horrors now taunted and haunted him, driving Stannic slowly insane.

His metal heart pounded with pain. The rhythm of Lydia's tin lid drum seemed to compel him on. *Left right. Left right.* Running truffle-terrified. Hopping like a jerky puppet. Driven mad and paranoid. This raving man in shabby clothes. Scared his own robots would tear him to pieces.

Alazandr met them in the dining hall courtyard. The area glowed with incandescent jelly steam wobbling up from the underground kitchen. The explosive cake was just about to detonate.

The Tin Man stutter-ran, then fell with a whimper to the courtyard, trembling uncontrollably, racked with cramps and fits of fizzy dizziness, his metal heart ticking erratically.

Alazandr stared at the skeletal ogres, quickly assessing the situation. 'Lydia!' he cried. 'Give me your tin lid!' Lydia ran over, and her father snatched the lid from her hand.

The loathsome knife-and-fork-limbed robots screeched ever nearer, scraping along on their cranky legs. Razor knives. Razor teeth. Jagged jaws drooling fudge.

Alazandr seized Stannic by the collar, and dragged him back to the dining hall, bashing the lid against his head. *Lik-rish clash. Lik-rish clash.* Drawing the robots back to their master.

Still the monstrous ogres advanced, thirteen vile metallic skeletons, steadily converging on their prey, towering above them, cutlery limbs poised to strike.

Stannic cowered. Stannic screamed. So feeble now that Alazandr was able to pin him in a headlock. Hold him against the wall of the hall. The windows behind them, glowing glowing. The jelly-cake so close to exploding. '*Elixa! Lydia!*' Alazandr called to his daughters. 'You two scoot! Go! *Now!*'

With the jelly-cake at critical heat, Elixa scooped Lydia up in her injured arm and, wielding the diamond sword, she sought a way past the perilous skeletons.

'No, Daddy, no,' Lydia wept, catching one last sight of Alazandr as he vanished in a corona of jellied gold.

Lydia held on tight to Elixa while she darted into the robots' midst, slipping through the twists of metal. Her shoulder bleeding, her heart racing, Elixa used her sword against the skeletons, parrying the knives and forks, chopping with ferocity, fending off the crisscross cutlery stabbing all around her. Agile, lithe, slithery quick, she dodged the lethal knifing fingers, misshapen blades that cut the air, threatening to chop her limb from limb. With a sparkly *clash-clash-clash* of knives, Elixa squirmed a way through the robots, wriggled clear of the skeletal ogres as they clattered past en masse to the dining hall. Tearing at the walls with their knives and forks. Tearing into the screaming Tin Man.

Elixa was soon away. Racing at a breakneck pace. Through the gates. Away from the factory. The nighttime orchard whipping past. And behind them, the almighty roar of a cake-bomb coming from the Burnville site.

Elixa's liquorice hair streaked behind her as she dashed between the trees, with Lydia in her arms. Citrus scents slicing past them, orange lemon citron lime—

Now came a series of flashing explosions. The ground around her trembled and rumbled. Elixa fled the fiery destruction, sprinting past the sweet fruit-trees.

Lydia saw the distant site, witnessed its dramatic light. Burnville's buildings burned and raged. The factory site consumed by flames; and all its skeletal metal horrors melting away in a sizzling blaze. Spears of jelly fire filled the sky. Glowed like candles on a birthday cake. Bright against the winter night.

Afters

With Stannic's factory HQ in ruins, so all his operations came to a halt.

Thousands and thousands of Karamesh snakes were unleashed across the Candi-Lands, hissing out, spitting out scrambling signals to hypnotize the robot army: the sentries in confection camps, those policing prison zones. All were reprogrammed to free the people. To help keep order, help rebuild. Until the lands of Candi were returned to their sweetest, once more.

Across Redberry Common, the sounds of children could be heard. Children playing around a lovely marquee, enjoying a tea party with their families.

Most of the children there were girls, and eleven of them were really half-sisters, wearing paper crowns and their fanciest sweetie outfits:

One of them was called Alma. Alma of Franjipan, no more the wood-skinned Marzipan.

Another was a shy little Frozan girl Liise, no longer cursed by her icy persona.

There was Donna Ganash, once a tomboy called Jawbreaker, now the best of sibling friends with a hazel-haired dancer Shelley Janduya.

And then there was Suzette Éclair, no longer a ghostly buttery girl, but still full of mischief and cheeky as ever.

Also there was a girl with pastel purple hair, a girl called Sophie Münch, who used to resemble a giant marshmallow.

Now she booted a gobstopper-beachball to a smiling ginger-haired girl called Dinah. Bull's-eyed no longer, Dinah was able to feel the redberry grass between her ten toes.

A giggly girl, that Lydia used to know as Dolly, stumbled about and fumbled with a frisbee; a candy mixture of a sister no more, she was just plain Candice Battenberg.

Candice played catch with a child called Katti. Katti with her humbug eyes and pretty skin of peppermint blue. Once mute, she was now the most vocal of them all, erupting with peals of flameless laughter.

A girl from Layakayk, whose name was Gluca, looked on from a motorized wheelchair, her brilliant mind alert as ever, her sugary senses almost restored.

Indeed, all the sisters were able to live more normal lives, free from their freak-of-nature powers.

And Lydia. Who had found a new family. And helped to change her world for good.

Lydia looked towards her home nearby. Maple Syrup House, where her sister Celine, Uncle Terri and Morella, and her foster daddy Petro waited.

Waited for the arrival of their special guest, Elixa.

Elixa, wearing a dark cocoa-cloak, gathered everyone in the Maple Syrup garden; she said some words to honour Alazandr, a man who'd played a part in all their lives.

Elixa then handed Lydia a bag. A blood red bag of toffee tiles. Lydia put her mother's crystal heart inside, tying the bag with an emerald ribbon, sealing the heart with her favourite confection. Lastly, Elixa used a bronze toffee-scoop to chisel a hollow in the Maple Syrup soil—a grave of sorts—where she placed the bag of tiles.

Then Lydia took the toffee-scoop, and buried the heart in the earth.